ERIC IS AWAKE

ERIC IS AWAKE

DOM SHAW

ANONYMOUS PRESS

First published in Great Britain in 2013 by Anonymous Press
www.anonymouspresspublishers.com

Cover illustration by Dominic Thackray

Source ISBN 978-0-9926115-1-4
Ebook Edition 978-0-9926115-0-7

To my grandfather Leonard Moore,
who believed in always standing up for the working man

Contents

Look back in memory and consider when you ever had a fixed plan, how few days have passed as you had intended, when you were ever at your own disposal, when your face ever wore its natural expression, when your mind was ever unperturbed, what work you have achieved in so long a life, how many have robbed you of life when you were not aware of what you were losing, how much was taken up in useless sorrow, in foolish joy, in greedy desire, in the allurements of society, how little of yourself was left to you; you will perceive that you are dying before your season
Seneca – On the Shortness of Life

Prologue

IT IS A cold bright January day and the bells of St Mary's Church Islington have just struck thirteen. A few of the shoppers in Upper Street look up at the clock on the spire, noting the hands set correctly at half past six. But most, deadened by the weather and footsore from January sales, don't even notice. It is a Thursday and therefore a day when the bars and restaurants staggered along the street can be patronised for a mildly bibulous night, knowing that the fully unfettered release of the Friday debauch is only a hangover away. A few brave white-collar proles quiver in red blankets on sofas outside the Turkish cafes, puffing on hookahs and looking like the casualties of a particularly languid road accident. They blow apple flavoured smoke across the pavement and the two homeless men trudging slowly past the church, sniff the air hungrily, but remain invisible to all.

Both men are in their late forties. Pedro, short and ratty in a tattered lumberjack shirt beneath a stained fake sheepskin bomber jacket, scuffs along on a twisted right foot. His trousers are multi-pouched army fatigues and his sneakers are thin and bolstered beneath by two layers of football socks. His friend Lewis wears a hooded top beneath what appears to be an army greatcoat. His long face seldom emerges from the shadow of his chain-store cowl and a straggly anaemic roll-up, burning between his thin lips, lights the hollows of his cheeks. He feels tired and his chest is heavy with the familiar blade of pain blossoming fiercely beneath his breast with every breath.

'Early night, Pedro' he rasps and spits into the gutter. Pedro stares sadly at the ruby red streaks visible in the glistening oyster and pats him on the back. 'OK, Lewis. You want to go Camden. Try Arlington House?'

Lewis coughs for almost thirty seconds before answering wearily. 'You need a referral.'

'We can go up the housing people and get one. You not well, man. They got to priory you'

'Prioritise'

'Yeah, yeah. Priorise.'

Lewis pauses on the pavement and seems to sway slightly as he considers the journey down Copenhagen Street and out behind York Way to Camden Road. 'Too tired. Let's get some cardboard from the bins out back of the furniture shop and find a space out of this wind.'

Pedro rubs his hands and stares up at the white sky. 'Maybe going to snow. Probably cold weather shelters still open tonight, innit?'

'Don't let me stop you.'

Pedro shuffles awkwardly, his pock-marked jowls turning red beneath his light black beard. 'I won't leave you, Lewis. Not when you feeling bad. You know that.'

'I'll be alright'.

'No. I stick with you. Bastard shelter people get on my nerves anyway. Cheesus, what you have to do for a warm place and a lousy meal'. He pats his pockets, either side of his jacket. 'Anyway I got prawn cocktail crisps this side and cider this side. We going to be OK, man. Poco dinero, pero mucho de corazón. You know what this means, Lewis?'

'Of course not.'

'No money, but plenty heart. Yes?'

Lewis coughs painfully and rubs his belly. 'I could eat a heart'.

Fever Diary – 22 January 20--

I have stepped off the end of Wigan Pier. The last time I remember the nurse taking my temperature, it was 104 degrees. If this is a fever dream, as I have surmised, then this ethereal journal may not last very long. Every week one reads in the newspapers of such cases. A man disappears from home or work or somewhere in between and isn't seen for months or years. He comes to a realization, in the street perhaps that he doesn't know where he has come from or where he is going. Just as one may enter a room and forget entirely why one came. In such cases, the victim gradually comes to understand that he doesn't know who he is. But although I have no memory of how I got here, I believe I am acutely aware of who I am, although, naturally in a dream one may be convinced of a fact that on waking turns out to have been a complete fiction.

There have been fever dreams before, of course. Some accompanied by vivid hallucinations and an undercurrent of dread or menace. Whilst lying in a Cologne hospital ward, I once experienced a long and complicated scenario accompanied by the pervading smell of burning onions and a malevolent toad slithering beneath my bed. But this current episode is a curious hybrid of dream logic and sensory excess that I know I have not experienced before, whatever my temperature. In the hallucination that I find myself enjoying (and occasionally suffering) I seem to be able to think and feel as ever I did. Curiously, a kind of detachment that I always strove for in my waking life seems to come very easily now. This may well be the over-heated brain playing philosophical tricks on my perception. But I suspect it is more the collision between the very familiar landscape of the England I know and the profoundly alien intercision of the fever world I now inhabit. I both know and do not know this world as the delusion lays a curious topography over the once familiar contours of a landscape skewed by my affliction. Although, I'm not sure affliction is the right word. I find that although I can touch and feel in this largely benign fugue, I am completely free of disease for the first time in nearly twenty years. I felt that instantly. It's true, I bleed if I graze my knuckle against a wall, but the previously constant shard of ice beneath my breast is mercifully absent here. Perhaps if it returns, I will know that I am about to wake up or die. Neither option appeals to me at present. I am tired of the tedious routine of the chronic patient. In this respect, the dream is a welcome relief, whatever it signifies about my current state of health.

There are still newspapers here, at least. They speak to an extraordinary explosion in telegraphic means which as I always suspected, tend to retard rather than enable international communication.

Looking back through the diary I kept during the war, I find that I was usually wrong when it was possible to be wrong. I hope that I can write a little longer and with a little more prescience for whoever seeks me out in the universe of perpetual dialogue I seem to have projected for my own amusement or torment. The electronic cacophony that this world now seems to endure is a hard place to be heard. Perhaps I have made it deliberately so, as a reflection of how my political writing is treated in the real world. Amidst the largely docile and benign headlines from my own country of the imagination, I perceive the ominous soccer-rattle of ravens beneath Britannia's skirts, the malignant clatter of the machine gun behind the arras. I have not left Albion as it was. But what have I done to it?

NB: I have just eaten prawn flavour potatoes.

JOURNAL ENTRY ON INTERIOR SURFACE OF A TORN ENVELOPE FOUND
AT BARNHILL, ISLE OF JURA – 12 MAY 20--

Lewis always chooses the place. Pedro concedes that his friend's superior experience of living rough, together with his army training, give him a kind of authority about such things and normally he would trust his compadre's judgement. But tonight Pedro realises that Lewis has opted for the nearest possible option, which turns out to be a narrow alley between the rear of a row of modern houses facing on to Upper Street and the side of the Compton Arms pub. They lay out their cardboard nests in the bin space of one of them, beneath a closed-circuit camera fixed to the door above the pub's side entrance.

Pedro shivers, realising that the chosen spot is relatively sheltered between the rows of buildings, but not as protected from the biting wind as a snug cubby-hole in one of the abandoned squats up on the Balls Pond Road might be. For a moment he considers calling an ambulance and at least getting a few warm hours accompanying Lewis to A & E. But one look at his friend's exhausted face as he tucks in his tattered sleeping bag persuades him that the best thing is to bed down here and think again in the morning.

He sighs, fumbling for one of the bin-salvaged cigarette stubs in his pocket and daydreams fondly of a warm square in Vallcarca i els Penitents. His birthplace calls to him at such times and he struggles to avoid thinking, once again, about all the muddled circumstances and miscalculations that have taken him away from warm Catalonia to cold and heartless UK Plc. He looks up at the street sign on the wall of the alley opposite. Hyde Place. Not much of a hiding place, he thinks to himself. It's going to be a long night.

'What did you do in the army, Lewis?'

'Fought and slept and ate and nearly died, all for money in my pocket. Pass me that cider.'

Pedro wipes the neck of the brown plastic bottle and passes it to Lewis. 'Where?'

'The desert, Angola, Mongolia. Wherever they sent me.'

'Did you like it?'

Lewis swigs and shivers in his thin coat as the liquid courses past his wounded lungs and into his belly. He feels feverish and the shaking in his arms and legs seems unstoppable. 'I suppose I didn't have to think for a while. I didn't like that part much. I like to decide my own destiny.' He laughs bitterly. 'Look where that gets me.'

A black Labrador lopes out of the encroaching darkness and sniffs expectantly around Lewis's sneakers. He draws them out of reach and raises a foot to kick him away. But Pedro holds a protective arm between them.

'Don't. He's just cold like us. Come, boy, sit down here next to me.'

Lewis eyes the dog hazily as it instantly curls around Pedro's feet. Then, as if from a great distance, he senses the scene fading and melting into a grey blur. Very suddenly he feels his limbs loosening and the empty cider bottle falling from his hand as he slips under a blanket of darkness and into a coma. Pedro, thinking he has merely fallen asleep, curls along his back; the dog's body nestled against his thighs, and shivers into fitful slumber beneath a heavy sky, waiting for the snow to fall.

January 1950 – London

Eric was alone in the side ward and for once his coughing had subsided. He felt serene and at peace beneath the moonlight streaming through the window. Visitors had crowded him out recently and he was even glad to see Sonia finally leave after what seemed hours of stilted jousting concerning Ricky visiting one more time before they departed for the continent. His adopted son seemed to have grown away from him in the last few months and whilst he didn't want to risk infection, he missed the little imp and wanted him here, on his bed, playing games and laughing. Poor little sod loses his new mother and now has to worry about his ailing new father. Not much of a start to life so far, Eric mused mournfully. It was he that was supposed to die, not Eileen.

He tossed aside the Baedeker, suddenly sick of the bloody Alps and picked up his notebook. He wanted to write down a more descriptive passage about his fever dream. There was a good essay there about everyone having one peculiar to him or her alone. Somehow they reflected the patient's innermost dread. Perhaps in a fever, you go into your very own Room 101 where the worst thing you can think of is right in there with you. Cyril said his was always a feeling of being trapped in a lake between two mountains with a huge finger and thumb coming down between them to pluck him from the water and crush his head. The sense of rising panic as the digits bore down upon him filled him with that curious combination of dread and fear that always accompanied this raging rebellion of the body. An absurd pantomime image, Eric thought, reminiscent of Jack and the beanstalk giant; but seemingly none the less frightening for the habitually implacable Connolly.

Eric's fever dream seemed benign in comparison but no less terrifying. He is always lost in a huge city with enormous buildings all around him. No one knows him and no one cares and yet he feels observed and hunted by lions prowling unseen amidst crowded streets. His overheated brain seemed capable of the most remarkably vivid hallucinations and he strug-gled to record them; but only after the fever when the images had faded. The amnesia of the cooling brain.

As Eric pulled himself up on the pillows to start writing, something deep inside wrenched and tore away from its moorings. He felt an implosion in his chest that filled his throat with the familiar metallic surge. But it wasn't like the other times and he knew as the blood poured from his mouth and nose that something was irrevocably broken. He wasn't afraid, only desperately sad not to have seen Ricky one more time. As he gave in to the collapsing lungs and exhaled, knowing that he would not, could not, draw another breath; he remembered being shot in the throat while standing above his dusty trench in Spain and how, as he fell, his one thought was simply a profound regret. There was still so much he wanted to do.

He made a half-hearted attempt to stretch out for the nurse's call button, but couldn't reach and turned on his side to avoid choking on his own blood. The last thing he saw as the darkness closed over him was the fishing rod falling from the end of his bed and clattering onto the polished lino.

Lewis awakes from his coma briefly, struggles for breath and fails. As Pedro sleeps soundly on beside him, his final breath rises as a cloud of misty vapour in the snowy air. Only the black dog and the closed circuit camera are there to watch him die. Lewis lays with his glazing eyes half shut, blue with cold, his mouth open.

The cloud of vapour coalesces in front of the lens and slowly starts to dissipate in wispy tendrils. Just as it seems to have completely melted away, it suddenly reappears and sinks down towards Lewis's open lips. It seeps into his lungs and he takes a breath, and then another and, without waking, gently starts to breathe again. The dog's ears prick up and he watches intently as the chest rises and falls and the lips turn from blue to pink.

Eric is awake.

*Life is divided into three periods – that which has been,
that which is, that which will be. Of these the present time
is short, the future is doubtful, the past is certain*
Seneca – On the Shortness of Life

1 Reveille

The first sensation was of numbness from the neck down combined with a tremendous ache in the glands at the back of the head and nape. Prior to this, a complete blackout. No feeling, no pain, no distant voices of hospital staff and, mercifully for an agnostic, no shining light or choir of angels. In fact, if I were an unequivocal believer in some eternal after-life, I would have considered myself, as Carlyle, 'to a certain extent bilked' by the first sight of my new fate.

As I struggled to open my eyes, I appeared to be lying in a foetal posture to the lee of two metal dustbins sited in an alleyway between a public house and a row of new brick-built houses. Looking at me across a bundle of shabby blankets was a glossy black Labrador, his deep brown eyes watching me intently. For quite a while, perhaps ten minutes, I could not move and remained paralysed and helpless, my eyes locked on the dog. He also seemed curiously still, as if in silent empathy.

I experimented at first simply with the motion of my eyelids. Closing and opening them seemed to be as much as I could manage and I started to suspect a stroke. But why deposited unceremoniously in an alleyway? As far as I was aware, my medical bills were paid up and although I knew in theory that they often discharge seriously ill but penurious patients, I could not believe they would have done so in this instance. There is usually some foundation or other that allows at least a few days grace. But then, how long had I been unconscious and in what mental state? For all I knew, I could have discharged myself, wandered into the street and suffered some sort of episode in a remote part of the city. In which case, I felt I had better try and get to my feet and seek help before the snow that I could perceive on the pub windowsill at the corner of my vision, started to work on my extremities.

When I did begin to move, it was my fingers and my torso that first felt the damp of the thawing snow beneath me. What I had first thought were a shapeless bundle of covers, turned out to be another sleeper, his face obscured by a woollen hood, his breath sending cloudy messages into the freezing air. As the sensation returned to my legs, I began to shiver uncontrollably and felt certain the movement would wake my slumbering compatriot. But he remained insensible and I smelt a sour alcoholic odour from him, mixed with the sweat and urine combination of the long unwashed. It was almost a relief, as I knew stroke victims often lose their sense of smell. But movement was returning and despite the cold, I felt euphoric and foolishly happy that I was going to be able to walk around on my own two feet.

The first effort was profoundly painful as I levered myself up on one arm. The cold air razored the damp of my clothing and forced a deep shuddering breath that would have seemed impossible only an hour ago. Cramp turned the screws on my elbows and shoulders as I laboured to inch around on the palms of my hands to a more comfortable sitting position. Blinking with the effort, I stared comically at the great army boots I seemed to be wearing on the two inaccessible peninsulas of my feet. As I looked them over, it occurred to me that I could remember little about the immediate past. I knew I had been in hospital and I knew I had been there some time. Memory and detail were largely absent, although I was angry with the staff for having somehow allowed me to be in this state.

Another quarter hour seemed to find me in a much improved condition and I was ready to try standing up. As I did so, my boots scraping noisily on the cement, the sleeper grunted and cocked a bloodshot eye in my direction. He yawned and sat up, seemingly unsurprised to find me standing above him. He had dark eyebrows that almost met in the middle and the same dark brown eyes as the dog.

'Feeling better?'

His accent was unmistakably Spanish and I hesitated before answering, as my throat seemed dry and clogged with phlegm. Turning aside, I spat into one of the bins and cleared my throat with a rattling cheer. 'Yes. Yes, I think so.'

'Good. I was really worried about you, man.' He patted the dog, which opened its mouth as if laughing and then suddenly raced off. The sleeper laughed and tossed a cigarette butt after him. 'Fair weather friend, eh? He get warm from us then he bugger off, isn't it?'

I reached out a hand to the rim of the nearest bin and held myself upright, swaying slightly with the effort. I shook my head slightly to try and relieve some residual dizziness and my companion cocked his head to one side in a concerned fashion. 'You OK, Lewis? You still sick?'

I contemplated the question for a moment and then smiled, my lips feeling stiff and unfamiliar. 'No. No, I think that's all finished now.' I held out a hand. 'I'm Eric. What's your name?'

The Spaniard looked at my hand as if it were a dead flounder and frowned. 'You still got the fever. We got to get you hospital.'

I withdrew the hand and ran it over my chin, which seemed to have been a stranger to the razor for some time. He sounded like he was from the north. Barcelona, perhaps? I searched my memory for forgotten phrases. 'Molt de gust de conèixe'l. Com es diu?'

He looked mildly surprised and stood up, revealing a bizarre outfit of army surplus trousers and a lumberjack style shirt. 'I din't know you speak Catalan, Lewis. You OK?

It was then that I saw the box like contraption above the door of the pub behind him. At the centre was the unmistakable double ellipse of a camera lens.

JOURNAL FOUND AT BARNHILL, ISLE OF JURA – 20 NOVEMBER 20--

FOR A WHILE, the two men faced each other and said nothing more. Pedro remained bemused and wary of this startling new development in Lewis's increasingly fragile grip on reality. Eric simply reveled in the sensation of breathing normally and evenly without pain. Avoiding the vacant glare of the boxed camera, he looked all around and behind Pedro and noted the familiarity of the pub's side door. He glanced up and almost clapped his hands. The Compton Arms. For a reason yet to be explained, he had been deposited outside his old local.

'I say, what does your watch say?'

Pedro gave an exasperated sigh at the sound of the fluting, faintly upper-class rasp of Lewis's latest affectation. 'What does my watch say? It say, 'Bye bye Pedro. Uncle buys you a winter coat, that's what it say. What you talking like this for?'

'Pity. I could have done with a pint of brown about now.'

'Lewis we really got to get you hospital. I worried about you, man'.

Eric, feeling stronger and livelier than he had in a long time, shuddered slightly in the cold and clapped his hands together for warmth. 'Last thing I need is another bloody hospital. All I really want is a wash and a shave. Come on.'

He set off at a brisk pace to the end of the alley.

Pedro trotted anxiously after him. 'Where we going?'

Eric stopped and looked back at the bedraggled Catalonian with a smile. 'It seems I owe you a debt. Not sure how at present. But clearly you've been watching over me while I've been ill. But I'm better now and the least I can do is to show you a little hospitality. My flat is just around the corner. Please, be my guest. We can get a cup of tea at least.' He turned and strode confidently out on to Canonbury Lane and turned left towards the square.

Pedro stared after him for a moment before following. He shook his head, his jet-black greasy shoulder-length hair swathing his bewildered brow. It was going to be another of Lewis's off days. 'If you got a flat, I'll kill you, crazy bastard.'

As Eric walked, he looked down at his flapping trouser legs with interest. It was so easy to stride energetically down the icy flags with no pain or effort. His feet seemed small inside the army boots, which were of a slightly different design than he remembered from the Home Guard. His physical vitality seemed utterly restored and it filled him with a euphoric giddiness. The last time he remembered feeling like this was after a particularly good breakfast one October morning on Hampstead Heath with Eileen. Dear God, kippers! He stopped, the thought of them making him salivate. Breakfast of Kings! What he wouldn't give for a kipper right now. He laughed aloud. He felt like a small child let loose in the park without Nanny. Trivial things gave him huge pleasure in a way that would have seemed inconceivable only a lifetime ago.

He strode on, kipperless, and was brought up short almost immediately by a rectangular metal box. He peered at the tiny label of instructions, which appeared to be a set of times related to when one could park. They appeared next to a tiny grey windowpane. The time, according to the extraordinary display, was 06:08.

He looked more closely at the street as he continued along and found a row of cars, their surfaces covered in a layer of frost and snow, parked end to end. It was hard to make out their contours beneath their white eiderdowns, but something about them struck him as odd and unconventional the shape and construction slightly off-kilter. He realised, in his usual doggedly methodical way, that he was going to have to decide, minute by minute, what to discard and what to retain. At present, the air and the low hum of the city were vibrating his senses and singing in his head, preventing serious evaluation. There simply wasn't space to think about everything his senses were telling him. He suddenly remembered Pedro and wheeled around to see his reluctant companion trudging morosely after him, stepping with careful concentration in his footprints to reduce the slush leaking into his shoes.

'Do you like kippers?'

Pedro sighed and skidded on a frozen dog turd.

'Gentleman's relish? I think I still have some somewhere.'

'Whatever, Lewis. Whatever. I like anything you can eat.'

As they neared the square, Eric ahead of Pedro by yards, the gap between them widened, until both were puffing with the pace, their breath feathering the air with hoary billows. Behind them, a little way back, the black Labrador followed, his paws leaving no impression in the snow.

March 1945 – Paris

Paris had not changed as much as Eric had expected, although the atmosphere was depressing and oppressive, the uncertainty of the situation making the people watchful, nervous, and unwilling to give away any emotion or opinion. He had wandered down shortly after his arrival in February to his old billet in the Rue du Pot de Fer. The building had survived, albeit with a bombed exterior either side. He did not go in and returned to the hotel feeling tired and feverish, pausing to dispatch an article back to 'The Observer' before retiring to his bed for several days to recover. It was one of the great advantages of the place that each room had central heating. But when you are lying drenched in your own sweat with the window open to the winter wind, it has its disadvantages.

He had not been at the Hotel Scribe very long before he realised he was being watched. One day at the beginning of March, this came home to him with particular force. The lobby was littered, as usual, with journalists from all over the world, drinking, meeting consular officials, flattering army contacts, and entertaining prostitutes. He nursed a contraband whisky in the bar whilst observing the delicate profile of one woman, her shaved head ill-concealed beneath an incongruously jaunty cloche hat with her pretty face bruised and burnt from a vigorous application of tar by a vengeful mob in the Rue St Honore, eager to show the Allies their abhorrence of sexual collaborators. She was weeping quietly as an elderly Swiss Embassy official gently stroked her arm with one hand and his own neat grey beard with the other, his pince-nez sparkling with tears. Eric speculated on their relationship and eventually chose to imagine they were father and daughter.

Sitting at the bar next to a pair of drunk American Infantry officers, was a man in a flat cap and a heavy coat, his face partially obscured by a woollen scarf. His back was to Eric, but his eyes regularly checked the mirror behind the bar and fastened on the lone Englishman sitting at one of the booths. After a while, another man, their exchange accompanied by a few words of Russian, relieved him. The replacement was slimmer and taller with a full set of whiskers, but the first man who had followed him from the Latin Quarter, was squat and bulky, as if concealing a bolster beneath his coat. Eric tried to get a closer look at him as he passed out of the entrance to the bar, but he turned his face away.

Chatting shortly afterwards with a middle-aged liaison officer from the French sécurité militaire who introduced himself as Malcolm Muggeridge, Eric received the distinct impression that pretty much everyone in the hotel was under surveillance. He always felt a slight frisson on first meeting a writer he had reviewed, but Eric found Muggeridge to be relatively sanguine about it, given that it was at least five years ago. However, the fact that the Russians seemed to be taking a particular interest in 'The Observer's' latest Paris correspondent, made him unusually jumpy and watchful with strangers. His new friend confirmed that Russian surveillance was a distinct possibility and after a few glasses of wine and some gossip about certain Soho luminaries, became more loquacious.

'I suppose, in a way, I am also supposed to be watching you. Well, frankly, my orders are to watch every bugger around here. Particularly journalists and writers, as it happens.'

Eric was amused by the indiscretion, realising that their shared irreverence about mutual friends and literary figures had helped to foster a lazy, collegiate atmosphere. 'Who, specifically?'

Muggeridge eyed one of the Yank Majors snoring loudly with his head resting in a pool of ice on the bar. 'Well, silly ass Plum, for a start. Wodehouse has blotted his copybook with those damn silly broadcasts he did from Berlin. I have to give him a talking to and, if possible, rehabilitate the BF before he ends up shot. Would you like to meet him?'

'I'd love to. But I have to go to Cologne for a while. Some mopping up going on that Astor wants me to cover. Perhaps you have orders to follow me?'

Muggeridge snickered like escaping air from a bicycle tire and raised his glass in appreciation. 'Not this weekend. I'm afraid I'm detailed to watch over frère Hemingway's crimes against the Geneva Convention.'

Eric tried to appear nonchalant but his heart leapt at the thought of a fellow writer and Spanish War veteran on hand to help him with the watchers. 'He's staying here?'

'Until early tomorrow at least. Not sure if I'm supposed to follow him or not. Waiting for orders. Room 132, if you want to knock him up. He knows I'm detailed to be his sneak, so don't feel constrained.'

'What's all the Geneva Convention fuss?'

Muggeridge signaled for another drink. 'Looks like the Nazis drank all the best years, doesn't it? He drained his glass with a grimace. 'Your fellow traveler seems to have overstepped the mark, Blair. Foreign correspondents aren't generally supposed to take command of resistance groups and go around blowing up the Hun. Not that I'm at all affronted personally. But it is rather naughty and everyone is terribly exercised because he's so obvious about it. There are some higher-ups who resent having their snouts tweaked by a bohemian scribbler of such notoriety. You might think about that, Eric, if you're planning any more books.'

'Too late, I'm afraid. I take it there's a file on us both?'

'I'm sure the domestics have one on you. You're a bit small beer for my chaps. Are you quite well? You look awfully hot'.

Eric rubbed a hand across his forehead and finished his whisky. 'Always. You should put that in the file.'

Fever Diary – 31 January 20--

There has been some debate about this journal, revolving principally around its distribution. My first reaction to the idea of some sort of private therapeutic diary for the benefit of Dr Statton and my own 'recovery' was lukewarm. After realising the accessibility of the messages hanging in the ether to anyone who cares to stumble across them, I insisted that the entries should be as public as possible. On the basis that I would not show her any of my writing otherwise, she reluctantly agreed.

I have always regarded myself as a political writer. Even in my dreams, it seems, I insist on bludgeoning the reader with my own unfashionable views. The journalist's malaise.

It is said that great and enduring writers are a product and a reflection of the age in which they live. Political and historical context is all. These being the case, I currently find myself a man

without context. A large fragment of the world my mind has created for me to experience, contains a wealth of new chapters that
I appear to have slept through. To this end, I am rudderless and
voiceless, unable to express any view that is not coloured by my
own brief sliver of perspective. Faced with a world of choice that
does not immediately announce its significance to the age, I find
myself falling back to my fellow journalists for guidance.

I begin with the Times newspapers' contentious list of the 20
greatest British writers since 1945. A handful are familiar, the rest
necessarily unknown to me, apart from one name that I shall resolutely ignore as unworthy of the accolade. A reading list made up
of their greatest works gives me a literary perspective as well as
one that throws a light on the development of the novel, of poetry
and of the essay as a craft, even if the selection is subjective to
fashion and partiality.

For the political, I draw upon an old friend. Tribune. Bevan's baby,
it seems, has died and its last issues looked somewhat dog-eared
and class war-weary. But I am gratified to see easy access to its
back issues remains at the newspaper library, which no longer
stands in Colindale, but hangs, like everything else, in the ether.

I have, under Miss Statton's guidance, also snatched a glimpse
of this invisible library at my disposal through the device she constantly carries around. As I have since discovered through my introduction to the contraption I am using for this entry; a window on
the world shows you only what passes from one side of the pane
to the other. It does not discriminate and therefore paints a constantly shifting picture of the universe in which it exists. Without
preparation, she advises, I can find myself disappearing up arcane
cultural cul de sacs that will serve only to confuse my desire to
obtain a modern overview of all that has occurred since the war
or, in her words, to regain my memory. I am therefore restricted
to this journal or 'blog' (derivation?) and 'The Times' news page.
It is tempting to venture further, but I am slightly cautious having
only recently emerged from what may best be described as a
semi-catatonic state.

I find this experience both frustrating and exciting. Overwhelmed with all that I have to absorb, I find it difficult not to leap to conclusions that are instantly gainsaid by Emily's dogged recitation of past events that render both my view and my method of expressing them invalid and patently inaccurate. I have already been upbraided for referring in conversation to the 'negro view of colonial power'. The altered orthodoxies of language are probably the most noticeable and, for the most part, welcome. Some, less so, being simply the usual tools of euphemism, devised to give the lie to some unpalatable truth. I am fortunate that she is highly educated in both social history and psychology with a younger person's encyclopedic knowledge of popular culture that I find constantly surprising and helpful. Her articulate and measured responses to my endless questions are thoughtful and eked out like morphine to an addict, constantly aware of my being overwhelmed. She is not typical of her generation, whose argot appears largely indecipherable and delivered as a babbled lingua franca of restricted code.

In a way, I resemble a patient with brain trauma, (that is certainly her view) except instead of learning to walk or speak again, I am being 'brought up to speed' in a measured and careful way by a guide of some sensitivity. I am not comfortable with what I reveal to her, unintentionally, about my own psychological barriers. But in a sense, this is the only way in which I can repay her. The quid pro quo is painful but necessary and relieves the loneliness I find creeping up on me, like a baleful burglar in the night.

Below is the Times' list, found amongst old copies piled in the corner of Miss Statton's consulting room. I have started to read them in the order in which they are listed, although there is a temptation to leap to familiar friends to see how they developed in later years. One imagines Anthony Powell would be quite incandescent at the ranking. I will skip Tolkien, I think. I am heartily at one with Eileen's fellow Inkling at Oxford who greeted yet another reading by the earnest Professor at a literary discussion group with the words, 'Not those bloody elves again'.

1   Philip Larkin
2   George Orwell

3   William Golding
4   Ted Hughes
5   Doris Lessing
6   JRR Tolkien
7   VS Naipaul
8   Muriel Spark
9   Kingsley Amis
10 Angela Carter
11 CS Lewis
12 Iris Murdoch
13 Salman Rushdie
14 Ian Fleming
15 Kurt Vonnegut
16 Roald Dahl
17 Anthony Burgess
18 Mervyn Peake
19 Martin Amis
20 Anthony Powell

ericisawake.blogspot.com

POSTED BY H LEWIS ALLWAYS AT 10:30 0 COMMENTS

The crows in the trees above Canonbury Square set up a clattering salutation as the two men trotted briskly around its genteel northern edge. Eric decided to cut through the centre to his flat, as the two gardens bisected by Canonbury Road appeared to have been beautifully transformed. The buildings too, seemed cleaner, with Blitz-damaged end terraces restored and repainted. He rattled the gate but found it padlocked with a stout chain, which infuriated him. A sign indicated that the London Borough of Islington would deign to open them from 8am to 6pm only.

'Look at this. Disgraceful.'

Pedro caught up with him at last and bent over, hands resting on his thighs, while he recovered from the effort. 'If they didn't, we would sleep there, wouldn't we?'

Eric batted the padlock in irritation. 'And what if we did? They should be accessible to all people at all times, instead of only those who can afford to have a square in front of them.'

He peered through the railings and was puzzled to see two vine frames with metal grapes adorning them. Trotting across the Canonbury Road to the other gated garden, he perceived well-planted flowerbeds around the white urn on a plinth in the centre.

He grunted and walked on around towards 27b. That cup of tea and the roaring fire were calling him now. It was only as he found himself wondering if his sister Avril or Miss Watson had remembered to order some coal; that he started to feel something vital had passed him by. Surely, Susan Watson, his young housekeeper, had left the flat? He remembered a formal but polite farewell and watching from the window as she limped across the square towards the tram stop with her battered bag. Then he remembered his own trunk and Ricky's neat little valise resting on a ferry luggage rack on the way to a cold island far away with Susan promising to follow soon. Did that happen or was it going to happen? For the moment, he could not be sure.

He shrugged off the dislocated feeling in his haste to get up the stairs. As he drew level with the front door he fumbled in his pockets for his keys. He didn't find them. Suddenly weary and disappointed, he sat down on the stoop to rest. He felt his wrist and was not surprised to find his pulse racing, his temples pounding in syncopation.

Pedro sat next to him and started to roll a cigarette. 'We got to get you to a Doctor, Lewis. This crazy stuff is worse than usual.'

He felt Eric's forehead and tutted as he spat the end of a cigarette paper onto the pavement. 'You really, really hot, still.'

Eric looked at his hands with their filthy fingernails and the nicotine breach between his index and forefinger. What was he thinking of? He gave up this flat two years ago. Of course he wouldn't have the keys anymore. What the devil was wrong with him? Looking up to the first floor window, he squinted at a sign that stated entrance to 27b could be achieved around the back through Alwynne Villas, which, of course, he knew. His eyes moved alongside to a small blue lozenge on the wall above the front door. All the breath went out of him and he leapt to his feet, his knees quivering and his throat dry and constricted. He swallowed and closed his eyes for a moment. In a few moments he managed to regain some composure. He looked at Pedro and pointed upwards, his voice as calm as he could make it. 'Can you read that?'

Pedro shook his head without even bothering to look. 'You know I don' read English so good.' Nevertheless, he got to his feet with a sigh and turned to look up at the plaque. 'Heestoric House – George Orwell (1903 – 1950) Novelist & Ess… essayeest lived at 27b. 1945–1948 – London Borough of Islington'. He looked quizzically at Eric who was frowning, one hand at his throat, and rubbing at the old scar. 'What about it, Lewis?'

Eric felt suddenly angry and failed to control the giddiness and nausea that seized his chest and stomach. 'My name isn't bloody Lewis. My name is Eric.' He lurched across the road and grabbed the railings surrounding the garden. With a manic surge of energy, he levered himself up to plant one foot between two black spikes and grabbed wildly at the overhanging branch of a tree. His skinny legs swung completely over the barrier and he hung limply from the limb, one un-laced boot starting to slide from his left foot. Dropping to the snow-covered grass before it fell off completely and winding himself slightly as he hit the lawn with his shoulder, he got up and walked quickly towards a bench nearby and swept the covering of crystals away with one hand. He sat, facing the white urn and buried his head in his hands, blotting out the impossible.

A wrinkled Burmese Hindu clerical officer had once tried to get him to meditate in the prison courtyard outside the Adjutant's office. His querulous accents came to him now, across the years, as he struggled to control his breathing. 'Take the time to clear your consciousness completely. If you feel a thought starting to establish itself in your mind, push it away. Concentrate only on the rise and fall of your chest. Inhalation, exhalation. These are all that exist at this moment and they are completely in your power.'

But there were too many thoughts and he couldn't push them away. Every time he tried, others clamoured to get in front, like a theatre queue for the last night of a particularly scandalous revue.

Eric vaguely perceived Pedro cursing as he struggled to follow him over the railings. After a moment or two, he felt him add his weight to the bench beside him.

Pedro picked up a stale piece of Greek bread from beside the litter bin and tore off a few crumbs to throw at the birds around their feet. Eric heard the gentle coos and glimpsed through cracks in his fingers the blue and grey sentinels pecking the sesame seeds from the soft white shrapnel. He felt a nudge and drew his hands away from his face to look down at Pedro's outstretched hand. 'Take some.'

Eric reached for the torn fragment of seeded loaf and contemplated it for a moment before crumbling a little between his fingers and dropping it around his boots for the robotic, hungry pigeons and nimble, darting sparrows. As he worked his way down the bread, he looked carefully around the square, avoiding the front of 27b. Several of the houses opposite and traffic lights at the junction with Canonbury Lane had rectangular boxes fixed to them. Across towards Canonbury Place there was a newsagent and a large building that had once hosted meetings of the Freedom Defence League, which now called itself a Conference Centre. They too had the ubiquitous boxes, their lenses staring blankly at the street, the pavement, the rear of his old flat and the square itself. He realised that he was completely under the eye of at least four of them. 'What are they looking for?'

'What?'

Eric nodded at the nearest box. 'All the cameras. What are they for?'

Pedro shrugged. 'Security, innit? Chinese bombers and Hoodies and the war and that. You know.'

'War?'

'Is no secrets since Altay. Big Brother thing, y'know?'

Eric stared at his companion and dropped the rest of his bread to the snow, one hand reaching up to tug at his hair. 'Sod it. Just stop.'

'What? What I say? Hey, look. How he get here?'

The black Labrador had appeared beside the bench and sat placidly alongside Pedro who tickled his ears affectionately. Eric tilted his head back; his fingers locked in his hair and tried to breathe out steadily into the grey atmosphere. There were patches of icy blue now as the snow clouds burned away in the morning sun. He watched the fog from his resurrected lungs streaming up from his trembling lips towards the yellow disc and saw a crisscross pattern of white trails making billowy chalk marks in the azure. At the end of one was a tiny dart, impossibly high, choking a slender wound across the winter sky. As he closed his eyes against one more impossible vision, he heard a thudding combustive beat approaching from the east. Inwardly he tried to push it away. Inhalation, exhalation. 'God knows', he muttered to himself, 'you've found that exercise hard enough these past few years. Relish it now, while it lasts. Whatever this is, it is less painful than all our yesterdays.'

The Labrador gave one sharp bark, like a full stop at the end of a short sentence. Eric opened his eyes and saw the helicopter hovering above nearby Essex Road. It was, like the cars now emerging in the thawing snow, odd in contour and construction, but still recognisably a helicopter. In the distance several sirens could be heard in the same vicinity.

At that moment his brain seemed to click into a place the old Hindu would have recognised. He was detached at last and the rising panic he had felt since the unsettling arrival in the square had quite gone. In its place was a curious remove – a brown study of the soul, where he retreated to consider all he had seen. It was a familiar place. One he was well used to. 'Is it a raid?' he said to Pedro calmly. 'We should get under cover, maybe.'

Pedro chuckled and offered him a flexible metal cylinder with a tear-shaped aperture at the tip. Eric drank a little, despite some initial distaste and felt the cheap sweetness of strong cider, unnaturally effervescent, coursing through his throat and warming his belly. He passed it back, relaxed and tried to blot out the noise. Looking down at his discarded lump of bread, he realised that it was as important as anything else. In fact, far more important, because feeding the birds was a clear unequivocal activity, easily understood and with no complicated purpose or meaning. He bent and retrieved the flaky offering. The pigeons strutted over expectantly, vying for Communion. He made a mocking obeisance and distributed his stale favours with careful regard to an equal allocation of what wealth he had to redistribute.

Pedro noticed the change in him and was quietly relieved that the manic period seemed to have been replaced with a more stoical and familiar Lewis. 'You better now? No more nonsenses?'

Eric smiled. 'Yes. I think I understand now. Rather slow on the uptake, I'm afraid.'

'Good, good. You understand, eh? That's good.' Pedro watched his friend with one eye, swigged the last of the can, crushed it and tossed the crumpled cylinder expertly into the bin. 'Now, just so we clear, man. What is it you understand?'

Eric gestured to the cameras, to the door of his old flat and finally to the dog. 'Despite a lifetime of trying to maintain absolute discipline, it seems the prosaic and ham-fisted imagery you've always suppressed, will filter through your subconscious, however hard you try. Just look at him.'

Pedro stroked the dog that arched its neck in pleasure, eyes closed. 'Perro? What's wrong with him?'

'He's a cipher and a bloody obvious one at that.' Eric was still feeding the birds leisurely, his hands gesturing as he spoke, his voice quiet and measured. 'Observe the rest of these symbols; all the cameras straight out of '1984', my old flat where I started the novel, the plaque, and my favourite pub. Forgive me Pedro, but the Catalonian tramp with a limp reminding me both of my crippled housekeeper, my Spanish Civil War years and my down and out rags and soup days. Last time the nurse came to check on me, I had a raging temperature. All of this jumbled up nonsense from my life is a vivid but obvious dream. A fever dream. I'm in my bed at UCH, waiting for this to end, one way or the other.'

Pedro was silent for a while and opened his mouth several times before he finally spoke. 'Well, I'm glad we clear that up. I was really worried you might be a little hot in the head. Turns out you completely loco. Great. That's great, man. How you feel?'

Eric threw the last of the bread to the wind and bent down to cup the dog's muzzle in his hand. 'I'm glad there are dogs here. Clichéd dogs, but dogs nonetheless. It's a relief, Pedro. It means I'm alive.

In a coma perhaps, but alive. All I have to do is wait around until I wake up'.

Pedro scratches his head. 'Or until you die. You need to get to a hospital, Lewis. That bang on the head keep giving you trouble in the brain.'

'If this is dying, it's not bad, not bad at all. Everything is so real. The bread in my hand, the sound of the pigeons, the wind in my hair, the snow underfoot.' Eric suddenly stood up, excited. 'Good God, I can have a drink. I haven't been allowed a ruddy pint for ages'.

'I don't like to say nothing to bring you down, man. But in case you don't notice, we got no money.'

'The landlord of the Compton Arms knows me well. He'll stand us a drink or two. If not, I'll dream us up some cash'.

'And I'm a dreamed up man' said Pedro glumly. 'That's nice. You think you can get me some dream vodka?'

Eric set off for the railings, Pedro followed, muttering unhappily. 'Hospital, man. We got to get to hospital'.

'No, Pedro. We have to get to the pub.'

'Hospital.'

'Pub.'

2 Assembly

The door to Room 132 of the Hotel Scribe was partially ajar and as Eric arrived, he could see a loaded kit bag and a battered suitcase half-filled with shirts, cigarettes, a long saucisson and a couple of whisky bottles. He knocked lightly on the door and it was instantly jerked open by a stocky dark-haired man in a crumpled correspondent's uniform that looked like he'd slept in it several nights running. He looked Eric up and down and spoke from around a cigarette stuck to a bruised lip beneath a bushy unkempt moustache. His eyes were bleary and he emanated an energetic hangover.

'Who the fuck are you?'

Eric smiled uncertainly. 'I'm Eric Blair.'

Hemingway frowned, removed the cigarette and cocked his head on one side, looking at the uniform. Eric noticed the whisky smears of grey just beginning to appear at his temples. 'So what, Captain?'

Eric's smile slipped slightly and he stepped further back into the corridor. 'Um. No reason you should know, of course, but I write under the name George Orwell.'

Hemingway blinked. 'Why the fucking hell didn't you say so? Get in here.'

He reached out a hand, which instead of being shaken was tugged heartily as Eric found himself being propelled through the door and deposited on the bed next to the luggage. Hemingway grabbed a bottle from the suitcase and produced two tumblers from the side table. 'Have a whisky. I got no soda. I'm out of this dive in a few moments. You should have caught up with me before now. Really liked your Spanish book. Looks like you hooked up with the wrong guys over there. Those fuckers killed Nin didn't they?'

Eric accepted the whisky gratefully and felt like he was already running to keep up with the energetic American whose thick strong arms seemed ready to burst through his tunic. Not for the first time, he envied the way other people wore their good health and vitality with ease. 'The Fascists? Yes, it would appear so.'

Hemingway snorted derisively. 'Fuck, no. Andres wasn't killed by the Fascists. I heard from a good source that the Russian NKVD was in charge of the whole damn thing.' The American drained his tumbler and poured another, collapsing heavily on the bed. 'Who told you it was the Spanish?'

'An old friend, Georges Kopp.'

Hemingway frowned. 'I heard of Kopp. He was in the Maquis before the British got him out. You want to be careful of that guy, Eric. Shit, do I call you Eric or George?'

'You of all people had better call me George. I hate Eric. I've spent forty years trying to escape from him. What do you mean about Kopp?

'He was tortured in Barcelona too, wasn't he?'

Eric nodded. 'Absolutely. I tried to get him released, but Eileen and I had to leave in a hurry, before we ended up in the same cell.'

'That your girl?'

'My wife.'

Hemingway grunted thoughtfully and cocked a finger at him like a man aiming a revolver. 'If I'm right about Andres, then Kopp was tortured by the same NKVD guy, Grigulevich. He was doing all the P.O.U.M guys around then. He would have loved to have gotten a hold of you.'

'Did you ever see him? What did he look like?'

'Tubby, shortish with a bushy 'tache. He'd be about thirty now, I guess. Speaks good Spanish. Supposed to have been raised in Argentina, I heard. Uncle Joe's favourite killer. Fat greasy little fuck, but meaner than a scorpion. Rumour is he's hooked up with the Mafia too.'

Eric gulped his drink and held out his glass for more, his hand shaking. 'I think he's here.'

Hemingway paused, the bottle hovering over Eric's glass. 'For you?'

'Seems that way.'

He filled the glass to the brim and refilled his own for the third time in as many minutes. 'Ever ask yourself why Kopp was released after everyone else got burned?'

'He fought very bravely in Spain and in the Maquis from what I heard. I would trust him with my life.'

Hemingway leaned towards him, his weight making a large indentation in Eric's side of the bed. He could smell the whisky on his breath and realised the American had maybe already been a little drunk before he arrived. 'But would you trust him with your wife? George, you can't trust any bastard here. Why do you think I'm getting out? Some guy I know ratted me out. If Grigulevich is here then you better get out too.'

Eric nodded. 'I know. I'm heading for Cologne for a while. Hopefully I can shake him off. But I could do with some means of defence. Do you happen to have a gun?'

Hemingway rummaged in his kitbag and came up with a Colt 32. He threw it on the bed and extracted some bullets from his belt. 'Not much ammo left, I guess. I used up most of it with the Maquis. Listen, if you tell me when you're leaving, I'll get a few of them to tail you out of town and check he's not right behind you with a garrote.'

'Thank you. You should know there's a British Army Intelligence officer called Muggeridge watching you. Apparently he's waiting for orders.'

Hemingway laughed and tossed his glass into a waste bin. 'Fuck 'em, George. They're all watching us.'

University College Hospital
Preliminary Assessment – 29 January 20--

Patient E.583 – Caucasian with dark wavy hair greying at temples. Height: 1:82. Blue eyes. 45–50 years of age. Prominent brow and nose. Blue dot tattoos along knuckles of each hand.

Prior to section, patient first presented with manic delusional forced speech and hyperventilation followed by temporary catatonic state lasting 48 hours. After sedation, patient was calm but depressed and uncommunicative for a period of three days. This reverted to a second period of manic and potentially violent behavior requiring restraint and further sedation for a further 48 hours.

Medical assessment of his physical condition, (Dr Edward Martin) revealed emaciation, mild anemia, varicose veins and substantially-sized healed lesions on both lungs indicating some history of previous tubercular condition that is now absent. Large scar on neck and substantial esophageal trauma now partly healed – unable to determine cause. Evidence of Dengue fever in the past also indicated. Blood and urine tests showed trace alcohol but suggested no prolonged or excessive use despite the prevalence in homeless patients of this age and condition. Would have expected a high level of kidney damage, but, again, very healthy function, which, along with liver test result, suggests no prolonged use of drugs beyond traces of Streptomycin.

Neurological tests (Dr Khin Ei) showed no physical brain damage and a wake-and-sleep EEG identified no psychomotor epilepsy. CT scan and MRI did not indicate brain tumour or any other causes of organic brain syndrome. Dr Ei suggested a lumbar puncture would be helpful in diagnosing central nervous system lues. But patient is still showing severe PTSD indicators that suggest the procedure would prove counterproductive to recovery at this stage. Dr Ei mentioned also that the patient conversed in Hindi and Burmese with her during examination suggesting an army career may have encompassed postings in Asia. She said that he was still very feverish and delirious during the examination and at one point he ordered her to bring him a whisky and to undress as 'we still have some time before morning parade'.

First stage assessment interview was conducted on 27th January 20-- at UCH (Rosenheim) with patient calm and apparently alert. Wary from his treatment on first presentation, he was, at first, reluctant to discuss any aspect of his delusional indicators. However, after reassurance that provided no violence or distress was displayed, restraint or forcible sedation would not be utilised; he became more forthcoming. The subject of his delusion was stimulated almost immediately by his complete denial of the identity of Harold Lewis Allways, given by the other homeless man in his company – Pedro Abbad.

The patient believes he is in a coma or dream and will either wake or die in due course. His principal construct is that he is Eric Arthur Blair (real name of author George Orwell) and that he has created a version of the world during a fugue or fever in which he finds himself dumped in an Islington alleyway some distance away from the hospital where he was receiving treatment for tuberculosis from a Dr Andrew Morland.

Given the wealth of easily accessible material available on Orwell, first impressions suggest that the patient has absorbed and memorised many biographical details, including the name of his surgeon and the number of the private room at this hospital in which Orwell was treated and later died. All indications suggest that he absorbed an autobiography on the subject before an episode or breakdown that jolted his consciousness into the subject of the book. Homeless for some time – (according to medical and DWP record entries for Harold Lewis Allways) – patient has been subject to violent attack in the past and once sustained a serious head injury (Whipps Cross Hospital 29/05/20--) that may have triggered the current psychotic episode. No mention in UK medical record of neck wound. But if incurred abroad on active service, may not feature in history. Army records not currently merged with NHS and may not be accessible without some bureaucratic wrangling. Will only request if necessary.

First session was short as patient rapidly became frustrated with any reference to his true identity. Next session will be focused on avoiding the delusion and all references to it; concentrating instead on his feelings and anxieties.

CONSULTANT PSYCHOLOGIST: DR EMILY STATTON

THE PUB, OF course, was closed and they sat on the stoop outside to wait. Eric asked Pedro for his tobacco tin which was reluctantly surrendered. As he watched his fevered companion expertly building a tube from the makings, he suggested that perhaps, after coughing blood last night, he should stay away from cigarettes. Eric looked at him with amusement. 'Probably do me good. Open up the lungs a little. Anyway, I feel fine now.' He lit the pillar of peace and took a long drag like a dying man on an oxygen tank. It felt good although the brand was not as strong as he was used to. 'I normally favour a Nosegay Black Shag.'

'I'm no surprised' grunted Pedro.

They sat in silence for over two hours as the streets came alive around them. Eric took pleasure in watching the various outlandish vehicles driving past and was enlightened as to the source of the screaming sirens when a police car sped by. European individuals of various nationalities, dressed in a complex variety of styles, mostly bareheaded, walked around conversing on minute portable radios of myriad colours and design. Car radios were loud with booming bass tones that shivered the windows of the pub. The number of Orientals interested him. Chinese and Mongolian faces, the women with Islamic style scarves around their heads, the men with small embroidered round hats walked with slow familiarity on the snow.

Looking around furtively at the camera trained on the large bins opposite, Eric extracted a portion of newspaper from the detritus. Returning to his perch and spreading it out on to his knee, he was disappointed to see very little actual news. What he did see made little sense to him, but seemed familiar in its way. There was a war far away, an economic crisis at home, a terrorist outrage, a celebrity scandal, a political scandal, a Royal scandal. Every now and then a smaller story suggested something more overtly authoritarian – a court report about a Terrorism Act suspect and the raiding of an East End factory under the provisions of the Nationality & Identity Act, the banning of a play that was said to incite religious hatred, the cancelling of a film production at the request of the American intelligence services. Further on, he found a directory listing of radio and 'telescreen menus' that went on for three and a half pages. The choice was bewildering and his former employers the BBC were the only recognisable name amongst them. The whole thing seemed to indicate a society in a state of perpetual communication. One section seemed particularly disturbing with programme title such as 'Pre-Teen Binge Drinkers', 'Fucking Miss Daisy' and 'The Uyghur with Three Brains'. The date on the upper edge was randomly impossible but he acknowledged that it was purporting to be 20--. The paper seemed more durable and silkier in texture than he remembered. When he was only halfway down an intriguing review of a Humphrey Bogart film that he had once reviewed himself, the words melted away and the entire surface of the paper became blank. It seemed his imagination could encompass an entire world of alien experience, but could not maintain one page of a newspaper populated with text. He crumpled the annoyingly un-informative sheets into a ball and threw them with a familiar spin-bowl action back into the bin opposite.

Gradually, the smoke, the strong sunlight melting the snow around him and the soft caw of crows in the trees nearby sent him into a calm and tranquil reverie. He wondered if some inverse internal logic would see him wake up in his hospital bed if he fell asleep in his dream. But there was too much stimulation for him to test the equation.

He thought about Cyril and what he might say about this experience when he had the chance to recount it to him. They had discussed his fever dream essay only the other day and it seemed to be a perfect introduction to the topic, provided he could remember it all when he woke.

He patted his pockets and found a small pen marked 'Lazarenko Betting' and a small torn brown envelope with 'Department of Work & Pensions' below the rear flap. He paused for a moment as he regarded the odd writing tip and considered making a few notes for his journal. Who knew if this exercise within his dream would help his memory afterwards, but writing something, anything - was such a compulsion that it seemed natural to try.

He tore open the side flaps of the envelope to form one longer surface and scribbled – 'Fever Diary' at the top of the page. 'Pedro, do you know the date?'

'22 January. 20--'.

Eric pondered this for as a moment and laughed. 'There is a certain element of my own contrariness operating this thing. Yesterday was the 21st January 1950. I somehow expected it would be 1984 here. But it seems my imagination is rebelling against the obvious in one sense at least. I'm quite disappointed with the whole black dog imagery though. Very much a blue pencil.'

Pedro looked around. 'Hey, where he gone?'

'Well, I'm feeling quite well and moderately contented so naturally he's disappeared. Believe me if the beer isn't as good as I remember, he'll be back.' Eric wrote out the date and began to scrawl in a small spidery hand across the envelope.

'I have stepped off the end of Wigan Pier.'

A startling siren accompanied by ringing bells made him jump and look up at a woman across the street that seemed to be the source. She scrabbled in her handbag frantically and produced a small box to silence the din. He watched her look around furtively and a group of builders on their way to work laughed and pointed at her with hands formed into pistol shapes. She looked mildly annoyed and nodded in a resigned fashion at this apparently threatening gesture.

Eric was about to return to his writing when he saw the ghost. Luminescent and seemingly floating along the pavement, was the unmistakable figure of Winston Churchill. He swallowed a familiar feeling of panic rising in his craw and blinked twice as the phantom approached, the wrinkled face impassive, like a portrait. As it neared, he realised there was something more substantial inside it. As the sunlight hit the glowing contours, he could see glimpses of a black burka and a hennaed hand. As the figure passed him, Churchill flickered momentarily like a light bulb just before it dies and Eric clearly saw the bulky Arabian woman's back receding before the luminescence engulfed her again. He looked across the road to another pair of glowing visions; a huge praying mantis swaying behind a gigantic beetle in stately procession along the pavement. As the creatures reached the entrance to a café, the images flickered off and he perceived two ordinary middle-aged men in paint spattered clothing.

Pedro, apparently unperturbed by the apparitions, sighed and looked away. He had begun to feel hungry now all the cider was gone. He suddenly remembered the crisps and fumbled in his trouser pouches for the precious shards. He opened the packet noisily and offered some to his friend.

Eric took a few of the salty flakes and placed one experimentally on the end of his tongue. 'Pork crackling?'

Pedro thought that very soon he was going to become a sigh. One enormous slumped shoulder, permanently exhaling until his wrinkled deflated skin blew away in a breath of exasperation. He decided it wasn't going to happen today and answered enthusiastically through a tight smile, like an indulgent adult to a child. 'Is fried potato, Lewis. Prawn flavour'

'How do they combine the prawn flavour into the potato?'

Pedro could feel himself getting smaller, air escaping like a punctured tyre on a worn ramshackle bicycle. 'Is petrol. Er... petroleum by-product. This potato don' see no prawn or nothing. Is a chemical thing, I don' know. Is no real prawn, y'know? Am I really talking about this crap, man?'

Eric munched thoughtfully and continued scribbling.

They sat for four hours, Pedro dozing fitfully, Eric alternately writing and staring at passers-by or their projections, which seemed to be the exception rather than the rule. At around a quarter to eleven, several old men, their faces beer-cracked and purple, joined them; smoking, spitting and still smelling of last night's ale. At eleven they heard the bolts on the pub door being drawn and the patrons entered like greyhounds from the trap as the landlord drew away from the door and sighed his way behind the taps to draw the first pints of the day.

Pedro nervously kept behind Eric as they waited their turn. Eric was mesmerised by a large rectangular picture on the wall in the snug with powerfully colourful moving pictures. A debate was going on with a sneering mediator abusing two obese women and a sheepish slimmer male seated on a podium. He found it difficult to drag his eyes away as the young barman raised an eyebrow and asked dubiously in an Australian accent what he wanted. Eric cleared his throat and tried to smile with confidence.

'Is Toby about at all? Mr Anscombe, I mean?'

The barman frowned and shook his head.

'Jeff's Grandad? Not for years, mate. He died ages ago. Name's still over the barrels downstairs though. You knew him?'

'I did. He… well he would often stand me a pint on the slate when I was locked out or waiting for a cheque. My friend and I… um… Jeff here at all? I remember the little fellow used to run about the cellar. I suppose he's the landlord now.'

The barman's expression changed and he looked pointedly at Pedro's tattered trainers and Eric's shabby coat. 'Alright mate. Piss off out of it. There's no freebies going.'

Eric was affronted and drew himself up to his full height as Pedro plucked anxiously at his sleeve. 'I assure you I'm good for the money. I have just sold a book for American distribution.'

'Yeah, yeah and you've a giro coming tomorrow. You can stuff that bullshit right up your arse. Go on. Rack off. We're not a fucking charity.'

'You sir, are not a gentleman.'

'And you're an arsehole.'

Pedro pulled desperately at Eric's coat as the barman emerged menacingly from behind the bar and shepherded them out of the door.

Outside, Eric struggled with a sudden panic as he hit the frozen air once again. Looking at his ashen face, Pedro decided the time had come to be firm.

'OK, Lewis… Eric… whatever. We going to the hospital, alright? You got to be checked out right now. No argument?'

Eric passed a shaking hand across his forehead and nodded. 'No argument. We can walk to UCH from here. I'll be glad to be back in my bed again.' The thought cheered him and he as he allowed the sun to warm his face, he wondered what his room would look like in this dream. 'Maybe when I get into it, I'll wake up.'

3 Sick Call

AFTERWARDS, ERIC REGARDED the walk to Room 65 of the Rosenheim Building from the Compton Arms pub as being like a journey through his own mouth. Gaps had been filled in and blackened decay had been bleached to paler shades. The whole smoky hole of London seemed to have been hosed down and repainted. Where were the sooty windows and roped off bombsites? Where were the pools of water leaking from cracked down pipes? Where were the horse and carts trotting across the side streets with milk churns or scrap? Where were the tramlines and indeed, the trams?

At first, as they trudged across Upper Street, past the Hope & Anchor pub, little else seemed un-familiar barring the unnatural cleanliness of the buildings. In fact, as they hit the Liverpool Road, he started to feel more confident. A sign above a pub terrace read 'This could be your party' and at that moment, he really felt that it was. The air was so much cleaner than he remembered and his lungs felt like a new pair of bellows in an old fireplace. The sun was warm and the gutters ran with the thaw.

As they turned right into Cloudesley Square, he was reassured by the familiar solidity of the villas. He had often cycled past when he still had the wind for it and they seemed well preserved with their blank-eyed windows unperturbed by his impossible presence in the square. By the time they hit Copenhagen Street and headed left on to the long twisted eel of Barnsbury Road, nothing disturbing to the eye had given rise to a recurrence of the panic he had felt outside the Compton Arms. It almost seemed as if the city was wiping itself clean to provide a trauma-free route back to his bed. The air quality was notable for the absence of soot or smog; although a metallic chlorine taste tinged the back of his tongue when a black cab or bus growled by.

The placidity started to erode as they approached the Mount Pleasant sorting office which was now some sort of museum. At the end of Lloyd Baker Street as they breasted the rise at its centre point, a large hotel of alien design rose white and ghostly at the junction with Kings Cross Road. It echoed a Wellesian vision of sleek featureless modernity that disturbed him and as they passed and turned left into Cubitt Street, he was comforted by more traditional LCC styles in the low dwellings that now filled bombed terraces that he remembered as a haven for stray cats. Only the plethora of Chinese graffiti marred the familiarity. He noticed the black Labrador following them and wondered how long he had been there.

The long tramp down Ampton Street, Sidmouth Street and Tavistock Place tired him enough to falter at the gates to Tavistock Square. Pedro, sensing the need for a break, led him into the well laid out green and steered him towards a bench before exploring the bins nearby for cigarette ends. Eric hoped he found some more potato flakes. Their chemical salty tang was a nostalgic memory now and his stomach was starting to rumble again. His rations at UCH had been bolstered recently by additions from Sonia and Astor that included tinned liver pate and champagne. But these treats failed to stir his taste buds and he thought about what to order when he finally woke up. Damn the UCH kitchens – he would have kippers whatever it took to obtain them.

He closed his eyes and felt the warmth of the sun on his face. The wind blew a chill through the saplings planted across the wide sward by the Hebrew Palestine League, various charitable committees and other political worthies. A small orchard of piety and remembrance.

It struck him that reincarnation was inadequate to describe what had happened. But when he tried to think about it, to define it, he felt old and tired and his attention drifted. He seemed to snooze for a while and when he came to again, his chin had slumped onto his chest. He contemplated Poe's concept of dreaming within a dream and decided that if his theory were correct, he should wake to the real world again.

But when he opened his eyes, a plinth with a green statue of a bald cross-legged figure confronted him. Eric stared for a moment at the head with its lowered eyes apparently regarding the small posy of flowers left in his lap. Then he laughed. The old Hindu reactionary – a graven idol at last. The idea of the tribute intrigued him. Was his sub-conscious teasing him again? He had always rejected the sainthood thrust on the old pacifist by others and yet here he was, Mohandas Karamchand Gandhi, docile and meditating on his own elevation in the quiet English square. Long dead, the bespectacled old crow had inveigled his way into Eric's fevered mind without a by your leave.

He shivered in the wind and decided with a nod to Pedro that it was time for him to complete his quest. He levered himself from the bench, past a curious black basalt square labelled simply 'Altay' above a date and ambled towards Gordon Street.

As they reached the edge of the pavement, another alarm sounded with the now familiar combination of siren and bells and a tall commuter in a business suit cursed before silencing the control on the box in his pocket and looking around. A woman on the top deck of a bus made the pistol gesture with her hand at him, without any expression on her face. He nodded ruefully and continued on his way.

It was now a short hop along Gower Place to the hospital and Eric stopped briefly at the tall windows at the rear of the Wellcome Institute to absorb the pictures displayed. They were of dividing cells positioned next to a short paragraph on 'gene therapy' and 'genetic coding' that held shades of his old tutor at Eton. The reluctant and frankly inept teacher had written him a supercilious letter recently, assuming wrongly that he had intended '1984' as some sort of prophecy, telling him he was wrong about the future being a boot stamping on a human face forever. He suggested a radical and more scientific transition along the lines of his Brave New World. The dream, Eric noted ruefully, had decided to side with Huxley. He remembered Eileen being very affected by Huxley's dystopia and tried to recall the words to her poem 'End of the Century, 1984', but his memory was fogged and sluggish.

There was nothing subtle about the huge tower of chrome and green glass that faced him as he turned to walk the rest of the way towards Gower Street. Pedro followed his gaze to the towering tip of the edifice and grunted. 'Plenty room for you, man.'

'What do you mean?'

'That's the hospital, innit?'

'UCH? That? Are you sure?'

Fever Diary – 6 February 20--

We are going to have to come to some convention on time. I favour BW and AW – Before Wigan and After Wigan. AW, of course, used to denote everything that comes after the moment I stepped off the end of the pier and into whatever this turns out to be. It allows me to write, without fear of the usual rolling eyes and discreet tapping motion at the temple, about the wake state and the dream scene in a fashion that satisfies anyone reading this journal. BW for the life I remember up until 25th January 1950. Those of you familiar with the pier's place in dubious local folklore, may remember that the most salient feature of Wigan Pier in my time was that it did not exist. Although in this world, of course, it might.

I have had doubts about my own subconscious. Some of the things I have seen here seem unlikely to have emerged from my own mind, despite the wealth of Verne, Wells, Huxley and Zamaytin that I know I absorbed over time.

One thing, however, convinces me that this world is of my own construction. Here, in the AW, there is no such thing as an out of print author. I have just used a machine that acts rather like a literary jukebox. All English language texts of any age are contained within it and can be printed (complete with glossy cover and binding) or transferred to a hand-held device where they can be read at leisure. Who else but a vainglorious author could conceive of such a thing? To never be so lacking in readership that your oeuvre is pulped and forgotten, but to live on, for any individual of any period in subsequent history, to hold in their hand as if newly published. If only the lost library of Alexandria could have been preserved in this manner for subsequent generations, we could have been bored by several more Greek tragedies and a Rameses pyramid inventory.

I have used the machine to transfer the principal works of every author on my reading list to the device lent to me by Miss Statton. I would have preferred the printed option to the glowing screen, but I was shocked by the costs involved and opted instead for the ethereal versions.

One of the titles I have obtained by this method is 'A Brief History of Time' by Stephen Hawking. In it, there is much on the subject of infinity and of the beginning of all things. I have no way of knowing if the ideas contained within it, as arcane and peppered with diagrams and equations as an Aleister Crowley notebook, are credible or not. But they are unsatisfactory.

Scientists are measurers. They mark out the world in increments that please themselves. They like numbers and proportions and if no scale exists against which concepts may be weighed, they will invent one. Therefore, the concept of one 'big bang' to jump start the universe is a comforting one – just as the idea of a flat earth beyond which nothing can exist, was comforting to the ancients. But to the rest of us, particularly those who live through their imagination, it is, as I say, deeply unsatisfactory. A poet has no problem with infinity. Writers have dealt with eternity far longer than Copernicus. But ask a scientist what comes before the primary combustion and you will see a tidy collection of shifty eyes and vague gestures accompanied by mumblings concerning cyclical entropy and chaos theory.

I, for one, have no problem at all with the eternal. A random bacterium on a random rock near a viable star in one small speck of an infinite universe is a concept I can both conceive and appreciate. But perhaps, only After Wigan.

ericisawake.blogspot.com

POSTED BY H LEWIS ALLWAYS AT 12:31 0 COMMENTS

March 1945 – Paris

Eric had a little trouble with the stairs after he left Hemingway. A combination of whisky and fever had him negotiating the final flight down into the lobby like a bomber missing an undercarriage. As he struggled to maintain his dignity, the maitre d' hôtel called him across to the desk to accept his post. Eric surveyed the lobby for his watcher but he didn't seem to be in attendance. As he tore open the letters, he wondered whether he were imagining the whole thing. He was feverish after all and often felt some increase in paranoia when these sweats were upon him.

The first letter was from Fred Warburg confirming that 'Animal Farm' would now be published in August, paper supplies permitting. The second was a long one from Eileen and he decided to sit down in the lobby to read it at leisure. He knew it would carry lots of news about Ricky and he wanted to enjoy it. He sensed his wife had been ambivalent about the adoption, but it touched him whenever he saw them together. He knew she was now genuinely as fond of the child as he was. Every letter so far had been filled with the little boy's latest exploits and he kept them in his breast pocket where he could read them whilst travelling. As he selected an empty couch near the entrance to the bar, the words 'Richard sends you this message' caught his eye on the seventh page of her eight page typewritten epic. He settled himself down and drew a cigarette from his pocket and read the rest of the paragraph.

'He has no conflicts. If he gets a black eye he cries while it hurts but with the tears wet on his cheeks he laughs heartily at a new blue cat who says miaow to him and embraces it with loving words. Faced with any new situation he is sure that it will be an exciting and desirable situation for him, and he knows so well that everyone in the world is his good friend that even if someone hurts him he understands that it was by accident and loses none of his confidence.'

Eric felt tears prickle and lit his cigarette, turning to the beginning of the letter. How beautiful a child's mind. How wonderful to believe the rest of humanity bears you no malice and for this to be true. He felt Eileen was perhaps chiding him for his own bleak view and wishing he could be more like their son. He scanned the first page whilst still thinking about Ricky's face and the sound of his giggles when he tickled him. He almost missed the words 'growths' and 'tumours' and had to go back and read the passage again.

'The operation costs fifty pounds! But this thing will take a longish time to kill me if left alone and it will be costing some money the whole time.'

He read on but the twisting blade of fear in his belly that had been absent for this brief moment, returned with a bitter familiarity. Part of him was profoundly angry with her. She must have known she was ill before he left, but had said nothing. He quickly abandoned this feeling and reassured himself that she was right to be practical. She was strong, far stronger than he. He was grateful in a way. One of them had to be. He glanced up and met the eyes of the man in the flat cap sitting on a chair across from him, his newspaper partially lowered, covering his face from the nose down.

The Accident & Emergency department of University College Hospital was an antiseptic open-plan green and chrome coloured expanse of fixed seating and telescreens at the base of the huge tower. Pedro steered Eric into a chair and went to talk to the receptionists at the ice-blue console to one side. Eric slumped gratefully into the bucket-shaped mould and looked up at the impossibly thin screen above his head. A whale was breasting the waves in a glorious slow-motion sequence that made it seem as if the Leviathan were flying impossibly high above the blue billows. An earnest, elderly voice told him that the creature was now reduced to a population of 200 and returned each year to the Gibraltar Straits to feed and to be counted by marine biologists from all over the world. He marvelled at the detail of the image as every last glistening droplet seemed to hang like crystal shards in the shadow of the rock. He felt his eyes closing, the image still on his retina, flying in an endless arc across his mind. He could hear Pedro's conversation with the receptionist and allowed his immediate history to lull him into a doze.

'My fren' needs to be treated. He talking crazy and he got a fever.'

'What's his name?'

'Lewis. Lewis Allways.'

'Who's his GP?'

'He don't got, I think. He been in hospital before. Whipps Cross. Some bastard druggies beat him up bad by the canal. Bash him in the head. He don' wake up for a week and he get… er… what you call… Epileps.'

'But he's never been here before?'

'No. He say he had a room here. But I know him for six years and he never been here before. That's what I mean. He say crazy stuff. Thinks he was here yesterday. But he was with me last night. We sleeping rough, you know. So I know where he is all the time. We stick together.'

'Take a seat and the triage nurse will call his name. '

'I got to go with him. He don' know his name or nothing.'

'Take a seat.'

Eric slumbered on as Pedro returned to the seat beside him. He sat whale watching for an hour before a middle-aged nurse called out the sleeper's name. He shook Eric awake with difficulty and walked with him to the side cubicle for assessment.

The nurse was intensely pretty with a nice smile and Eric, dazed with exhaustion, smiled back almost involuntarily as Pedro started to describe his symptoms. She nodded every now and then as she listened and took his temperature and blood pressure. Her perfume made him giddy and her soft brown neck as she listened to his chest was close enough to see the smooth curve of her jaw rippling when she ground her teeth in concentration. In his half awake state, he imagined they were married and living in his ratty old room in the Rue du Pot de Fer. He met a beautiful brown Algerian girl in Paris once and had fallen in love with her almond eyes almost at once. She had stroked his head and promised without hesitation to accompany him back to his room. Later when she went for an unfeasibly long powder room break, he realised his wallet was gone and he hadn't the means to pay for his pastis or her abandoned cognac. He still loved her though. She had allowed him a kiss, at least, that had stayed with him forever. It was the same with his favourite prostitute in Burma. It was so easy to fall in love with the young, the healthy, the beautiful. He did it all the time. He read the nurse's name on the badge pinned above her breast. Joy Adedigba.

'I'm a private patient, Miss Adedigba.'

Pedro paused in his narrative and sighed.

Nurse Joy looked at Eric's grubby clothing, smelt the odour coming from it and contrasted both with his cut-glass accent. She surmised an ex-army officer taken to drink and the street. Smiling tolerantly, she felt his pulse. 'Course you are. Why not?'

'I have TB. Very advanced I'm afraid.'

She frowned at this and went across to a set of keys seemingly detached from a typewriter that lay before another of the ubiquitous telescreens.

'Curiously, I've been feeling very much better since this morning. I am very tired, though. Can I get back to my old room?'

She noted the 'vair tarred' and the 'beck to my own rum' and thought perhaps a Colonel or, at least, something quite high ranking. Not a prole. "What's your date of birth, Mr Allways? I need to track down your medical record and National Insurance number.'

'25th June 1903.'

She arched one beautiful eyebrow at Pedro who shrugged. 'How old are you?'

'47'

'Your full name?'

'Eric Arthur Blair'

She smiled as Pedro shook his head. 'Any relation to Tony?'

He looked puzzled. 'To whom?'

Pedro coughed and beckoned the nurse over so he could whisper in her ear. 'Harold. Harold Lewis Allways. But he like to be called Lewis. This Eric thing start up this morning.'

Eric, annoyed at the whispering, tried to regain her attention. 'My surgeon is Andrew Morland.'

Nurse Joy straightened and opened the door. 'Take a seat. I'll do what I can with the database and track down his records. I'll tell you when you can go through. We're not so busy right now, so it shouldn't be long.'

Pedro shepherded Eric back to the bucket-shaped seats for more whale watching.

It was only thirty-five minutes before they were called to the curtained cubicles of the A & E ward and for a tired looking young Doctor called Edward Martin to rally enough enthusiasm to examine him thoroughly. Listening to Pedro as he worked, he concentrated finally on a few neurological tests. After asking the patient to follow a pencil with his eye and to raise and lower his limbs, he sat on a metal-framed chair beside the bed with some obvious relief dragging a hand through his unruly brown hair and assessed the medical record for Harold Lewis Allways, which had been printed out and passed to him at the allocation desk.

'Well. You've got a slight temperature and a bit of a crackle in the chest, although nothing that sounds as bad as TB. Your friend here says you've been having a few funny five minutes in the memory department and you're looking a little anaemic. Tell me about this head injury.'

'Never had one, as far as I know.'

'Your friend says you were badly beaten up a few years ago. In here it says fractured skull, swelling and an operation to relieve the pressure followed by some medication to suppress some recurrent epilepsy.'

'I don't remember.'

'No mention of TB here either. When did you last have a fit?'

'I suppose it was in the hospital at Hairmyres. I had a bad reaction to the Streptomycin and I think I had some kind of seizure at one point. My hair fell out.'

'You don't think you might have checked out for a while last night?'

Eric paused before replying. Something had definitely happened last night.

'I suppose it's possible. Things haven't been quite right since then with my... perception. The things I see.'

'My talking to you now, does that seem real?'

'In a way. Everything seems real. But it clearly can't be. Things are so... different from when I went to sleep last night. Everything is skewed and... wrong. Rather like I stepped through the looking glass. Interesting really. I've felt curiously elated for most of the day until just before we set out to come here. Now I'm just exhausted.'

Dr Martin looked searchingly at him for a moment, noting the almost academic detachment as the patient described his condition.

'A bit hyperactive perhaps and then a feeling of deflation afterwards?'

'Not deflation exactly. I'm just very tired. Look, can't I just go back to my room?'

Martin ignored this and to Eric's amazement, took out a blue box that wasn't metal or wood and started tapping on the screen with a stylus that looked as if it might also be made of white bakelite.

'I think we'll give you a bit of an MOT. Bloods, urine, imaging on that chest and your head. I think we'll also need to send you up to neurology for a full-blown assessment once we have all the results. Are you up for that, Lewis?'

Eric frowned and instinctively patted his pockets. 'How much will all this cost?'

'Cost?'

'I am a private patient. The Rosenheim Wing. I've got a bit of money coming. But I like to have the invoice in advance if I can.'

Martin looked nonplussed for a moment and then decided to wrap this one up before the patient got any more confused. He turned to Pedro who was writhing uncomfortably in the second chair. 'Are you staying with him? Make sure he gets to where he has to for these tests?'

'Sure, sure.'

The Doctor patted Eric on the arm. 'We'll sort you out, Lewis. Don't worry. There's no charge. You don't look like you'd fail the means test.'

'It's Eric, actually.'

4 Recall

OVER THE NEXT four hours they traipsed along escalators and polished corridors following confusing signs to get Eric imaged, tested, sampled and analysed.

Pedro remained nervous and complained that the hospital was the best place to catch something serious. Eric didn't doubt it. Relieving himself in the public lavatory on one floor had been quite an experience with urine and blood sprinkled across the floor with no obvious sign of any cleaning staff. A telescreen above the cistern extolled the virtues of a company designated to carry out these services for all London hospitals.

The odyssey was proving to be frustrating and very tiring and Eric felt himself getting angrier and angrier as they journeyed around the small un-connected hamlets of treatment specialisms that rarely seemed to communicate with each other. Whatever the Doctor had tapped into his Bakelite box seldom seemed to have been conveyed to the dismissive guardians of each department gate. He wondered at the appearance of efficiency being undermined by such obvious lack of co-ordination and remembered the dream logic that usually characterised such vivid fever images. He started to think that the dream was trying to prevent him from waking by delaying the moment he could return to his bed for as long as possible. Finally, after a blood test had to be repeated because the blood type did not correspond to his medical file, he could bear it no longer.

'We're leaving' he said to Pedro as he limped behind him down one more featureless corridor.

'Look, this is just what they do. You'll get a bed, man. They got to keep you in. We pick up your head tests next and that will tell them they got to keep you. Stick with it, Lewis.

'I already have a bed. I know where it is. Come on.' Eric followed the exit signs for more than fifteen minutes, Pedro protesting all the way until at last they emerged on to Gower Street. They passed the Cruciform building that had been the main hospital and Eric saw that it was now called the Wolfson Institute for Biomedical Research. Ruddy Huxley, again. He scanned Gower Street and found the corner of the Rosenheim building where the private wards of UCH were to be found.

Getting past the reception desk was easier than they expected. A knot of mostly elderly people clutching appointment cards were waiting to be checked in and Pedro quickly steered Eric over to the lift before they attracted any attention. Eric allowed himself to be manoeuvred past a fascinating sign suggesting patients might 'Drop-in for Cancer' and surveyed the long menu of medicine that presented itself on a black plastic background beside the lift.

Ground Floor – Department of Medical Physics and Bio-Engineering, Cancer Information Centre

First Floor – Haematology Daycare, Complementary Therapy: Aromatherapy, massage, reflexology, reiki, healing

Second Floor – Children's Outpatients, Departments of Medical Physics & Bioengineering and Maxillofacial Surgery, Assisted Conception Unit

Third Floor – Private Patients Wing, Clinical Audit

Fourth Floor – University College London Hernia Clinic, Department of Urology

Fifth Floor – South Camden Mental Health Liaison Service, Department of Psychological Medicine and Psychotherapy, Neurology and Neurosurgery

Pedro, knowing it was only a matter of time before they were thrown out, frowned at the various departments and nudged Eric. 'You look like a fifth floor kinda guy, Lewis'.

Eric pressed the call button and said firmly 'Third floor.'

As the doors hissed open at the third floor, they were faced with a large Lucian Freud print of a naked girl lying on a couch. It was called 'Euston Road Venus'. Eric eyed it with distaste and decided the dream was now deliberately tormenting him. The woman's voluptuous breasts, rendered yellow and flocculent as a drowned corpse's, were Sonia's. Her face, turned slightly away from the viewer, was flushed as if she had just made love. As no doubt she had.

Eric walked rapidly down the thickly carpeted corridor, shedding his army coat in the heat and passing another series of prints, all of them Freud nudes and all of them sickening to him with their oily lubricious limbs reaching, stretching, reclining in attitudes redolent of rotting corpses scattered in the bombsites of Barcelona.

By the time he reached the last turn leading to his room, he was sweating and manic in the hooded top, his fists pumping at his sides as he ran towards the door. He banged through it intending to leap into his bed and pull the covers up over his exhausted head and sleep the whole mess away. But there was no bed. Only a startled balding man in a suit and tie sitting at a curved desk, who looked up and rose quickly to catch him as he fell forward. Pedro limped up behind Eric and held him by both arms.

'Lewis, please.'

Eric wrestled free and pushed Pedro to the floor, suddenly furious.

'Can't you get it into your head? I'm not Lewis.'

He was utterly devastated not to find his bed and an end to the confusion. He realised the dream would not let him wake. Not yet, maybe never.

The startled man stood up. Self-consciously brushing his hair across the bald patch, he made what he imagined was a calming gesture with his other hand. 'OK. How can I help you?'

Eric took the man by the collar and slammed him up against the open door. Pedro whimpered from the floor as he realised that things had, at last, got way beyond his control.

'This is my room. I paid for it. Who are you?'

The man's eyes tilted upwards to the sign on the door. Eric read it and shouted hoarsely into his face. 'What the devil is a Clinical Governance Facilitator? Where's Morland?'

The shorter man struggled to break free from the tall, thin attacker and threw himself back behind his desk, reaching for the telescreen. 'Just take a seat and we'll try and sort this out. OK?' He stabbed at the screen.

Eric's insides turned to ice and his normal detachment was out of reach as his mind whirled into a terrifying fear of the room, its occupant and every unfamiliar light fitting.

'Security? Third floor.' The harassed administrator turned slightly away from Eric and murmured in a low tone. Only snatches of his conversation were audible. '… middle-aged loony… playing at down there? No I don't know who…'

Eric screamed across the desk, his body bent and contorted. 'I'm Eric Arthur Blair.'

The Clinical Governance Facilitator stepped back from the screen and gave a short nervous laugh as he read the legend 'Arsenal FC' across the intruder's hooded top. 'Oh, I see. Been reading a guidebook have you? Well it isn't his room anymore, I'm afraid. The Orwell Archive is across the road if you really wish to know more about him. But this sort of thing is quite wrong, you know. You're not supposed to be able to just walk in here.'

Pedro clambered to his feet. 'Look mister, we going to go. He got confused. He got… er…head bang, y'know? He's not well.'

Eric struggled to contain a rising heat that seemed to begin from his feet and travel up to his knotted fists. 'Of course I am not well. That's why I came to hospital, damn you. I am supposed to be in your care.'

The Clinical Governance Facilitator decided enough was enough. He had tried to play the concerned, calming influence in the face of madness. But he was not a patient man and several Key Performance Indicators were due for review before he went home. 'You people make me sick. Bloody play-acting fantasists, literary researchers and documentary film crews every anniversary. When are you all going to realise he's not worth all this fuss? In my opinion, the most absurdly overrated writer in history.'

The security men arrived shortly after Eric had smashed his bruised fists into the man's doughy face for the third time.

March 1945 – Cologne

Eric, spitting blood, got himself admitted into a hospital in Cologne after putting up with the fever for almost a week, even whilst he stumbled over the rubble of bombed out buildings in the city. He endured the place for a few days before checking himself out, even though his chest still felt weak and painful. The public ward was intolerable with filth and he dosed himself up with the limited supply of drugs and walked unsteadily out, grateful to be free of its fetid atmosphere.

He arrived back at the Hotel Scribe lobby the following day to find an urgent telegram from Eileen's sister-in-law Gwen, via the Observer. His consent was required for the hysterectomy. He replied immediately and asked for a porter to help him up to his room. The stairs were beyond him, as the typewriter weighed down his bag.

As he climbed slowly behind a spotty young yokel from the Auvergne, he spotted the man in the flat cap sitting in his usual place on the chaise longue near the entrance to the bar. He nodded at the watcher, wondering whether he had missed him. His putative assassin, amber eyes bright and impenetrable above a copy of 'The Road to Wigan Pier', nodded back.

In his room, he collapsed on his bed after removing his clothes with difficulty and slept on and off for nearly ten hours. The next morning, lying swathed in linen like a holy relic, he realised he was going to have to get up and eat something. The thought made him feel nauseous and he became fixated on the notion of a reviving coffee in the Café Lumiere. This thought got him on his feet and into his uniform. There were several people he wanted to catch up with in the bar later and an assignment for the paper to be completed before tomorrow. He wondered if any of his fellow correspondents had peached on him to Astor about the state of his health. He didn't want to have to deal with embarrassing pleas to return if he could help it.

He took his temperature before he left his room and found that the fever had subsided considerably overnight. He felt a lot better now he was upright and stepped down the stairs to the lobby with confidence knowing that, for the moment, the crisis had passed.

In the Café he politely acknowledged a table of hacks including previous drinking companions Capa and Duff, but chose a table on his own with a copy of the Times. As he sipped his coffee with quiet appreciation, a porter told him there was a telegram at the desk and that several calls had been made to his room. He debated whether to wait until his toast arrived, but in the end told the waiter he would be back shortly and headed to the desk.

The lobby was buzzing with activity and uniforms of various hues were huddled together in informal gossip camps, most of them fuelled, even at this hour of the morning, with wine and Calvados. Another picture of De Gaulle was being hoisted into position by two liveried functionaries. He felt, as always, that the General looked down his considerable nose at all of them.

At the desk, he was handed another telegram from Gwen, presumably telling him how the operation went, along with several messages from Astor asking for him to call. He opened the telegram immediately, in case a reply was required. The message was short and couched in the usual abrupt language of the telegraph. Although Gwen had tried to soften the blow, it was clear that the operation had not gone as planned. Eileen was dead.

5 Parade

EMILY HAD ONLY heard the alarm once before, when she had accidentally pressed it whilst chatting to an attractive radiographer who had, quite unnecessarily, brought the head scan of a patient she was treating. They both knew it was accessible on the hospital's intranet minutes after the scan. But she gave him marks for initiative and kindly and calmly deflected him with confirmation of a currently fictitious boyfriend. This was somewhat undermined by the screaming siren triggered by the back of her briefcase against the panic button. The subsequent lecture by the breathless head of security, Mr Bellamy, after a headlong rush up the stairs, was no less humiliating.

'That button, Dr Statton, is called a panic alarm. There is a reason for this name. Can you guess what that is?'

This time, she sensed that someone was genuinely in need as the accompanying sound of running feet and the bellowing of a man on the floor below, seemed to indicate a panic at the very least. She tried to concentrate on her case note, but was interrupted about ten minutes later by a telephone call from Bellamy.

'We have a bit of a situation on the third floor in Mr Dellow's room. Can you come down for a sec? We're in the side ward off the Nurse's station.'

'Me? What for?'

'I think we're looking at a section and the police attending need an assessment.'

'God. I suppose so.'

Fever Diary – 9 February 20--

When I first saw her, a 15 stone police officer was sitting on my back and a somewhat smaller security man lay across my legs. She had her blonde hair pinned back in the fashion I remembered from the last time I saw her. It was such a relief to see the familiar golden halo as she entered the tiny one-bed ward where I had been dragged. Pedro was shouting loudly in Catalan to anyone who would listen. But he too was stunned into silence by her entrance. She was beautiful as always and I knew if she were really here with me in the After Wigan, that all would be well. Absurd notion, but somehow it seemed to be true.

I confess all this is in retrospect. At the time I was seized with a violent seizure that only slightly abated when I saw her face. I hardly remember now why I lost my reason to such an extent. I called her name. No. I am ashamed to say I screamed her name and struggled to reach her, to hold her in my arms. On the whole not a sane or rational response that is likely to find favour with any woman. But then, as many women have told me, par for the course in my relations with the opposite sex.

It is at this point that my memory has a gap of some days where I retained nothing beyond a series of moments that seem to have survived a period of complete nullity. A glimpse through a car window of a towering structure at the junction of Lower Regents Street and Charing Cross Road during a struggle with several heavy men in the back of a police vehicle. The screaming of a man in a prison cell that grated on the nerves until I realised it was me and asked myself to stop. Another glimpse through a van window at a Government department apparently called the Ministry of Sound. An injection and a courtroom. An injection and a hospital ward with locks on every internal door. An injection and Sonia's face. An injection and Sonia's voice. An injection…

ericisawake.blogspot.com

POSTED BY H LEWIS ALLWAYS AT 12:31 0 COMMENTS

The gates of the Inner London Crown Court sagged with the weight of the pathetic and appalling stories that entered and were despatched from their embrace, five days a week, nine to five. Emily had been there only twice before. Once for a preliminary hearing, to be cross-examined by Counsel for the Defence on why she had scored his deranged client a 21 on the Hare Psychopathy Checklist. Then, to give evidence in respect of a former student, a psychiatric nurse of Uyghur origin, who jumped from his 21st floor flat after an argument with some violent neighbours.

She had been walking away from his tower block in Swiss Cottage after responding to a tearful phone call and had just spent an hour calming him down. Before she reached the end of the road, she heard the sound of smashing glass as he pushed his head through his bedroom window. She turned to see him reaching forward with both hands for the sill beneath the shattered aperture. As she watched, unable to move, his body tumbled out over the frame and he hung from his fingers to the narrow strip of weathered wood, before finally letting go. His pyjama bottoms and ragged tan dressing gown fluttered in the breeze like pennants on a battlefield as he fell 21 storeys in what seemed to be an eternal flight. She lost sight of him below the 4th floor and heard the fleshy smack of an obese diver belly flopping into the deep end of the pool.

She was the first to reach him. One of his tormentors; a builder with a shock of dark hair, came out to watch as she climbed awkwardly over a steel rail that barred entry to the narrow trench bordered by a low concrete wall that encircled the base of the block. He was lying on his back and breathing in great heaving gasps as his punctured lungs poured blood into his chest cavity. One arm, knotted with fractures, waved slowly above his head and one eyeball lay on his cheek, the right side of his face shattered by the wall as he landed. The builder looked shocked but muttered 'Fucking Uglies. They're all crazy.'

A neighbour called the ambulance eventually and Emily was found by the paramedic, cradling the victim's head as he died with a grunt and a grimace. She felt responsible, of course. She always felt responsible. Part of her understood that this was eternally true, even if she were clearly not to blame. She was, after all, a murderer.

The taxi crawled into Southwark allowing Emily to touch up her make-up and gather her notes into some kind of order. As far as she was concerned, she was killing two birds with one stone. Having to submit reports and attend the hearing was not the chore it might have been. The tall blue-eyed gentleman who kept calling her Sonia was an interesting case and she found herself curiously eager for the section to be extended.

In addition, she had promised her annoying little brother for some time that she would one day see him in action and still hadn't done so. To find Simon as the appointed representative for the patient was fortunate indeed, although she had to inform the Clerk of the Court in case of any perceived conflict of interest. Judge Ely regarded himself as a wag and found it amusing to send back a message asking if there wasn't another member of the Statton family in the police force to complete the set. He regarded himself as a charming roué when in fact, she knew him as a slimy lech that had sued a newspaper over a messy affair with a woman thirty years his junior. Apparently they alleged that he enjoyed being urinated on, when, in fact, rather disappointingly, he accepted the usual clichéd beatings with nylon whips purchased from chain store sex shops. It was important that the newspapers got these little details right and were legally com-pelled to apologise for such gross inaccuracies. Otherwise people like Simon would be out of work.

Simon met her in the large chamber at the front of the building with its motley collection of nervous plaintiffs, defendants and wit-nesses littering the padded seats of judicial purgatory. As usual she found it impossible to think of him as anything but the snotty-nosed tag-along from their youth. The idea that this skinny, confident floppy-haired advocate was anything to do with the image in her head was always difficult to believe. He hugged her perfunctorily and nodded at her notes.

'All over as far as that stuff goes. Your report accepted and con-sidered last time.'

'I know. I just like to have it to hand in case something comes up and they want me to speak. Will we get an extension?'

'If you really want one. Why? English literature course at evening class?'

'Funny. I just think he's good value.'

'As nut jobs go.'

'As a case study.'

'Ah, writing a book are we?'

'I've considered it, cynical toad. But that's not why I think it should be extended. He still has a long way to go.'

'All the way to Wigan?'

'Says the failed English A level. He's not a danger to himself or others anymore and the assault charge has been dropped, so...'

'Has it?'

She frowned and rummaged in her notes. 'Didn't they tell you? I asked Charlie Dellow if he really wanted to piss off the administrator by drawing attention to the lapse in security and he decided, on balance, that he didn't.'

'Why should he care?'

'Improving security was one of Charlie's Key Performance Indicators. Bit like the safety officer falling down a lift shaft.'

'Only himself to blame?'

'Precisely.'

'It's probably in my brief. But I haven't read it yet.'

'Do you remember leaving your DH Lawrence essay until three hours before it was due?'

'Briefs are different, Sis. The Section 136 has reached the time limit so at this hearing the best you can hope for is referred for hospital treatment, but entered as an 'informal' patient on a voluntary basis. In this case he won't be subject to detention and would not be prevented from leaving if he wants to. Plus, his consent would have to be obtained before treatment continues.'

'Not a problem.'

'Really?'

'Really'.

The case was pushed forward into the afternoon to deal with an urgent Terrorism Detention Act extension that required a Mandarin translator and when they finally trooped into the court, the air of postprandial torpor pervaded the Judge and counsel's oratory whilst the short and relatively simple matter of Emily's care extension was drawn out like taffy on a hook, until all present were sticky with boredom.

A crumpled court reporter, Derek Sallon, found himself trapped in his seat after falling asleep during the TDA proceedings and waking far too late to get out of the room without a sarcastic response from Ely. He smouldered in frustration as the next case inched on with a staggering indolence only matched by his own.

Prosecution counsel Mr Bowling, bored and middle-aged, outlined the Crown's abandonment of the assault charge and sat down again, hoping he wouldn't have anything more to say or do until an early afternoon knock off for drinks with Ely at the Windmill Tavern followed by a cheap but satisfying working girl before the long train ride home to West Bletchley.

The only moment of interest, for Sallon at least, came as the patient himself asked for an opportunity to be heard. Emily's own sleepy calm was disturbed by this indulgence and she didn't quite see why Ely was allowing it. She watched Eric, his tall lanky frame fidgeting slightly in the donated suit trousers, jacket and long sleeved white shirt. He cleared his throat and the high, fluting whisper began its susurration around the panelled walls.

'I really don't know if what I now believe is what I have always believed. As I have no memory of this existence and this place, I cannot truly determine whether I am deluded or dreaming. If the former, it appears a curiously convoluted fantasy rooted in an arcane knowledge of an all too well documented life. If the latter, then nothing you recommend about what people choose to call my 'care' will make any difference at all. We occupy two opposing perceptions of existence, my Lord. To you, I am an ex-army petty offender with a medical record and a history as Harold Lewis Allways. To me, I am who I have always been; or, at least, who I now perceive myself to have always been. Although a courtroom is no place for a discussion on the nature of existence, I would recommend, if you are at all interested, the works of phenomenologist Maurice Merleau-Ponty. He has some interesting things to say on how we may be in a position to undertake actions that transcend the organic level of the body.'

Sallon snorted involuntarily and scribbled on the smooth screen of his MC's notepod. He was beginning to see an amusing word sketch in this. Perhaps a column on a 'day in the life of the Inner London' piece, tangential to the TDA hearing he was supposed to be writing about. He watched the lanky, ravaged individual as he faltered under his gaze and then appeared to rally.

'More prosaically, I can't convince you that my perception is any more valid than yours. On the other hand, you cannot convince me that I am anything other than Eric Arthur Blair. We are, as far as I am concerned, in a stalemate position, existentially. But as it has been explained that I do have some choices, whoever I turn out to be, I am happy to accept the continuing care of Miss Statton, provided some kind of accommodation can be found for myself and my friend Pedro.'

Ely raised an eyebrow at Simon who rose quickly in response.

'I understand that Mr Abbad is in temporary accommodation in Stamford Hill and that Hackney Social Services have arranged a room for Mr Allways in the same building on his release from the Acute Assessment Unit. Miss Statton has said that she is happy to receive him twice a week at her therapy room at UCH and to supervise and monitor his medication.'

Ely looked at Emily and grunted, non-committal, before rubbing his eyes tiredly. 'I'm not sure I'm happy about that, Mr Statton. Although assault charges were dropped, we are talking about a patient who has shown some violence in the past.' He smiled slyly at Simon.

'I'm surprised you aren't more concerned about your sister's welfare, Mr Statton.' Simon smiled back indulgently and turned to Emily, his teeth grating in suppressed irritation. 'As my Lord will perceive, Dr Statton is alive and well after four weeks working with the patient. The Rosenheim Building at UCH has a fine figure of a security man, therapy rooms with panic buttons and there seems no likelihood of a recurrence of the crisis that led to Mr Allways' disoriented, distressed and uncharacteristic outburst against Mr Dellow. This is due, in no small measure, to the work she has done with him since that time and reflected by the advice received on the relaxation of the section we dealt with at the last hearing'.

Ely's eyes twinkled suggestively at Emily. 'He still thinks he's George Orwell.'

Simon bowed his head in acceptance of the inescapable. 'Perhaps, my Lord, that is more of a problem for us than it is for him.'

Sallon chuckled to himself. Better and better. Orwell in the dock. Even looks a bit like him. Positioning his MC discreetly at the end of the bench, he snapped a front view of Eric as he waited impatiently for the deliberations to end. The high forehead and the piercing eyes were unmistakable to Sallon's memory of Orwell's famous image. This had potential.

Fever Diary – 16 February 20--

I have my Rocinante at last. Donated by Miss Statton's brother, who apparently gave up cycling when he entered the Inns of Court. A far cry from the touring bicycles of my youth, but a worthy steed, I think. The gearing is more complex than I am used to, but I was absurdly pleased when I saw it and couldn't fathom why, until I realised that it represented a degree of freedom – a ticket to explore the changed city now that I seem to have regained my health.

A further degree of liberty has also been afforded by the arrival of bi-weekly payments from the state. They seemed like a fortune until I discovered the cost of living, but this is to be expected. Tobacco and tea are my chief indulgences and oh, how I have missed them.

The process of applying for such assistance was possible only by accepting and acknowledging my identity as Lewis Allways. I objected to this, but as I retain none of my own identity documents, I could see no other option. In the end, rather in the manner of my acceptance of a position as a propagandist at the BBC, (making the message marginally less disgusting than it might otherwise have been) I came to an all too convenient accommodation with myself. Rather more persuasive than my own ethical pirouetting, Pedro pointed out that our rent and minimal living expenses would be guaranteed on the basis of my alleged 'mental incapacity'. Armed with a written diagnosis from Miss Statton that was treated like a Papal edict by the local authorities, we were soon on Easy Street as far as I was concerned, albeit with an uneasy conscience and the perception that the decision was likely to come back and haunt us before long.

I find that cash is regarded as the currency of the poor and very much looked down upon even by the smallest corner shop. It used to be a sign of conspicuous wealth (or spivvery) to go around with a bankroll of crisp notes. Now you are regarded with suspicion and derision if you do not pay with your MC. The MC is a hand-held device activated by a thumbprint (I am not entirely certain of this) that effectively supervises your entire life. The most common versions are thin rectangles of hard material, the more luxurious, transparent squares of indestructible 'paper' that can be folded or rolled. As well as communication, entertainment, projection and diary functions, it also serves as a means to pay bills. Transport is accessed by simply passing it across a barrier and shop purchases are made in the same manner. Simply proffering a note or coin across the counter is enough to provoke an exasperated sigh followed by a head to toe appraisal of your exact value in Eurodollar, creditworthiness and social status.

The crumbling converted Edwardian maisonette, in which Pedro and I are currently living, encourages an early exit after waking, if only to eat and get a little heat into the bones. Every Monday, a plastic container of milk and a wrapped loaf of bread are left by the landlord in the hall and apparently fulfil his legal obligation to provide daily bed and breakfast accommodation. These offerings constitute breakfast provision for the week and may be regarded, I think, as an inedible loophole in the contract he has with the local authority.

The bread is a an unnatural white colour that reminds me of the chalk and flour loaves meanly got up by famine hit villages in Spain during the worst of the blockades. There are few cooking facilities beyond an electric kettle and a luxuriously appointed pop-up toaster, a necessity when all of the existing fireplaces in the Edwardian house conversion appear to have been boarded up. Pedro has shown his ingenuity by use of the small metal frames that are built into the top of the device and enable him to heat broth in the opened can. It's a perilous exercise which I am certain will eventually lead to a spillage that, if we survive, will see us imbibing a form of electric soup. He has since constructed a small grill with salvaged bricks in the tiny walled yard in front of the house facing the towpath.

The room itself is, of course, very small with a single bed covered by a puffy stuffed material that replaces the normal blanket and upper sheet. There is a telescreen as there is everywhere, although it is quite small and battered looking. The programming is commanded by the ubiquitous jukebox method of selection, which affords me a seemingly endless choice of viewing. Pedro is contemptuous and complains that it is a very restricted menu and that they only have one in the room because access to mobnet is considered to be some sort of civil rights issue. Evidently people are still allowed to starve, to be unemployed, to be homeless and to roam the streets baying at the moon, but they cannot be deprived of the right to a virtual world that bears no relation to their own.

Remembering my whale watching in the waiting area of UCH, I have successfully programmed the device to show me only wildlife documentaries and a single BBC News Channel. Here I can flip between the naked savagery of animal interaction and the natural history programmes.

The draughty window, stuffed around the edges with paper, looks out over the Lea Navigation Canal. The view in the mornings when the mist is rising from the Walthamstow Marshes is eerie but beautiful. It also means that the room is almost permanently damp. A heating panel against one wall affords a cosy but intermittent comfort after eight in the morning until around noon. Even so, I can honestly say that it ranks highly over my Canonbury Square flat in winter.

The Hasidic Jews congregate by the waters of the canal to

feed ducks, ride bikes and to pray. I understand they even have a separate Stamford Hill ambulance service. There is something disorienting in the sight of people dressed as 18th century Polish aristocrats to a man wrenched out of my own century into an already chaotic future. Nonetheless, I find a curious comfort that they too are out of their time and have struck up many conversations as I loiter on the towpath, forced to smoke outside by a draconian and frankly mystifying prohibition on any inhalation of tobacco in areas that possess a roof. It is in this way that I discover they have far more capacity to assimilate than I. Many have more devices in their pockets and in their homes than the average scientist. Nonetheless, they eschew them all on the Sabbath as they have always done and I was amused by the ingenuity displayed by one trader who employed a gentle Hindu tobacconist to press the required buttons on a Saturday when international trade dictated that some business courtesy had to be performed for his foreign clientele. The compromises of faith are evidently encroaching in the face of a society that never seems to be at rest.

I rejected the bizarre head protector offered to me by Miss Statton and opted for a balaclava from the charity shop in Stamford Hill. The formidable German lady who sold it to me remarked that they were seldom found these days and Miss Statton, seeing me arrive for one of our sessions still wearing it, remarked that I was likely to be mistaken for a burglar or paramilitary terrorist. This pleased me very much and I tried to ride my bicycle with the air of a seasoned fighter that should not be trifled with. Using some cable ties liberated from the lethal wiring in my room, I secured a stout stick beneath the crossbar and felt myself well prepared for any challenge encountered on my long canal towpath rides.

On one occasion, I rode past a group of black, white and oriental teenagers near the small railway tunnel that leads to High Hill Ferry and the pub at the foot of Springfield Park. They appeared to be rehearsing a complex rhythmic rhyme that combined percussive vocal impressions with a stream of unconsciousness narrative from a young girl with startling facial tattoos. Several of them accompanied themselves on MC's that emitted string and brass simulations of remarkable quality.

I passed them slowly without meeting their eyes and entered the tunnel, only to find a group of Orthodox youths, their beards wispy and patchy beneath their long curled side-locks, doing exactly the same thing. I stopped and asked what was going on and a ginger-haired young Ashkenazi told me brusquely that they were about to 'have a battle'. I reflected on the eternal verity of racial and ethnic conflict and contemplated which side I would choose to defend, until the 'battle' itself began.

I found the cable ties around my only defence extremely reluctant to release their charge. I am not sure I fully understood their construction. Given the police sirens and regular news bulletins of shootings and knifings amongst the youth of East London, I expected therefore to be ill equipped for the melee and tore off a branch of an innocent cherry tree that overhung the dull waters. By the time I returned, prepared for whatever injustice was to be meted out, I found myself in the urban equivalent of a chamber concert. The tunnel resounded to the sounds of both sides taking it in turns to improvise and expand upon a sophisticated melody with a reflection on the differences and similarities between them. True, their approach and demeanour was aggressive and a degree of insult was exchanged, but it never seemed set to develop into the physical.

I was both charmed and ashamed that I had misinterpreted the situation and when they perceived me standing in bicycle clips with a raised branch in one hand, I thought I had succeeded in raising the metaphorical to the literal. Fortunately I presented such a comical sight, that they dissolved into gales of laughter and the collapse of stout party was the only sensible response.

This is my life now, the betrayal of the senses.

ericisawake.blogspot.com

POSTED BY H LEWIS ALLWAYS AT 12:31 0 COMMENTS

6 Therapy

THE SESSIONS, EMILY mused, were interesting, even if progress was almost imperceptible. Every two days, the patient wobbled in on her brother's ancient bicycle and rested it trustingly against the UCH cycle park bollards without any locks and spent at least an hour with her.

The room was furnished with three or four padded blue chairs and a series of Magritte prints on the walls which clashed with the institutional green of the walls.

He always sat coiled in a knot of legs and arms with one hand rolling a cigarette paper between two fingers. Emily watched the delicately rolled sliver of white skin as he manipulated two rolled ends against each other – a substitute for actually filling it with the cheap tobacco he favoured. Sometimes he looked out of the low window to one side at the Cruciform Building opposite, his right knee juddering up and down like a jackhammer.

As always, he maintained his position that he was not Lewis Allways, but had ceased to refer to her as Sonia. Development of a sort, she thought.

His talent for misdirection was limited, but he attempted it nonetheless. Today he had arrived breathless with the discovery of an old table football game salvaged by Pedro from the canal and installed in the tiny hall of their digs. She was amused that even this seemed to provoke a lecture on the history of the game; beginning with its invention by a man trapped in the rubble after the bombing of Madrid during the Spanish Civil War. As he spoke, she discovered from her MC that this was not what mobnet said about the origins of the game. She put this down to his Civil War obsession until she stumbled upon a competing (though largely discredited) claim by a Spanish inventor called Alexandre Campos Ramírez, that was indeed exactly as he described. He reminded Emily of her Grandfather, a self-educated manual worker who once gave an impromptu lecture on the history of the bicycle to her hapless date who had made the fatal mistake of arriving on one. Eventually, she managed to steer her charge round to the central issues.

'How are you settling in at Stamford Hill?'

'Very equitably, thank you. Almost luxurious, in a basic way. But I'm used to that. I very much enjoy the bicycle. Please thank your brother for me.'

'He doesn't know about it yet. I don't think he knows how it works. And the medication? How are you getting on?'

He tugged at his nose impatiently and avoided her eyes. 'I'm getting on very well without it, actually.'

'Lewis, it really is very important that you take it.'

'Why? Specifically?'

'Because you are still hallucinating and that really isn't where we want to be now that we've got you more settled.'

'It's where I want to be. Is there some sort of legal compulsion here?'

'Not now. No more than there is for you to come here.'

He grunted and brushed lint from his trousers. 'I don't mind that so much. Pedro is a limited conversationalist and not as pretty.'

'You come for conversation and for the view? You don't think it's doing you any good to come to terms with your condition?'

'It's you who regard me as a 'condition'. I am very content with my delusion, if that is what it is.'

'What do you call it?'

'The end of the pier. A show taking place inside my head. Moderately entertaining but also quite uncomfortable at times.'

'Where did you get your costume?'

He looked down at his smoking jacket, tweed trousers, Argyle socks and creased brown brogues. 'Costume? The hooded garment and the Arsenal shirt seemed far more of a pantomime to me. Both elicited a fair amount of hostile comment and general disapproval. I found these in a charity shop on the Seven Sisters Road. A very comforting smell came with them. Old tobacco and mothballs. The odour of dead old men. I'm beginning to think of this as my personal cologne.'

'Why do you think I regard it as a costume?'

'Because you believe I am playing a part. But then, aren't we all?'

'No philosophical sidebars please. Let's discuss that perception.'

He sighed and rubbed his long jaw reflectively. 'I sleep very well in the skin of Eric Arthur Blair, though you believe this to be wrong. I cannot help how you feel about it. Are you familiar with milieu therapy?'

'In what context?'

'In the context of taking the madmen and teaching them to be silent on the top decks of buses and to only talk to themselves when no one is listening. Making them presentable in a public milieu. A Victorian innovation, I think.'

'Not quite the definition I was taught. You think that's what's happening here?'

'I think you need me to be Lewis Allways. I think anything less than this is an affront to your sense of order.'

'I don't need you to be anyone but yourself.'

'And here, once again, we buy a ticket for the number 29 bus along the Moebius strip.'

'You seem to think I'm trying to compel you to be something you're not.'

Eric sighed. 'You want to pull me back to the centre. I prefer the edge. You can see further from there.'

'What if I were able to prove it to you? Beyond doubt?'

'How?'

'Scientifically. DNA. Genetics. Whatever.'

'Is that possible? What do you mean by DNA?'

Emily frowned. 'As I'm sure you know DNA is a kind of unique genetic fingerprint that can be tied to one particular individual. What would you say if it were possible to match your DNA with that of Lewis Allways?'

'Then I suppose I would be swayed in the direction of my being under the influence of a defined mental illness, rather than at the end of my pier.'

'And might therefore make some progress in your perception of who you really are?'

'Perhaps. I really don't know. If both the past and the external world exist only in the mind, and if the mind itself is controllable, what can either of us prove beyond doubt?'

'Have you always spoken like you do now?'

'I had more volume before I was shot and Eton grinds out an RP that seldom leaves you once it has been beaten into place. But, in general, yes. Why?'

'Because Pedro's perception is that your voice has changed, radically. He doesn't recognise either your vocabulary or your accent. It has a 'Brief Encounter' timbre that comes from another age, so you are to be congratulated for studying it to such a degree.'

'That would bear considerably more weight if I didn't believe Pedro to be a product of my own subconscious.'

'And me? Your bike? Stamford Hill?'

'I believe so. I recognise, of course, that if I were sitting in my hospital bed listening to Cyril or Malcolm telling me I was merely a product of their fevered imagination, I would suggest they take a little more water with it.'

'Cyril and Malcolm?'

'Connolly and Muggeridge. They've seen me in the raving hours and still, bizarrely, remain my friends. You know that phrase 'fair weather friends'? Those two are some of my hot and cold fellows. Always willing to talk to you regardless of whether you are running a temperature and waffling about running a tobacconist kiosk or stone cold sober and asking for the cricket score. I've watched them making exasperated moues at each other during the fevered hours, and then having a little fun with my memory whilst they can. Another friend, Paul Potts, once swore he'd lent me two pounds the previous day and only relented when you...' He paused and looked away. '...when Sonia slapped him on the back of his hand and told him he was a devious bastard.'

'I've looked at photos of her. I can see the resemblance.'

'I'm sorry. I promised not to make that mistake again.'

'Why is your identification of me as Sonia Orwell…'

'Brownell.'

'…Brownell, a mistake and your identification of yourself as George Orwell a fact?'

'Although you are the living image of her, you have none of her personality. That's not pejorative, by the way. Sonia simply isn't like you in nature.'

'I don't think you or I can possibly know what she was like. You accept that the general consensus in society would be that you cannot possibly be who you think you are?'

'Being in a minority, even a minority of one, does not make you mad. In any case, according to the National Health Service I am a 'service user' not a madman.'

Emily smiled ruefully. 'The jargon of healthcare can be woefully euphemistic at times. Wouldn't you rather be a 'service user' than a madman?'

'Frankly, no. Language is important. When someone seeks to dissemble in prose or in life, their vocabulary betrays their true intention. Collateral damage, quantitative easing, service user, empowerment. You know they are calling Pedro my carer?'

'I'm sure he's happy with the label. It means he may eventually get a carer's allowance from the Department of Work & Pensions'.

'I thought I detected a new glint in his eye. Tell me about this device.' He pointed to her MC resting on the nearby desk.

'It's an MC. You've seen them, I'm sure.'

'Oh yes. They seem like the keys to the door for most people. But why MC?'

She cocked her head on one side and looked him in the eye. 'Do I really need to explain that to you, Lewis? Don't you already know very well what it is?'

'Can we assume, for a moment, that Eric does not know what it is?'

Emily sighed and picked up the slender silver device as if seeing it for the first time. 'It stands for Mob Console.'

'Mob?'

'Ministry of Business. You remember the attacks on the cloud servers and the power supply after Altay?'

'I am sure you expect me to.'

'We still get power cuts every now and then. But the infrastructure suffered, businesses were paralysed and transport, communication and civil administration at a standstill every time we lost power. The country virtually shut down. Chaos. Some of it engineered by terrorists hacking into the providers and sabotaging it deliberately. As a consequence the Ministry of Business was formed out of the old Home Office and Treasury with a mission to ensure the constant maintenance of consistent power to the network and therefore the economy. Effectively they took responsibility for the regulation and security of power supplies to every Interverse Provider and corporate cloud server in the UK and as signatories of the Moscow DAT1 Accord, filtered all traffic with the rest of the world. They provide the access technology and therefore these devices, which are always able to connect anywhere in the country and abroad. They are licensed to commercial providers very cheaply by the MOB to ensure the security and consistency of the infrastructure.'

'And the control, of course.'

'Well, that's mostly anecdotal paranoia from conspiracy theorists who know nothing about how the UK works. People claim they are screening out sites and information that isn't helpful to the state. But frankly, given the criticism meted out to politicians in the Interverse, that's difficult to believe.'

'If you have control, you can allow all manner of irreverence. Ultimately those who criticise within a system controlled by the state are powerless to organise.'

'This, I think, is you theorising as Eric, not Lewis.'

'And therefore 'not helpful' to your purpose?'

'Or to your recovery.'

'Aren't there alternatives?'

'To recovery?'

He smiled. 'To the state controlled system.'

'A few entrepreneurs and press magnates with enough money to launch their own satellites and networks and many foreign providers of course, although the US has a similar regulatory authority. One Irish billionaire, John Carolan, makes a point of his independence from state control and hosts a portal that contains numerous civil disorder and climate hactivist sites. But of course, his network is less stable and prone to sudden unexplained crashes at crucial times.'

'Just as certain stories fail to find their way into supposedly independent newspapers?'

Emily put the MC down with a faint click against the table surface. 'Are you going to take your medication?'

'Would you?'

'Of course.'

'No. I mean would you if you truly knew that you were who you claim to be and not subject to any delusion?'

'Given the impossibility in time and space, I would assume I was wrong and needed help.'

He gazed at her intently and slowly tapped his head. 'I have all the time and space I need up here.'

March 1945 – London

After Eileen's funeral, Eric waved goodbye to a weeping Gwen and travelled back from Newcastle in an empty train compartment.

Looking out at the blacked out countryside, he felt utterly alone. It had been a good decade of marriage, all in all. He had not been faithful the whole time and he knew the business with his secretary at Tribune had upset Eileen greatly, although they had seldom talked about it. He suspected she had also had at least one affair after this, perhaps feeling that he needed to know the pain of betrayal. But, to his mind, that was simply what they did with their bodies. The fidelity of their minds was absolute.

Without Eileen's razor-sharp acuity, he could not have written at least two of his novels. She had always managed to coax him out of the darkest hours and gently deflate him when, in a pompous, drunken mood, he allowed his more ridiculous notions to take hold. Who would do that now? Who would love him? Who could love this sickly, moth-eaten relic? How could he find his way to the mountains and the sea without her? 'Every man is an island unto himself' he had said once when chided for his reticence. She had smiled and replied 'Yes, dearest, so they tell each other. But they always seem to be building bridges on the quiet and there's usually some poor benighted woman at the end of it.'

The following day he went to Soho and had lunch at Czarda with David Astor. Astor thought the food unusually appalling, the chef presumably driven to desperation by rationing, but Eric ate so voraciously that Astor began to think he did not taste it at all. He realized with amusement that anyone looking at the shabby figure eating with the neat gentleman sporting gold cufflinks would have no doubt who was paying the bill. As usual he felt overly ostentatious next to Eric and found himself almost shrinking into his Savile Row suit.

He studied his friend as he ate and sipped a dubious Hungarian wine whilst they dissected the latest rumours, gossiping about Connolly and others. When they reached the stage of smoking and studying the limited dessert menu, he offered his condolences again for Eileen. Eric looked uncomfortable as he had managed to go a whole hour without mentioning her once.

'You don't look well, Eric. This must have been a terrible shock. Why don't you take a rest?'

'I got Eileen to write to the Fletchers about Barnhill. It seems I get could rent it very cheaply now.'

Astor looked exasperated. 'Barnhill? Good grief, man. It's miles from anywhere. The remotest house on the island. There isn't even a road to it, just a track. No electricity, no telephone, the mail only delivers once a week, if that.'

'Sounds wonderful. I can bury myself there'. Eric seemed to brighten for a moment but then his shoulders slumped. 'I would like to go. The Isle of Jura sounds just the job. But I don't think I can do that right now. I need to be occupied and isolating myself on a remote rock, although attractive, is probably not the ticket just yet.'

'You're not thinking of going back?'

'I must. A few weeks of bumping round in army jeeps will restore me a bit, I think. After all, the war is petering out or rising to a crescendo depending upon your point of view. Either way, I'd like to bear witness

for a bit longer if I can.'

Astor sighed and glanced over at a nearby table where a distant relative was entertaining a stunning girl with a halo of blond hair and sparkling blue eyes.

'Eileen gave me quite a hard time about giving you this job. She felt journalism was a waste of your talents. I think she held me personally responsible for taking you away from your true calling. Perhaps I'd be doing a favour to her memory if I just told you to go and write your novels and forget Fleet Street altogether.'

'I will. But this is probably my last opportunity to be anywhere near the front line before the whole show is over. A journalist, even a reluctant one, can't turn down that sort of opportunity.'

'Promise me you'll let me find you a more hospitable cottage in the West Country or somewhere when you get back. I think you need a good long rest and it really is quite temperate down there.'

'Sounds ghastly. Too easy for people to drop in on you uninvited. At least at Barnhill you know that every visitor has to have gone through an ordeal to get there. In the meantime, can you get me a passage to Germany?'

'What about Richard?'

'I've asked Doreen Kopp to take Ricky on for a bit. She and Georges have a child, so he won't be lonely.'

'Is she still with Georges?'

Eric looked away. 'He's away a lot. But I think they stagger on. She told me...'

It was Astor's turn to look uncomfortable. Their conversations ranged far and wide, but seldom edged into more intimate areas. In truth, Astor felt ill qualified to intrude on the complex knot of relationships Eric maintained with women. Nonetheless, he felt curiously protective of the shabby scribe and hated it when he appeared vulnerable. Eric was the most self-denigrating man he had ever met and it sometimes distressed him to see such a destructive lack of confidence in someone so talented. He had once told Connolly after sitting through another of Eric's self lacerations over one of his novels that it was 'like watching Eeyore repeatedly lashing himself with a riding crop.'

'I think I know what she told you.' He said carefully. 'Eileen loved you very much, you ass. You know that. Whatever did or did not happen

with Georges.'

Eric drew deeply on one of his appalling roll-ups and squinted at Astor through the plume of acrid smoke. 'The trouble is, I had enormous faith in Kopp. Now I don't know what to think.'

'It doesn't change anything. Not really. Good God, Eric. It's only sex, damn it.'

Eric smiled wryly. 'It may be more than that. You know they are trying to kill me, don't you?'

Astor frowned. 'Who? Kopp? Ridiculous.'

'No I don't think he'd go that far. But the Russians let him go and they never let anyone go without a reason. Now I think they are coming after me.'

'Evidence? Someone shoot at you?' Eric laughed. 'At the army. Not at me particularly. But there were several characters around at the Scribe. Russians hanging around, watching people, watching me.'

'Sure you're not imagining it?'

Eric took several seconds to think and the ash of his cigarette fell into his coffee without comment. 'It's possible. My nerves haven't been at their best. Maybe it's my ego. Stalin probably doesn't even care about Spain. But I am still down as a Trot on their lists. These days that's a death sentence.'

'Only in Russia' said Astor disdainfully. 'I can think of a dozen more important targets than you.'

Eric roared with laughter and dissolved into a fit of coughing, his eyes streaming. 'You really know how to hurt a chap.'

Dr Ed Martin came up to Emily's room one Thursday after her session with Lewis and sat in a puzzled slouch in the chair occupied by her patient only an hour before, his white coat hanging over the arms. He stared at his MC in a perplexed manner and said nothing. Emily coughed and leant down to catch his eye. He seemed to suddenly remember why he had barged into her office and straightened up a little.

'Bit of a cock up. I think. Yes, I think it's a mistake.'

'How unusual around here. Software again?'

'No. We trashed that system after the supplier went bust. It went out to tender again and I think Mickey Mouse got the contract.'

'Run that by me again?'

'Disney work either. Ho, bloody ho. Humour, even in the face of adversity.'

'Of a sort.'

'Of a sort. Harold Lewis Allways. Bloods were wrong so we went for a walk around the test schedule.'

'Infected?'

'No, no. Very healthy. No trace of anything current as we found on first examination. Just wrong.'

'How?'

Martin slumped again, frowning. 'Wrong blood type. Wrong medical history. Wrong guy.'

'Not Harold Lewis Allways?'

'Not according to the numbers on the file from Whipps Cross. He checked in there with his head injury years ago and they gave him three pints of blood and ran all the usual tests for HIV and allergies before the operation. At one point they thought both kidneys were shot and tested him for the transplant list.'

'And?'

'Kidneys partially recovered, but the tissue samples… Not a single number matches and no head injury showing on the scan.'

'Computer error?'

'Not on every test done by different people at different hospitals. Checked out his archive and found a visit to St Thomas's after a binge. Belted a charge nurse and had to be sedated to stitch up his right arm. Again, matches all the Whipps Cross numbers, but not what we took from your fella after the section.'

'So, not who we say he is. Not who he says he is.'

'I heard about that. Very literary schizophrenics we get in Gower Street. Bloomsbury Group for Bedwetters.'

'So what now?'

'Police? Full DNA test? Missing persons?'

'You're stumped.'

'Any ideas?'

'His friend, Pedro, met him five or six years ago. Called himself

Lewis, said he was ex-army. Had no ID when we found him though. Maybe just decided to be this guy for a while. Escaping some dodgy past or memory.'

'Sure. Makes as much sense as anything else. But Allways was close to liver failure from cirrhosis and had an ulcer. He once had the clap. Your man, sober as a judge and no ulcer. Had the clap once too. But different kind of clap.'

'What do you suggest?'

'I think you're obliged to inform what they call 'the proper authorities' that your patient doesn't exist.'

IT WASN'T THAT Derek Sallon hated Merrett specifically. He hated pretty much every human being he met and therefore Michael Merrett was simply another cylinder of chemicals that engendered a general repulsion within him. Listening to him holding court in the White City Tavern with two young researchers, Sallon reflected on their long disassociation as he tapped absently on his MC.

Long, long ago, when they were both narrower and less toxic tubes of vitriol, Sallon had employed Merrett as a writer of obituaries at the West London Gazette. He had been a long-haired, fogeyish young man with a keen literary wit and rather more education than the usual applicants. In the intervening time, their waists thickened whilst their fortunes waxed and waned in diametrical opposition. Merrett went from local to national obituaries on the 'Independent' and then progressed to television where he summarised, with a supposedly engaging irreverence, the lives of the recently expired. 'Boxed Lives' ran for seven years and became a column in a satirical magazine, a book and a mobnet resource.

Sallon went from lead reporter on the West London Gazette to sports editor at the 'Guardian' followed by a period of drunken disgrace via divorce, AA and extreme debt and finally to court reporter for the Associated Press where he had lodged, like a cuttlefish bone between two rocks on a deserted shore for years and years and years.

Merrett had since evolved, further up the beach, as a television historian; his talent for summary employed in reducing the giants of culture and politics to digestible lumps, leavened with his customary flip satire. His unnaturally brown hair remained long, his teeth were whitened and his waistline fluctuated between liposuction appointments. He deflated criticism by satirising his own narcissism and regularly updated his fan site with his latest surgery or enhancement remembering always to do so in an amusing, self-deprecating manner that defied further comment. The White City Tavern lay a short distance from the offices of the production company that licensed his efforts across the Interverse and provided endless supplies of nubile young researchers to impress at lunchtimes.

Sallon registered that Merrett was engaging them with the same six well-worn stories of rich and famous indiscretions that had helped ease the knickers off countless production staff over the years and struggled to ignore him, trying once again to reconfigure a paragraph on his 'Orwell in the Dock' piece that had eluded his gin-fogged skills earlier in the week. Not that he still drank gin. But at the height of his habit, he had kept two-litre bottles in his wine cellar and gone through two in a day. This inevitably had a permanent effect on his intellect and motor skills, leaving him struggling for words that had once flowed as easily as sapphire into quinine. Now that he drank only tonic, some wondered why he bothered to frequent pubs at all. But he was no longer tempted and drew great comfort from the smell and memory of alcohol, without actually having to indulge. This was his little victory and one that he was proud of amidst the tedium of his post and the loss of his ambition.

There was something quite satisfying in the fact that the style he was trying to adopt was decidedly Merrettian in tone. Arch and casually disrespectful with occasional scatological asides designed to make the reader feel they were part of some wiser, more knowing elite, far above the regular observer. Sallon had failed to notice Merrett at his shoulder until he heard the famously nasal delivery in his ear reading the last paragraph.

'Mr Orwell asked for several other offences to be taken into consideration. Namely a hit list of Stalinists supplied to MI5 and some juvenile poesy entitled 'England Awake!'

Sallon shrugged off his arm in irritation and tried to shut down the document, but Merrett slipped the stylus from his arthritic grasp and hit the scroll control to expose the rest of the article, including the photograph.

'What's this, Derek? Imagination? Humorous sketches from the Bench? What an innovation. Shades of Dickens or of Mortimer?'

'Neither. Just a little tomfoolery up at the Borough. Thought I'd give it a spin as a colour piece.'

Merrett frowned as he read down the screen and grunted in amusement. 'Not bad, Del. Orwell delusions a bit thin on the ground in your game. Don't all your mentals usually aspire to divinity? Bit adventurous for you these days but a very creditable little sketch I think.'

'I'm so glad you approve, Mickey. Maybe one day I can write a whole page on some dead actress's tits for the Sundays.'

Merrett tweaked Sallon's ear lightly and tutted. 'Now that was a very long time ago and, if I recall, deeply appreciated amidst the sanctimonious garbage others were heaping on her botoxed little head at the time.'

'Off you fuck, Mickey. I'm trying to focus.'

'Always a struggle, Del boy. Laters.'

Sallon grimaced as Merrett strode to the toilet door. Defunct teenage jargon from the lips of the over forties. Always pitiful.

Thirty minutes later he had edited a thousand words to his satisfaction and sent it to the usual suspects with the photo attached before ordering another glass tube of quinine. He had hardly sipped down to the lemon of his straight tonic water before his MC bleeped with an acceptance and a warm note from some sub on the better of the remaining tabloids. He smiled to himself and ordered some Thai fishcakes. A back pocket bonus was handsome recompense for a wasted afternoon in the Inner London. He logged on to AM/FM and scanned the pub for victims. He quickly located a target with a lower score than his own with no shield up and a bounty of fifty points and pressed the 'AM' button. As he hoped, one of the two researchers turned out to be the target and he looked away as she cursed, acknowledged the hit on her MC and killed the piercing alarm. A round of applause from the rest of the bar's clientele and several pistol gestures from some, disguised her assassin, but he felt her looking at him suspiciously as she whispered to her friend and then giggled indiscreetly as Merrett returned to their ringlets and high heels. 'Someone dead, girls?' he leered. 'I do love a spot of necrophilia.'

Fever Diary – 6 March 20--

I have abandoned my reading list today quite by accident. Wandering around the charity shop on Stamford Hill for a decent pair of Wellingtons, I browsed the dusty paperbacks at the rear of the store. A copy of 'Crime & Punishment' fell to the floor as I attempted to lever out a neighbouring collected edition of the 'Girl's Own Paper'. Under the admonishing gaze of the fearsome Frau Leiberman, I bent down to replace it and found that it had fallen open on a page that instantly drew me. Before the murder, and after a drink of vodka and the consumption of a pie, Raskolnikov turns off the road into the bushes and falls asleep.

'In a morbid condition of the brain, dreams often have a singular actuality, vividness, and extraordinary semblance of reality. At times monstrous images are created, but the setting and the whole picture are so truth-like and filled with details so delicate, so unexpectedly, but so artistically consistent, that the dreamer, were he an artist like Pushkin or Turgenev even, could never have invented them in the waking state. Such sick dreams always remain long in the memory and make a powerful impression on the overwrought and deranged nervous system.'

Standing in the 21st Century in a charity shop on Stamford Hill after waking in an alley behind Upper Street, this passage held more than a little resonance for me. The final stages of tuberculosis could definitely be described as morbid and there is no doubt that the AW appears substantially real. However, Raskolnikov's feverish derangement seemed a world away from the way I have felt since billeting with Pedro. I am content to participate whilst still standing slightly outside all I experience. At first I was profoundly angry that I could not get back to my own rationed, grey, grubby little world. Now I am simply grateful for an unpredictable dream existence where I am seldom surprised by the twist and turns of my fate, being conditioned to expect some things to be unfamiliar and conforming to a certain internal logic.

It is no surprise, for example, that this particular book fell open on this specific page and that I happened to read this passage at this time, in this place.

Re-reading that last sentence, I realize the AW has turned me into the kind of superstitious idiot I despise.

The Wellingtons available did not fit.

ericisawake.blogspot.com

POSTED BY H LEWIS ALLWAYS AT 14:32 0 COMMENTS

8 First Call

23 April 1945 – Stuttgart

Eric entered Stuttgart over the Berger Stag footbridge less than three hours after the French Army entered the town. He took his time, cautiously on the watch for any remaining snipers and wondered whether he should have waited until he could actually see the troops on the opposite bank. But the pain of Eileen's loss was reduced to a dull background ache when he put himself in danger and therefore he sought out such opportunities rather more than was healthy.

The rubble and scorched ruins resulting from a brutal RAF bombing made him think of London, although the devastation seemed more severe with most of the city razed to the ground. He imagined there would be a billet somewhere but it was hard, looking at the blasted horizon, to see where.

As he stepped off the end of the bridge across the river, he saw an expanse of rubble and twisted iron ahead of him. He felt tired and decided to try and proceed rapidly, leaping from flat to flat like a mountain goat.

From above and to the west of where Eric stood, in the shattered shell of a bourgeois drawing room opened on one side by the impact of a blockbuster bomb, a young Wehrmacht officer lay on the scorched carpet, bleeding to death from a stomach wound, his ammunition spent and his eyes glazing. One of the last images on his fading brain was of a tall un-shaven scarecrow in a long army greatcoat teetering across the uneven surface like an un-coordinated ballet dancer, leaping from promontory to precipice and finally falling in a graceless arc to a pool of oily water.

Eric lay up to his sleeves in filth for a moment before levering himself up and leaping the last foot and a half to the flat unbroken flags of what had once been a city square. A newspaper lay on the ground nearby and he used it to wipe some of the muck from the arms of his greatcoat. He threw most of it away, but was caught by a propaganda picture of the perfect German Mutter standing with a child on an Austrian hillside, her hair and rosy cheeks rendered by the artist in the usual idealized Aryan fashion.

Despite the obvious Nazi fantasy of Teutonic womanhood, he was drawn to the image in quite another way. The woman and the child, even the rolling mountains behind them and the distant image of the sea, all seemed to him to represent everything he had lost after Eileen died. He had imagined such a life for them once and yearned for it still. Had she lived, by now all three of them might be living in the country somewhere on a farm, perhaps, or on Astor's secret island far away. He imagined himself retired from journalism altogether and working on another book in the neat room of a whitewashed cottage whilst Eileen sat smoking in an easy chair in his study, listening as he read out passages for her customary critique before Ricky ran in from a day spent chasing rabbits in the fields or fishing, demanding his supper and laughing, laughing, laughing. He tucked the page in to his breast pocket along with the hard lump of sorrow rising in his heart and moved towards the sound of tanks.

Later that afternoon, when the Americans arrived in Schillerplatz, furious at the French for disobeying orders and entering the town before them, he perched on a broken altar table lying outside the blasted Stiftskirche and observed a vigorous argument between a French colonel and an American major. He contemplated offering his services as trans- lator of the obscene curses offered up by the Frenchman beneath the gaze of Schiller's statue, but instead reached into his pocket and smoothed the crumpled propaganda advertisement on his knee. He extracted a salvaged German cigarette from his tunic pocket and smoked for a while, quietly contemplating the picture and wondering how it could be achieved before the end of his life.

IN THE END, Emily did not have to contact the 'appropriate authorities' as they called on her. As it happened, Simon was in the office, lolling in the chair normally occupied by her patients, waiting for her to accompany him to a drinks party at their parent's house in Islington. He was carping at the recent discovery of the involuntary donation of his bike and an old MC to her patient.

'Why must you keep giving him things? '

'He has nothing.'

'A lot of your patients have nothing. Not even their wits. You don't normally filch half my possessions for their benefit.'

'You haven't ridden that bike in years and the MC is outmoded and barely functional.'

'You didn't even ask. That's what I… Oh. Hello.'

A large man in a dun coloured overcoat stood in the doorway like a lost rugby player. He was of heroic proportion and had a brutish chin below large grey eyes and a shock of salt and pepper hair. The voice she expected to be loud and estuary. It was neither and the quiet Oxford accent took her by surprise. 'Dr Statton?'

She glanced at the visitor's pass in his hand and nodded.

'Sorry I didn't ring ahead. But I happen to be based down the road and it seemed a bit pointless when you're just around the corner.' He held out one huge hand and enveloped hers in a light feathery clasp. 'DI Gerry O'Brien. Here's my card.'

Emily took it and waved at a chair opposite Simon. 'My brother, Simon. What can I do for you?'

O'Brien sat gingerly on the edge of the tubular steel chair and reversed his MC to use the notepod.

'Lewis Allways. I understand he's a patient of yours.'

Simon laughed explosively. 'Bloody hell. Now what?'

O'Brien turned his bulk towards Simon's slouched lean figure and frowned.

'You know this man too?'

Emily sighed and cut off Simon before he could comment. 'My brother was the state appointed representative in court. We had to section Mr Allways after an incident here a few months ago. Look, I'm limited in what I can officially tell you, but can you tell me why you're interested?'

O'Brien looked carefully at Simon and seemed to contemplate various issues of disclosure before deciding that he could waive some Data Protection distractions for the moment. 'An alert was flagged on the system by a Dr Martin.'

Emily moved Lewis's file tablet beneath several others on her desk and leaned back in her chair. 'Ed. Yes. He said there were some questions over his test results. I think he may have jumped the gun a little though. How did you get involved?'

'The alerts are sorted by category to the appropriate department or agency. ID usually ends up in our lap. Are you saying you knew of these anomalies? Did you think of reporting it yourself?' His tone was gentle, but his gaze was a copper's stare, designed to provoke a defensive response. She refused to react and drew her own MC towards her.

'Ed mentioned something about the test results possibly being mixed up. They didn't seem to match our man. As the man himself did not admit to the name of Allways, I assumed that perhaps it was our error rather than his. I was waiting to see if any more ID possibilities turned up. Memory loss isn't all that common, but there's often a problem with medical records when such patients do enter the system.'

'Not just patients' interjected Simon. 'I wasn't paid for nearly eight months after the MOJ introduced new systems. Apparently they had me down as Simone Sprattow.'

O'Brien smiled. 'National databases can be very unreliable. But in this case we have some additional information at Border & Control.'

Emily could see he enjoyed the tiny frisson of apprehension that the name of his agency produced in the rest of the population. She decided that she wasn't going to like O'Brien and smiled tightly, refusing to ask. He waited for her to do so, nodded briefly and continued anyway. 'Mr Allways is a South African ex-mercenary, born in Bloemfontein, with no leave to remain.'

Simon barked his appreciation. 'Bloody classic. He's an illegal un-person. No one would appreciate this more than him.'

'How do you mean that?'

'Well, you do know who he thinks he is, don't you? Isn't that in your database?'

O'Brien looked down at his notepod and scrolled back a few screens and then reluctantly shook his head at the grinning barrister. Simon was ecstatic and practically writhed with pleasure, his legs wrapped around each other in a paroxysm of delight. 'Tell him, sis. You have to tell him.'

Emily sighed and folded her arms, shooting Simon the evil eye. 'The patient, whoever he is, labours under a complex delusion that he is a literary figure. He calls himself Eric Blair.'

O'Brien noted the name carefully down on his notepod. 'What leads you to believe he is delusional?'

Emily paused. 'Well, what leads me to this conclusion is that Eric Blair is George Orwell.'

O'Brien raised an eyebrow. 'He thinks he's two people? Multiple personalities?'

Simon spoke to his own tie, sotto voce. 'No book clubs down the old B & C then?'

O'Brien abruptly stood up, flipping his notepod into his pocket and leaning down, his arms either side of Simon's chair. 'Now it could be that you may have some useful information, Mr Statton, you knowing this man in one context and your sister in another. But I would be prepared to forego whatever fragments of fact you may hold if you waste my time. If you have nothing useful to say, you may leave now. Are we clear?'

Simon did not shrink from the meaty intimidation shoved up against his delicate features. If anything, he moved forward slightly and smiled sweetly at O'Brien, his nostrils flaring. 'Actually, that wouldn't suit my purposes very well. You see, you are discussing my client and I believe his interests are not best represented by emotionally incontinent police officers with anger management issues. So I will be staying to ensure that his liberty and his human rights are respected. Are we clear?'

O'Brien straightened up and contemplated the skinny obstruction lolling in the tubular chair like a resting salamander. He smiled unconvincingly and raised an eyebrow. 'Client?'

'Yes. I represented him at the last hearing and I don't believe we had a conversation about further representation, so as far as I am concerned, I am still engaged.'

O'Brien's smile became even tighter. 'You're off the state clock now and he couldn't afford your private fees.'

Simon flipped his own MC over and took out the stylus. 'Such is the yawning chasm of social conscience within me that I lay down my fees for a worthy pro bono client. You are to be congratulated, Inspector. Prior to your little tantrum, Mr Allways was a pain in the proverbial as far as I was concerned. But after your impressively regressive hissy fit, I have decided that he will be my number one priority.'

O'Brien pocketed his MC and nodded curtly to Emily. 'I don't think I need bother you any further.'

Emily stood and shook the proffered hand. 'What happens now?'

Simon also stood, his stylus poised and his head tilted enquiringly. 'Yes, what does happen now, Inspector?'

'Mr Allways will need to attend the nearest ID interrogation centre to establish his identity. '

'You will, of course, inform him in writing 30 days in advance as the Immigration and Public Order Act dictates?'

'Of course'. O'Brien deliberately turned his back on Simon and walked to the door. Emily followed him, waving Simon back into his seat. 'Inspector? Mr Allways is a patient of mine. I think that some account needs to be taken of his condition.'

'His rights will be respected Dr Statton. We aren't in China. What exactly is his condition?'

'Delusional, as I said. Also, Mr Allways, or whoever he turns out to be, apparently suffered a severe head injury a few years ago. I'm pretty certain that any confusion over his identity is not deliberate.'

O'Brien opened the door and filled the aperture with his bulk before replying. 'Deliberate or not, false identities mean false pretences. Fraud, illegal benefit claims, illegal immigration and illegitimate tax status. The kind of thing that we are set up to control.'

Simon turned languidly in his chair. 'But not to abuse.'

O'Brien stepped lightly but rapidly across the room and, for a moment, Emily thought he was going to swipe Simon across the face. Instead he held out his hand. Simon went to lightly touch the proffered digits and found his own hand enveloped in both of O'Brien's paws. 'My apologies, Simon. I behaved like an idiot. The worse kind of stereotypical government snoop. I hope you can forgive my rudeness and indeed my lack of control. I really didn't come here intending to intimidate. You see, I lost three of my colleagues last year in the bombing at Canary Wharf.'

Simon blinked in bewilderment, uncertain how to respond. 'Well, that's very…'

'The reason I'm slightly sensitive about following up these things… well. Truth is I dropped the ball at South Quay. I had an ID alert on the bomber and I didn't follow up in time. It has caused me some sleepless nights and shortened my fuse, I can tell you. Not a sensible thing when you're my size. Puts people's backs up. Totally counter-productive and, I assure you, quite out of character. Believe me, I am the last person to abuse your client's civil rights. I studied law myself before I joined the agency. Only a 2:2 but there were some very distracting girls on my campus. My thesis was a history of miscarriages of justice from Hanratty to the Haringey Five. You were a junior on that case weren't you?'

Simon withdrew his hand and narrowed his eyes at O'Brien. 'I won't be played, Inspector. Many have tried.'

O'Brien chuckled and nodded. 'Of course not. I understand. Look, I'll make sure you get an invite to the interrogation centre when your client is scheduled. I'm afraid it's likely to be a few months because we're backed up. I may be allocated elsewhere, but if I can, I'll try and take on the interview myself. Then we can both try and unpick exactly who your client is supposed to be. Yes?' He waved a hand to Emily and left.

She sat down opposite Simon who was scribbling furiously. 'That was a rapid reverse ferret. What are you doing?'

'Just a memo, sis. I'm going to have a little peek at O'Brien's credentials. He's certainly looked at mine. Very few people know I was a dogsbody on the Haringey Five case.'

I met 'Scratch' when I was caught short one day after a disappointing visit to the Scandinavian supermarket on the Upper Clapton Road. One feature of the AW is the lack of any public conveniences. The nearest one has been converted into a Chinese butchers and another further down Kingsland Road is now some sort of underground nightclub.

I had just toured the aisles of the shop looking for anything that might constitute provisions for the week, only to realise, not for the first time just how little the money we receive could buy. I decided to abandon my search and walk down to the market at Ridley Road. But, emerging into the cold wind, I was driven down the side alley next to the supermarket to the rear where I hoped to find a discreet corner to relieve myself.

As I finished availing myself of the lack of facilities, I noticed a young man in a woollen hat sorting through one of a trio of large metal bins next to a set of fire doors belonging to the shop. This was my first sight of Scratch. He was olive skinned, with dark heavy eyebrows, a slight figure and large emerald eyes. His features were delicate and his teeth misaligned at the front, but he was handsome and young and healthy. Rather too healthy, I thought, to be grubbing around in bins.

I don't know why I walked across to join him. Maybe I was curious about the plastic trays he was studying with such intent before stuffing them into a battered green rucksack covered with scribbled drawings and mysterious slogans. Maybe I was just drawn to his smile as he glanced at me in his amiable way as he sorted.

I asked him what he was doing and he looked me up and down, no doubt taking in my battered shoes and the mud thrown up from the bicycle on my trouser cuffs. He decided, there and then, that I needed educating.

Later, much later, he told me that unlike most people his age, he often spoke to 'Olders' on the street and that I seemed so skinny and lacking in means that he instantly felt responsible for me. So it was that I was introduced to the stunning level of waste in the

AW and the art involved in taking advantage of it.

For nearly an hour, I learnt the arcane symbols, colours and dates on the labels of the film-shrouded food items and what they signified. I learnt to discard mostly according to Scratch's own set of rules that involved not indulging in any product he disapproved of ethically and ones that were obviously rancid. Products from certain countries were not even offered for consideration and at the end of my impromptu lesson, I realised he had sorted two piles, one for him and one for me. I noticed mine were primarily meat based and when I queried this he held up his two index fingers in a cross formation.

'Don't eat the flesh, mon cop. But I know most Olders are cannibal protein monkeys. Got you some veg too though, look. Those tomatoes just need the black bits cut out and that jar there is pickled red peppers. No sense dating them really. But they got a corporate policy, see? Every day around this time, they clear out. You got to be here though. The good stuff is gone by tonight. S'cocktail hour. You wanna come down the towie for a drinkie poo? What's your tag, Older?'

I smiled, engaged by his cheery, cheeky charm. 'That's currently under debate. But you can call me George.' He cackled in delight and held a mango in his hands, stroking it gently and intoning in a low American drawl, 'I'll hug him and I'll pet him and I will call him George'. I laughed and pointed at his dazed expression.

'Steinbeck. Lenny from 'Of Mice and Men'. No?'

He stabbed his broad nose with his finger and pointed back. 'Zackly. And a Warner Brothers classic cartoon of course. But we are literary men, right?'

We sat shivering at the gouged metal tables outside the 'The Moon Under Water' down by the canal so that we could both smoke. We drank cheap dark ales and spoke for some hours after our finances ran out and the lights above the tables shone sodium saucers in the water.

He was a musician of some sort and lived in an abandoned house off the Seven Sisters Road. He was, as he said, a literary man; a voracious reader currently obsessed by Baudelaire and Kurt Vonnegut. I had just started Vonnegut from my reading list, drawn by his experience of the Dresden bombing and we talked for some time about 'Slaughterhouse Five', debating the advantages and disadvantages of the author's fey mannerisms. It was the first literary debate I'd been able to have since I woke up. Pedro didn't read and grew impatient with any serious discussion on politics. Scratch's knowledge was mostly derived from an eclectic and somewhat chaotic self-education. His mother was a Filipino cleaner who barely spoke English but his father had been a Cambridge don and therefore his reading was wide and varied, taking in everything from Gissing to the 'The Hotspur' comic from my own era and much else besides. He was appalled that I hadn't yet been to the cinema and insisted that he would 'score' us a couple of tickets one Wednesday.

I didn't fully understand his name. He told me it was derived from his habit of fighting with his brother in a manner that resembled some legendary animated cartoon combatants. His friends found their frequent wrestling bouts amusing and christened them after a particularly destructive contest in a lounge bar of a hostelry that had subsequently barred them for life. He refused to give his real name saying it gave people 'power over you'.

At one point he mentioned H.G. Wells and I let slip that we had once had an acrimonious lunch after which he had written me a letter calling me a shit. Scratch looked at me with some amusement and passed no comment. But as we parted, promising to meet again at the bins the following day, he pulled up my hair a little at the front and put his head on one side, his eyes twinkling.

'That's better' he said. 'Makes you look more like the man.'

'Who?' I asked.

He laughed and walked away, waving. 'The only George that matters.'

   ERIC IS AWAKE

9 ID

THE WINTER MONTHS turned into spring and Eric enjoyed the calming domestic routine of living in the cramped maisonette at the bottom of the hill next to the canal with Pedro. They played table football every evening and, each morning, covering the field of play with a sheet of salvaged wood and a bed sheet to eat what Eric regarded as truly majestic breakfasts. As it grew sunnier, Eric cycled daily to the Middlesex filter beds where he climbed down into one of the empty sunken reservoirs to sit with a notebook amongst the dried bulrushes, writing his journal and listening to the waterfall in the nearby river. It was here he would occasionally browse the battered MC given to him by Emily and where he made his first decision about what he would and would not explore.

Part of him desperately wanted to know what happened to Ricky in the AW. Part of him knew that whatever he found would upset him simply because he was not there through the formative years of his son's life. He started to read a potted biography, but closed the MC firmly after only a few lines and cried a little, his sobs echoing around the sloping cement walls, startling the thrushes swaying atop the bulrushes. He had established that Avril and Bill Dunn had taken Rick on. That was enough. In his heart he knew Sonia would not have changed her mind. The AW was a dream and one that seemed to flow contrary to his own desires and instincts, perhaps through some subversive action of the subconscious that remained out of his control. Whatever the AW said had happened, had not happened as far as he was concerned and so, why torture himself with whatever his mind had decided as a fate for his beloved boy?

Even the description of a life well lived would distress him because he wasn't there to be a part of it. It was not easy to suppress his curiosity, but he felt it very necessary. The AW said (amongst many other startling things) that George Orwell died in 1950 and yet here he was. So any information gleaned from it was suspect at best.

With occasional forays to the charity shops and some long tours around the city with a sandwich and a flask, he experienced a gradual flowering of equilibrium as boredom and the slow pace of unemployed life on a limited income, seeped into his bones with the sun.

His needs were few and he obtained a guilty pleasure by simply entering the local supermarket. The array of indulgence and unheard of foodstuffs shocked him and he felt like a maiden aunt touring Pompeii as he indulged himself in the salvage of kippers and discounted packs of shredded smoked salmon from the 'near expired items' area of the refrigerated shelves and from his daily bin rendezvous with Scratch at the rear.

He had always felt civilisation overly soft, but the AW was flaccid with decadence. The general shape of people on the street was radically different from the lean frames he had come to expect amongst his rationed contemporaries. They spoke to an attitude of utter indulgence and no shortages of anything substantial.

For his part, Pedro marvelled at Eric's apparent budgeting genius as he returned from Scandinavian chain stores with an array of riches that they eked out over the week with little difficulty. One week, Pedro managed to fashion some albondigas from the discounted minced beef and on another occasion, delighted Eric with a poor man's paella from a pack that laboured under the name 'seafood medley'.

In general, Eric felt they rubbed along together rather well, although Pedro's rough and ready way of living after years of homelessness needed a little getting used to. He seldom tidied up the living space, although both of them were meticulous, some might say compulsive, about the washing up, both having once worked in this capacity in dubious restaurants around the world. Eric's desire for order in his room was not particularly strong, but he gradually impressed upon his companion the need to occasionally do their own laundry and to at least shave regularly, now they had the means.

His hardest task had been the attempts to teach his housemate to make tea in the correct manner. These lessons were fraught with irritation as Pedro found exhortations about taking the teapot to the kettle rather than the other way around, utterly pointless. After a tense afternoon going through Eric's eleven-step process, Pedro vowed never to drink or make tea ever again and thenceforth it became Eric's task alone.

For a while Eric believed that he might begin his book. He had been fascinated and a little disconcerted to find that there was an Orwell Archive that contained some of the rough notes and synopsis for 'A Smoking Room Story' that he had been planning to begin when he was well enough. He contemplated visiting the University that held the archive, located conveniently near to Miss Statton's office, to refresh his memory and perhaps also to peek at the indulgence of his every written word stored in the Cruciform building like sacred icons at the base of a pyramid. He even made an appointment to do so with his MC; entering his occupation as 'Hagiographer'. But he never got to attend the appointment.

The letter came on benefit day. He had a MOB cash account that he was forced to open in the name of Lewis Allways with the aid of a battered National Insurance card that had been secreted in the greatcoat (now abandoned in the warmer weather for a charity shop suit jacket) in which he found himself when he awoke in the AW for the first time. The money appeared like magic every two weeks and he was given a talismanic blue card that he could use to withdraw hard cash from the machines. It still startled him that so much money was provided by the state for a man judged too mentally unstable to work. His Incapacity for Employment Allowance would have kept him for months in the BW.

He had just returned from the post office trip via his favourite supermarket where he had liberated a pair of vacuum-packed kippers and some flour that Pedro liked to use for frying churros on the makeshift barbecue. Pedro was standing at the football table, drinking hot chocolate and staring with trepidation at a letter lying on the wooden table cover next to an election leaflet extolling the virtues of the local Councillor. He looked up as Eric entered and shook his head. 'Always bad news from those bastards.'

Eric removed his twill suit jacket and placed it on the back of one of the two battered kitchen chairs, turning his head sideways to read the name on the envelope. It was addressed to Mr L Allways as usual and he could see nothing to distinguish it from the official communications from the Department of Work and Pensions that dropped through their letterbox with some regularity.

Pedro pointed to the printed postmark that incorporated a logo with the letters B & C interwoven. 'That's Border & Control, man. If you got business with them then you got trouble.'

'What sort of trouble?'

Pedro shrugged and handed him the envelope. Eric put the kettle on and opened the letter. An address in Holborn seemed to be the Headquarters of the Border & Control Agency and the signature was a printed facsimile that smacked of a thousand form letters generated by machine.

Re: Verification Interview
National Identity Register

Dear Sir,

You are required to attend for interview at the Camden ID Interrogation Centre, 140 Hampstead Road, London NW1 2BX on 28th September at 9.30am. Please ensure that you bring the following documents, if available:

Passport
Driving License
Medical card
National Insurance Card/Number
Birth certificate or certificate of naturalisation
UK leave to remain or visa confirmation

You are entitled to bring a representative or solicitor with you, but must give the name and address of this person at least ten working days in advance of the interview.

If you are unable to attend you must call this office on the number above at least ten days before the interview to arrange an alternative date.

Please be advised that failure to attend a verification interview may lead to arrest and committal under the provisions of the Nationality and Identity Act 20—

Yours sincerely,

Mr Mohammed Hanif
Branch Officer
Principal Identification Dept.

ERIC PUT DOWN the letter and reached down the teapot from the windowsill above the sink. As he warmed the pot, he was pensive and did not speak until he had the tea poured into the pot to brew.

'What happens if I ring up to rearrange it for a few months later?'

Pedro snorted derisively. 'Then they come get you. Vans, dogs, batter ram for doors, handcuff. Everything.'

'How do you know? Have you had trouble of this kind?'

Pedro looked affronted. 'No way, man. I am European Citeezen. I am free to go anywhere I like to starve. I had a fren' called Salim. He was from Algerie, y'know? They get him good. He don' come to ID and they take him on plane with big straps and a gag over his mouth. Take him right from next to me in the alley up Shoreditch Church. We was sleepin', man and the dogs nearly bite our faces off. You got to go, Lewis. Don' mess with B & C.'

Eric poured the tea, one eye running once more over the letter. He sat down and sipped contemplatively at the Assam, his hands cupped around the large chipped teacup. 'I don't have anything beyond the National Insurance Card I found in my pocket. But that's in the name of Lewis Allways.'

Pedro rolled his eyes in exasperation. They had managed to avoid the subject for several months as Eric allowed Pedro to address him by the name he had always known. 'You see?' Pedro said shrilly. 'You see what happen when you keep doing this shit about your name? They heard that. That psycho lady you go to. She told them and now you got problems, man. We don' need this trouble, Lewis. We got it good here, y'know? I got used to sleeping in a bed again. We got money, we got a roof, we got a football table. What more do we need?'

'Poco dinero, pero mucho de corazón' murmured Eric.

Pedro looked at him strangely and stroked his chin. 'Now that is very coorios, Lewis. Very coorios.' He aped Eric's favourite phrase with relish and his own particular intonation.

'Why?'

'Because I said that to you the night before you go crazy. You remember that?'

Eric considered this. He did have a memory of the phrase but couldn't recall from where. Pedro drank the last of his chocolate and started washing up his cup.

'Anyway, what the hell, eh? You European Citeezen too, isn't it? They got nothing on you really. Where you born, Lewis? Scotlan'?'

'Motihari'

Pedro dropped the cup and juggled with it in the suds before spearing the handle with his smallest finger. 'Moti-what? Where's that?'

'India.'

The dripping cup dropped from Pedro's wet finger and shattered on the kitchen floor. 'Oh, shit, Lewis. We got trouble.'

Eric sipped calmly at his tea. 'It's perfectly all right. India was a possession of the Empire at the time.'

Pedro clapped a hand to his head and slumped over the table. 'We got big trouble.'

10 Hack

ERIC TOOK THE letter from the Border and Control Agency to his next appointment with Emily. He sat, one knee jiggling up and down as usual, as she read it. When she had finished, she folded it and handed it back without a word.

'I'm wondering why they are writing to me and who told them my address?'

Emily thought for a moment about how best to respond to the mildly accusatory tone. 'Dr Martin was obliged to report it when your test results came back. I think he was a little premature, but I can see why he felt he had to.'

'I see. You tried to prevent him?'

'I didn't know about it until a B & C Officer came to see me about you.'

Eric's leg stopped jiggling and he sat back, his fingers interlocking over one bony knee. 'What did he say? This officer?'

'That Harold Lewis Allways was born in Bloemfontein, South Africa and has no leave to remain in this country.'

Eric laughed. 'All this he gets from my test results?'

She shook her head. 'Ed found that your blood type and pretty much every other detail did not conform to those of Lewis Allways.'

'Isn't that what I have told you from the start?'

'You have certainly told me that you were not who we said you were. It seems you were right. But I think you should acknowledge that this does not mean you are therefore, by default, who you claim to be'.

'Then it seems you have a problem.'

'We have a problem' Emily emphasised. 'I registered you as a patient and as a national insurance number under the name of Allways in good faith. If that's not who you are, then we do need to quickly find out your true identity.'

Eric rubbed the two-day growth on his chin reflectively, his thumb rasping against the grey-flecked stubble. They had run out of razors and money was going to be short until Thursday, which meant an unshaven and tobaccoless day. 'You also helped me to apply for state assistance in that name, despite my concerns about the deception'.

Emily frowned. 'I didn't think it was deceptive at the time. But you're right. I might be in a spot of bother too.'

'I'm a bit puzzled too, about how I ended up becoming the responsibility of Hackney Council for my accommodation? Wasn't I sectioned under the Health Act in this hospital which, I believe, comes under the aegis of the Camden Local Authority?'

Emily looked nonplussed. 'Why does that matter? I mean, why is that important in the great scheme of things?'

'I'm interested.'

'The last known address you, well, that Lewis Allways, could be traced to, was a hostel in Clapton. It turns out that he left there just as his visa ran out. The National Insurance card was a forged clone, probably purchased in a pub.' She smiled. 'Why? Don't you like Hackney? Is it not Orwellian enough for you? Would you have preferred Hampstead or Islington?'

'On the contrary, I'm very grateful for our billet and I don't believe I have the income for those boroughs these days. But even there, I seem to be an exceptional case. Pedro tells me most people end up, if they're lucky, in a large hostel or boarding house of many cramped rooms with little or no privacy. We end up in an admittedly small and run down maisonette by the canal, sharing with no one and largely un-disturbed, until now, by any official interference.'

'I did a fair amount of form filling independently. I argued that your mental condition required a certain degree of unusual accommodation'.

You arranged everything whilst I was… well, in the realm of the senseless. Suddenly, I seemed to be equipped with a roof over my head, a bicycle, an MC and money to sustain myself all because of your magical letter of diagnosis and your generous wire pulling. Why are you doing this?'

Emily slowly turned her MC over in her fingers. 'My brother was asking the same thing the other day. I don't really know. Maybe I knew you were not going to turn out as a typical amnesia case. Habitually patients I've had in the same category don't know who they are. You have a very clear sense of identity, even though it's clearly impossible. I… took an interest in you, I suppose. You are an interesting case and I wanted to make sure that you continued to come to these sessions. In order to ensure that, I went out on a limb to get you a place of relative safety and shelter so that a kind of routine could be established. There. I've confessed. I feel cleansed. How about you?'

Eric smiled and held out a hand in mock blessing. Emily, thinking he was offering a 'high five' slapped her hand into his. Startled, he closed his open palm, gripping her hand in his. After a moment, Emily gently disentangled her fingers.

'I think we need to clear this up on a medical rather than a mental level. '

She produced a pair of plastic tubes, each containing a long swab. 'Ed has suggested we start from scratch with a DNA test to establish some kind of match with the national medical record database. I believe you and I might also take the opportunity to establish beyond doubt that you cannot be Eric Arthur Blair.'

Eric took one of the tubes from her and regarded the label of the sample along the side. 'How would that be achieved?'

'We take two swabs; one to be matched, as I said, with the medical database, one across the road to the Wolfson Institute, where my colleague Professor Goldstein works. He has access to the Orwell Archive and could attempt to match your DNA with the real thing.'

Eric glanced out of the window at the Cruciform building opposite. A middle-aged man in an old fashioned flat cap stood in the shadow of the portico, his lower face masked by a scarf. It seemed to Eric as if he occasionally glanced upwards at the window. 'I don't quite understand how that could be achieved.' He said absently. 'According to you, Orwell is dead.'

Emily watched his face. He seemed to be regarding the red brick crenulations of the old hospital. His face appeared to have filled out somewhat, but his frame was still that of the ragged stork. 'Orwell's letters are stored there. Professor Goldstein is suggesting that sufficient DNA might be contained in traces of his saliva on the envelopes and stamps stored with them.'

Eric looked at her and she noticed again how his cheeks had lost their lined and sunken appearance. She also noted that his eyes, usually clear blue amidst wrinkled brows, were tired and dull. 'It doesn't really matter, does it?'

'I think it does' Emily said quietly. 'I think it would help.'

Eric glanced up at one of the Magritte prints between the windows of the room. It was the one called 'La Reproduction Interdite' and showed a man looking into a mirror and seeing only the back of his own head. He sighed and gestured towards the swabs. 'Very well, let's get it done now.'

As Emily gently swabbed the inside of his cheeks, she leant over so that her face was close to his and the top of her blouse bowed outward slightly. He closed his eyes to avoid seeing any more of the gentle slope rising from her neck and breathed in her perfume, his belly aching with a longing he could barely control.

Later, some thirty minutes after he left, Emily walked down to the private wards on her way to a clinic. Freud's nude portrait of Sonia had been turned against the wall. It had taken some trouble as the picture had been secured at all four corners. He must have had a screwdriver in his pocket, she thought. She decided not to call maintenance right away. Ed Martin had frequently remarked on her resemblance to the splayed figure and it made her uncomfortable, but probably not as uncomfortable as it made her patient.

Fever Diary – 9 May 20--

I have solved the mystery of the disappearing newspaper. I have hungrily searched for them on the streets, but soon after acquiring purchase, they become blank and I find myself absurdly gloomy about the failure of my imagination in this one regard. I laboured, often reluctantly, at the coalface of journalism for a very long time, but now found myself with a literary blind spot. Although the fancier MC's deliver a bulletin digest daily, many people do still desire a solid paper in their hands on the tube or the bus, but I can't seem to keep one in my eye.

I told Pedro of my experience. He looked at me in the usual pitying manner, picked up a discarded paper from the pile of waste in the Council recycling compactor kept in the front garden and took me down the road to the paper kiosk at the entrance to Stamford Hill station. Inserting coins into the kiosk he showed me two black dots in the lower left hand margin of the paper and placed them in a gap between two protruding spurs of metal on the side of the kiosk.

The spurs came together over the dots and the newspaper's surface instantly filled with text, colour photographs and advertisements. He showed me how I could make certain pictures move by tapping them to trigger a short documentary. It seems my imagination did not have a leak after all. It had filled the gap with something even more alien than the overt sexual language and depiction that seems ubiquitous in the media of the AW. Now that I know the costs involved, I will have to budget for a daily paper reload as well as everything else.

However, there are other allocations in our meagre economy that are probably more urgent. This afternoon, I visited my preferred Scandinavian chain store and invested in a tent and a small rucksack. Tomorrow I am going to search through what the AW calls Hackney's Civic Amenity site, which, in the BW we called a rubbish dump.

Five Nigerians hold sway over the site and sift the goods arriving for disposal like city antique dealers at a country auction. I have cultivated their leader over the last few weeks and am promised a robust recycled bicycle for Pedro. Preparations are almost complete. I have felt for some time that our time here is almost at an end. I sense surveillance. I am almost certain that I saw the middle-aged man in the flat cap again hanging around the station. Once again, the lower face was covered so it is difficult to be certain.

Yesterday, there was a knock on the door around lunchtime. Pedro and I were washing up after an Irish stew that had left me feeling indolent and bloated. A young woman stood on the door-step, a tartan coat over a pair of white trousers and tousled red hair above startling green eyes. I guessed she was in her twenties and almost certainly from the west of Australia, judging by the twang. She introduced herself as Helen Boden, a reporter from the Hackney & Haringey Advertiser. She held out her MC and said, 'I wondered if I could talk to you about this? 'On the screen was a picture of myself in the dock at the Inner London Crown Court beneath an article headlined 'Orwell in the Dock'.

I invited her in and she sat sipping tea whilst I read the rest of the piece – a mocking sketch on the kind of entertaining eccen-trics that occasionally pass through the courts. It reminded me of Dickens' 'Sketches by Boz' and perhaps this was the intention. It instantly sent a frisson of foreboding down to my belly as I realised that I was now attracting far too much attention for my own good. The most unsettling part was a reference to a 'Stalinist Hit List' for MI5. My game with Rees was hardly that, but it seemed to me as if Celia might well have had such connections.

'It's been picked up by quite a few people' she said. 'People like the idea, you know, that he's still alive somewhere, watching us all.'

I observed that she was wary of the madman, but also clearly wanted something. I presumed it was a story and told her bluntly that I wasn't interested in being interviewed and parodied for the benefit of the local newspaper. I told her, somewhat unconvinc-ingly that I no longer laboured under the delusion. This was not helped by the act that we had purchased new razors that morning and, for the first time in the AW, I had shaved all but my favoured line above the top lip. She looked at me with an impishly amused scepticism and told me that she wasn't really thinking of rewriting a national story for the locals. What she really wanted was for me to write a weekly column for the paper. I was taken aback and slightly suspicious. What made her think I could even write? She read from my impromptu meditations on the nature of existence in court and pointed out that it sounded like a writer speaking, if ever she had heard one.

'You may not be him, but there's an angle here. A view of the world from an unusual place.'

'Diary of a Madman' I suggested. She smiled and said she was thinking of something more like 'As I Please' or even 'Blair's Diary'. I told her coldly that a literary bedlam where readers passed by to see the mentally defective rend their garments was not an attractive proposition. In truth, I was intrigued by the idea of having a column again, but not the attention that it would bring. Pedro, ever the pragmatist, asked how much I might be paid. She told him and he did a little mental gavotte as he juggled with reducing our benefit payments over being comparatively better off.

I cut them both off by saying that we would be leaving the area soon. It was not the best way for Pedro to hear of my plans, but he betrayed nothing to the journalist. She seemed un-perturbed and pointed out that I could write from anywhere I pleased. I quickly, but politely, declined. But as she was leaving, she left me her card and told me that if I changed her mind, all I had to do was send the first column to the e-dress listed.

After she left I apologised to Pedro and told him my intention. I made it clear that he was under no obligation to go along with it. After two hours of wrangling, he convinced me to wait and see how the B & C interview went, before making a final decision. Conscious of how long he had lived without comforts before I came along, I reluctantly agreed. I hope it will not be too late by then.

I put Miss Boden's card in the small pouch that contains my puncture kit below the saddle of Rocinante.

11 Fugue

September 1945 – Isle of Jura

Walking in stout boots down the barely discernible track from the farm-house at Kinuachdrach, Eric skirted a small cove and headed in the direction of the white house, Barnhill. He knew that Astor had only conceded and arranged a fortnight's stay on the island 'to try it out' in the hope that a visit would discourage him. In fact, the temperate climate, the stunning views and the wandering herds of wild deer only served to convince him that this was the place for him.

His breath came in heavy rasps, but he knew that the London smog was gradually being leeched from his tattered lungs by the clean air. The food was plentiful and fresh, but, most of all, it had been the devil's own job getting here, which meant it was safe.

He rounded the final bend in the track and could see the roof of the house and then the whitewashed walls. Beyond it was a sloping boggy meadow and then a drop down to the startling deep blue of the sea.

He walked up to the house and peered through the windows. He could see a living room and a kitchen, sparsely furnished, but neat enough. He sat down gratefully on a bench to one side of the front door and looked back along the track. One way led to Kinuachdrach and the other towards Ardlussa and miles beyond that, the ferry.

Narrowing his eyes, he tried to imagine an approaching figure in any of the surrounding country. They would be visible from quite a distance in daylight and would need a light with them to make their way at night. He would know if they were coming. He raised the walking stick he had found at the farm and pointed it at the horizon, one eye sighted along its length like a gun barrel. With a decent rifle he would be able to pick them off.

He sat contentedly in the autumn sun and penned a letter to Arthur Koestler accepting an invitation to spend Christmas with he and his wife Mamaine in Wales. He also responded in enthusiastic terms to Arthur's recommendation of a woman called Celia Kirwan who would share the railway carriage with he and Ricky on the way down. She was Mamaine's twin and therefore would have the same look of the film star Vivien Leigh. Arthur seemed to be suggesting that she would be a good possible candidate having recently left a disastrous marriage to an Irish writer. Arthur knew that Eric was profoundly lonely and had tried out several other deeply unsuitable names on him in earlier letters. But Celia, a woman who moved in the same political circles as they did through a period working at Cyril's 'Horizon' magazine, seemed ideal.

He sat for almost an hour until, lulled by the distant sound of waves, he fell asleep. He was woken by the roar of an animal and for a moment after his eyes opened, he quickly scanned the heath for any signs of deer. But it hadn't sounded like the raucous bellow of the stag.

'THERE'S SOMETHING I'VE been keeping from you in these sessions.'

Emily cocked her head on one side and pursed her lips. 'I never doubted it'

Eric frowned and shook his head. 'It's physical, not mental.' He glanced up at the Magritte, his gaze fixed on the hair on the back of the head of the subject.

Emily leaned forward and waited. When nothing was said, she tapped her nail on the arm of his chair to draw his attention back to her. 'Is it medical? Something you're embarrassed about? We did go through some of the side effects of the medication.'

He grunted. 'Impotence, nausea, headaches. No. None of the above.'

She folded her arms, remembered her body language and quickly unfolded them again. 'Then what?'

He paused and looked down at his shoes before gazing at her directly from beneath his brows, without raising his head. She remembered an old acting master class pod from an aged actor demonstrating just such a technique. The actor had called it the 'cobra eyes' method. It was effective and she found herself holding her breath.

'Twice or more a week, I don't wake up. '

She relaxed and smiled. 'The occasional lie in, is, I believe, quite common amongst the unemployed.'

'Not asleep. Unconscious or comatose for up to four or five hours. Pedro finds he can't wake me even by drenching me in water. Effectively I pass out several times a week. I awake feeling slightly disoriented but more alert and…'

She scribbled 'fugue state' on her notepod. 'And what?'

He struggled to find the word and she saw that the deep furrows either side of his mouth had begun to fade as his face became fuller. 'Hungry?' she suggested. He laughed. 'Never that. Not anymore. No. It's as if I've been recharged or… reset somehow. I feel better able to cope afterwards.'

'Sleep refreshes. That's what it sounds like.'

'But not to be able to wake? That's not the same. I can't control where or when. It feels as if it happens when I am particularly bothered by something.'

She smiled slightly. 'Bothered?'

'You would call it stressed, I suppose. You label everything either stress or depression. Your profession has a limited lexicon.'

She called up his prescription list on the MC and tapped experimentally at some alternatives. 'We can adjust some of your medication. Could be that the side effects are beginning to…?'

Eric waved a hand impatiently and shook his head. 'It's not that. I haven't taken any of the damn pills and I won't. I relented for one day and took everything you gave me. I felt completely drained of energy. I was awake but not awake. Couldn't move from my chair. A zombie drawing the dole.'

Emily sighed. 'We've discussed this before.'

'I made no promises and I have kept all my promises.'

'I think these episodes may be evidence of some neurological damage. We may need to run some more tests.'

'Balls.' Eric stood up abruptly and went over to the window. He held one of his roll ups in his hand as he gestured to the Cruciform building opposite. 'I am done with hospitals. Spent far too much of my time being punctured, prodded and doped. I know what these comas are about. Every now and then the world I am experiencing becomes too much. The mapping of the human genome gets tangled in my head with the price of own brand haddock goujons and Chinese terrorists. I find I can't encompass everything and my thoughts become incoherent, disconnected. The train of thought continually comes off the rails, so that just as I set off down one track, a score of branch lines appear. I can't keep a single idea in my mind for longer than a few seconds before it runs off in another direction. I met a drunk on the towpath a few weeks ago who kept up a stream of unconsciousness that in one minute encompassed the memorized commentary of the 1999 Derby, a refrain about how his sister stole his money when he was ten and the rising price of barley wine. I've always had something of a gadfly mind in conversation.' He noticed her grin and nodded sheepishly. 'Well, you've seen that, constant tangents taken in our little sessions that finish a long way from their root. But never like this.'

'Look Lewis…'

He held up a finger and waved an admonishment. 'I thought we'd both established that I am not Lewis.'

'We also agreed that you could not be Eric.'

He smiled tiredly and ran his hand through the shock of untidy hair. 'We agreed to differ, I believe. Either way, the state hopes to decide that for me next week.'

Emily suddenly remembered and called up a message from her brother, turning the MC to show it to Eric. 'Simon will come with you on the 28th. He's contacted the B & C to notify them that he will be attending and he suggests you meet for a half hour beforehand so he can prepare you.'

Eric sucked on the unlit cigarette absently and watched an old woman sitting at a bus stop whilst slowly wrapping and unwrapping a packet of sandwiches. She was clearly looking forward to sinking her dentures into them but had lost her way somewhere in the process and now couldn't remember now if she was starting her lunch or finishing it. There was no sign of the man in the flat cap.

'Eric?'

He turned and raised an eyebrow at her. 'I beg your pardon?'

She rolled her eyes and smiled grudgingly. 'Well, I have to call you something. Might as well be your choice for the moment. At least until the DNA tests are back.'

Article – 'As I See It' column
Hackney & Haringey Advertiser 1 October 20--

The Ministry of Business has this week issued an edict against the Telvetica Gaming Corporation over the AM/FM game that has so seized the public imagination. Apparently the noises produced by MC's when someone falls victim to the contest has the potential to be what they call a 'dangerous misdirection of resources' in that the sound of the alarm can be taken as a genuine emergency, such as a rape siren or medication alert. In many ways, I find this to be entirely appropriate. A game that has become so addictive to so many and yet exists only in the mind of the participants may very well be taken as a cry for help.

For those still living in the real world, AM/FM stands for 'Assassinate Me/Fuck Me' and is the fastest growing craze on the Interverse with over 28 million users so far. The function is to stalk victims registered in the game as you go about your daily routine. Scanning the immediate vicinity alerts you to possible assassination victims or potential sexual partners. In the killing mode, certain rules apply to the vulnerability of a victim and their 'value' in points to the assassin. If you have the sufficient credit of points, if the victim has been allowed the appropriate time 'alive' in the game and is vulnerable to your particular combination of weaponry, advantage and tracking visibility, you may attempt a 'hit'. If you are successful, you gain points that allow you to accumulate money, prizes and/or further advantages in the game and your victim loses the equivalent privileges.

In the 'Sex' mode, the scan produces compatible partners from a set of characteristics entered by the user and validated or downgraded by previous sexual partners. This is rather akin to reading the reviews of a play you might want to see and making your decision on the aggregate opinions of the critics. If you are impressed, you can issue an invitation and your potential partner can 'view your stats' and see various photos of yourself before deciding to accept an encounter. If they do, both MC's emit something akin to a cooing turtle dove, so that as you walk around the city, London's pigeons find themselves once more in the firing line for eradication as pests, this time for misdirecting our more amorous citizens.

This form of sexual radar is said to banish what one writer has described as the 'curse of mixed signals' in human intercourse, but of course, it does nothing of the kind and not just because of the poor pigeons. You can lie and so indeed can your previous lovers and therefore the way you present yourself is subject to just as much fantasy, misdirection and embroidery as the conventional approach.

All of this seems designed to connect with one's fellow human beings in an increasingly dispassionate manner. On the one hand, you are indulging in proxy genocide with all the satisfaction of it being an apparently victimless crime. On the other you are making yourself available for sex without the complication and obligation of a relationship. Neither approach encourages anything close to a meaningful interaction. In fact the encounters become mere transactions, some of them purely financial, as if all contact may be entered into a ledger and totaled up at the end of the quarter to find the sum of human happiness.

Of course, there are great attractions to both of the modes offered by AM/FM. Most of us dream of the casual encounter with no real consequences, but they are lurking there nonetheless. So far, twelve people in America and five in Europe have fallen victim to players who choose to take the assassination mode from the ethereal to the literal. A far larger number of women have found that the 'Sex' mode has become a tool for rapists and obsessive stalkers.

It seems as if people have become so bored with their actual lives that they are increasingly casual about how much of their inner selves they are prepared to cede to complete strangers. So starved are people of genuine sensation, that these dangers are seen as acceptable risks in return for the thrill of the chase.

Predictably the game has an illicit attraction because it is subject to disapproval and calls for its prohibition. Those who demand that it is banned are playing into the hands of the Telvetica Gaming Corporation. In the Blitz, many citizens found it more stimulating to forego the shelters and make love as the bombs fell around them. Their bodies were often found the next day, covered in white dust and frozen in the throes of passion like citizens of Pompeii. There is a death wish at the heart of every man and woman closely allied to the sex urge. AM/FM simply caters for this darker side of human nature and therefore will resist all attempts at suppression, championed as it is by such a vast population of users.

However the most disturbing message it sends is the posture of the MOB. They have the means to wipe AM/FM off the Interverse completely as they have ultimate control over almost every MC in the UK and through the Global Communication Control Commission over nearly every device in existence. Yet, they fulminate against the game in public whilst allowing it to continue growing and gaining in popularity.

The truth it reveals is that the state needs games like this in the same way that they need the soap operas and Staycation domes. They cherish anything that distracts the population from engaging with the world in any meaningful manner, hence the legalization of high grade opiates and the promotion of alcohol to the detriment of smokers who are driven to indulge only in designated areas, wearing the mark of Cain. It may be coincidence that the social evil nicotine is a stimulant whilst state endorsed alcohol and heroin are depressants, but I suspect not.

Bedsit Soup Recipe
Ingredients
Dried Vermicelli Pasta
Meat or Yeast Extract
1oz Butter or Margarine
Water
1 Spring Onion

This recipe is for those, like me, with limited access to cooking facilities. The best kind of pasta to use is the packs of broken short strands used for soup that may be found in Turkish grocers.

First, balance a soup or baked bean can on the upraised metal arms of the toaster. Then add a small quantity of butter or margarine and depress the sliders at the side to produce heat.

Slice the spring onion and add to the can until they are coloured and bubbling.

Add a small quantity of Bovril or Marmite beef or yeast extract.

Take off toaster. This step is very important – I'd hate for any of our more impoverished readers to perish from this recipe. Add vermicelli. Add boiling water from the kettle. Stir. Season to taste.

Editor's Note: Readers should note our usual disclaimer that 'Mr Blair' is a local writer who has adopted the persona of a more celebrated and dead author. It is in this guise that he has been commissioned to write for this paper. Please note that his perspective and indeed his adopted identity are literary devices that do not represent the views of this publication.

12 Retreat

AT AROUND 4am, lying in a bed of furs in a rural log cabin beside Lake Khoton in the Altai Tavan Bogd National Park of Western Mongolia, Michael Merrett was playing 'women are another country'. This was not a metaphorical game. It involved lying on his side in the dark and tracing the naked contours of his latest conquest. Maya, a 22-year-old Welsh TV researcher was snoring ever so slightly as he drew the sheet down to expose her thighs. He sighed as he saw the breast minarets lurch drunkenly in the direction of belly salt flats, a raised left leg hill sloping above the burnt stubble field of pubis beneath. Somewhere in Afghanistan perhaps?

Last week in Beijing's finest hotel, he had been impressed by a 29-year-old Uyghur political activist's rising belly meadow plunging gloriously down to an old-fashioned luxuriant copse at the head of the dark canals of her legs. Provence, maybe? The Rhone or the Lot? A medieval French town in a rural setting; Carcassonne or Puy L'Eveque, Merrett had decided.

He smiled in the dark and his eyes glittered. To objectify women was a mortal sin. An accusation levelled at him more than once in the copious e-barbs thrown up by his television broadcasts or his written outpourings. If only they knew how his topographical survey of women took objectification to an entirely more frivolous level of dispassionate appreciation. I am far, far cruder than anyone imagines, he thought to himself. Maybe all men are, he thought. He hardly knew.

He had been raised with four sisters and a mother, his father having died young. Men were a mystery to him in his youth. Their motives, how they were supposed to behave, had all been learnt long after his formative years. He had worked his way into the skin of male behavior, struggling to appear natural. He had failed and yet his style and his expressive, empathetic delivery, attracted some women, despite his less than impressive physical charms.

Occasionally his historical subjects, Alexander the Great, Caesar, were more comprehensible to him as sexual beings than he thought they were to other popular historians. He found himself attracted to 'handsome' women, often Chinese or Filipino, with short hair, tiny breasts and lithe bodies. Androgynes, in effect, without the disturbing maleness of an adult man.

In his youth, when he too was hairless and lithe and muscled with youth, he loved his male friend's bodies, their faces, and their smooth thighs. Beyond teenage fumbling, he had never truly consummated this side of his sexuality, but knew that he could if he chose to. There was little or no stigma to bisexuality any more. It seemed as if they had returned to the Greeks on that at least. However, he knew he was too old now to be chasing young boys. The priapic elder satyr pursuing young female nymphets was a classical image that seemed more acceptable to society at large and he was grateful for that, at least. It was part of his brand.

He couldn't sleep now and decided to read the paper lying folded in crisp lines on his bedside table. He gently passed a hand over the reading globe and unfolded the evening edition loaded three days ago in Beijing Airport. Almost immediately he spotted another article with poor dear Sallon's byline about the Orwell obsessed eccentric. His follow up piece revealed that the man could not be officially identified and was being investigated by Border & Control. An amnesiac, it was rumoured, who had somehow opted to inhabit the guise of his favourite long dead writer. Others, Merrett observed, seemed so struck by his physical resemblance that they were prepared to assist him in this fantasy. A local paper had offered him an opinion column to expound on 'matters of local interest'. His psychologist's name was quoted and Sallon signed off with a wish to be a fly on the wall next to that particular couch. 'Or better still', he thought, 'a closed circuit camera.'

Merrett gently eased his MC off the table and made a quick note of the psychologist's name. He had been commissioned to write yet another Orwell biography almost 16 months ago and had plunged himself into research at the archive and amongst the great-grand-children of the writer's peers. He had yet to decide on a tone or style now that the research was complete. People would be expecting something arch, clever and left of field from him. He was known for a certain stance. A previously un-discovered letter retrieved from the Buddicom family archive would help to push some press and fuel an accompanying documentary, once it was published. But perhaps this fantasist would be a framing device, an example of how the country was still openly obsessed with Orwell and wanted to believe that his views about the modern world were he able to express them, would accord with their own.

Afghanistan stirred and rolled over, exposing a whole new nation. Merrett waved off the light and lay back on his side, eager to map the new frontier before the alarm rang and the local driver arrived to take him to the site of the explosion.

Scratch bashfully invited Eric and Pedro to his new billet, a house-boat moored on the Hertford Union Canal amongst a rag-tag convoy of barely buoyant narrow boats near the crumbling Olympic site. His new girlfriend Mo was an angular Irish woman with crow black hair and startling green eyes who welcomed them aboard a smarter and larger bottle-green barge with the name 'Hoodwink' painted along the hull and flying a pirate flag neatly emblazoned in one corner with a shamrock. She served them cocktails and set up a parasol over the front decking.

Pedro was quiet and said little, sipping his Mojito whilst perched uncomfortably on the prow as the other three reclined on a padded bench facing the broad wall between two lock gates that was com-pletely covered with murals, graffiti and cartoons. Eric knew from his uncharacteristic reticence that Pedro did not approve of Scratch, but was prepared to be civil by keeping his mouth shut.

Eric noted that the other vessels were covered in a layer of fine white dust which Scratch told him was the residue from the demolition site. He proudly pointed out that only Mo's boat was hosed down daily and therefore gleamed like a wet frog in the sunshine.

Seeing the unofficial name of the mooring had been spray painted against the metal pilings, Eric tapped the name 'Nagasaki Towpath' into his MC to see if it had any significant meaning. He had started to do this sort of thing almost automatically at any time of the day and he was suddenly embarrassed when he saw Scratch shaking his head.

'I'm so sorry. That's very rude isn't it?'

Scratch and Mo looked at each other and smiled secretively. 'It's not that, George. I don't like to see you owned by an MC, that's all.'

Pedro stiffened when he heard Scratch addressing his companion as George and scowled at Eric. Scratch stretched over and topped up the Catalonian's glass. 'Your friend Pedro's got the right idea. Stay off the grid, right?'

Pedro nodded reluctantly. Eric frowned and placed the MC outside the shady parabola of the parasol so that the solar cells would benefit the battery.

'The Grid?'

Mo cocked her head on one side and spoke as if she couldn't quite believe such ignorance, even from an 'Older'. 'The Grid. The Watchers. You know when you use that thing you give away everything about yourself. It's the state's remote control you've got there.'

Scratch sniffed and examined Eric's device carefully. 'Bit of an antique though, this one.' He pointed out a serial code on the side of the casing. 'Version 6! If you are being watched, it's by someone in the last century.'

'Can it do those… projections? The creatures, celebrities that… cloak some people I see on the street. Or is that… is that just me?'

Scratch grinned. 'Privacy Projections? No. Yours is too antique for that kind of 'versetool. Did you think you were hallucinating again, auld fella?'

Eric suppressed any signs of relief and listened to several more jokes at his expense, sipping serenely at his rum and Coke, wishing it were a pint of warm ale. Looking around him as they laughed and kissed, trying to avoid the sight of their young tanned arms around each other, filling him with longing, he noticed each vessel displayed a red cloth hood on a pole or aerial. They hung like sleeping scarlet bats in the windless air and he gestured at the one at the far end of the 'Hoodwink'.

Scratch smiled and tapped the side of his nose. 'Well, George, we're Hoodies, innit?'

'What does it signify? A flag? A club?'

Mo laughed and Eric saw her teeth flash as she turned her smile on him like a searchlight on a moonless night raid. 'Yeah, a club. A Hoodies club.'

Eric restrained an impulse to grab the MC and search for something half remembered. 'Have you heard of the Cagoulards?'

Scratch lit up a kif cigarette and squinted through the pungent smoke. 'Are you about to try and educate me again, Georgio?'

Eric smiled and accepted the proffered kif, drawing cautiously on it, remembering a more careless evening outside the Ferry Boat Tavern when he had mistaken it for tobacco. In truth his experiences in Morocco had determined that he was not a great fan of the effects, but in the absence of whisky or ale, he sought some loosening of the tense knots in his shoulders and neck and a glimpse of the cocooning effect of being slightly drunk on a warm day.

'They were a secret revolutionary Fascist group in France before the war. We had one… I believe they had them during the Spanish Civil War. They tried to infiltrate the International Brigades, but I don't think they succeeded. They were effective though, on occasion. They blew up boats intended to aid Republicans, assassinated prominent communists. Their name meant… well… hoodies, in effect.'

'It's a long way from being Fascist, but it is secret' said Mo carefully. 'Maybe if we get to know you better we'll tell you about it.'

Scratch seemed about to speak, but a glance from Mo was enough to make him wipe his face as if clearing a table and stretch languidly, pointing to the end of the lock. 'We're off soon, mate. Going to be away for a while. Festival season, see? We like to get around. Do some gigs. Spread the love.'

Eric looked around at the other boats. 'All of you?'

Scratch nodded. 'All Hoodies together. I read your column in the paper. Sweet. They pay you for that?'

'A little.'

Scratch seemed to hesitate, looking hard at Eric's eyes, searching for signs of madness. 'You really think you're him? Reincarnation and crap? Something like that?'

Eric looked him in the eyes and nodded solemnly.

Scratch whistled through the gap in his front teeth and rubbed his spiky black hair. Leaning together, their arms touching, Mo and Scratch looked to Eric like a pair of Indian braves. Brown and long-limbed, cheekbones sharp beneath large bright eyes, they were, he realized, so beautiful that it made his stomach ache.

'As it happens, we might be moving on ourselves.'

Article – 'As I See It' column
Hackney & Haringey Advertiser 10 October 20--

A propos the ID interview I mentioned in my last column and the hysterical news reports of my escape. For the record, I genuinely intended to keep the appointment, despite all the reservations I expressed in that article. But, a curious incident intervened; symptomatic of the authoritarian state we now endure. No doubt some of you are now aware that I am obliged to file this column whilst 'on the lam' so to speak. My apologies for this.

On the Monday before the 28th of September, I went for my usual ride to the Middlesex filter beds and found lines of frock coated figures assembled along the canal, praying and rocking, small black books in their hands. I weaved slowly amongst them until I found a face I knew. I recognised Nochem Rubin of the Stamford Hill Shomrim, a kind of unofficial Orthodox police patrol that I once encountered in our back yard, apparently search-ing for a mugger. Regular readers will recall them as the subject of a previous column.

The young man was preoccupied and reluctant to break

off his prayers but told me somewhat brusquely that it was Rosh Hashanah and that they were required to perform prayers known as Tashlikh, besides flowing water. Many of my regular readers will already know all this, but I was fascinated and asked about the significance of the ritual. Nochem looked nervously around at the Rabbi of his synagogue who was watching him from the corner of his eye as he prayed. 'We are casting our sins into the water. Do you mind, Mr Eric? I can't really talk now.'

I looked along the canal at the scattered lines of black clad figures and watched several of them throwing bread or pebbles unto the water as they rocked. Behind them I could see a line of police officers walking down from Markfield Park. I asked Mr Rubin why they were present. He explained that last year, Polish workers, working on the Olympic Park demolition, attacked several people.

'About thirty of them took it into their drunken heads to come down and throw several of us in the water. Typical Catholic Anti-Semites. A prominent Lubavitcher died.' He seemed suddenly very passionate and muttered 'If I'd been there...'

I left him to his prayers and continued on my way. Progress was slow as I tried to wheel unobtrusively past the long lines of fellow sinners. As I reached the Princess of Wales pub below Lea Bridge Road I was startled to see two rubber dinghies containing armed police officers slowly cruising up towards Stamford Hill. A couple of police vans on the opposite bank trundled slowly up the track through the marshes in the same direction.

When I reached the filter beds, it was as deserted as ever. Throughout the spring and summer it has been flooded with blackberry pickers, fishermen and mothers with children taking the sun. I have made little progress with a novel but have written numerous essays and journal entries and indeed this column on my experience of the modern world. The book, 'A Smoking Room Story' now seems irrelevant. Recent events in my life render my proposed story a relic of a long forgotten time that doesn't relate to the current political situation in any regard. I am loth to spend months producing a kind of antique curio. You are to be spared.

Instead I am currently engaged on an essay about the concept of democracy that I hope will wipe out any memory of my regrettable paean to a new British character, 'The Lion and the Unicorn' that now seems so very, very wrong. In fact, it seemed wrong almost as soon as it was published and after the war I did try to rewrite it, without success. Perhaps now I will have the time.

English identity has become such a riddle and, since I started this column, I have tried to record my observations of London as a microcosm of the way it has altered. The capital has always been a melting pot, a terminus, a true version of Airstrip One, if anything is. But what it boils down to is that wherever you come from, you became imbued with a distrust of authority and a cynicism allied to a general apathetic malaise that seldom rises above the level of complaint. But through my conversations with Scratch, (issue 1507 passim) I am beginning to see a whole new concept of active democracy in the next generation and long to see more of its character at close quarters before coming to any political conclusions.

All of these thoughts were pushed out of my head by the time I arrived at the filter beds and remembered that my former refuge amongst the reeds of the reservoir were now in two feet of green rainwater.

I retreated to a seat amongst the preserved millstones that are scattered around near the sluice at the head of the old mill run. One of them has been sculpted into the shape of a huge armchair and readers may have seen me perched comically on the seat, working on the MC. I have only recently been shown how to lay the device on its side

ERIC IS AWAKE

and activate the mode that projects a keyboard on any flat surface in front of it. It has taken time to get used to the lack of resistance to my fingers on each character, but now I have discovered a function that produces a slight feeling of pressure on the projected letters accompanied by a satisfying range of sound effects. I have selected one that sounds like my old Remington typewriter and at last feel I can safely abandon my clumsy thumb ballet over the tiny keypad.

I worked for most of the morning and then decided to make my way back for lunch with Pedro who had been preparing a set of chicken pinchos morunos with rice (recipe given in last week's column) when I left the house. I had to drop by the supermarket for potatoes first. Pedro's growing worry about my B & C interview is assuaged by spending each day planning our menus with military precision which has him sending me out with detailed shopping/scavenging lists. He also nurses the back yard barbecue like it was a sickly pet and obsesses about collecting wood and charcoal.

As I cycled along the bottom of Springfield Park and on to the canal path in front of the rowing club next to the footbridge, two armed police officers with Heckler & Koch carbines stepped into my path. To my right I could see one of the rubber dinghies moored at the marina on the opposite bank. I realised that this was the first encounter I have ever had with the Police. It actually began quite well.

The lead officer seemed perfectly civil and relaxed, despite the lethal weapon resting along his arm. He gave me the full tip to toe appraisal to which I have become accustomed.

'I'm afraid this path is closed sir. You can go up Spring Hill and around by the Clapton Road if you need to get any further.'

I glanced behind him where there seemed to be some

commotion amongst the lines of men who were gathering into clumps of furious discussion as officers stood taking statements. 'Has something happened? Is anyone hurt?' I asked.

'Can't say. Do you live here, sir?'

I chose to ignore the question and struggled to identify Nochem amongst the milling throng in the distance. 'I have a friend up there.' I explained. 'Was it the Poles again?'

The officer was older than his colleague and less jumpy, it seemed as the younger one sweated profusely in his vest and moved impatiently from foot to foot.

'Answer the question please. Do you live here?'

I looked from one to the other and decided to placate him with an answer. 'Yes, I live back along this path just before the park.'

'Then you don't need to be going this way at all do you?' said the younger, sharply.

I ignored him and addressed his colleague. 'I was on my way to the supermarket, actually. I simply wanted to know if my friend was alright.'

The older officer frowned and seemed to be giving me a closer inspection. He took in the odd clothing and the thin moustache and cut the other man off as he moved forward to shepherd me back towards Spring Hill. 'Can you show us some ID please?'

I paused and threw one leg over my crossbar. As readers will know, identity is a sore point with me. I sighed and decided this was not going to go well. 'I'm afraid not. Why? Is it an offence to be here?'

The younger officer barred my way and half raised his gun. The older moved to his right side and gestured for me to dismount. I didn't. 'Are you refusing to identify yourself?' he said firmly.

I found myself getting angry. Very well, someone had obviously been attacked. But I was clearly not a serious

                                        ERIC IS AWAKE

suspect and I felt strongly that I didn't have to identify myself to anyone unless I was arrested. Even then I had certain rights. Or at least I felt I should have. I said calmly 'Even if I could, I wouldn't. I'm a libertarian. I'm against that sort of thing.'

I note that reports of this incident in the popular press now has me yelling this defiantly, hitting the officer and riding away with bullets ringing around my ears. This no doubt serves a need for sensation and justifies my description being circulated shortly afterwards by the Metropolitan Police as a suspect in the attack on the unfortunate Rabbi, despite his detailed description of the assailant as a short man with a foreign accent.

In fact, the officers each took hold of an arm and attempted to lever me off the bicycle, whilst struggling to hold on to their weapons. It was relatively easy for me to wrest myself free and to wheel around, pedalling furiously for the bottom of Spring Hill. They ran after me, calling their colleagues for assistance and probably getting other units to be deployed at the top of Springfield Park.

Spring Hill is steep and although I was in relatively good condition after several months of exercise, I knew I could not maintain my lead indefinitely, even though they were weighed down by weapons and body armour. I cut right along a back street and abandoned my beloved steed in a gap between two garages for later retrieval. I turned my jacket inside out and rolled my balaclava into a kind of hat pulled down low around my ears. I then climbed over some allotments and weaved in zig zags across various back gardens and over fences until I could double back to the house.

That is what actually happened. There was no violence on either part and I have read that the actual culprit has now been identified. However, I also read that I am now sought for a number of offences including 'failure to attend an interview' and 'procuring a false identity'.

As a consequence, I intend to remain on the move. I hope to continue my reflections for this column, which I have greatly enjoyed these past few months. I am informed by the editor that the paper is happy to resist police requests to curtail them and that each of my articles is now to be disseminated to the Interverse via the Carolan Portal.

I did not mean to become a renegade from Justice, but it seems impossible not to these days. Political power may sometimes emerge from the barrel of a gun, but democracy seldom does.

Albondigas Abbad
Ingredients
Minced Beef, Lamb, Chicken or Turkey
Stale Breadcrumbs
1 Medium-sized Onion
Garlic Paste
Tinned Tomatoes
1 Red Chilli
Flour
1 tablespoon of vegetable or olive oil

This recipe was achieved in an army surplus billy-can on a home-made barbecue grill over a wood fire.

First add sliced onion and oil and fry until coloured.

Meanwhile, in a bowl, combine the minced meat, garlic paste, breadcrumbs, chopped chili and one egg.

Shape into small pebble sized balls and roll in flour.

Add meatballs to onions until browned.

Add tinned tomatoes.

Season to taste.

Serve with rehydrated pot noodle

Editor's Note: Readers should note our usual disclaimer

that 'Mr Blair' is a local writer who has adopted the persona of a more celebrated and dead author. It is in this guise that he has been commissioned to write for this paper. Please note that his perspective and indeed his adopted identity are literary devices that do not represent the views of this publication.

13 DNA

Life at Canonbury Square was beginning to achieve some degree of equilibrium. Eric found he had enough work to keep them going in relative comfort and Ricky was getting on well with his new housekeeper Susan.

Eric hadn't been entirely sure how to interview her for the position but, noticing she was to a certain extent crippled, he asked her to give the child a bath and observed how she coped. She seemed to be determined and firm with him and she had a little girl of her own, Sally, who would be good company, so he took her on at five pounds a week with bed and board. This was probably over generous but he wanted no cavils over pay when the working hours were extended, due to his own prodigious workload.

As the months passed, he found they became a little universe of their own. He formed a routine that allowed him to work from very early in the morning until midday when he cycled or travelled on the underground to Soho and met friends and employers for lunch. In the afternoon he resumed work until early evening where he played with Ricky or took him out for a walk before Susan put him to bed and he could continue typing until the small hours. His health remained relatively stable; with occasional lapses into fever that he felt did not merit more than a cool flannel on his neck whilst working.

All the time, he planned his route to the mountains and the sea. He kept the scrap of newspaper he found in Stuttgart in a drawer of his desk and imagined the face of the woman who lived in the downstairs flat superimposed over that of the Aryan woman on the hillside. But Miss Popham, lonely as he thought she was, did not respond in a promising fashion and after lunging clumsily at her one evening, he realised that he was about as unattractive a proposition as could be imagined. He wrote a note to her setting out his stall, as it were. But it was the usual self-pitying drivel and he knew it.

Susan watched his various pathetic attempts to snare a woman with unease and might have said something about his approach if she hadn't felt constrained by the formality of their relationship. She felt he was scaring most of them half to death with the sour odour of his desperation. She knew Celia Kirwan had gently let him down but managed to preserve an affectionate friendship without once taking offence at his sudden and typically clumsy proposal. Susan liked Celia enormously and admired her astounding beauty, but knew as soon as they met, that her hapless employer was never going to land the graceful and sophisticated ex-debutante.

One day towards the end of February Susan came home after a walk with Ricky to find the house silent, the absence of the usual clattering of the typewriter instantly telling her something was wrong. After knocking tentatively at his bedroom door, she found Eric shivering in his bed dressed in an appalling set of woollen combinations. She fetched an icepack and begged him to call the doctor, but he got very angry and refused. She considered calling Celia at one point when she found a bloodstained handkerchief in the dustbin, but she feared his reaction. She knew he was afraid of being put away in some sanatorium or hospital and that this would put paid to the Jura plan. Maybe, she thought, it was better for him to get away from the city and all its demands, even if it hastened his death. She could tell that if he continued working at his present pace, little Ricky was going to be an orphan before long.

MERRETT WAITED IMPATIENTLY while the crew fiddled with lights and squares of polystyrene. Behind him, the waters of the lake were black and malodorous and he felt his sinusitis coming back. He went over his lines again in his head, trying to filter out Maya's Welsh whine droning on about the dark clouds overhead. What did she expect less than 100 kilometres from the epicentre? Did she not see the cindered ash of the once verdant forest around them? Had she not inhaled the polluted air as she panted beneath

ERIC IS AWAKE

him last night? Or was it all a bit too similar to Swansea to notice?

He glanced down at the radiation patch hanging from his belt. They had been here for over 12 hours and had to leave the area within 24 to avoid any significant contamination. The time had come to turn over, get it done and bugger off. The director, a bright young thing from the ranks of the film school hopefuls they employed for next to nothing, noticed his impatience and quickly shut Maya down.

'Ok, let's get on' he said imperiously, trying to impress Merrett with his steely resolve. 'Michael, are you set?' Merrett nodded in irritation. Maya clicked on the live Interverse link to his fan site and positioned her MC to frame presenter and crew. The cameraman closed in on the radiation meter and then pulled right back to reveal him with the lake behind him, the Altai Mountains showing up as a ragged obsidian line below the dull orange morning sun.

Merrett looked over his shoulder at the black water and turned to the camera.

'Lake Khoton in the Altai Tavan Bogd National Park is as close to the epicentre of the Altay disaster as we are permitted. Even here the radiation level is still dangerously high some twenty years after the explosion. It's in the blighted wasteland of Mongolia that Chinese society and indeed, world politics, changed forever. This man-made disaster zone remains a mystery. Nuclear experts say the Altay facility was old and badly maintained. As with Chernobyl and Three Mile Island, an accident waiting to happen. The Chinese government blamed Islamic terrorism; militant Uyghur activists, finally tiring of the massacres and repression meted out to them by the military, opting for a devastating display of martyrdom designed to destabilise the regime. Conspiracy theorists spin ever more fanciful stories about alien attacks, US missiles going off course and deliberate Chinese government sabotage designed to vilify the Uyghurs, many of whom were wiped out or exiled. All we know for sure is that a huge explosion triggered a global economic and political meltdown, dwarfing the nuclear disaster that destroyed this beautiful wilderness forever. The reverberations of that warm spring Saturday 12th May are still being felt here, here and here.'

He stopped, his edit point reached. Later each 'here' would see him standing in a different part of the world, his travel budget, like an isotope, seemingly never depleted. He ran a hand over his expensive hair implants and walked over to the Land Rover, ignoring the director's plaintive request for another take as his MC's message alert rang. He opened it to find a missive from one of his more pneumatic interns now based at UCL. The young medical student was apt to be rather too free with her exclamation marks and this was no exception.

Re: Your Orwell Biog

Dear Sexy,

Thought you might be interested in this! Working in the lab with old Goldie for extra bunce. Turns out Orwell has a previously unknown living relative! Call me when you get back. I want mucho credit and kisses for this, papa bear.

Candy xx

Emily met Simon outside the Cruciform building and as she spotted him strolling nonchalantly along Gower Street, she waved impatiently. Ever since Eric's disappearance, she had been under intense pressure from O'Brien, the hospital board and ironically, the Clinical Governance Facilitator. Now Goldstein's cryptic summons had further interfered with her schedule and she was eager to get it over with and discuss her legal position with her brother. Things were now getting decidedly sticky for her professionally and she felt angry that she was forced to waste yet more time with the Professor when she should be trying to save her career.

As they walked up stairs to Goldstein's office, she showed Simon the message she had received from the Professor. 'Interesting and disturbing. Please can we meet to discuss?'

Simon scowled. 'Probably related to Orwell after all. Some long lost illegitimate grandson or something. Prof likes to hype it up, doesn't he? Any more from the board?'

Emily sighed. 'An internal enquiry into my treatment plan, the help he got with his accommodation and whether it was 'appropriate' to assist him to commit ID fraud.'

Simon laughed. 'They'll be lucky. You weren't to know he wasn't who he appeared to be. He had someone else's National Insurance card, so if anyone is guilty of ID fraud, it's him.'

Emily wasn't convinced. 'O'Brien is telling them that I dragged my feet and should have alerted them when Ed told me about the test results. '

'Bollocks' snorted Simon as they emerged on the first floor and walked along the waxed floors to Goldstein's office. 'They can't claim you weren't justified in delaying whilst the tests were done again for certainty.' Emily knocked on Goldstein's door and sighed. Simon patted her on the back. 'What you need is a first class lawyer.'

Goldstein was a twinkle-eyed bald man with a ginger beard and a belly, accentuated by a paisley waistcoat that made it look as if he were carrying triplets. Despite his bulk he stepped nimbly around an office crammed with telescreens, gene analysers and piles of paper towering over half eaten sandwiches and empty coffee cups. Placing them on a pair of folding canvas chairs normally used by him and his wife at Glyndebourne, he called up two DNA profiles on a pair of large monitors. Swinging around to face them in his favourite padded chair, he twinkled away without speaking, waiting for them to acknowledge the impossibility of what they were seeing. Emily struggled to see the two profiles with any degree of clarity, but after an uncomfortable silence smiled at him indulgently.

'So, he's related to the Blair family? A direct descendant or an indirect genetic match?'

Goldstein shook his head and giggled like a teenager. 'What does he look like, this chap?'

'There is a resemblance' said Simon dryly. 'But then in a certain light, I am often compared to a young Franz Kafka'.

'Kenneth Williams' remarked Emily and received a shove in the bicep in response.

Goldstein gestured at the images behind him. 'These are not related, they are an exact match. We ran parallel tests as a control, taking saliva from envelopes, hairs from a jacket and the residue of a biopsy slide held by UCH. It is 98% certain that your patient has identical DNA, primary and secondary genetic indicators of Eric Arthur Blair aka George Orwell.' He paused and seemed utterly delighted with himself. Emily and Simon looked at each other and then at the beaming Professor. He appeared happy to simply sit there like Buddha, serene in his inner joy at a perfect scientific conundrum.

Emily shifted uncomfortably in the sagging chair that made her feel like she was at a particularly unsuccessful rock festival and pointed at the screens. 'Have you got any theories? I mean, could he be some sort of, I don't know… a clone or something?'

This seemed to send Goldstein into ecstasy and he whinnied like a horse, shaking his head, almost bent over with mirth. 'Someone extracts the DNA of a long dead author and grows a new one? Deeply hackneyed movie plot.'

Simon leaned forward eagerly. 'That's possible isn't it? Haven't they already done that sort of thing? In Russia?'

'Oh yes. Somatic Cell Nuclear Transfer and the like. Embryos have been produced for their genetic material for years by many countries and Pharmacoms. We've done some here. The Russians got a little further, but their experiment ended in the usual way. Abnormalities caused by the process rather than the transferred DNA, resulting in death at an early age. There are rumours that they have a seven year old with one lung stashed somewhere. No one has yet produced a 46-year-old man however.'

'There's also the fact that for most of those 46 years he was another person' remarked Emily. 'According to him, he woke up and instantly knew who he was. That's quite a delay.'

Goldstein nodded. 'True. But a clone wouldn't necessarily know anything about the persona or identity of the donor. There's talk of something akin to a race memory in descendants. A transferable sense of being that echoes that of the person from which they are derived. But none of it is science based. Few clones, illegal or legitimate, have survived long enough to find out if the same applies. Fun though, isn't it?'

Emily frowned. 'I can think of better ways to enjoy myself. This gets me nowhere that makes any sense. He can't be who he claims to be, whatever your tests say. How could he?'

Goldstein swivelled in his chair pensively and sat back, hands folded over his belly. 'Well, let's think about that. It is agreed, as far as we can be sure, that reincarnation is not a possibility. Therefore, scientifically speaking, we have to posit a theory that fits the known facts. He is genetically identical to a dead man. He has not always claimed to be Orwell. In fact, as far as we know, he only came forward with this idea in January this year after some traumatic event, possibly of a neurological or psychological nature. Correct?'

Emily shook her head. 'Not neurological. He was fully examined and there were no physical indicators on the scan. No haemorrhage, no stroke. The nearest I could get was a previously unheard of form of Transient Global Amnesia that substituted someone else's long term memory for his own.'

Goldstein shook his head. 'Not typical. I think if we really wanted to crowbar a scenario that explains the way your patient presented, we could argue that he is an experiment that took place 46 years ago and abandoned as a bad job or that became misplaced somehow.'

'Misplaced?' Simon said incredulously. 'The first fully grown clone experiment, lost on a shopping trip or down the back of the sofa?'

Goldstein smiled. 'Perhaps he escaped or was abandoned as a child and then adopted. Maybe in South Africa, as that was his nationality for most of his life. Or perhaps he never really knew who he was until an accident jogged his buried memories and triggered him to start behaving in a manner that he thought corresponded to his genetic identity.'

Emily stood up and paced to the window over Gower Street. She looked down at the row of metal cycle posts and wondered if she should have given O'Brien a description of Simon's bike. 'The man woke up in an alley 46 years after he was supposedly created in an experiment no one has ever heard of and that, despite never having been achieved before, is inexplicably abandoned. He becomes a South African mercenary and travels around the world thinking he is someone else and after a bump on the head or some sort of mental breakdown, suddenly remembers he is a long dead writer. There must be a mistake.'

Simon watched Goldstein's twinkling little eyes moving over the screens, enjoying every striking similarity. 'Presumably they would have had to do what you just did? Find some DNA from Orwell to reproduce?'

The Professor nodded. 'Of course. But the sample would have to better than I've salvaged from the relics we hold in the archive. These smidgens are OK for finding a DNA match, but I doubt they'd be sufficient for an experiment as advanced as this. Even digging him up and taking a direct sample wouldn't be good enough, in my view. But then I'm not in the forefront of this sort of science. My speciality is chromosomal replication and medicinal chemistry. Preventive rather than creative, I suppose.'

Simon grinned mischievously. 'Curing cancers rather than whipping up bestselling authors in a test tube?'

'Something like that.'

Afterwards, they repaired to a down-at-heel cafe on Percy Street and Emily stared glumly through the window at the tourists heading for the British Museum as Simon laid out her options.

'They can't pin much on you beyond an unusually personal investment in your patient. At best, that could be characterised as unprofessional. But it's not against the law.'

'When O'Brien came to see me he suggested I might be in big trouble now that our man has become a hunted fugitive. Aiding and abetting or something'.

Simon snorted derisively. 'He's flying a kite and he knows it. The worst your charge can be accused of is fleeing an ID interview and that's not down to you. Anyway sis, the fact is, this won't last long. Nobody disappears. Not really. O'Brien will pick him up before long and I'll do my best to make sure he behaves himself. Interesting thing about him actually'.

'What?'

'He has a history with the intelligence services according to my tame spook. Apparently B & C is just a temporary secondment after he blotted his copybook at Canary Wharf. They wanted him out of the loop for a while.'

'He was the one who shot those kids?'

'Not on paper. A junior armed officer carried the can and will be giving evidence to the inquiry. O'Brien, according to my man, was the shooter. Five shots, five dead. All in the back and all allegedly while surrendering. No camera footage because they were deliberately placed in a blind spot. I don't envy your lad when he catches up with him.'

'Oh, I can't have that. I have to find him. I'm responsible.'

'Bollocks you are. He's an un-person, Em. Very dodgy to be around now B & C has drawn a bead on him. Don't be silly.'

'I mean it. This genetic thing is serious nonsense. Goldstein must be losing it. I really think Eric may be some sort of descendant. But his clone idea doesn't make any sense. If he is a genuine relative then he is going to be public property once people find out. I'm not sure that's the best thing for someone in his condition.'

Simon sighed and shoved away his half finished coffee in an irritable gesture he'd been idly rehearsing for a few minutes.

'Well its academic, isn't it? You couldn't possibly know where he's gone to ground.'

Emily shook her head. 'Like you say, no one truly disappears. Your old MC can be tracked by anyone with the right programme.'

'True. But O'Brien is far more likely to have done that by now. Forget about him, sis.' In an uncharacteristic gesture of tenderness, Simon took her hand in a way that made her eyes suddenly fill with tears. He wiped one away and held her chin so that she looked straight at him. 'This. Is. Not. Your. Fault. Neither was the other thing and you really have to let it go now you boring, boring little freak. You were a kid for Christ's sake. Are you still seeing that shrink?'

She smiled bleakly. 'I am a shrink. No, I stopped all that. He couldn't get me any further. It's not as bad as it was. But this has made me feel ten years old again and I don't know if I can shake it off this time.'

14 Pseudonym

**IntelPod Ref: BAC501/DO/INTELDIVMARK 2.2345
Back Ref to Security Service archive tag
— 301/NWC.683**

Origin trigger as ID alert via UCH. Later, failed to attend ID interview, absconding after secure uniform unit check failure to produce. Then status level 5 with a low level beta priority until further ID alert follow-up from Wolfson Institute MedResearch Data-Trak. DNA match negative – but positive for Ref 301/NWC.683 despite inactive status (deceased) since 1950. Possible illegal clone activity or ID fraud and so upgraded to status level 7 high level alpha priority. Data-Trak UK initiate with Ground Agent status active.

Assigned: O'Brien 25643
End

May 1946 – London

Eric felt strongly that now was the time. Work was suffocating and he had thought to try and earn a little more before leaving London. But with his sister Marjorie dying suddenly and unexpectedly of kidney disease, he became convinced that he needed to get as far away as possible from the rising tide of grief and loneliness that threatened to overwhelm him. Worst was the constant need to appear unaffected. The stiff upper lip was necessary for Ricky's sake and to deter the painful attempts by friends and family to offer pity, that most scouring of sentiments. But, Christ! How wearing it was.

One Sunday, he could bear it no longer and borrowed a motor cycle to visit Shiplake. It was an aimless trip and it simply made him more depressed and lacking in energy. He had taken Hemingway's gun with him. He hadn't seen the man in the flat cap for some time.

His attempts at finding a mother for Ricky had been repeatedly and robustly rebuffed although he was hopeful that once lured to his island hideaway, certain women might be seduced by the beauty and serenity of the place. His one shining hope was Sonia Brownell who he had met at a dinner party at Connolly's house. She was incandescently beautiful, with a crown of blonde hair and a seething sexuality that Connolly readily admitted had kept him 'on the boil' ever since she came to work for him at the magazine.

She had been attracted to him right away, he was sure. Mostly by his work and reputation, but a man must accept his advantages where he finds them. They had continued to see each other over several weeks and finally he had made love to her at the flat.

Beguiled by the way she stripped off her clothes and stood like a statue on display before him, unabashed and brazen, he virtually pounced on her, driving her on to the bed and holding her hands pinned above her head as he thrust luxuriantly into her alabaster white body, feeling as if he were pouring all the pain and grief away like water into the desert sand. She bucked beneath him and fought him on to his back, crushing his hands onto his chest. Looking up at her, he felt as if she were utterly free and utterly corrupt. The way she used her body told him he could do whatever he wanted to her. Even kill her. Her youth, beauty and lack of inhibition both frightened and entranced him.

Afterwards, she fished some chocolate from her bag. It was dark and expensive and in a way, as sensual as the sex. They held it on their tongues and lay naked, as it melted into their throats.

'Where did you get it?'

'On the black, of course. I winked lasciviously at an old docker and he

                                                          ERIC IS AWAKE

promised me some more if I promised him a kiss.'

'Will you kiss him?'

She turned and placed a hand across his heaving chest. 'If I feel like it. I kissed you didn't I?'

'I'm sorry if I… I know it wasn't very good. Next time…'

She arched her back and stretched luxuriantly before looking over her shoulder and arching an eyebrow at him satirically. 'You were a little selfish, you know. What makes you think there'll be a next time?'

'If you marry me, there will have to be, if only for consummation purposes.'

'You are a bloody fool. I don't want to marry you. Why are you in such a tearing rush?'

He stroked her back and felt like hugging her to him, letting her youth and energy flow into his rotting innards.

'Because we may all be dead tomorrow.'

She laughed. 'We could all be dead tomorrow. Perhaps we already are. Maybe we all died in the war and no one told us. Maybe all this is just a very vivid dream and you and I are lying in the rubble after the Blitz, imagining the lives we might have had in the last remaining seconds before our hearts give out.'

'My heart already gave out, along with my lungs. I am as near to dead as makes no odds.'

She leaned back on his arm and laid his other hand on her breast. 'My heart still beats, despite my demise.' She laid her head against his chest. 'So does yours, old man. Just.'

Eric plunged his face into her hair breathed deeply and whispered 'We are the dead.'

She murmured sleepily, her eyes closing. 'We are the dead.'

She left him then and didn't contact him again for several weeks, beyond a short note. After a few days of packing, he departed with Ricky and Susan for Jura on the 22nd May, picking up his friend Paul Potts on the way. His sister Avril was to follow once they were settled. Maybe then, he would ask Sonia to come and perhaps, if she cared for him at all, the dead would come together.

PEDRO WAS NOT happy. Eric knew this, because he had said nothing since he bought their bicycles from the Nigerians at the rubbish dump and loaded up the saddle bags with a tent, groundsheet and a camping stove reclaimed from Scratch's store of recycled festival goods.

As they left, Pedro wobbling uncertainly after his more experienced companion, Eric realised he had forgotten completely about his friend's lame foot. He dismissed the thought almost immediately, reasoning that it was far better for him to have some kind of conveyance than to attempt the journey he had in mind as a pedestrian. Judging by his slow sullen progress from Hackney to Richmond, Pedro did not agree. He was more comfortable on his imperfect foot. He had walked London for years and before that had tramped from Vallcarca to Perpignan twice. He had not been astride a bicycle since he was seven years old and he did not approve. His silence, as they cruised slowly through the backstreets sticking closely to the canals and the river where possible, told Eric clearly and concisely that he did not approve of the manner of their frenzied departure, of bicycles or of Eric's latest bout of madness.

They camped in Richmond Park, setting up the tents well after the gates closed and concealing their fire behind the thickest screen of bushes at the centre of Sidmouth Wood. The camping stove and small gas cylinder provided a warm meal of beans and chorizo before they wrapped up for the night. But it was cold and the sleeping bags offered limited protection despite the relatively sturdy two-man tent. They both smoked intermittently throughout the night which warmed them a little and around 2am, Pedro finally thawed his mood long enough to ask if Eric had any particular destination in mind. Eric didn't answer immediately, perhaps punishing him for his long silence. They lay for a while, each in his sleeping bag, watching the frost forming on the grass visible through the tent flap.

'Shiplake.'

'Where's that?'

'Near Henley.'

'Means shit to me. Why?'

Eric's eyes narrowed to slits as the smoke from his cigarette was blown back into his face by a cold breeze. He sat up and zipped the flap shut.

'I left something there. I want to pick it up on the way.'

Pedro sighed. 'On the way to where?'

Now that the moonlight was no longer illuminating the interior, they couldn't see each other. In the sudden darkness, Pedro heard Eric's habitual clearing of the throat. The one he had become accustomed to hearing right before he received the latest piece of bad news.

'Look, Pedro. I know you're angry and I quite understand. As you said, we had a good comfortable billet there, but we both knew it was never going to last. However, as all our difficulties stem from my identity problems, you are free to go, you know. I won't hold it against you if you want to go back. After all, they might let you stay on, despite my disappearance. You haven't done anything wrong as far as they are concerned.'

Pedro laughed bitterly. 'You think they let me stay in a place like that on my own? They only gave us this place because you fren' say you are crazy. She fix up a good thing for you and I just came with the package, you know? I don' go nowhere, OK? I got nowhere to go. If you say we goin' fuckin' Shipshape then we go Shipshape. What else am I goin' to do? But do me a favour, OK? Stop asking me to call you Ereec. I don' know this Ereec. I don' want to know him.'

There was a pause after this passionate declaration during which Eric cleared his throat again.

'Very well. But you can't call me Lewis. That's established. How about… George? How do you feel about that?'

'Yeah, yeah. Jorge. Why not? And you can call me Julie, OK? Whatever make you happy, man. Now let's get some sleep.'

'Good night, Pedro'.

'I tole you. It's fuckin' Julie. That's establish.'

Within two hours of arriving back in the country, Merrett had visited Professor Goldstein and several doctors at UCH before tracking down Emily to the staff cafeteria where she toyed with a seafood linguine as he quickly set out his proposal. She knew him from his TV appearances, of course, and was as wary of his charm as he expected her to be. His plan was for her to help him track down Eric. The search and discovery would all be filmed as part of a documentary on both the Orwell obsession and the database society.

'I see this as the modern dilemma in microcosm. Here is a man who has a proven genetic connection to Orwell being tracked and hunted by the authorities because he cannot prove who he is.'

Emily lost interest in her plate and pushed it away, wondering how the staff could categorise a spongy soya substitute flavoured with fish oil as seafood.

'You're writing a biography of Orwell aren't you?'

Merrett, still dressed in a somewhat inappropriate safari style jacket, leaned back defensively in the flimsy plastic chair and smiled tightly.

'As it happens. Is that somehow dishonest?'

Emily shook her head. 'Not if you're straight with me. You see this as a promotional tool for your book and your television show. I see it as the exploitation of a vulnerable patient.'

'Quite a case study this chap, isn't he? An unusual psychological profile.'

'He is quite an interesting patient, yes. That doesn't mean I lose perspective and forget my duty of care or confidentiality.'

Merrett smiled and she noticed that his eyes appeared to be almost entirely black. She wondered idly whether he was on any kind of medication. He leaned forward conspiratorially and whispered.

'You think he's special. You went overboard for him. Could it be that you were ever so slightly attracted to him?'

Emily laughed. 'You haven't seen him, have you? He looks like a wrinkled mackintosh on a bent coat hanger. Is this the depth of your analysis? I'm a woman so naturally I will be attracted to a male patient? Sounds like a bit of middle-aged male fantasy projection. Wouldn't you say?'

'Then why did you sort out his benefits and get him a cosy little villa down by the canal? Do you do that for all your patients?'

'Hardly a villa. You've been talking to Ed who seems to have a problem with patient confidentiality'.

'There is no such thing. We all know that.' He straightened in his chair and proffered Emily his silkiest smile. 'Let's be honest, shall we? This man constitutes a very credible basis for an award-winning scientific paper, doesn't he? A complex scenario in which we are all characters in his dream. A classic philosophical model as well as a psychological one. Don't tell me you haven't considered writing something about that. '

'I can find a patient interesting and indeed write about him, disguising his identity, without exploiting him for commercial gain.'

'And you'd give that away free, would you? Publish it only to your peers and if an award comes your way, well, that's just the law of unintended consequences?'

Emily stood up. 'I think we've finished, haven't we?' She tidied her tray and lifted it up, intending to deposit it on her way out. Merrett didn't attempt to stop her but sat, pondering for a moment as she started to walk away.

'Under what name was he admitted?'

She paused and turned, spilling her unfinished carton of orange juice onto the linguine, turning the sauce a pale yellow. He didn't turn around so she addressed the well coiffed bald spot and wondered how much the thin covering had cost.

'Allways. Harold Lewis Allways. Why?'

Merrett turned and his black eyes glittered.

'That's one of the names Orwell used when he was posing as a down and out in London.' He gestured to the chair she had just vacated. She didn't move.

'He would have known that. He has an obsessive, biographical knowledge of him.'

'Orwell had a set of blue dots tattooed along his knuckles. Got them done in Burma because tribesmen believed they protected them against bullets. He joked after he was shot in the throat, that their efficacy was somewhat impaired'.

Emily blinked. 'He does have tattoos like that, but...'

Merrett turned away from her and read a message on his MC.

'But he would know that too and perhaps had some done to back up his story. Before he bedded down in a gutter and washed up at the hospital. Hmm. I suppose it is possible. Rather thorough of him though, isn't it? Your patient is using a very old MC, I understand. Apart from the fact that they don't know he has it, their software doesn't automatically track the old GPS style location of those early models. I still have a program dating from my investigative journalism years. If your brother still has a record of the user ID, I… we, can find him before they do.'

Emily sat back down.

15 Down and Out

We ran out of money around Heathrow. I checked my account on the MC and was not surprised to find that benefit payments had been stopped. The Hackney & Haringey Advertiser however, had faithfully deposited my extremely modest fee for the last column and this allowed us enough to buy a new butane bottle and some provisions.

As we sat out in front of the tent in a patch of green called Cranford Park, I calculated that we had enough food for another three days before becoming completely destitute. This didn't fill us with despair. Both Pedro and I had been in this position on the road before (albeit in different centuries) and knew that there was always a way of picking up work for cash in hand. In addition, we sought out supermarket back alleys for the usual scavenged items among the daily food dumps, so we were a long way from starving. If we were in Kent, I might have found us some hop picking, but when I suggested this to Pedro he just laughed.

At Pedro's suggestion, a tour of the industrial estates surrounding the airport produced a couple of days working alongside a dozen illegal immigrants spraying car windshields, windows and other glass surfaces with a coating of what was described as 'permeable nanomaterial'. The Turkish supervisor of the crowded workshop was harassed by an impending deadline and happy to see another pair of hands. We received a quick safety instruction that consisted mainly of a warning that failure to wear a thin waxed paper overall and flimsy face mask would render the firm's insurance invalid. No one commented on the unlikely prospect of any of us being covered by any sort of legitimate policy, whether we wore a paper overall or a beekeeper's outfit.

The work was hot and stifling but lasted just over a week whilst we 'drummed up' in a different corner of surrounding fields every night. One day whilst smoking a cigarette on the forecourt of the warehouse, I overheard the supervisor being warned of an impending B & C raid on the entire business park that had us cycling quickly towards Datchet, leaving that day's wage irrecoverable.

We camped that night next to a reservoir at Wraysbury where I despatched my column to the Hackney & Haringey Advertiser. It contained an account of my escape and informed readers that I would, in future, be submitting via the Carolan Portal. I had read that this alternative to mobnet afforded a more secure method, making it impossible to reveal our location. But afterwards I fretted that I had given away too much information and contemplated throwing away the MC in case it contained a treacherous element that would help the B & C to track our progress.

It was then that I experienced a wholly bizarre sensation. Despite standing at the water's edge, the device in my hand, Pedro urging me on, I couldn't destroy it. I likened it to the pang I felt when they confiscated my Remington in the sanatorium. I realised I had developed a peculiar attachment to the smooth lines of my MC. To drown it, seemed like sacrilege. I have not been averse to pissing on the altar when the need arises, but this seemed altogether different. More like pissing on myself.

I had taken the precaution of establishing an Interverse mailbox that functioned as the equivalent of a 'dead letter drop' using the ID tag 'Winston' for my own absurdly romantic reasons. I rationalised the decision by convincing myself that the B & C were not aware that I had an MC, although I could not be certain that Emily's brother hadn't revealed this to them. I assumed not, as he messaged me to say that he still regarded himself as my representative should I wish to 'turn myself in'. He emphasised that my offence was a comparatively trivial affair in monetary terms. The benefits fraudulently claimed under the name of Allways would not bear a custodial sentence, although it could mean me spending some time in a detention centre whilst my identity was established.

In a way, I can see the advantages of this. I cannot prove who I am, no more can the authorities. There is a temptation to let them sort it out and bugger the consequences. But something tells me that the wheels of bureaucracy turn ever more slowly here and I might be rotting in chokey for a long time before they found a suitable explanation for my existence. Not a sensible option.

Also, I am very eager to be on the tramp again. I knew it would come to this in the end and it's almost a relief to be forced to rely on one's own resources and cunning to get by. I am challenged to evade the many methods that now exist to pin a citizen down to a fixed space and I am curiously cheerful at the prospect. It feels like the old days in the LDV in St John's Wood, where we planned a British Resistance trained to attack and evade an occupying German army.

I find my many conversations with Scratch have given me a picture of the complex and subtle structures of authority in the AW that isn't immediately apparent to the casual observer. Of course, I noticed the surveillance cameras, the armed police officers, the press reports of random censorship on 'security' grounds, the hyped menace of armies of Chinese / Islamic / Zionist / Uiguyr / Russian terrorists threatening everything we hold dear and the obsession with identity, immigration and nationality. But he made me aware of the more ethereal battle going on in the Interverse for personal data. In so doing, he helped me to find the missing context that has been nagging away at me for so long. Previously, it seemed that every time I thought I had a grip on what the primary issue was in the AW, it slipped away from me in a shower of disputed history and fact. In a sense this was entirely expected. If the AW is a delusion of my madness, then it seems only right that I should tilt at a few windmills before finding my true quest.

I knew fundamentally that the real driver for authoritarian behaviour was capitalism, but Scratch (wish I knew his real name) made me aware of how this manifests itself. Under the guise of anti-terror measures and efficient delivery of municipal services, more and more information is required on each individual. The technology for obtaining this information, and indeed the administration of it, is handled by corporations. The Government, driven always by a creed that suggests private companies are better administrators than civil servants, has auctioned off the job to a dozen or more favoured corporate giants who are, as always, beholden not only to the dividend takers, but to their patrons within the Government itself.

Inevitably, capitalism demands more than one method of exploitation and most citizens don't appear to have consented (unless implicitly) for their personal details, credit record, purchasing choices, health, wealth, secret perversions, criminal records, DNA, sexual preferences and political beliefs to be hawked amongst the corporations as currency. By this method they are approved or denied insurance, employment, housing, benefits, education, health services, transport, passports and patronage of any kind.

At the same time they are touted by the same corporations or their clients for everything from luxury apartments to pile ointment depending on the 'profile' the accumulated data procured on them draws in the ether. I had thought the frontier of this battle against intrusion and personal liberty lay in the area of identity cards or passports. In fact, the authorities do not need such things. Everything a citizen does or says, every offence committed, every book purchased, every trip taken, every song composed, every article written, every subscription, every Saturday night observed on camera, tells them all they need to know.

The only problem the state has, is managing the scale of the information gleaned from so many people in so many forms. Judging by my experience at UCH, the fault lines lie in the technology used to collate or collect and the inefficiency or competing interests of the corporate systems and processes that interpret that information. In a sense, and perhaps not for the first time, the bureaucracy is the citizen's best bulwark against intrusion.

Needless to say, I did not throw the MC into the reservoir. Had I done so, I would not have been able to collect a message from

Emily. It was short, but expressed concern and a healthy dose of guilt for my 'predicament'. I replied with some reassurance that I did not blame her at all and that all choices had been made by me alone and with a realistic knowledge of the consequences. She asked to meet and although I long for this, I had to put her off for now. I think there is a danger that she will be followed and I am not ready to surrender my liberty so soon. I have been in the AW for ten months, but I feel as if I have only just woken up.

BEFORE MEETING MERRETT, Emily, toting a small holdall, called at Simon's ancient chambers at Verulam Buildings in Grays Inn. As she was shown into his office, the stripped trees of Grays Inn Field visible through his draughty window, she thought he looked like a bespectacled praying mantis, cocooned in piles of paper and files. He was bored and therefore pleased to see her, if only as a distraction.

Hearing Merrett's plan, he reclined in his creaking chair and cackled loudly, much to Emily's annoyance.

'You and that media whore on the hunt with a cameraman?'

'In fact he operates the camera himself. He says a full documentary crew might slow us down. '

'I bet he does. So why are you telling me this?'

Emily paused and smiled weakly. 'I don't really want to be on my own with Merrett.'

Simon suppressed another guffaw and adopted a solemn expression.

'You want me to chaperone you? To protect your virtue? Will I need a can of CS Gas and some chemical castration tablets?'

Emily swung her handbag and narrowly missed her brother's head as he darted sideways to avoid it.

'Idiot. I can handle that myself. I just think it will be easier if you are along. If we do find… Eric, then he's going to need some legal protection from O'Brien, but also from Merrett.'

'Have I got time to nip home and pack a spare pair of knickers? Or am I expected to drop 'em and scarper?'

After getting him to retrieve the MC user ID, Emily grabbed his jacket from the back of the door and manhandled her brother into it whilst pushing him towards the door. He managed to shout to his secretary as she dragged him out of the building and hailed a cab to Chiswick where Merrett was due to meet her at his flat in a red brick Edwardian mansion block beside the Great West Road. He looked momentarily downcast when he saw Simon but quickly pulled himself together and shepherded them into his Bentley.

'Where are we going?' asked Emily, running her hand over the expensive upholstery after skilfully eschewing the offer of a front seat. Merrett donned a pair of Aviator sunglasses and popped some Breth-Fruit gum between his veneers. He stuck an antique looking MC almost identical to the one donated to Eric to the dashboard and switched it to the old GPS beacon search program. Somewhere above them, long defunct satellites turned tattered solar panels to the sun and subtly altered direction. He spoke over his shoulder to the siblings in the back seat, adjusting the rear view mirror to get a better angle on Emily.

'Do you have the user ID?'

Simon rifled his wallet and produced an old registration token. He read out the code and Merrett tapped it in. After a few moments a map appeared with a single marker. Merrett smiled.

'This thing has a limited range but the last trace was from a park near Heathrow so I think if we head towards that, we'll pick up the next way point.'

Emily looked puzzled. 'They're not there now?'

Merrett shook his head. 'The trace will pick up the last time the MC was in range and in use. This thing says they were there yesterday. You didn't pass on this code to anyone else did you?'

Simon leaned forward, blocking Merrett's view of Emily. 'Don't you trust us, Mickey boy?'

Merrett looked pained. 'Michael, please. I don't trust anyone over five and I'm not entirely sure about the toddlers to be honest.'

Simon grinned evilly. 'Ditto.'

Article – As I See It column
Hackney & Haringey Advertiser 10 November 20--

Weight to height ratio has an enormous effect on a cyclist. This non-sequitur of an opening will suggest to the reader that I am still on my involuntary UK tour. My fellow renegade is a good foot shorter than I and feels the difference on the flat, but I find he is at an advantage on the steeper hills. The bicycles now resemble ailing relatives in that they require constant nursing. They still make our progress somewhat faster than it might be, even taking into account the many stops to adjust or repair tires, inner tubes, brake pads and the like.

It is a curious thing that when cycling alone, one can be gripped with a kind of l'esprit d'escaliers en avance that manifests itself in a range of imaginary violent scenarios where the authorities, the police, random fellow cyclists or passers-by attempt to impede one's progress and are dispatched with foul rants and extreme violence. The motion of cycling, its solitary nature and the isolation of the rider on small paths or at the margins of major roads makes possible all manner of placid contemplation, but instead fills the mind with imagined slights and outrages that can only satisfactorily be dispelled with assault and battery. I can't count how many times I have imagined fights with muggers and obstreperous dog walkers whilst travelling quite without obstruction along the tow path or through a sunny park. It is only when you are travelling as a pair that such odd thoughts are prevented as you inadvertently find yourself defused by the fellowship of a companion on the road. I have no idea why this should be or if I am alone in these regards, but I would be interested to hear from you if you share the experience. I would be equally interested if you don't.

We camp as much as possible on common or remote land or in woods, but often find ourselves moved on by private security guards or Civil Wardens, both of whom wear uniforms designed to resemble legitimate police attire as closely as possible. This ruse seems entirely designed to intimidate obedience from the general citizen, as most assume that they carry some degree of authority and seldom question it. In most cases they are simply un-trained employees of private companies or municipal volunteers with no official capacity at all.

In our desire to be unobtrusive, I curb my natural tendency to challenge this authority and, therefore, we frequently find ourselves turned from our beds in the middle of the night. 4 am seems to be a popular time for rousing the itinerant and setting them on the road.

Travelling through urban areas at this hour, you see only one set of people still upright; young women attired for the previous evening, alternately crying or vomiting at bus stops. This along with the homogenous nature of small towns leads to a constant feeling of déjà vu as one trundles through the same shopping malls, past the same ten high street chain stores, past the identical just out-of-town business park and the same clusters of crying, vomiting girls. One wonders where the men are at this hour. Still drinking or asleep, lacking the stamina of their paramours?

Pubs, in the form that I would recognize are few and far between and breweries almost non-existent. The country appears to be in a rush to be generic in every aspect. The effect of this is that, far from taking advantage of the many opportunities to travel, I read that more and more people are remaining in their own communities for pretty much their entire lives. This was not unusual prior to the Great War, but after a subsequent period of booming rail and air travel, it seems as if most people, constrained not only by expense but by a view that everywhere else is pretty much the same as where they live, are now staying put.

In addition, the Government have so terrified the population with armed police and army operations amidst constant reports of thwarted terrorist outrages at airports and railway hubs, that remaining in your own village or town precinct seems to be infinitely less perilous than expanding your horizons into the frightening wider world. The frequent accidental shootings of innocent citizens only serve to reinforce the dangers of wanderlust.

The only possible motivation to travel, it seems, is better weather, which can be found, if one chooses, in the vast Envirodomes run by the Staycation Corporations which, the brochure assures us, offer 'all year round sunshine, salt water bathing, sandy beaches and water sports in ventilation controlled, solar and wind powered environments, centred around a bio-diverse mini rain forest park that contributes to carbon emission reduction and provides a haven for numerous endangered species.'

Those domes run by the more media-oriented corporate giants even offer the ironically named 'reality experiences' which centre round several of the more popular soap operas. The holidaymaker 'relaxes' amongst the hysterical melodramas of their favourite characters in 'Hope Bay' or 'Riverbank Railings', reduced to playacting a far more glamorous life than their own. There are plans; I regret to say, to build one of these artificial nightmares on the old Olympic site, the theme to be a living breathing simulacrum of Tolkein's 'Lord of the Rings'. I can hear my late first wife groaning at the prospect of being trapped amongst the old bore's elves for a self-catering fortnight.

Over all this diversion is laid a fetishistic obsession with the King and his photogenic daughters that is enough to drive a stake through every Republican's heart and simply serves to perpetuate the view that the only thing that would drive the British people to revolution would be the Romanov style execution of all four of them and their dogs live on every screen in the country. If this could be achieved by interrupting a particularly overwrought episode of 'Riverbank Railings', the country would be alight before supper.

All of this suggests that this is a Government who follow a well-worn path of control through fear and distraction. If no one moves around and spends all of their money at the 'Company Store' on cheap alcohol and fantasy games, consuming every salacious detail of the next empty-headed celebrity's sex life, stuffing their homes and adorning their bodies with the latest technology, shopping as a leisure activity rather than as a necessity, vacationing in their own heads, then they are easily monitored, limited, distracted and manipulated into a subservient torpor. Resistance or dissent becomes rare and difficult and therefore does not really need to be prohibited. It is easy to trumpet a benign society that welcomes and facilitates protest if those who choose to avail themselves of the privilege are a tiny minority not trapped on the treadmill of working to fuel perpetual consumption and thus appease the shopping gods. T'was always thus, of course, but is now magnified to the nth degree.

It seems modern education teaches citizens all of their civil rights and how to exercise them in the same way that it teaches first aid. They use them only in the direst circumstances and seldom more than once in a lifetime. Curiously the most rebellious act of an Englishman in today's society is not to storm Parliament or hang the last priest with the entrails of the last banker. It may simply be to never accept credit, never to shop beyond your immediate needs (and then only in cash), never to appear on a database for any product or service, never to use the Interverse and most importantly, never register to vote. It seems the greatest threat to a Bureaucratocracy (a horrible term invented by leftist sociologists) is not to participate. This is a deeply unsatisfying method of dissent because it is so passive, although it would be a pleasing phenomenon for a revolution to be achieved purely by indolence. 'Yes, he was a model revolutionary. He wilfully neglected his admin.'

According to this morning's newspaper, there is to be a General Election on January 12th. None of the main centre or centre right parties has addressed any of the above. None even acknowledge that this situation exists. Indeed, few of you reading this column ever even discuss it and yet it is the most important political issue in the country.

Earth-Baked Toad in the Hole Catalunya
Ingredients
2 Raw Chorizo Sausages
1 Large Onion
Water or Stock
Potatoes

Whilst, strictly speaking, toad in the hole should at least incorporate some batter, we are obliged in present circumstances to bolster the sausages with slow roasted potatoes that eventually reach the consistency of a soft mash that encase the chorizo in a fair simulation of the traditional 'toad'.

First, dig a small pit in the earth and lay wood and straw in the bottom. Light the fire and feed with medium sized branches or logs until blazing. When the fire has been going around an hour or more, it will eventually reduce to glowing embers.

Place the sausage and onion in a sealed army-surplus billy-can or Asian tiffin tin along with sliced wedges of potato and a little water or stock. Place the container in the embers of the fire.

Place a layer of branches over the fire and the tin. Then bury with a thick covering of earth and leave for one hour.

Exhume the tin from the pit and serve direct from the container using stale brown bread as trenchers.

Editor's Note: Readers should note our usual disclaimer that 'Mr Blair' is a local writer who has adopted the persona of a more celebrated and dead author. It is in this guise that he has been commissioned to write for this paper. Please note that his perspective and indeed his adopted identity are literary devices that do not represent the views of this publication. This is especially true now that our eccentric contributor has attracted the attention of the authorities. Judging by your feedback, we have chosen to continue to offer him space in the paper although we are not permitted to offer any financial remuneration under the new provisions of the Proceeds of Crime Act and have agreed to donate a sum to charity. The syndication rights to his column have now been passed to The Carolan News Network making his words available to the wider Interverse. We cannot obviously control any monies paid by them to our correspondent.

16 Shipshape

The atmosphere at Barnhill was beginning to fester and Eric found himself making frequent forays outdoors to shoot rats or to fish with Ricky as his sister Avril and Susan, bit lumps out of each other over the housework. He knew Ricky was used to Susan having spent so much time with her at Canonbury Square after Eileen's death. But he could also see him becoming attached to Avril and wished that the women could both get along, for his sake at least. He had hoped for some peace after the acrimonious departure of Paul Potts who was forever blowing up about some imagined slight and who finally left in fury at about midnight after Avril had deliberately (he claimed) used a manuscript of his novel to light the fire. Eric felt some sympathy with him having once rescued the only draft of 'Animal Farm' from the bombed remains of a flat in Kilburn, but he knew it would never have worked with Paul, who, though amusing, was always volatile. A Canadian anarchist poet was never likely to find favour with Avril's sense of order.

In truth, the constant disputes caused him far more angst than it did Ricky who happily played inside and out with a kind of reckless headlong enthusiasm that often resulted in cuts and bruises borne out of a piratical disregard for physical preservation.

Things did not improve when Susan asked if a friend could visit her on the island and stay for a week or more. Eric sensed she needed an ally against Avril's sniping, and reluctantly agreed. But later conversations revealed that her young lover, David Holbrook, was a member of the Communist Party and Eric instantly began to regret his decision.

Since the publication of 'Animal Farm' he had become aware of a growing movement amongst the Stalinists to discredit him. Letters from Anthony Powell relayed some strained conversations amongst the literary set Eric labelled 'Stalin's Nancy Tendency' much to Rees' amusement.

Muggeridge wrote intimating that British Intelligence were aware of a Russian NKVD file on him dating from the Spanish Civil war and that at a recent meeting of their Inostranny Otdel unit a man called Iosif Grigulevich had mentioned him by name along with a poet called Guy Leland. As the death toll mounted in Russia, Eric knew there was every possibility that the safety of he and his family, could be at risk. It was said now that the Inostranny Otdel had murdered Andres Nin in Spain and Trotsky in Mexico using mobile groups of assassins under Grigulevich's command as Hemingway had suggested. Trotsky's assassin, Mercader, had been Eric's Spanish tutor in Barcelona, so they undoubtedly knew what he looked like. They weren't restricted from travelling either, it seemed. Even the remote islands of Scotland were not beyond their reach. Who was to say Grigulevich, who masqueraded as a Costa Rican, could not convince a young Stalinist member of the Communist Party of Great Britain to wield the axe?

On the day that Holbrook was expected, he hid an old service revolver beneath a piece of sacking in a drain outside the house and ensured the shotgun, the air rifle and the hunting rifle were all oiled and loaded.

The women didn't notice his anxiety and knew that they would put it down to paranoia. But he had been in this position before in Barcelona. Eileen had known they were in danger and he had ignored her, only realising the peril they were in when every member of the P.O.U.M militia were suddenly deemed to be Trotskyite Fascist collaborators and Georges Kopp was arrested for being a member of the newly proscribed organisation. They barely escaped joining him there. Back then Eric had been a name on a list along with thousands of others. This time, because of his long awaited success, Stalin and Beria knew him by name. Paranoia, yes, but perhaps with some justification, particularly now he knew that Kopp too, may have been playing both ends against the middle.

He spent the afternoon pretending to tend the vegetable garden, watching the horizon for a car or the pony and trap. Around three he saw a speck a few miles distant and shading his eyes, watched, as it became a figure stumbling under the weight of an army kit bag and a cardboard suitcase.

He ducked inside and picked up the shotgun from just inside the back door. He stepped out towards the field behind the house and spotted a couple of ducks approaching in a V formation from inland. He waited until Holbrook was close enough to see him and to raise a hand in greeting. Eric pretended he hadn't seen him, put the gun to his shoulder, took aim at the lead duck and fired. Holbrook flinched and dropped his kitbag, his hands shooting up in the air. Eric walked calmly over to the middle of the field where the duck was falling. A shot across the bows. He was no Trotsky.

Holbrook stayed only a few days, leaving late one afternoon after Eric had some fun menacing him with an ostensibly guileless warning that he shouldn't go too near the cliffs as people had been known to fall. 'Sometimes quite unexpectedly.'

Sadly, Susan went too, finally unable to bear Avril's attacks any longer. He gave her a little money and was sorry to see Ricky clinging to her tightly as she said goodbye. The child was soon distracted and Eric felt very relieved that the atmosphere had lightened at last.

Being with Avril again was rather like it had been when they were children, all those years ago in Shiplake, playing with the Buddicom children by the river as he fell deeply in love for the first time with Jacintha. Back when it was all so simple and joyful and free, before the innocence was lost and the shadows fell across all their lives. The only thing missing, as far as he was concerned, was Sonia.

ERIC AND PEDRO did their best to avoid Windsor Great Park, but, footsore and weary after a difficult ride from Shepperton, they opted to camp very close to the outer walls of the King's well-guarded estate in a wood near Cranbourne.

This would not have been a problem, if Pedro had not found Eric in one of his fugues early the following morning. Cursing loudly, he failed to rouse him through shaking and slapping and decided that the safest option was to cover the tent with a layer of foliage and hope that the regular patrols of the perimeter would not stumble across them.

Four fraught hours of near discovery eventually forced him to quietly dismantle the tent around his unconscious companion and roll him into a thicket where he also stowed the packs and bicycles whilst he reconnoitred the route and timing of the patrols.

He sat at a rural bus stop that had been quaintly furnished by locals with cushions, a padded bench and even a picture of the King surrounded by dried flowers. He was able to relax a little, sinking back into the bench and resting comfortably from the brisk wind whipping around the little wooden shelter. He watched several army trucks go by and tried to look as if he were studying the timetable with great concentration when they were followed shortly afterwards by two police patrol vehicles. He knew he didn't look like a local in his mud-spattered jeans and tattered trainers, but the police seemed to be more interested in a camper van illegally parked near to the perimeter wall. He watched them lecturing the elderly couple and helping them to get the engine started. The Olders were grateful, respectful of authority and scandalised that they might have been taken for terrorists, their battered Volkswagen stuffed with explosives rather than sleeping bags, digestive biscuits and sacks of their favourite tea.

As he watched, he contemplated the future in a way that he rarely ever had. Before his old compadre had started to act up, he had never thought beyond the next day, the next meal, the next bed for the night. Now, after tasting the good life in the little house by the canal, he found himself wondering about what would happen to them both, in the end. A street life can be a short one, even if you are careful. But a street life as a fugitive, with people writing about you in the Interverse and the police breathing down your neck, was likely to be shorter still.

Sitting in the pale winter sun, he tried to pin down what life he wanted and decided that the only thing that made sense was to go somewhere far, far away where no one else could bother them or care. Somewhere where Pedro, Lewis, Eric and Jorge could live on the land, all four of them. He did not know where this place might be, but after a conversation with his companion one night, he felt very strongly that it should have the sea on one side and the mountains behind.

After a while, the road seemed to be clear and he walked back to the hedgerow above the embankment opposite where he had left Eric cocooned in his sleeping bag, the hood pulled up around his head. He was awake, but motionless, his eyes open, slowly thawing his frozen limbs. Pedro helped him out of the bag and poured some cold tea from a flask and held it to his mouth. Every time he had one of these periods of oblivion, his hands and limbs shook uncontrollably for a while and Pedro had to help him to stand, to walk, to wake back up to the world as it was, not as he would have it.

He allowed him half an hour, seated on a tree stump whilst he heated up some soup and passed it to the tangled arrangement of shivering bones. When he felt the focus had returned to the flint blue eyes, he placed a cigarette between Eric's lips. As he leant forward to light it, he said quietly. 'Where you was?'

Eric smiled. 'Another place.'

Pedro nodded sagely. 'Better?'

Eric shook his head. 'No. Just different.'

'We nearly there, Jorge? Shipshape?'

Eric grinned. 'Nearly shipshape, Pedro.'

They packed up and mounted their rickety steeds within an hour and moved unsteadily along the lanes and on to the main Ascot Road.

IntelPod Ref: BAC501/DO/INTELDIVMARK 2.23456
Back Ref to Security Service archive tag
– 301/NWC.683

Status level 7 high level alpha priority. Data-Trak UK alert – Ascot Road – Windsor Golf Club CCTV – ID facial recognition: Pedro Urquiza Abbad – Euro itinerant back ref UKBA entry 15 years. Associate BAC501 accompanies. Ground Agent alert. Trace and collect.

End

In fact, the place near the river where Eric used to play as a child was a little way out of Shiplake, beneath a thin shade of skeletal willow and ash, the cool shallows dark and green with weed. Eric took off his shoes and socks and waded out knee-deep to the centre of the tiny brook tributary that ran parallel to the river. Pedro sat watching him from a carpet of winter moss on the stone-hard bank. For a while, Eric just stood there, his thick trousers rolled up, feeling the bitter chill of the water working its way up his legs, enjoying the gentle pull of the flow around his pallid shanks and the growing numbness of his toes.

Pedro lay on the rolled tent beneath a willow, head propped on his backpack, trainers next to him, his filthy heels lying in the freezing water. Eric, swayed slightly, his eyes closed, recalling the sounds of his playmates splashing about after frogs amongst the slippery green stones. In the veins of his eyelids, he saw Jacintha, Prosper, Guiny and little Avril watching him as he stood on his head, his chubby face turning red whilst his legs wavered unsteadily above his chin. This is how he always saw Jacintha in his mind, upside down with her head turning curiously to try and encompass the strange boy who stared back at her with Oriental eyes, his breath coming in gasps as he strove to maintain his balance.

To Pedro he looked like an old stork, his ragged jacket flapping like tattered wings, oblivious to the silver darts flying between his spindly legs. They stayed like this for more than an hour until, as if waking from a Hindu posture, Eric strode back to the bank and put on his shoes and socks, his feet blue with cold. Wordlessly, they both gathered up their possessions and draped them once more around the rusting frames of their bicycles.

Pedro waited patiently as Eric looked around at the leafless trees, searching for some point of orientation. He seemed to find it and they walked their bikes away from the brook towards a wooded copse at the edge of a bleak ploughed meadow, the mud frozen into brown icing sculptures beneath their feet. Ahead, was an almost dome-like tree or bush of a species that Pedro could not have named, its evergreen leaves still concealing its core even at this time of year.

Ducking underneath the curtain of foliage, they found themselves in the heart of an almost impenetrable green bower, the ground dusty but dry beneath their feet. Pedro approved. The place was hidden and they would pitch the tent here for the night, knowing they could not be seen from outside the canopy of thorn and thicket. He set about preparing the camp as Eric explored a bank of nettles to one side. He beat at the green fronds with his bicycle pump until he had revealed the lip of a low cement storm drain. Satisfied, he retreated and helped Pedro to erect the tent. Within an hour they were eating baked beans heated on the tiny gas ring, the last of the butane sputtering out just as the mixture began to bubble.

They smoked in the dark afterwards, wrapped in their sleeping bags. Pedro waited until then to speak for the first time since they left Windsor.

'Why we here, Jorge? Where we going?'

There was silence and when Eric's voice whispered out of the murk, it seemed as if it came from a long way off.

'I used to play around here as a child and as a teenager. It was a good time. I wanted to come here on the way.'

'On the way to where?'

'To the mountains and the sea.'

Pedro was ecstatic. 'Tell me about it again, Jorge.'

'It's an island. There are more deer than people. It's lonely and isolated and the house has a meadow that runs right down to the sea. You can see the islands opposite and the mountains are behind you. No one can touch you there. They could drop the bomb and you'd never know.'

'Sounds good, man. We goin' there now?'

'Yes, we're going there now.'

'How far? How long will it take?'

'It's a long way, but we'll make it there in time.'

Pedro absorbed this and analysed it for meaning. Finding none, he farted and turned over on his side, pulling the bag's head over his eyes.

Later, as Pedro slept in the fastness of the dark winter night, Eric rose with a torch in one hand, crept as quietly as he could back over to the bank of nettles and struggled to enter the grave-like pit between the two cement walls. There was barely enough space to turn around and the drain was covered at the farthest end with a concrete lid that blocked out the moonlight. He ranged the torch around the muddy covering of leaf mould ahead of him and measured out two hand breadths from the back wall. Reaching into his trouser pocket, he managed to extricate his penknife, pulled out the largest of the blades and began to dig into the soft loamy mush. It was a hard and lengthy job to reach the satisfying metallic solidity of the ammunition box in its wrapping of oiled cloth. Working around the edge, he managed at last to lever it up, only shreds of the cloth shroud still clinging to it.

As he heaved the box onto the side of the pit, scraping away the dirt covering the LDV crest and legend C Company, 5th County of London Battalion, he looked up to see Pedro gazing down at him, his hair tousled with sleep and his trainers half-laced.

'I knew you was up to sumtin', Jorge. Shipshape business. I knew. What you got in there? Cash?'

Eric levered himself out of the drain and sat on the cement lip, next to the rusty box. Pedro hunkered down beside him and watched as he scraped away at the dirt clinging to the catch on the front of the box. As he opened it with the edge of his penknife, he leaned forward and was disappointed to see a canvas bag. Inside the bag was a roll of yet more oiled cloth.

'What woke you up? Was it the digging?'

Pedro shrugged impatiently. 'No. I thought I hear grass swish, swishing outside, you know?'

Eric gently un-wrapped the cloth covering to expose a rectangular wooden case. As he opened it to reveal the small oiled corpse of Hemingway's Colt 32 and a clip of ammunition, Pedro sat back on his haunches and hissed curses in indecipherable Catalan. He looked at Eric reproachfully and shook his head.

'You goin' to get us in more trouble, Jorge. What you have a shooter for?'

Eric looked levelly at his short, dirty companion with his wayward outcropping of wiry black hair and said quietly 'I don't know that I was thinking that clearly, actually. After the war, I came back here, to the camp, to see how it looked. I had just lost my wife and I felt… I felt I needed to see it again before I died. It was in my pocket. I don't know why I decided to bury it here. I did it knowing that you can never go back. Not to the past and not to how you were, and yet here I am. I did get back.' Eric expertly opened the gun and loaded the five remaining, well-oiled bullets into the chamber.

Pedro's eyes widened and he sighed in exasperation. 'Now, we are as good as dead.'

'Now, you are as good as dead.'

They both swung around to see a dark figure stepping from the outer circle of the bower into a shaft of moonlight spearing through a gap in the canopy. He was tall and broad and dressed in a dark jumpsuit, festooned with radio, night goggles, earphones, shoulder holster, handcuffs and a length of nylon rope. All this they saw in the moment before his torch caught them in its fiery halo. Their pursuer perceived Eric blinking behind the crouched figure of Pedro, but could not see what lay between them. His hand rested lightly on the barrel of his carbine, which was slung across his chest and he waggled the torch up and down indicating that they should both stand. His hand left the carbine as he reached up to the button by his throat mike to relay his discovery and froze as he found himself staring down the barrel of a small handgun. It never occurred to O'Brien that either of them would be armed. Another black mark on his resume. The voice behind the gun was curiously refined and archaic.

'I really would prefer it if you didn't. Drop the torch and put both hands behind your head.'.

He complied, knowing that when the gunman was close enough, he would be able to reach the knife sheathed behind his collar.

'Who are you? What's your name?'

'DI Gerry O'Brien. B & C. Why don't you wind your neck in before someone snaps it off? You're already in the shit, don't make it worse.'

Pedro picked up the fallen torch and trained it on the visitor. Eric moved behind O'Brien, which annoyed him as he knew it restricted his planned strike. The low guttural chuckle from behind his ear momentarily unnerved him.

'O'Brien? How stupid this is. Put your hands up, high.' He removed the carbine, looping it quickly and deftly over one of the raised arms. O'Brien's right hand moved imperceptibly towards the back of his neck until he felt the cold barrel of the Colt shoved directly into the base of his skull.

'Why are you following me? I'm nobody.'

'That's kind of the problem, sunshine. You aren't nobody. You are very much somebody.'

'I'm small beer for you, O'Brien, if that really is your name. Failure to attend an ID interview? Benefit fraud? They don't send out men like you for people like that and we both know it. What's going on?'

'When were you born?'

'1903' Eric breathed quietly in his ear. 'And I'm aware of people's views on that.'

O'Brien shook his head, feeling the barrel scrape the hollow at the base of his cranium. 'We reckon about 20-- at the latest. You're an experiment. That's the theory. An illegal bit of genetic kite flying that got out of control. Russian Big Pharma, possibly. They've been messing around with this shit for decades. Nice bit of mindfuck by the Oligarchs, using Orwell's DNA. You shouldn't be here. Most clones die young, usually in agony, great disabling errors in their make up. You survived. We need to have a bit of a look at that.'

The torchlight was quivering in Pedro's shaking hand and he whispered plaintively 'We're dead, we're dead, we're dead' until Eric shushed him.

'You were the one who visited Emi… Miss Statton at UCH.'

O'Brien opened his mouth to shout his answer, knowing it would alert the rest of the unit and draw them to his position. But Eric had not really asked a question. The metal sheathed rabbit punch to the back of his head told O'Brien that it had been purely rhetorical. He fell in a heap, his throat mike coming adrift and slipping between his teeth as they connected with the dirt and snapping in two. Pedro hopped hysterically from lame hoof to good hoof, his face contorted with fear. A look from Eric silenced him and he turned off the torch.

Standing quietly in the dark, they could both hear the rest of the unit tramping through the grass fifty yards away. Putting his finger to his lips, Eric gestured with the gun at the tent and backpacks behind them, making a cutting motion across his throat. Those were to be abandoned. The noise would give them away.

He placed the Colt in his trousers and lifted O'Brien by the shoulders. Pedro grabbed the legs and they gently lowered him into the drain. Eric found the knife in its concealed scabbard at the nape of the uniform and took it with him. He un-slung the night goggles and peered with them out of the bower's foliage at the dark shapes walking slowly towards them from the river. They were a heavily armed troop of six with the last one on point and he assumed O'Brien had been the forward scout and that they were now advancing after failing to hear from him over the comms.

Taking Pedro by the sleeve, he pushed through the thicket at the opposite end of their refuge and headed in a long circle further south and downstream of the main river. Using the night goggles to determine the pursuers' position, he was able to slowly draw away from their slow progress and make it to the river itself where he eased himself into the freezing water up to his waist, prodding and kicking Pedro ahead of him.

They waded laboriously, keeping close to the bank for about three quarters of a mile before Eric thought it safe to emerge from the camouflage of the babbling waters and back up to the road. They were shivering and sodden in the winter air, but he drove them on along narrow country lanes, pleased to discover that the night goggles contained a digital compass that allowed him to keep their progress northwards. The aim, such as it was and in the absence of any other course of action, was to get to Barnhill. Eric did not know why it was important. But he wanted to go home, to the mountains and the sea.

In his sodden ditch, O'Brien came to an hour later, the serial number of the MC he had spotted dangling from Eric's belt imprinted irrevocably in his cortex.

Fever Diary – 25 November 20--

The priority on that dire day was to either dry our clothes or obtain replacements. The cold cloth was debilitating in the wind and slowed progress. In the end, I found, to my shame, that I could go no further and huddled, utterly miserable in the lee of a dry stone wall, waiting for the end. When one is profoundly end-of-tethered and cold to boot, there is something comforting in the slow shut down of exposure. They say the feeling of cold slowly recedes and a kind of drowsy numbness takes its place. Nature's blanket gently being drawn over the head.

However, just as I began to find the sleep of the eternal an altogether attractive prospect, (and one I may well have experienced before) Pedro, to his everlasting credit, took charge and disappeared towards a distant farmhouse. All in all we had travelled less than five miles from Shiplake and I knew that they would track us down soon enough if we couldn't leave the area rapidly. All seemed lost and, in truth, I wasn't entirely unhappy. I had died once. I could do it again.

He returned within half an hour carrying two pairs of running shorts, a pair of baggy jeans, some army camouflage trousers and two heavy woollen hoodies, the legend 'Working for the Clampdown' on the back and 'The Clash' on the front of one and the superfluous legend 'HOOD' on the other. He had wrapped the shorts around each hand and draped the jeans and trousers over his shoulder. Balanced on his swathed palms was a foil tin that smoked slightly. He placed it down to reveal a portable disposable brazier of smouldering charcoal beneath a wire mesh upon which rested two of the most delicious smelling pork chops I had ever seen.

We fell on them intermittently as we stripped off from the waist down and donned the running shorts beneath the clothes. I eschewed the baggy jeans and chose the army trousers as they felt more natural. Although I hated the hoodie and its eccentric, indecipherable decoration, I was cold enough to find its material a comfort and relief. I was loath to put the soaked boots back on, but Pedro produced two rolls of long socks from his pockets and I almost kissed him. His raid on an empty farmhouse had produced nothing, but a foray to a temporary caravan in the field behind had produced the contents of a washing line and a barbecue whilst the inhabitants squabbled over a TV programme inside the tiny mobile home that apparently played host to a pair of raggedy builders converting the abandoned farmhouse into a habitable holiday home. The chops were still warm and we ate like pigs, the juices coursing down our faces until, warmed by this and the new clothes, we felt we could go on and find shelter.

What happened that evening as we entered the town of Shipston-on-Stour will now be well known to most of the Interverse. It might appear from the footage of my impromptu appearance on the hustings, (now ranked as the most viewed vid in the Europe section of the Viewsites) that I had intentionally sought out this meeting to put my point, but nothing could be further from the truth. In fact, the rich and mostly undercooked meal stolen from the builders had an unfortunate effect on the stomach and the only reason we entered the community centre was to use the lavatories. Viewed historically, it might be seen as entirely appropriate that some political passions may be put down to the bowel and the stridency of some speeches to diarrhoea.

Having availed ourselves of the facilities, we noted that hot teas were being dispensed at the rear of the political meeting that was taking place in the main hall. We quickly snaffled a scalding beverage in an inadequate plastic beaker with a slice of fruit cake and sat with some relief on a pair of free seats at the rear.

Only then did I realise that the four main political parties were hosting a local debate on the most vital (!) issues of the impending election. Four representatives and a dowdy chairwoman sat on a shabby stage before drab red velvet curtains tied back either side to frame a painted flat of the London skyline on the back wall that had obviously been used for a recent 'Dick Whittington' pantomime.

The drone of uninspiring discourse had the usual soporific effect and I sat drowsily aware that both the sitting MP and the three challengers could all be described as sitting firmly on the centre right and centre right right of the political compass. One younger fresher faced candidate tried to curry favour with a slightly libertarian view undercut by an emphasis on home security that seemed guaranteed not to frighten the horses.

However as the debate went on, I noticed that all were focusing on the situation in China, terrorism and the need for constant awareness of all manner of potential threats. The Chinese debacle, of course, was not described by any of the politicians as a war. The phrase 'peacekeeping' was used throughout, despite the news reports of active British campaigns against various factions in the territory since the break up of the country into its respective UN cantons after the collapse of the Revolutionary Government. There was an underlying implication that the Altay disaster which precipitated the fall of China could very well happen here in Europe and that the security of nuclear power facilities needed to be ramped up and improved against those who sought to bring about change via the atom. No one but the quasi-libertarian suggested closing them, of course, and he was quickly shouted down.

All in all, there was few of what one might call 'local' issues, the emphasis being entirely on outside forces. All of the whey-faced career politicos darkly hinted at impending threats against which we would be defenceless unless a new Government were elected or a 'fresh approach' to security introduced. At the same time, technology and the Interverse were cited as the tools to empowerment and change that would make 'Digital Democracy' a reality at last, with even the Olders assisted into participation. At one point, in a rare departure from the enemies without and within theme, a candidate seemed to be suggesting, to much applause, that 3D wallscreens in every home was not only some kind of civil right, but a necessity for any functioning democracy.

It was at this point that the local Mayor who was chairing the farce threw the floor open for questions and I committed what may now be regarded as the most foolish act of my life in the AW. At a time when we were effectively public enemies, on the run from all manners of covert authoritarians and with a need to be as invisible as possible, I got to my feet, Pedro pulling desperately on my jacket. I did not know what I was going to say. In fact, without notes of any kind, I was not as incoherent and rambling as I expected. Nonetheless, in the end it was ridiculous, nebulous nonsense. The kind of thing one might say in a dream.

17 Hustings

Handwritten Notepod entry
MOBCOM No.872 -7685-6245 2 December 20--

O'Brien,

If you are reading this, it means you have found the MC you have been using to trace us in a litter bin by the roadside, this last notepod entry uppermost, the stylus very pointedly broken in two. I am done with this device.

By now, you will also have surmised that I do not intend to give myself up. Pedro is not a party to any of the alleged crimes of which I am accused. I therefore ask that you exclude him from your thoughts whilst you attempt to find and arrest me. He has not made any of the decisions that bring me to this point beyond wanting to stay with me for whatever fate or the B & C have in store. The gun is a memento, but useful in that it is the only accessible form of defence I could find in the AW. Pedro now tells me I could have had an AK47 from one conversation in a Hackney pub. But I doubt we had the cash for that. I know for you it conveniently raises the stakes, but Pedro is no part of the battle between us.

The story you told me lacks conviction, smacking as it does of half-remembered science fiction and barely credible cinema scenarios. You know as well as I, that I am no clone or genetic experiment. We will no doubt meet again, but I think it fair to say that I regard you, along with everything else in this fantasy, as a figment. Therefore, you will catch me or not according to my own subconscious whim and it seems that neither your nor I are wholly in charge of that.

You see, I know full well who you really are. In effect, Detective Inspector Gerry O'Brien, guileless literary taunt and gaunt authoritarian, you are disease. A living, breathing tubercule, chasing me across my dreams as you harried me in my waking life, a constant reminder that whatever fantasy I may harbour about a life with a woman, a child and a house by the sea, you will be lurking somewhere, trying to leech the breath from my lungs, the joy from my love, the light from my life. But I am not ready for you now. There is so much I still want to do. I am awake. I am alive, even if it is only in my mind. You shall not have me yet.

EAB

PS: Have you noticed how no one mentions the significance of your surname to me? Another salutary reminder that many people have heard of my work, parroting phrases like the lyrics of popular songs, but not a single one of you has actually read it. One might almost cite this as evidence of the fantastic and hallucinatory nature of the world I am in. But regrettably, I suspect it may be further evidence of this fever world being rooted in some sort of reality.

IT WAS EMILY who found it first. She and Simon were sitting on Merrett's bed at the Birmingham Marriott, waiting for him to complete his complex toilette in the en suite bathroom. The MC they were tracking had died and they were rudderless, not knowing how to find the trail. They were going to head north on Emily's instinct alone. She had been searching the towns they had been to and in the area around where Eric had actually been seen. The direction seemed to be generally upwards. She was hoping that something may turn up in local news sites. Two itinerants arrested or turned off private property, perhaps.

The county of Warwickshire in conjunction with the names Eric and Orwell brought up a dozen Viewsites and the same clip over and over again. 'Shipston-on-Stour Community Centre. Eric or is it George?' the most common tag. The one she chose to run was tagged 'Our favourite Orwell doppelganger, columnist and minor mentalist celeb crashes the hustings.' The clip on this site alone had been viewed 150,000 times in the 48 hours since it had been uploaded. There were links to the article 'Orwell in the Dock' that had first brought him to public attention and then a directly sponsored Carolan Portal click-through ad for his column in the 'Hackney & Haringey Advertiser'.

Emily and Simon watched the shaky and slightly murky camerawork in the dimly lit hall as the Mayor of Shipston-on-Stour, a dumpy middle-aged woman who looked the image of Margaret Rutherford, fielded questions from the audience including one earnest young man spouting planted entreaties for more access to the hi-speed Interverse for poorer Olders in the area. The Mayor cut off the response from the middle-aged sitting MP to say that there was time for only one more question.

At first, Emily could not discern Eric's face amongst the serried ranks of spectators, their plastic cups rising and falling in rows. Then he stood up right at the back and she was shocked to see him wearing a pair of army camouflage trousers beneath a thick hooded top of the kind she knew he loathed.

He cleared his throat in that familiar fashion and started with his usual diffidence and apologetic posture, hands cupped around his plastic beaker like a supplicating penitent, his resemblance, as she remembered, eerily unmistakable with the unruly shock of dark hair, lined jowls, piercing blue eyes and thin ridiculous moustache. His voice was fluting and higher pitched than anyone might expect from such a face. He started quietly and the audio failed to pick up his first words. She heard an old woman in the audience mutter 'Nutter' to her neighbour and, nearer to camera, a man who looked like a farmer nudged his ruddy faced son and said loudly and boisterously 'That's that loony from the paper thinks he's Orwell.' His boy, chewing fruit cake, responded with a puzzled look on his wind-burnt face 'Isn't that a song? Like the boy down the chip shop thinks he's Elvis?'

Eric seemed to falter and the Mayor leaned forward to her microphone and said primly 'Please can contributors state their name before they ask their question. Thank you.' A nubile blonde volunteer shoved a portable microphone into his hand and Emily saw Eric blanch slightly before reluctantly accepting it, his other hand still clasping his tea. After a moment's pause she sensed him taking a deep breath as people craned their necks to see the country's newest celebrity madman.

'My name is Eric and I am barely a citizen. I don't even know if I am allowed to vote. Several times in this meeting, you have talked about voter apathy. A couple of the audience members have said that they feel it a waste of time to vote. You have all responded with predictable piety that people died for that right. This is true, of course. They did so because it was the most credible route to emancipation, to be heard. It was important. It mattered, because there were polar opposites on the ballot paper, but not anymore. Politicians don't seem to realize it, but everyone else has known for some time that voting is futile, moribund, and redundant. It may be resurrected someday when the contours of our politics have been levelled and rearranged. But for now, it's dead. That is due to your apathy, not the voters'.

'As far as I can tell, no one voted for the seemingly perpetual wars in China, Iran or Afghanistan. No one voted to bail out the financiers and enrich the dividend takers, leaving the rest of society to face cuts in services and lower wages, all the time being told that they had been living for too long in a fool's paradise, that they were to be punished for their profligacy even though they did not engineer the reckless barely regulated lottery of the gaming houses in the City.

'No one voted for means testing in the National Health Service, traducing the main principle of the single greatest post-war achievement of the British parliamentary system. No one voted for low-grade proletarian exam factories in place of schools. No one voted to make protest of any kind mostly illegal, all the time being told that it is to prevent terrorists hijacking legitimate dissent. No one voted for the database state, a network of information slowly joining up across Europe and the world to spy on entire nations of the apathetic voters you so disdain. No one voted to arm our law enforcement officers and to forget that they are supposed to police with our consent, not their contempt. No one voted for celebrity culture instead of a genuine news agenda. No one voted for the basic necessary things of scale that the state controlled like transport, health, power, education, the mail, the rubbish collections, the army and the municipal services to be auctioned off to a thousand private companies and entrepreneurs only to watch them deliver disastrous results at a far higher cost which only serves to drive down an already unsustainable rampant capitalist economy.

'Those people who died for the right to vote, they also died for the right to choose. That includes the right not to vote. The future isn't an X in a box. None of you truly offers a genuine choice. Not until a significant proportion of the population come together to demand one and you respond enthusiastically to meet their desires by including political aims that are not filtered through your perception that the middle ground agendas are always safe and will not frighten the horses. It is a well-worn cynical cliché but nonetheless true that most citizens believe there should be a box on the ballot paper that simply reads – 'None of the above'. Your lack of political courage is to blame for that.

'I can tell from your rhetoric that not one of you entered politics to change the world. You came to make careers, not vocations and to better yourselves, not the country. I do not condemn. It is a natural atavistic streak in human nature, hard to resist. The wrong sort of people are always in power because they would not be in power if they were not the wrong sort of people.

'But forgivable or not, it is you, the power seekers, who lulled us into a dreamless sleep and stole our souls while we slumbered. Maybe the tipping point has finally been reached. Maybe now is the time, I don't know. I could be wrong. But I feel it and I think you do too. That is why you are panicking in this election, ramping up the fear and calling for more bread and circuses. Maybe they will swallow the ruse again. They have before. But looking at the news that does still filter through, it is clear that some, at least, mostly the young, are not as dulled by television, vacuous celebrity and total immersion games as you might have hoped.

'I think much of the more restless population, increasingly separated from the conventional political process, un-cowed by the slow subliminal removal of their civil liberties are stirring in their chambers, having slept too long.

'There are poems from the past that might, half-remembered as if from a dream, express the taint in the air. "For we are the people of England; and we have not spoken yet. Smile at us, pay us, pass us. But do not quite forget."

'Loudly and clearly from every rooftop one feels more and more that we should all be shouting the truth of Juvenal. Asking who will watch the watchers? Who has taken our lives and sold them to the highest bidder? Is it possible, as I fervently hope, that some are rising, stretching and asking bleary-eyed, 'Is it time to call a halt and reverse the tide? Is it now? Is it today?'

Emily watched Eric hesitate and the audience filled the silence with a mixture of jeers and applause. She saw him hand back the microphone and walk crab-like along the row of plastic chairs, the smaller figure of Pedro following quickly behind. Someone threw a cup at the stage. Another followed and as the clip came to an end, the camera panned to the podium where the four politicians and the Mayor sat glumly whispering to each other, a few laughing wryly as the white plastic shrapnel began to fall around them, some bouncing off their heads. Simon pointed at the date below the clip. They had been in Shipston-on-Stour only five days ago. They were still heading north.

Emily knocked on the door of Merrett's bathroom. Receiving no response and nervous of discovering him nursing his hair plugs or worse, she urged Simon to push open the door.

They found him watching his MC as he carefully shaved around his facelift scars. He gestured to the screen as he rinsed the foam from his cheeks. It was a celebrated artist's montage of scenes from around London intercut with the actor Peter Finch shouting from the scenes of a long forgotten Seventies movie 'We're as mad as hell and we're not taking any more.' The scenes, blip edits and longer pans, showed graffiti and Banksy style portraits sprouting the same theme across the city over the last five days. On a tow path wall – 'Wake up. Voting is dead' next to a small man in a strait jacket holding a ballot paper in his teeth beside a vast booth emblazoned with the picture of a face with dark hair and a truncated moustache. On the metal shutters of a Shoreditch bar – 'Orwell is alive and well. Big Brother has TB.' On a draped banner from the lower tiers of Tower Bridge – 'Eric is awake. Are you?' Across the paving stones in front of the Tate - 'Is it time? Is it today?' On the three white sails of the windmill off Brixton Hill – 'Eric is Awake' gently turning in the winter wind. Etched in weed killer on Lords cricket ground's wet green sward – 'Big Brother must die. Fratricide UK'. Finally, shot from a traffic helicopter, scrawled in ten foot high letters on the roof of the Greenwich Dome, so that travellers coming in and out of City airport could see – 'We are Eric. We are awake.'

Merrett dried his face and smiled at them as they watched the screen. 'Your patient seems to have embraced one tenet of the twenty first century at least, Emily. He has become a brand. I think, darlings, that one or both of you should sleep with me as soon as possible. This is your last chance to fuck a Pulitzer.'

18 Hoodie

THE EX-MINER, WHO acted as custodian and guide at the long defunct Black Country pit, wore a costume straight from a theatrical costumier, designed to portray a working man of the late 1930's. Depression wear, it seemed, de rigueur for this sort of occupation. He hated its artifice. He was therefore more than happy to enter into a bargain with the tall man he recognised from the Viewsites and the Carolan News Network bulletins and swap his hated costume for Eric's camouflage trousers and hoodie. He was also happy to share a beer and his sandwiches with the odd duo amongst the well-lacquered tools placed amongst the tired waxworks at the foot of the column that housed the winding gear.

He tilted back on his seat as they all munched quietly, sipping their beer at intervals. He was nearly seventy and doing the job as a meagre supplement to his inadequate pension. His grizzled unshaven face bore a scar across the forehead from a cable that had snapped and hissed through the air like a rattlesnake almost fifty years ago. He saw that Eric was far more comfortable in the boots, thick trousers and woollen jacket than he ever had been and he looked down at himself, pleased with the legend on his newly acquired top. He had always been a fan of the Clash.

'Yow orta shave that silly arse mustache and cut yer 'air, mate'

Eric smiled and donned the studiously designed proletarian style flat cap.

'No need. They will find me soon enough.'

The mining man coughed for a long time causing Eric to gently ease him forward in his chair and pat his back, knowing that it did no good but needing to do it anyway.

At last the old man rasped 'They wun't 'ear it from me, son. Lot of folk thunk you wuz robbed. Put oop job, they say. Go to it and scarper, I would.' He gave them his flask of tea and a little cash, despite Eric's protestations and sent them off down a minor road that headed north. It had to be north.

It was the same in the next village. Recognition, an affectionate bit of leg pulling and then some donation or other that allowed the madman and his squire to press on with their quest. They were tired of walking and hitched rides from long distance delivery lorries, the drivers bored and needing the company, even of petty fugitives.

Eric took these opportunities to listen to news reports and found that there was never any mention of cloning or of O'Brien. They were just an amusing running joke on the bulletins, a growing Interverse phenomenon; the eccentric appeal of Eric's story somehow chiming with the growing cynical response to the relentless hectoring tone of the election campaign. Jokes abounded about Big Brother being unable to track down a ghostly reincarnation of Orwell. T-shirts were being produced and he found it disturbing to find his own face staring back at him, the BBC microphone in the foreground, his eyes amused but showing his impatience with the photographer.

The tone of the news reports threatened to alter a few days later when 'police sources' suggested the eccentric was armed and had assaulted a police officer, although the lack of any detail or indeed an officer to interview, further fuelled a general feeling in the media that this was an attempt by the B & C to quash a rising tide of sympathy. It seemed as if O'Brien was the only one really concerned with Eric's capture. The nation was happy for the fugitive to be running free and wanted to see him everywhere. Eric was reminded of the newspaper competitions of the Before Wigan. 'You are Lobby Lud and I claim my five pounds.' There were spurious reports of sightings at Glastonbury Tor, Lydd airport, Stonehenge, Canary Wharf, Canonbury Square, the Café Royale and once, accurately, from a lay-by on the A34.

Those who really did meet him were inclined to tell their friends and even the papers, but genuine sightings were subsumed in faked encounters and no one seemed to care very much. Everyone knew the joke would end soon enough and that eventually there would be an arrest, a magistrate, a fine or a sentence. A small, inconsequential novelty that would be wiped from the news by a fresher story and perhaps a better one. After all, he was no serial killer or mass murderer. What was he, in the end? He resembled someone whose name everyone knew but no one read. Some of the broadsheet columnist's jokes were completely missed as the majority of their readership had the key phrases memorised – 'Big Brother, 1984, some animals are more equal than others' – but little else. They were limited to these few cultural clichés because they had never read a complete Orwell novel.

It was all an amusing, harmless and entirely characteristic display of English eccentricity. Until Warwick.

January 1947 – London

Eric returned from an exhausting two weeks in Jura to the worst winter on record and a crippling fuel crisis, rendering Canonbury Square a deeply inhospitable prospect. He had planted fruit trees around Barnhill in preparation for his permanent move and the effort had left him feeling pale and lacking in stamina. When he thought of how easily they had gathered firewood from the surrounding fields, he wished he'd been able to carry some back. Back in the flat, he took to wearing fingerless gloves while writing and experimented with a peat fire when he had run out of furniture to break up.

A few days after he arrived, he invited a few friends including Richard Rees, Paul Potts, Connolly and Muggeridge to the flat to listen to a radio broadcast of 'Animal Farm' on the BBC's Third programme. He also invited Sonia although he didn't expect her to come. Letters from her bolthole in Paris had tailed off and rumours that she had taken up with a married Marxist philosopher called Maurice Merleau-Ponty filled him with despair. But as he arranged the tea things for his guests, he glanced out of the window to find her picking her way through the snow around the square, an outrageously expensive hat on her head and a deep fur collar on her coat.

She looked up as she stepped gingerly across the street to the pavement outside the flat and he smiled involuntarily. She grinned back and it was if they had never been parted. She was early and he virtually ran down the stairs. As he opened the door and her breath swathed his face in misty billows, he hugged her to him and kissed her cheek, whispering 'You've come. Thank God'.

After the broadcast, when everyone had made appreciative noises about his script and the actors, guests departed one by one, until Sonia and Eric were left smoking and adding brandy to their stained teacups, huddled next to the smoky fire.

Although she talked a little about working at the magazine and joked about Connolly's continued attempts at seduction, they spent long periods simply staring at the fire and each other.

After one of these tranquil moments, Eric stubbed out his cigarette and cleared his throat in a manner she had come to know. Significant pronouncements were presaged by this nervous, guttural tic and she closed her eyes, leaning back in the worn armchair, ready to be placed on the emotional rack.

'Do you love him?'

Sonia sighed. 'Yes. I wish I didn't because the situation with his wife is bloody and can only end badly. But I can't bring myself to give him up.'

Eric brooded on this for a moment and although he betrayed nothing as usual, inside he felt a dull ache beginning in his stomach.

'Does he love you?'

She laughed bitterly. 'He's a philosopher. The most he can say for sure is that he thinks he might possibly harbour some emotion for me. Of course he adds a number of clauses and perorations on the nature of lust, affection and obsession. None of which are a compliment.'

'I love you. I can say that without sub-clauses or conditions.'

'Yes, but you love every woman who ever showed the slightest interest in you and plenty that never have. Your proposals are legendary in Soho, Eric. Cyril told me he worried about getting one himself during one of your fevers.'

'I must cut a very dignified figure.'

'Actually, you do, when you're not firing off propositions like a Gatling

   ERIC IS AWAKE

gun. The book is a masterpiece. So straightforward, but devastating in its simplicity. I've been reading your 'Tribune' column as well. You make me laugh sometimes. I can hear you sounding off up here. Trying your outrage and your arguments on for size before you hammer them out on the page.'

'Do you care for me at all?'

Sonia leant forward and took one nicotine-stained hand in hers and gently kissed his palm.

'I worship at the altar of your talent, like everybody else.'

He withdrew his hand angrily.

'Eventually even the most frivolous of women has to be serious.'

She stood up abruptly and the thought that she would soon be gone made him utterly miserable.

'You know nothing about women, Eric. Not about their minds or their bodies. Most of us go for men who couldn't give a damn about us, not the doe-eyed mooning romantics. Confident, self-sufficient, ambitious and cruel men who can live perfectly happily without us, if they have to. That's our biology. We are shallow evolutionists. Didn't you always suspect it?'

'If I can only have you by driving you away, then you'd better sod off.'

She put on her ludicrous hat and, despite himself, he helped her on with her coat. As he stood behind her and placed it around her shoulders, his arms clamped around her torso like a drowning man.

She threw him off her with a shriek and her eyes were wide and terri-fied. 'Never do that. Never, ever do that.'

Eric stood back, startled. She was shaking as if he had beaten her and she almost ran to the door.

'Sonia!'

She turned in the open doorway and cast a wild look of fear at him, her lips trembling.

'You can't pull me down. I won't let you. Don't make me hurt you. Eric.'

Then she was gone.

Fever Diary – 6 December 20--

The red hoods started to appear shortly after we tramped into Stratford-upon-Avon. We had managed to hitch a few rides since we left the village hall but had been forced to rely on our weary feet for the last three miles.

The garments were placed on the tops of lampposts and perched rakishly on traffic lights at zebra crossings. As we passed the puzzling attractions of the 'Falstaff Experience' (a pub in a woodland glade?) I began to perceive a pattern to their placement. Looking down the street from the bridge over the Avon, I could see a long line of the red markers leading up the Warwick Road. As the direction was generally north, and not knowing their significance, I decided we would follow them as far as we could. Pedro was reluctant as he knew the hoods were somehow associated with what he called 'beeg hassle', but I persuaded him that if at any point they veered off a northward course, we would abandon them as a guide.

Our progress had so far been very slow and as we stopped at a garden centre cafe for tea from the ubiquitous plastic beaker, I reviewed our prospects while we sat on railway sleepers stacked around the car park. I estimated that if we continued at the present pace and with such visibility, we were unlikely to reach Jura any time soon. Either we would be apprehended or it would take a good month and a half to reach our destination with no guarantee that we would have the resources to pay for the ferry from the mainland.

I was finding the travelling extremely tiring and although I had so far been in general good health in the AW, I knew that the nights spent huddled without tents in bushes or bus shelters were taking their toll. The money from the Carolan Portal for the syndication of my column provided us with the essentials in the way of food and drink, but did not stretch to lodgings or a new tent. We found ourselves seeking out homeless shelters and finding them almost impossible to get into due to the vast increase in numbers brought about by a more severe welfare regime that had driven many from their lodgings and out on to the streets in great numbers. I began to realise how lucky we had been to have survived so long at the State's expense and thought once more of Emily who had sent daily messages up until I had been forced to abandon the MC. I was, as expected, almost in mourning for the ridiculous box of tricks, but this lasted only a few days as I took up my journal again with pencil and notebook, despatching my columns to the newspaper from post boxes along the way.

As we neared Warwick itself and passed around its southern edge, we found ourselves part of an increasing band of travellers, many with backpacks and tents, tramping along the red cowl route.

Finding no shelter that didn't risk exposure, we carried on walking well into the night until we veered off the main road and lost sight of the hoods in the darkness. We tramped for hours across frozen fields until we were utterly lost and bitterly cold. I even started to regret the loss of the hooded top I had been so eager to give away.

Finally, I could go no further and flopped down in the middle of a field, not caring if it snowed and covered me in the night. Pedro was eager to at least find some woodland where shelter might be found, but I was already falling into unconsciousness as I listened to his entreaties. I curled up like a chick inside the egg and fell into darkness, my hands clasped around my knees. In my head the lions roamed again, their hot breath on my cheek as they paced around my body, occasionally rasping their great tongues across my hands.

JOURNAL FOUND AT BARNHILL, ISLE OF JURA – 12 MAY 10--

Pedro sat beside Eric and shook him periodically to ascertain that he was not asleep, but sunk once more into one of his culture fugues. He sensed that this one could last a while and worried that the morning would find them exposed and prone to discovery out in the open.

He made a small fire from a few damp twigs and tried to curl himself and Eric around it in a complete circle. However there was a gap in the circumference at one end where the wind seemed to blow against them particularly hard. This was filled at some point in the night. Only half asleep, Pedro was woken by a snuffling sound and the sight of a low black shape easing into the gap around the fire and completing the circle. Kicking the embers into a flame that cast light across the radius, he observed the matt black fur of the sleeping Labrador. He shook his head. Obviously it could not be the same dog, but it certainly looked very similar to the one they had encountered before.

Pedro slept on fitfully, his jacket drawn over his head, trying to muffle the worrying sounds of distant voices and clanking metal around him. He imagined O'Brien preparing to rush them, guns loaded and ready on shoulders, orders whispered on radios amongst trenches and secret hollows surrounding their resting place. Outside the circle of fire, he sensed a gathering of forces and wondered if he was finally going as mad as his companion. Perhaps he would wake up tomorrow claiming to be Cervantes or Alcazar. He shivered at the prospect and tried to disappear inside in his jacket. If O'Brien was here, then they were finished, but he could not carry Eric and would not leave him. He fell at sleep at last around 4am and did not wake until the winter sun was quite high in the sky.

The first thing he saw as he opened his eyes, were flags fluttering over his head on long bendy poles that drooped in the wind. There were three designs dominant. One depicted a red hood on a white background above the legend H.O.O.D, the other was a graffiti style slogan 'Hands Off Our Data' with a hooded figure holding a spray can in the foreground and the third was a traditional pirate skull and crossbones. He glanced sideways to check on Eric and found him still unconscious, the Labrador curled along his back. He had come to know the subtle difference in the expression when Eric was sleeping and when he was in a temporary coma. Poking his head out of his hooded jacket like a tortoise from the shell, Pedro slowly sat up and looked around.

Once, escaping from a bitter winter a few years ago, he had managed to take refuge in the National Gallery for a while before security traced the source of the smell and ejected him. He had drawn their attention because he fell asleep on one of the velvet benches before a wall-sized painting of the Field of Cloth of Gold. Henry VIII's extraordinary display of wealth to the King of France was laid out in vivid colours with gaudy tents and waving pennants ranged across the landscape as brightly tinted courtiers and troops weaved in an out of the carnivale. As he looked now at the extraordinary scene around him, he felt as if he had stepped into that painting, swallowed by the canvas and absorbed into the oils.

At the far end of a broad avenue of trees, was a huge castle. Filling the space around it were islands of tents and vehicles scattered in profusion across the extensive grounds. The smoke from a thousand campfires, barbecues and spits rose above the flags and banners. Here and there, mobile commissaries and food stalls could be seen with people gathered around drinking coffee and eating what smelt to Pedro like delicious combinations of bacon, eggs, roasted hogs, bean burgers, mushroom omelettes and the unmistakable and familiar fried chorizo sausage.

Above the castle's main gate was a huge pig-shaped balloon, almost fifty feet across, bobbing gently against the cloudy sky, the letters HOODCAMP emblazoned in pink across its belly. Music clashed into one low rhythm from speakers and musicians all over the camp. The people wandering around were all characterised either by a scarlet hoodie or headscarf and seemed to be predominantly young, although there were also middle-aged and elderly figures scattered here and there, some in wheelchairs or mini golf carts. He estimated that there were close to a hundred thousand people swarming around the incongruous medieval fortress.

Nearby was what appeared to be a coffee shop. A hand painted sign above the rows of wooden tables and salvaged church pews read 'Starfux' and the smell emanating from it set Pedro's heart racing. He patted the pockets of his trousers, looking for any loose change and was disappointed to find only a few cents.

'No need, mate.'

He jumped and looked up to find Scratch leaning on an ancient bike near a tent offering massages and Reiki healing. He wore a pair of mirrored sunglasses that flashed arrows of sunlight into Pedro's eyes.

'Oh. It's you.'

Scratch let his bike drop to the grass and leant down next to Eric, feeling for a pulse in his left wrist. The black dog shifted to make room and looked up at the young man placidly.

'Is he OK?'

Pedro shrugged sullenly.

'He goes unconscious sometimes. I don' know if he wake up this time. He never been out so long before. What's the time?'

Scratch looked up at the sun. 'About 11, I reckon. How did you get here?'

Pedro pointed to his ragged trainers. 'Jorge say we follow the hoods, so we follow the hoods. What is this place? Festival? Hippy punky crusty party? What?'

Scratch massaged Eric's temples and smiled at Pedro.

'Yeah, like that. But we weren't invited so the Old Bill are a bit grumpy, like you. This is a sort of very, very, very unofficial festival, y'know? '

'Police?' said Pedro nervously, looking around. 'Where they is?'

Scratch pointed down the avenue of trees to a distant road surrounding the estate. A line of police vans could be seen along with a thin line of uniforms milling around the gates where streams of people were still arriving. A helicopter was approaching from the same direction and Pedro could see it would soon be overhead, photographing the crowds below. He stood up quickly, shaking the stiffness from his legs.

'Ok, look, we don' need trouble. Jorge he got a warrant and me too I think. We take a coffee maybe, but we got to get him under cover so he can wake up. Then we got to go.'

Scratch gestured towards the cafe.

'It's all free, mate. Help yourself. I know about the warrant. Everybody does. Your man here is a little bit famous. He could probably make it on to the guest list of several dodgy nightclubs in Essex. But they won't take him here. We're not letting them on to the site without negotiation and so far they are trying to keep it light to prevent any bad feeling. Georgie's safe here for now. You're far more vulnerable on the outside pissing in than on the inside pissing out, y'know? Go get a chino and I'll watch him. Bring him a latte or something. Smell will probably bring him round.'

Pedro was torn between leaving Eric with the dubious Scratch and the lure of free coffee and food. In the end, his rumbling stomach decided the matter. He walked tentatively towards 'Starfux' eschewing a competing establishment called 'Cafe Shithead'. He was welcomed by a young girl in a scarlet Chinese jacket and black skirt wearing a plastic lily in her auburn hair. Seeing a hand signal from Scratch, she loaded up a tray with a cooked breakfast and a large cup of coffee and seated Pedro at the end of a wooden form in front of a scarred altar table. For a brief but blissful twenty minutes, he forgot everything but the growing warmth of his belly and the warming unseasonable sunlight on his dew dampened back. The sound of plates crashing into water inside the tent and the excited chatter of the young murmuring around him formed a low buzz that sent him into a kind of stupor of contentment and calm.

Walking back to where he had left Eric, he was disconcerted to find a small crowd around his charge who had been lifted on to a wheeled stretcher attached to a tricycle and covered in Mexican style blankets. Several men with low slung army combats festooned with metal clamps and karabiners were raising a shelter over him and stretching canvas windbreaks around it. Scratch ordered a passage through the crowd for a young man in his twenties carrying an old fashioned Gladstone bag who stooped to take Eric's pulse and blood pressure.

Pedro elbowed his way to Eric's side and stood protectively next to the stretcher as the Doctor, a snake shaved into his blonde scalp and a tattoo of syringes on each arm, shone a torch into the patient's eyes. Scratch introduced Pedro and asked him to tell the physician about Eric's previous history of fugue states and comas including the amnesia and delusions that had become so well documented in the press. Pedro reluctantly responded to the Doctor's questions about frequency, diet and previous medical treatment as the unconventional physician removed one boot and sock to prick Eric's foot with a pin.

Finally, it was decided that the patient should be wheeled over to a medical tent where he could be monitored and a drip put in to prevent dehydration. The crowd cheered as a burly girl hopped on the tricycle and started pedalling uphill, her efforts assisted by a dozen helping hands on her ample rear. Pedro struggled to keep up as the crowd gained momentum up the hill and down towards the castle. Scratch dropped back and placed a reassuring hand on his arm.

'Chill. He'll be alright. Everyone wants to look after him. The girls especially. They like an Older to coo over. Come and find yourself a bed. We've got places on a few of the buses and there's a bunch of dormitory tents up there by the castle wall. Look for a sign for the 'Hotel Paradiso' or 'The Pitz'. They got a really nice lounge area with a sunken lava rock heater. Quite toastie, but the Older who runs 'The Pitz' is an old acid boy so you'll have to put up with banging house half the night if you pitch your kip there. There's showers up there too, but I think the wood burners are playing up so the water might be a bit fresh.'

Pedro looked around in confusion. The site seemed to extend all round the castle and beyond. At the centre were a row of large inter-connected black tents that extended into a vast canvas arena. The sides were still being constructed but he could see rows of computers and large cables leading to a nest of wheeled containers, solar panels gleaming above the squat rectangles of the generators beneath.

'What's that?'

Scratch grinned mischievously and waggled his dark eyebrows.

'That, me old cop, is the Lab.'

19 Corryvreckan

Fever Diary – 12 December 20--

I ran with the lions for almost a week and can remember little except the feel of fur beneath my fingers as I clutched desperately at their manes. Eventually I became aware of the low babble of a thousand conversations mixed with the drone of helicopters and indecipherable megaphone messages. There was an odd taste in my mouth and I struggled to open my eyes, the effort fading with each attempt until finally they flickered open of their own accord and I tried to focus on a bright square of whiteness ahead of me. I could still feel the lion's mane beneath the fingers of my right hand as I tried to bring the shadows and stark brightness into balance. Someone touched my head and breathed close to my ear. I smelt Sonia's perfume as a woman's voice said quietly, 'He's awake.'

I turned my head to the right and was elated to see Sonia looming over me, her face concerned at first, and then smiling as I started to take in my surroundings. I tried to touch her cheek with my left hand but found it was restricted by a canula taped to a vein. Glancing down at my right hand, I found it was knotted in the fur of a black dog standing docilely beside my bed. I wondered why the nurse hadn't closed the curtains on the window as the light was shining right into my eyes. I wondered why the walls of the ward seemed to shiver slightly and it was some moments before I noticed that the window had no frame and that the scene beyond was a snow covered field, as if the meadow behind Barnhill had been uprooted and placed in Gower Street, just below the private wards of the Rosenheim building.

'He's definitely awake. Eric's awake.'

Then I heard another, more guttural and familiar voice. A voice from my dreams, irritable and sulky.

'Jorge. You mean Jorge is awake.'

I tried to sit up and found Pedro's hand on my shoulder. Pedro from the AW. Impossible Pedro who didn't exist and next to him, not Sonia, but impossible Emily.

Behind them, his lanky form draped across a collapsible canvas chair was Scratch who said languidly, his tanned face splitting into a broad smile, 'George. George is awake'.

He turned to the open side of the tent and shouted out into the snow, 'George is awake. He's awake!' The call was taken up by voices outside and was repeated like a thousand echoes in a deep canyon. I realised then that I had woken once again in the AW and part of me was filled with sorrow. Then I saw Emily's relieved expression and she looked so happy that I was instantly calmed and accepting. Whatever this was, she was here with me and that seemed to be all that mattered.

Gently I grasped Pedro's hand and levered myself up to a sitting position. A young man with curious arm tattoos passed me a beaker of water and I gulped it down, my throat raw and tender.

As details began to emerge from the murk around me, I realised that I was in a large tent and that heads were appearing round the open flap as people wrapped in colourful winter clothing gathered around to stare at me. Some of them were snapping vids on their MC's and as I turned away to look behind Emily, I noticed a middle-aged man wearing a safari jacket training a sophisticated looking camera on me. I am in their eye again.

JOURNAL FOUND AT BARNHILL, ISLE OF JURA – 12 MAY 20--

Readers will be aware of the growing crisis here at Warwick Castle as police and armed forces gather to lay siege to the site after more than three months of what the Government calls an illegal occupation. The activities of the Hoodlab, I understand, are now classified as terrorist crimes and therefore all those participating in the camp management or facilitating the scores of data hackers are also classified as Terrorists. This is because of the state's interpretive clauses within the Terrorism Act of 20--. It is worth reproducing them here for reader's benefit as it is almost certain that many of you may well lie on the wrong side of the law under its provisions.

Terrorism: interpretation

Section 1
In this Act 'terrorism' means the use or threat of action where: the action falls within Section 2, the use or threat is designed to influence the government or to intimidate the public or a section of the public, and the use or threat is made for the purpose of advancing a political, religious or ideological cause.

Section 2
Action falls within this subsection if it: involves serious violence against a person, involves serious damage to property, endangers a person's life, other than that of the person committing the action, creates a serious risk to the health or safety of the public or a section of the public or is designed seriously to interfere with or disrupt an electronic system or universal communications technology.

It is primarily under Section 2 that the Government has been able to invoke certain measures under the Public Order Act. Apparently you may be said to endanger life and create serious risk to your own health and safety and that of your fellow citizens by releasing information the Government and Security Services wish to keep secret and by wiping out your membership of the Rotary Club and the way you voted in the last five elections. One Kafkaesque interpretation within a later section of the Act is pleasing in its circular logic.

'A constable may stop, search or arrest a person he suspects to be a terrorist to discover whether he has in his possession anything that may constitute evidence that he is a terrorist or that he is involved in the preparation or instigation of acts of terrorism.'

I am told that this clause once contained the words 'reasonably suspects' and that the interpretation of 'preparation or instigation' has been reinterpreted to include anyone who: 'reveals by speech or other method of expression that terrorist acts are contemplated.'

In other words, you may be arrested in the United Kingdom and Europe if a police officer thinks you look like a terrorist. Apparently the wearing of scarlet hoodies may now be interpreted as such.

Not only that, but it is enough to have expressed a desire to commit a terrorist act, even if you have no intention of doing so. In effect, you cannot think such a thing and express it, even as a joke or as exasperated hyperbole, without breaking the law.

So let us be clear, so that no faceless army of lawyers has to labour through the 120 clauses and subsections of the Terrorism Act, the Public Order Act or the Information Security Act. It is obvious to me as an observer, that the camp's sole purpose is to attack the cloud servers and repositories of information gathered and collated by the state on every citizen in the UK. It seeks to destroy it permanently if possible, or at least to send it into a chaotic spiral and to reveal the actual statistics and policies associated with current military actions abroad. That is why the authorities wish to remove it. The Hoodies have not only 'thought' the crime, they have put it into practice. In effect they are saying, 'We admit it. Come and get us.'

It was always known that the Police would eventually cease negotiating and start the process of forced eviction. But they are now painfully aware that their greatest tactical mistake was to allow the Hoodcamp to become a magnet for those disgusted by the election result and the blame heaped upon the movement, and indeed on me personally, for the lowest turnout in a generation. Had they made their move before the camp swelled from one hundred thousand to one and a quarter million people spread across the Warwick Castle grounds and the adjacent farmland, they might very well have forced the Data War further underground. As it is, over the last three months, the Hoodies Lab Rats have successfully cyber-attacked seventeen Government cloud servers and caused the collapse of any number of official databases. Although each was restored and made accessible again fairly quickly, the state has expended huge resources fixing the data and has not been able to repair the damage to their credibility in the face of the systematic leaking of the true casualty figures, operational errors and abuses committed in China, Iran and Afghanistan.

Even if they are successful in removing such a huge body of people without controversy, the genie is now out of the bottle. The Data Wars seem likely to continue until the state learns that the population is not convinced that holding such vast amounts of information on every individual is a viable protection against terrorism. In their view, they are attempting to take back their privacy and their liberty and this, of course, is not acceptable to a

Government that has spent many years slowly encroaching upon both.

There are no leaders here, but of course, a hierarchy exists. Most of those organizing the evening meetings have been schooled in the process throughout their youth. Regardless of whether their sympathies lie on the right or left they have experiences that range from University protests and direct action campaigns, attendance at various mass protests organised by an earlier generation of activist parents, mock parliaments at primary and secondary schools and, most satisfying of all, through the Woodcraft Folk who organized international camps shot through with educational exercises in economics, political systems and negotiation which many of the London Hoodies attended throughout their infant and teenage years.

The principals at the top of this unofficial hierarchy are determined by their presence on the lists of MI5 surveillance targets that have been leaked on to the Interverse, mostly through the activities of the Hoodies themselves. The higher your indices on the barometer of public menace, the more respect you command amongst your peers.

As is always the case with large debates, pre-meetings are essential for maintaining focus in the main discussion. Some see this as suppression of dissent, but the criteria seem eminently sensible. Scratch, who takes a lead role in these planning sessions, says they are designed to marginalize the time wasting diatribes of those he calls the 'NWO Illuminati'. These are the tangled knot of inchoate conspiracy theorists whose beliefs centre round a model I find altogether familiar from the pre-revolutionary Russian hoax document 'The Protocols of the Elders of Zion' so beloved of Ezra Pound.

They believe that the world is run by a secret cabal which they have given the collective term 'The New

                                    ERIC IS AWAKE

World Order' or 'The Illuminati'. The powerful elite is said to have a global agenda to impose a single totalitarian world government and are actively engaged in covertly moving the world towards this objective. Some variations in this theory are that the elite are primarily Zionists, (the Elders again) but the NWO crowd are quite happy to exclude any anti-Semitic undertones by emphasizing the difference between Jew and Zionist. Not always convincingly. As I have observed more than once, this is simply not the doctrine of a grown-up person. Variations cite Catholics, Freemasons or reptilian extra-terrestrials as the culprits. As one satirist observed, no one is more incompetent at keeping secrets than the state and if the Government really had captured an alien, by now it would be on a chat show seeking closure over its abduction trauma.

Apart from a generally distasteful melting pot that incorporates an overtly hysterical anti-state attitude, their belief in such a universal, successful and well organized covert plot is touchingly naïve. They fail to understand that the nature of power is that it corrupts to greater or lesser degrees according to the prevailing mores of the time and of the region. In effect, the failure of politicians is not an organized conspiracy, but a tendency that occurs in almost every power structure of any size. State kleptocracy is a fundamental element of all systems where inadequate and opaque controls allow the few to hold undue influence over the patronage and enrichment of the many.

Perhaps the most insidious nature of the tendency to become more authoritarian is that, like prejudice of any kind, it exists somewhere deep inside every individual. How often does one label some dime store martinet or minor railway bureaucrat a 'Little Hitler'? We do not need to be part of a Bilderberg Group or occult political coven to become so.

An example of this was made painfully personal by certain biographers. Despite a request (put no more strongly than that) that no biographies should be written after my death, I find that they grew like mushrooms after Sonia authorized the very first back in the 1970s. They paint a picture of a man who was homophobic, homosexual, anti-semitic, racist, misogynist, pro-imperialist, a Government stooge and a political naïf. All of which, you may be surprised to hear, are in various degrees, mostly undeniable. I am a bigot and always have been. I believe that you too, dear non-voter, are a bigot and that everyone currently breathing on this earth is equally mired in prejudice.

The resentment of 'other', that which is not 'I', is genetically encoded into our race memory and instinct. It is a measure of our personal development as human beings that one recognises this prejudice and strives to control it. The territorial instincts of the neolithic animal that ensured their survival in a more overtly Darwinian age, no longer apply to the same degree. Therefore suppression of the vestigial instinct is important if one is to behave honorably and in an egalitarian manner. I don't say it is easy. It is a constant struggle and we all have our blind spots. But it is an internal conflict that requires constant self-examination and vigilance.

In the coming more external conflict at Warwick, we at the castle will need to be on our guard against sacrificing our purpose and principle to another equally strong instinct, self preservation.

Pot Luck Pierogi
Ingredients
9 Strips Dried Lasagna Sheets
1 Jar Sauerkraut, Drained and Rinsed
2 Oz Lard
1 Large Onion, Diced

Salt and Pepper to Taste

2 Tablespoons Brown Sugar

1 Pack Instant Mashed Potatoes

8 to 10 Slices of Cheddar Processed Cheese

This recipe was compiled using only the available ingredients salvaged from the expired items bin of Café Shithead at Hoodcamp.

Cook lasagna sheets rinse and drain.

In billy-can sauté chopped onion in lard until onion is soft.

Add sauerkraut, salt, pepper and 2 tablespoons brown sugar

Cook for about 20 minutes.

Make instant mashed potatoes

Place layer of sauerkraut in bottom of billy-can

Layer lasagna sheets and sauerkraut alternately and top with instant mashed potatoes.

Lay cheese slices over mashed potatoes and place lid on billy-can

Bake in embers of fire for 30 minutes, remove lid and bake for further 15 minutes.

Editor's Note: Readers should note our usual disclaimer that 'Mr Blair' is a writer who has adopted the persona of a more celebrated (and dead) author. It is in this guise that he has been commissioned to write for this paper. Please note that his perspective and indeed his adopted identity are literary devices that do not represent the views of this publication. Episodes of Michael Merrett's reality show 'Looking for Eric' are available weekly on the BBC and on the Hood TV Interverse channel.

In retrospect, Eric knew they had stayed too long at Glengarrisdale Bay. His sister Marjorie's children were lively, stimulating company and Avril certainly enjoyed their visit, given what terrible company he was when he was writing. But after only a day into their excursion, he felt quite bloody. Teenager Lucy, her older sister Jane and their handsome brother Henry were having such splendid time fishing, swimming and exploring rock pools that he desperately wanted to stick it out for the full two days. Eric felt strongly that the Dakin children deserved a break from death and grief having lost their mother to kidney disease a little over a year ago. But he knew they saw the same etched lines of sickness and death in his face and he was sorry that he could not be reassuringly healthy for them.

Ricky was in his element. His chubby face absorbed in a goat's movements across the rocks one moment and a cormorant's darting arc the next. After the enforced isolation of his convalescence and the intense period of work, Eric felt at last as if he had been able to re-connect with him in the familiar way. They played on the rocks, hopping between pools with new discoveries, just as he once had as a child in the river at Shiplake with Prosper and Jacintha.

For a while, Eric felt the awful winter at Canonbury Square receding and enjoyed making campfires in the warm evening haze and kitting out the shepherd's cottage with bracken for mattresses at night. But the last few weeks had been bloody and exhausting as he struggled with the first draft. When longhand at his desk became too taxing, he had retired to bed and tried to type some sections rendered illegible with notes and revisions. His neck was aching and permanently tense from lying propped in his bed, the weight of the typewriter on his chest, like a stone strapped to a suicide. It wasn't until he stopped and stood up to go to the lavatory or pour another mug of tea that he really started to feel the effects. He realised that he entered a kind of trance when he was clattering away, that soon dissipated when the pain became intolerable. The book wasn't even half done and he already felt like a broken mast.

His original plan had to make at least a short foray across to explore the Isle of Scarba, but it had been a struggle to get through the notoriously treacherous Corryvreckan strait between home and the bay and he didn't think he had the strength for a diversion. In truth, he really wanted to hike the six miles back across the island to Barnhill with Avril and send Henry back in the boat with Ricky, Jane and Lucy. But, as well as probably being entirely beyond him physically, he knew this was irresponsible. Always a realist about his own fragile health, he knew that if anything happened to him, he wanted to be with Ricky.

He sensed they were dawdling over breakfast and, worried about the tide; he rallied them with some difficulty and packed their blankets beneath a canvas sheet in the stern of the boat.

As it turned out, Avril and Jane decided they would rather walk back and as they waved off his sister and his niece and started to pile into the dinghy, Eric realised this was for the best. Just manoeuvring the 12 foot vessel out past the rocky contours in front of the bothy made him feel giddy with exhaustion and Henry, hearing his heaving breaths, suggested he get in and start the motor whilst he pushed them free. Eric felt guilty and a little jealous, which made him guiltier still. Henry had just finished National Service. The young army officer was as hale as a man should be and Eric felt slightly emasculated and useless. Henry sensed this, of course and was kind enough to try and downplay the matter. Last evening, he had asked about guerrilla tactics in the Spanish war as if genuinely seeking advice for any future posting. Eric knew he was just striving to close the gap between them. But he appreciated the gesture.

The journey was choppy but manageable as they travelled northwards up the rocky coast towards the tip of Jura and the craggy outline of Scarba. But as they rounded the point he realised he had delayed too long. The swell was high and the tidal flow fast and reckless beneath them. He looked at Ricky trailing his hand in the water, saw Henry's concerned frown and decided to turn back. He wheeled the outboard sharply to port and the boat lurched but failed to turn. He realised they were being dragged towards the moiling turbulence of the smaller whirlpools at the edge of the larger more deadly vortex. Corryvreckan had them in its grip and wasn't letting go.

Since early childhood, Eric possessed the capacity to detach himself from fear or pain. An unwanted argument, a painful injection, a dangerous foray out into enemy lines; all could be put to one side if you knew how to distract yourself. He felt himself doing it now. Taking the heart-cramping dread that Ricky might be lost and pushing it down deep, deeper than the whirlpool within him, he continued to struggle with the motor as his eyes darted around for distraction.

A black shape surfaced amidst the turbulent waters and turned towards them, a pair of shining ovals dancing with lights above the whiskers. He pointed it out to Ricky, even as his other hand strained to twist the tiller arm to port.

'Look. Curious creatures, seals. Seems very interested in us'. Lucy looked at him as if he were mad and stifled a scream as the turbulence became unmanageable. Pitching and tossing, water slopping heavily across their faces, the boat span like a paper dinghy down a storm drain as it was tossed amongst the smaller whirlpools. Even as the current sucked the outboard from its rusty bolts and dragged it down to the bottom, Eric's set expression betrayed none of the fear rising inside him.

Looking across to Henry, he kept his voice level and matter-of-fact.

'Motor's gone. Better get the oars out, Hen.'

Henry nodded and unshipped the battered wooden lengths tied to one side on the dinghy.

'Can't help much, I'm afraid.'

It seemed almost superfluous to add this. The young man already knew. The struggle with the motor had quickly exhausted what little reserves Eric had left. They were in Henry's hands.

Eric kept his eyes on the main whirlpool behind Henry's head and watched as he pulled hard on the starboard oar to bring them around. By heaving hard on both oars immediately after a strong starboard pull, some progress could be made in lateral zigzags away from the lethal centre. But the going was slow and they seemed to be dragged back almost as much as they were making way.

It looked as if Corryvreckan was winning and Eric wondered whether he had the strength to fling Ricky far enough from the craft to be free of the currents. He even gathered up some rope and a float to bind to him. He realized that he would not be able to save the others in this way and decided in a pragmatic fashion that at least the youngest and smallest would have a better chance of survival if he threw him overboard.

It was as he was wrestling with this decision that he noticed Henry's face. He was rowing as hard as he could, sinews straining in his arms and sweat pouring over his eyes. But his expression was of relief and triumph.

Eric realized he couldn't see the whirlpool any more. Twisting around, he looked back and saw that its gaping throat was slowly receding. The waters around them were still rough and dangerously high. But they were no longer heading to the sucking maw of Corryvreckan.

Eric saw that Lucy in particular was struggling to remain calm and although gripping the rail firmly, looked pale and scared. The motion of the boat remained violent, although the intensity had eased somewhat as Henry pulled hard. Looking out behind his head, Eric spotted a long low outcropping of rocks and glimpsed between the rising swell that it was a spit of an islet around 75 yards long.

'Behind you, Hen. Make for it if you can.'

Henry twisted around to see the foam breaking on the black rocks and fought with the starboard oar to bring them around. Ricky laughed as the motion rolled him off his seat and Eric gathered him up on to his lap, tickling him playfully. He was utterly untroubled by the experience and Eric imagined that to him it was the same as an exhilarating ride on the see-saw.

As the current finally worked in their favour and carried them close to the island, Henry shipped the oars and took off his boots. Whilst the prow edged closer with every deep swell, the level of the island rose and fell so that he had to judge when he could make a jump for the rock. Eric held Ricky tight, realising that this part was as perilous as the whirlpool and smiled reassuringly at Lucy. He watched Henry hesitate as the boat dropped down about 10 feet below the nearest landing point and as it rose up once again, he saw that he had the painter ready in his hand and was poised to leap. All of them held their breath as his lanky form pushed off from the wooden rail, sending them rocking violently to one side. They never saw him land as the boat tipped rapidly over and they were all plunged into the violent green water.

In the dark beneath the upturned boat, Eric and Ricky came up into the hollow space. Lucy surfaced but quickly ducked down and out, kicking for the shore. Eric took a breath, held firmly to Ricky and then kicked down and under the edge of the boat and up to the surface on the island side. As they emerged, he kicked off his shoes, struck out towards the edge of a serrated rock and yelled to Henry who was reaching down to help Lucy from the water a few yards away.

'I've got Ricky.'

Lucy pulled her own way up the final incline of sharp rocks, her shoes lost in the struggle towards Henry's vantage point. She was shaking but relieved as she hobbled painfully to a flatter space about five yards from the edge of the island. Henry reached down to take Ricky from Eric as the deep swell brought them both up to the level of the rocks. Eric banged his knee painfully against the submerged outcroppings and shook off his trailing waterlogged socks, which were hampering his progress. But he felt exhilarated and energised by the peril and knew he had the strength to join them. Ricky was scared and crying now as he realised the game was over, the shock of the cold water making his teeth chatter. He scrabbled across to Lucy who put her arm around him and rubbed his back.

Eric felt himself sucked backwards and made a huge effort to push himself towards Henry's outstretched arm. He grabbed it and heaved himself up onto the rocks, his toes starting to bleed from tiny razor-thin cuts. Henry looked back at the boat, which was being drawn back towards the whirlpool. Eric helped him retrieve one oar and a fishing rod that were close enough to pluck from the waves. Henry tied the painter around a rock and decided to give up on their blankets, floating in sodden clumps around the upturned hull. They both teetered on the sharp surface as they made their way to where the others were gathered in a sodden clump of their own.

Eric tousled Ricky's wet hair and whistled cheerfully.

'I thought we were goners there.'

Henry laughed at his light-hearted tone and shook his head. Lucy, shivering in her thin summer clothes, wondered if Uncle Eric wasn't a little bit touched. Her Aunt Avril had told her that he often ran terrific temperatures and talked nonsense. He seemed positively elated by their near-death experience and even now was busy laying his lighter on a flat rock to dry as if he had just dropped it in the bath. As Henry stood to survey the distance to the Jura coast, Eric, restless and eager to keep moving, decided to explore the island.

'I'll see if I can find us some food or firewood'.

Lucy, wringing out her socks, muttered 'Not hungry. Just cold.'

The rest of the island was concealed by the rocky incline and as Eric stepped carefully on the flattest rocks up towards the centre, he gradually began to see that the spit of land was mossier on the far side and very narrow. He felt excited and vital in his bare feet and hoped he could find enough driftwood to get a fire going. They were probably going to have to spend the night. The thought pleased him as he envisioned a happy glow and some barbecued fish caught with the rescued rod. Probably should have set the rod out before he left, he thought, using urchins as bait, perhaps.

Henry watched his Uncle disappear over the incline and took off his shirt. He tied it by the sleeves to the oar and wedged it in the rocks as if claiming the territory for the Dakin Empire. With any luck a passing boat would see them although he couldn't see how they would get near enough to rescue them. He lay across the flattest of the rocks and felt the sun warming his chilled bones. His arms ached from rowing and he realised with some pride, that these two limbs were all that saved them from the whirlpool. He wished his mother could have seen him. Ricky watched him and, after freeing himself from Lucy's embrace, took off his little shirt and lay down next to Henry, shading his eyes with his hand to check his legs and arms were in the same attitude as his cousin.

On the far side of the rock, Eric teetered in his bare feet across the cratered black surface, occasionally trying to lever a limpet from its anchorage. He had heard you could make a nourishing, though disgusting, soup from them. Unfortunately there were no mussels and he wondered if they might need to collect crabs before nightfall. He pottered slowly about enjoying the prospect of gathering seaweed to dry for a fire, although he wasn't entirely certain this was possible.

A puffin perched on the precipice of the farthest point of the islet and he looked around for its burrow. He relished the surprise on their faces if he were able to come back with eggs for lunch. However, it seemed that the bird was merely pausing on a long search for sand eels and probably nested a long way off.

Some high-pitched squeals drew him to a tumble of rocks and moss that sheltered a nest of two baby seagulls; their mouths open for food. Their grey downy feathers were speckled along the wings. He watched them for a while, scanning the sky for their mother. But she didn't return. He would have to wring their necks and although he had done the same to chickens before now, it didn't seem quite right with gulls.

Bizarrely, he found a single potato lying on the moss. He turned and started back, the salt beginning to make the cuts on his feet sting and burn. His lighter had dried sufficiently to ignite some of the dry moss and he placed the single potato in the embers. Looking back the way they had come, he saw that a red lobster boat was approaching from around the point. He almost felt sorry as he saw that they would pass right by the side where the children and Henry were lying. He wanted to tell Ricky all about the birds and, of course, to warn Henry about the boat. But he felt suddenly very tired again as he realised this little patch of excitement was already nearly over.

It would be enjoyable telling Av they had been shipwrecked. He knew it was probably his last adventure before the end.

Transcript of 'Looking for Eric' – Pod 6

Presented, produced and directed by Michael Merrett for the BBC

INT. HOODCAMP. MORNING.

Camera travels through opening of yurt to find Eric, standing on his head, feet leaning against the central support, eyes closed.

Merrett

Good morning, Eric.
Why are you standing on your head?

Eric

Good morning. It aids digestion and is a good exercise. Also, you are noticed more if you stand on your head than if you are right way up.

Merrett

Is that an Orwell quote?

Eric

I think you know it is.

Merrett

Your knowledge of his life is encyclopedic isn't it?
You must have studied him for a long time.

Eric

I have not studied as much as I should have.
Self examination is rare and uncomfortable.

Merrett

Or were you taught? Didn't someone, the Russians
or the Chinese perhaps, school you in every detail?

Eric

Another aficionado of science fiction.
You and O'Brien should get together.

Merrett

O'Brien?

Eric

The B&C officer who seems to have
made me his personal mission.

Merrett

Does he really exist?

Eric

Miss Statton and her brother met him.
But a good question, quand même.

Merrett

It's what Orwell said when he met Jacintha
Buddicom in Shiplake, isn't it? She asked
him why he was standing on his head.

Eric

I thought it would be easier to start a conversation.
A desperate measure, but then, I once wagered a girl
a pound that she wouldn't go out with me.

Camera adjusts as Eric's feet come down and he stands
upright again.

Merrett
What did she say?

Eric
'How desperately sad that you have to pay
a woman to step out with you'.

Merrett
She turned you down?

Eric
Oh no, she took my pound.

Merrett
Jacintha Buddicom was Orwell's first love,
I think. Did you know that?

Eric
I suppose she was. I know it was the first time
I felt such a thing for a girl.

Merrett
You never forget do you?

Eric
Forget?

Merrett
Who you are supposed to be.

Eric
Do you? It must be difficult sometimes when you
look in the mirror, before the surgery has healed.

Merrett (Laughing)
Very good. Yes, you might think it would
sometimes be a puzzle. But I have always
known exactly who and what I am, whatever
I choose to rearrange on my face.

Eric
So have I.

Merrett
Assuming for a moment that in some
parallel reality you are Orwell, you agree
that you loved Jacintha Buddicom?

Eric
Yes.

Merrett
Then why did you try to rape her?

Eric
I think you'd better go now.

Merrett
Orwell would know that, wouldn't he?
He would know what happened out in the woods
when he pinned her down...

Eric
Get out.

Merrett
When she screamed and struggled and you almost...

Camera jerks right. A scuffle and the sound of several
blows.

Merrett
Eric..Ow! Don't... ah... ah. There's no point... ugh.

Camera falls to ground. Angle on Eric standing over it,
looking down slightly to left of camera.

Eric
I'm afraid I've ruined your new nose.

EMILY ACCEPTED WITH some disgust that Simon was finding camp life much easier than she was. He had attached himself to a bunch of Roedean girls, one of which he vaguely knew from a case involving climate protesters. She hardly ever saw him and when she did, he was the centre of a chattering phalanx of hyphenated 'gels' all obviously finding the rebellious atmosphere very stimulating.

She had opted for a spare bivouac near to Scratch and his girl-friend Mo and joined them for meals off and on. Now was definitely one of the off times. Mo had started off friendly and welcoming, but in the last few days had started to be a little cold and irritable. This, Emily supposed, was because of the way Scratch looked at her. She caught him glancing as she struggled in and out of the bivouac, when she queued for the showers and when she ate, cross-legged next to their homemade brick barbecue in the little area in front of their tent that Mo had corralled with a line of stolen police tape. She had therefore decided to keep her tanks off Mo's lawn for a while, but as she made her way to Eric's yurt to see if he would come and eat with her at the newly christened Chestnut Tree Cafe, she saw that Scratch was already there, reading the post-its and little scraps of paper stuck and pinned to the outside of the yurt. Eric stood with him and they shared a cigarette, passing it back and forth between them and pointing every now and then to the wallpaper of messages.

Since Eric had been resident, the yurt, previously a 'chill out' zone, had been decorated with quotes from Orwell's works and a single 'Big Brother' eye stenciled across the roof that owed rather more to a long defunct television programme than a dystopian novel. After this, camp dwellers who lacked the courage to express themselves directly, placed messages of support, the odd political argument, proposals of marriage, sexual overtures and a modicum of abuse on the walls of the structure until it was almost completely covered in fluttering and rustling layers of paper, flowers, flyers and photographs, left like Tibetan prayers on a mountain shrine.

She almost retreated, but Eric had already seen her, so she reluctantly walked up to join them. Scratch was wearing a woollen hat and, despite the spring chill, a sleeveless waistcoat over a thin shirt and a pair of black jeans. He gave her a smile that went right down to her belly and lay there aching. Eric watched them both and she felt him physically and mentally turning aside. Coughing slightly, he pointed out two notes alongside each other. One was a declaration of love accompanied by a topless photograph and the other was a badly scrawled death threat that read 'There are no leeders here. If you aspyre to bee wun, then you will desrve assisinating.' The anarchist symbol was drawn underneath. Scratch laughed.

'You're in the game, George.'

Eric raised an eyebrow, accepted the cigarette back from Scratch and drew deeply.

'The game?'

'AM/FM. Assassinate or Fuck. Or both. Some of these girls seem a bit confused.' He eyed one picture of a naked female performance artist of some renown, her body painted red, holding a knife to her breast.

'It raises a good point though. I'm concerned about the number of MC's still being used on camp.'

Scratch shrugged.

'We can't force them to give them up, George. The security services know where we are. We're not hiding are we?' He glanced at Emily, seeking approval. She swallowed and tried not to meet his eyes which, she noted, seemed to have impossibly long lashes.

'I really don't think it matters right now. It might be an issue later when this all ends and they start trying to trace the ringleaders.'

Eric frowned at her. 'You think this is going to end? The Data War will continue whether this camp exists or not.'

She looked at him, noting the ragged ends of his vintage jacket and the muddy ends of his archaic trousers.

'Surely the supplies will run out eventually. I mean, who pays for all this? The free food, the generators, the tents? '

Eric looked at Scratch.

'That is an issue. Scratch keeps telling me it's taken care of. But we never seem to hear how.'

Scratch looked up at the approaching roar of a helicopter.

'People contribute. They come with money or stuff. But the real money, the infrastructure stuff, that comes from the Devil. Come on.'

He strode towards a clear patch in a nearby field where a scarlet helicopter loomed into a bumpy landing. The surrounding tents were being flattened by the downdraft and paper cups and plates whipped past their faces as they followed Scratch out to the bottom of the meadow.

By the time they reached the foot of the hill, the rotors were slowing to a halt and the crew were disembarking. It was a huge craft, a Chinook style carrier with a large hold. Men in red jump-suits unlashed boxes and unloaded sacks of equipment and food. A middle-aged man with slicked back hair and a lightweight suit sauntered between them, shouting orders. Scratch whistled and he turned and smiled, his broad face red and sweaty as he stepped forward, a hand outstretched. Scratch had what Eric liked to call a 'hugging compulsion', but was curiously reticent and merely shook the hand once before quickly disengaging.

'You took your time, Mr Carolan.'

Carolan nodded absently, looking beyond Scratch at Eric.

'Well I thought I'd hold back from being too visibly on side. I get enough hassle from the Information Security gobshites as it is. I can do without aiding and abetting cyber-terrorism charges right now. This must be George. Delighted to meet you, sir. Last episode was a doozy. Huge viewing figures for you belting Merrett. We took it on syndication from the Beeb and it played just as well in Europe and Asia as it did here.' He grasped Eric's hand firmly. 'John Carolan. I'm a big fan. Christ, don't you look the image of him.'

'No leaders, Mr Carolan' said Scratch.

Carolan waved his other hand dismissively.

'Yeah, yeah, no leaders, just committees and endless feckin' talking festivals round the arsing campfire, I know.'

Scratch looked annoyed.

'Done OK so far, haven't we?'

Carolan reluctantly released Eric's hand and wheeled round to face him.

'Have you though, Scratchy boy? InfoSec has repaired every server and reversed every change your Lab geeks have made. You're costing them money but you're not shutting them down. I'm here to tell you, one of my hacks got a whisper that they are planning to wait it out. Not bother clearing you off at all. They reckon the rot has set in. People wondering how long they can camp in a feckin' field.'

'Summer soon' said Scratch defiantly. 'They'll stay for festival season. Half the major bands are coming here to play. We can keep up the numbers. Increase them.'

'Only if I feed the little sods. I'll not do that for ever, son. They won't stick around if they think everything the Lab destroys is up and running again less than a week later.'

'What else did you expect?' asked Eric.

Carolan turned to face him and eyed Emily and the distance between them. 'You must be his trick cyclist. The one who keeps covering her face on camera in Merrett's show. Emily, is it?'

Emily ignored the lecherous appraisal that ran from her hiking boots up to her sweatshirt.

'What did you expect, Mr Carolan? Why are you bankrolling all this? Must be costing you a tidy sum. What do you get out of it?'

Carolan smiled.

'Fuck all, to be honest. But it's in my nature to be up the Government's arse as often as possible. I offer an alternative. When you log on to the Carolan Network your personal information is anonymous. You can sign in as the Pope or a bear that shits in the woods, I don't care. Just so long as you use the network. '

Eric lit another cigarette and looked down at his boots as if contemplating the conundrum of his feet.

'There is always a quid pro quo. You are obviously an entrepreneur, the new euphemism for capitalist. You gain, you do not give.'

Carolan smiled and pointed at Scratch.

'He'll tell you. I've got some interviews to do. You lot need some new angles for the media to keep this going a little longer. If I break cover they'll focus on me. I can handle it, if it forces them to seriously consider changing the data laws. That's what I'll be telling 'em.' He glanced behind the helicopter at a figure struggling across the mud with a camera on his shoulder and a white plaster across his ruined nose. 'Merrett, get your arse in gear. I'm away back to Dublin tonight.'

Eric watched him go to meet Merrett and looked at Scratch who wiped his face in the sheepish gesture Emily had seen before.

'We leave his servers alone. In return he helps out with supplies and gear.'

Eric nodded slowly.

'That's known, is it, by the rest of the steering committee?'

Scratch shook his head.

'Not exactly. Look I told you he's the devil you know. Faustian pacts and all that. It's a bargain really.'

'There is always a price to pay. How does he extract his profit?'

Scratch squinted at the sun which emerged from behind a low bank of grey cloud and warmed the dew soaked grass.

'Say you like fencing, yeah?'

Emily blinked.

'Fencing?'

'Yeah. Or bowling. Or whatever. On the Carolan Network, you search for local fencing clubs and you find a neat little 'versetool that can tell you all the fencing facilities anywhere you happen to be in the world at any time. It can tell you the opening hours, the free slots and book them for you. Now mobnet will have the same sort of thing, but when you buy an MC you sign up with blood.'

'Blood?'

'You had an antique MC, so you wouldn't know. These days you don't just have to give your name, thumbprint, your bank details, your date of birth, all that. You give a drop of blood that they encode onto a personal micro sim that activates the console. Without it, it doesn't work. They use it for deciding what insurance they can sell you, whether you have a good credit record and whether your DNA matches the ID details you've given. The Carolan Network is anaemic. You sign up just by using the 'versetool. No personal details at all. People like that. It makes them feel private again. But Carolan can still monetise that.'

Eric wrinkled his nose disdainfully.

'Monetise? How?'

Scratch sighed.

'His system counts up the number of users, when they use the facilities, when they use the 'versetool, how often, in what areas.

Same as the mobnet bots. He links their MC address to other 'versetools they use, the sites they visit blah, blah. Now on mobnet they can sell that info to anyone and those companies know your name, your address, your genetic predisposition to disease, everything. Carolan just sells them the market figures. How many are buying this, how many are buying that. How many tried to buy something but found it wasn't possible. It's valuable information and if you're a new independent company not on mobnet's list of approved corporations you pay top dollar to them for that sort of material. Carolan gives it to them cheaper and faster than mobnet. He also uses it to target his own products and services. If mobnet is cocked up by our activity, he gets more punters on his network. That's all.'

'That's all?' Eric's voice was strained and angry. He looked at Scratch and opened his mouth, but nothing came out. It seemed to Emily that his whole lanky frame deflated slightly and his shoulders seemed to droop as he turned slowly and walked back to his yurt.

Scratch shouted after him 'It's whatchacallit, realpolitik, George. You know all about that.' He didn't answer and after a moment, Emily lightly touched Scratch's lean, caramel coloured arm and followed Eric.

Fever Diary – 12 April 20--

The meeting last night was probably the most acrimonious I have ever attended. Relayed across the camp through speakers, telescreens and personal receivers, contributors with allocated slots spoke longer and more passionately than usual.

By pure chance, the steering committee and main forum took place in the large canvas dome of the LAB tent. The Big Top atmosphere encouraged some to display fearfully inept theatrics with the NWO Illuminati and the black-bloc anarchists playing a particularly significant role, quite out of proportion to their numbers. Draped and seated around the solar servers and terminals, the debate raged on for nearly eight hours.

The cause of all this extended meandering was the proposal

that the strategy of the Lab should be altered. Scratch and many of the right wingers were expected to oppose, but he seemed very subdued as I stated the motion.

In effect I was suggesting that instead of attacking the government servers and disabling the databases, we should be sabotaging the actual information. Replace names and details. Mix them up, change them around. A bad insurance risk becomes a triple A 'person of high financial worth'. The subscriber to a Harrods site becomes the owner of a Lidl Cash account. The fencing enthusiast becomes a baseball card collector. The bid on the hoover becomes a bid on a hovercraft. A Coutts bank account holder gets entered on to a credit blacklist. The world turned upside down. A true counter-intelligence Data War. After all, you are noticed more if you stand on your head than if you are right way up.

Not surprisingly, this played very well with the anarchists who had previously threatened to disrupt the debate with complex and incoherent motions that would have taken days to decode and defuse. They realised quickly that the Government's capacity to 'monetise' the information ceded to them over years would be instantly worthless.

My final flourish before the vote was called, was to insist that this state of chaos should apply to mobnet and all other networks, including Carolan's.

Scratch seemed to come alive at this point and as he stood to speak, I braced myself for a rousing rebuttal. I was prepared to reveal the Carolan compact if forced to do so, but the wind was taken from my sails rather abruptly when he simply seconded and passionately endorsed my proposal before looking across at me, drawing the hat from his raven's wing hair and addressing the assembly through a battered microphone held together with gaffer tape and glue.

'It's hard sometimes' he began and I found myself suddenly wanting to look away. 'It's hard sometimes to do anything in a country that has sold itself to the corporations wholesale. You remember how they took over the free festivals we used to run in the City and around the edges of the climate camps in Scotland

and that mad, bad session on the Isle of Thanet back in 20--? One day I noticed that the performers, the bars, the food stalls, the games tents, the Interverse links, the toilets and the bands were all financed by a different brand. No one was turning up on their own account anymore.' He scratched his head and made that familiar gesture of wiping one caramel hand across his face like a cleansing flannel of flesh. 'It says a lot about UK Plc when the only state sponsored group in the field is the People's Republic of Korea's Acroslapstick Theatre Group.' The crowd laughed and someone shouted something in Korean and did a backflip off a speaker stack to a smattering of applause. Scratch smiled rue-fully. 'We can find ourselves turning into corporate whores almost without noticing. We should be harder about this stuff. We should have some principles, no matter how much money or payment in kind, the sneakiest kind, they offer us to be their shills. Eric thinks we should be pure and maybe he tries to be pure. I try too, but I reckon the best we can hope for is that we get away with fewer stains on our soul than everybody else. Nobody gets away un-marked. Maybe the best way, the only way, is to take what's offered and piss it back down their leg. It feels dirty, but at least there's some relief.' Then suddenly he was sitting down, throwing his arms around Mo and smiling sheepishly at me across the serried ranks of telescreens. Some people cheered a little, but others were hissing.

Just before the final vote, I attempted to instill some sense of responsibility about the information released concerning the wars in Iran, Afghanistan and China. I felt very strongly that nothing should be exposed that put British troops in peril, but beyond an expression of tacit support for some filtering of the material for 'current impacts', the motion failed. Maybe I was just trying to be pure.

The votes were taken electronically on MC's (regrettably) and I noticed the newer formats on clear paper like materials that could be folded and shoved into back pockets or slid into wallets. There were standing terminals also and it wasn't long before the results were quickly displayed on the large screens across the camp. It was a narrow majority, but the principal motion was passed. One Lab Rat shouted cheerfully 'Now fuck off out of our tent so we can get on with it.'

Merrett of course had been filming the whole thing. I arranged for a Lab Rat to cut his feed and someone then obligingly stole his camera and MC. Since our broadcast encounter, I had been subject to some minor vilification as an alleged rapist, but he had received no quarter from anyone in the camp. I later heard that he had been carried to the police barricade and dumped at their feet, bound in a lightly oiled sado-masochist rubber suit donated by the naked performance artist now hosting her own exhibition of paintings in Cafe Shithead. I did not quite see, artistically, why she insisted on being naked at all times, but I said nothing. As with Dali, one can be a disgusting human being whilst also being a great artist.

Pedro had been living with me in the yurt and I sensed he was brooding on something as he has been almost entirely silent most of the time. When I got back, he was waiting outside, his backpack stuffed with food and a new woollen hat on his head. I asked him where he was going. He told me he couldn't stay in 'this fuckup place' and that he wasn't going to wait around to be arrested. He tried to get me to go with him and we argued for some minutes until he finally accepted that he would not sway me. In a last appeal, he reminded me of the shared fantasy of the house under the mountain facing the sea. I told him he should go and find it. I had spent long hours telling him how to get there. We embraced and our voices cracked a little as we said our goodbyes. He has been my constant protector and guide in the AW and I was genuinely sorry to see him go. I hope he gets to the sea. I did not tell him that the average rainfall was a tad higher than he might be used to in Catalonia.

I have missed prawn flavoured potatoes since we have been here and this morning I found a packet at the entrance to the yurt, laid out by Pedro as a parting gift, like some sacrificial offering to a vengeful volcano.

As I munched them gratefully, I read the messages as usual

until a new one, high up near the entrance, caught my eye. It was written in a very neat Cyrillic hand and read simply, 'Anti-Soviet counter-revolutionary puppet of western capitalist capitulators. Your time will come. Grigulevich'. In the game, this would qualify as an AM high score.

JOURNAL FOUND AT BARNHILL, ISLE OF JURA – 12 MAY 20--

IntelPod Ref: BAC501/DO/INTELDIVMARK 2.2346
Back Ref to Security Service archive tag
– 301/NWC.683

Upgraded to status level 10 high level alpha priority. Data-Trak UK initiate with Ground Agent status active. INFOSEC cross ref alert now active with full deployment MOD and MI5. InfoSab activity authority trigger for active deployment under Section 44, Security and Public Order Act 20--- maximum engagement protocol. Primary directive for BAC501 capture and detention received and authorised.

Assigned: Cmdr O'Brien 25643
End

21 Rewind

HE WAS EASY to deflect, but Emily had been startled by the sudden change. One minute they had been talking quietly beside a campfire close to the eastern wall of the castle, the next she was fighting him off. The employees who ran the building for the National Trust had spent some time negotiating with the Hoodies over security and the castle had remained sacrosanct with no one camping within the walls or attempting to enter. The doors were all locked at the end of each day and the Trust maintained their usual complement of night security, so when Emily screamed involuntarily, a uniformed guard quickly arrived outside the perimeter, his torch flashing across the two figures hunched next to the dying fire, Eric wild-eyed and dazed in the bright light. The guard saw Emily holding up a placating hand.

'It's OK. I'm alright. Just got a bit of a fright.'

The light died and Emily heard Eric breathing heavily in the darkness beside her.

'I'm so sorry.'

'What the hell was that?'

'I really am very, very sorry. It was… shameful, disgusting. Please forgive me.'

'I take it that I have just experienced the Orwell lunge? Merrett told me about that.'

She heard him snort.

'The what?'

'He said you had a habit of launching yourself at women, trying to kiss them without preamble. He described it as the avalanche seduction technique where desperation led you to fall upon the objects of your desire without warning. He even named the women. Anne Popham, Celia someone and of course the one he mentioned before you hit him. Jacintha?'

'I was very young and stupid.'

'Do you want to tell me about it?'

'Not if we are still psychiatrist and subject.'

She paused. 'You know we've moved on from that. I know you aren't who or what I thought you were. I don't know what that means. But I wouldn't have chased any regular patient halfway across the country.'

She could hear him scrabbling in his pocket for a cigarette and presently she saw his grim expression in the flare of a match. The fire was a little way from the nearest set of tents and the perpetual rumble of camp noises was low and subdued at this hour of the night.

'As we are no longer in that patient doctor mode, I believe we should trade our very worst secrets on an equal basis. I will tell you of the most shameful episode of my youth and you will do the same. Agreed?'

Emily considered this. 'I suppose.'

'Jacintha was… a girl I really liked. When we got a little older, I wrote her poems, quite passionate ones, I suppose. But I was always confused with lust when it came to dealing with girls I liked back then'. He laughed. 'Actually it was no different later on. The BW is so bloody difficult unless you have somewhere to go. Landlady lurking, no place of your own. One is forced into parks and rural rambles into woods, haystacks and barns. Sex is an objective that can only be attained with military-like planning. One day, we went for a walk and I knew she wanted me to kiss her. We were next to a kind of mossy green bank and I convinced her to lie down on it with me. We started to kiss and I was happy, I think, that we were doing it at last. But I found myself getting very hot indeed, like the fevers that would later consume so much of my damn life. I… frightened her, pushing her back and tearing her clothes a little, not really listening to her protests. She hit me, quite hard fortunately, in the face. I came to my senses and then, of course, I was profoundly ashamed.

I was also desperately sad because I knew I had fatally damaged what might have been. We carried on writing to each other when I went to Burma, but she cut me off eventually. A slow and painful death. I don't think she really recovered. I wrote to her recently and I seemed to have been forgiven, but she wouldn't come to see me. And here I am, still lunging like that gauche young idiot, still fatally misunderstanding women and humiliating myself. If I could have one wish for myself in this life or the last, it would be that I was more attractive to the opposite sex.'

He fell silent for a minute or two, drawing heavily on his cigarette. Then, even though she could hardly see his face, Emily sensed him examining her.

'Why did you follow me? Wasn't it because you had feelings for me?'

She took a deep breath and realised that she had been asking herself this for some time. The truth would humiliate him again, but she couldn't lie. Not about this.

'I felt responsible' she said simply. He stirred and she saw the orange end of the cigarette arc across the dead fire as he flicked it away.

'An obligation, then? Some sort of duty of care issue that needed to be addressed?'

'No, you idiot' she chided softly. 'I felt responsible because I always do. I wanted to save you. Not in some evangelical way, but I felt your vulnerability, your naiveté. I knew you were going to be no match for people like O'Brien and I worried that whatever happened to you would be because of how I had treated you.'

'How you underestimate me. How infantile you make me sound. A helpless fool who can't fend for himself. Fond, then? Can you concede that, at least?'

'You know for such an apparently intelligent man, you have a remarkable capacity for self-pity.'

'And you for guilt. Not a noble motivator, one would say. I know what I'm guilty about. What about you?'

He thought at first that she had moved away and he restrained an impulse to reach out and check that she was still there. Then she spoke and her voice was somehow detached and distant, as if describing a half-remembered dream.

'I was about ten, I think. Simon was too small so I think he was with Mummy and Daddy back at the house. We were staying very near to a large lake in Cumbria. It was over the fence at the end of a long bit of woodland at the foot of an estate owned by my Great Uncle. You had to go through a gate and beyond some woods. Poor Daddy wanted us to have some independence, to roam and build dens and things like that. People are so risk averse these days that children are seldom alone. He was trying to give us some memories, I suppose.

'There were five of us, including me. My cousins, John and Michael and their friends Gillian and Ian, all about the same age. Ian was slightly younger actually. We could all swim, well, I had done my 100 metres I think and Michael was like a fish, always diving in to the pond near the house and swimming to the other side. But this was the lake.

'It was all very "Swallows and Amazons" and we built this raft out of plastic cooking oil barrels and nylon washing line lashed to long branches and a few planks we found in the barn. It took us ages and we had to drag it down to the lake. John, who I absolutely worshipped, had made a big punting pole, but we didn't realise that it was too deep out there until we'd already pushed ourselves well out into the water. The lake had a bit of a swell when the wind was up and we were getting swamped. The pole was worse than useless except as a kind of rudder and John struggled to turn us around and back to the shore because our feet were wet and we were getting scared. Then I noticed the barrels at one end beginning to work loose in the swell and I tried to retie the washing line, but it snapped. Then, before we knew it, we were all in the water and the raft was in pieces. We didn't realise the tops of the cooking oil barrels had vents in them, to allow for the release of pressure. They were sinking and taking the branches and the planks with them. I kicked out for the shore and didn't really look back because I knew everyone would be doing the same.

'I didn't notice that Ian was struggling until I was quite some way from the remains of the raft. I turned around treading water and he caught me up. He was splashing quite a lot and I reached out to help him keep his head above water, but he was grabbing me with both arms, pushing me under and I panicked. I tried to push him away from me, but he was so clinging and desperate that I couldn't get away. My face was in the water more often than it was out and I was really struggling for breath. In the end, I just needed him to calm down and be still so I could tow him on his back. I pushed him under for a bit, thinking this would stop him from struggling and that when he came back up I would be a little further away and could tell him what to do. But… when I kicked away from him and waited, he never came back up. He never…'

Eric heard her sob a little and reached out tentatively to take her in his arms. He felt her stiffen and then slowly relax, her head buried in his chest.

'I found out afterwards the other three had been tangled in the washing line and knocked about by the wood. All three of them drowned. They trawled for the bodies the following day and they were in very deep water. Ian wasn't found for a while. Apparently his body had been swept beneath an outcropping of rock. I didn't say anything. Not until a long time later when I was studying at Uni and had a complete breakdown. I was the secret murderer, the silent assassin. It all came out after that. No one wanted to take it any further. They made all the right noises about how we were kids and we couldn't be held responsible. But I was responsible and I still am.'

Eric didn't say anything for a long time. She shifted slightly and sat upright, his arms gently falling from her shoulders. She heard him rolling a cigarette and then once again saw his face in the sulphurous flash of the match. His cheeks were wet. After a moment, the smoke drifting around his bowed head, he spoke in that high, indeterminate voice that had altered subtly since they first met into a less refined, broader and more generic vernacular.

'With some variation, that is a story I've heard before.'

Emily was somehow outraged and betrayed by this response, but she kept her voice level, asking 'Where?'

'That, all of it, happened to Sonia. This whole bloody business, the AW, you, Pedro, all of it is my madness. You talk about having a breakdown. You are all part of my psychosis. It cannot be anything else. I refuse to believe it is in any way real. It feels real, but it can't be. I was dead, Emily. I know you don't believe that, but I was dead and gone. Now I'm here and I'm not sick or dying. I talk, I get involved, I ache, I… love. But it's all impossible. O'Brien, Scratch, the man in the flat cap I keep seeing on street corners and on the tops of buses. For a while I live my life as if it were real, believing it. Then something like this, some echo from the BW leaks through and it's clear that it cannot be.'

'Fuck you, Eric.' Emily stood and he realised that he could see her outline more clearly in the hovering lights approaching in the sky from above the tree line. 'Fuck you and whoever you think you are.'

Her voice was drowned out by the barking of a dog and a growing, pulsing sound. Eric looked beyond her and saw the black Labrador, snout pointed to the lights in the sky, barking again and again. She whipped around in time to see the first of the black helicopters roaring overhead. There was a chorus of dull thuds and canisters landed all around them, billowing white choking clouds across the camp. Eric grabbed Emily's hand and pulled her. 'They're here' he yelled above the increasing roar of the engines and as she felt herself being dragged towards the woods, she saw the first of the black figures abseiling down. The Lab tent in the distance flickered at one edge with bright orange fingers of flame. Then, she was pulling away from him, screaming curses and kicking out at his legs. Her eyes and throat were closing up, seared by the gas, but she ran in the opposite direction to Eric.

Looking back she saw him in a brief break in the smoke, the right side of his face lit up by an explosion over by the shower tents. He was staring at her, shaking his head and beckoning. He struggled to be heard above the chaos, but she thought she heard him yelling 'Please… please. Then the white clouds and the smoke from the fires obscured him and she turned and ran for the field behind the castle.

The ironic thing was, that apart from the usual weakness, Eric felt altogether quite well on the day he started coughing blood. A turkey had been arranged for Christmas from the nearest farm at Kinuachdrach and things, in general, seemed to be going well. Richard Rees was staying and, as one of his first editors from the Adelphi days, had helped to enthuse him about the job in hand, just as he was getting discouraged. 'The Last Man in Europe', was taking shape, but he knew he had a long way to go. In other words, although he felt confident in the idea, his treatment of it was a task he felt might be too much for him. He had convinced himself that he might be able to achieve another ten years of life, even with the likely degeneration of his lungs. After all, no one had ever actually diagnosed any specific disease. They tested for TB and almost everything else in Cologne in 1945 after he admitted himself to hospital whilst reporting on the last exhalations of the war. Every test had been negative. But even with an extended lease, he worried that he had wasted his time.

He spoke to Avril on the subject on the walk back from Kinuachdrach to Barnhill. There was a bitter wind as usual, but the sun was out and the waters of the Sound were incandescent in the pouring winter light. Avril griped that his motorcycle was broken once again. They had previously done the trip on the tired old machine, brother and sister clutching each other as they used to on horses long ago. He suffered the walk because, although the flesh was willing, the body weak, he preferred it to waiting for a horse and cart to return from the fields.

He had intended it to be a cautiously positive conversation – an affirmation of how much safer he felt on Jura with her, Ricky and her prospective young beau, Bill Dunn, who had arrived to take charge of the growing livestock experiment, financed primarily by Rees. But he underestimated how much the loss of their sister, their mother and their father in quick succession had made Avril impatient with any talk of death or failure. Instead of accentuating the positive, his bleak outlook overcame him once again and he told her he was thinking of giving up on the book.

'I'm making a mess of it, Av. It's too big an idea and I've started in such a stupid way. Half of it doesn't make sense to me anymore and I don't think I have it in me to straighten it out. It's killing me, that's the truth.

What's the bloody point?'

'Don't bring us all down, Eric' she grumbled as they stomped along the rough track. 'We're alive aren't we? Here and now, we are alive, after all the bloody disaster. That's something to be thankful for.'

'I am thankful, Av. I'm just saying that when we came here, for the first time since Eileen died, I felt like there was some sort of prospect to look forward to. A life, even. Now everything's ballsed up.'

She was silent for a while and, for once, failed to match his faltering pace, racing ahead with a sullen, dogged stride. Eventually she deigned to stop when he did, and waited for him to catch his breath.

'For Christ's sake, Eric, how can you be so selfish? Everything in the house is geared towards allowing you to work on the damn book. I take Ricky on, I entertain Rees and help Bill with the animals, I cook for us all. Dear God, I've never worked so hard in my ruddy life.

'If you hadn't driven Susan away…' he interjected, regretting it almost at once.

'Oh do wrap up. That's not what I mean. What I'm saying is I don't give up when I'm struggling with the Rayburn and wondering if it will ever stop raining. I put my head down and I carry on because I know…' She broke off, looking away at the bay, breathing heavily.

'You know what?'

'I know that if you stop writing, you stop breathing. I wonder if you realise it?'

He started to demur, to deny and to backtrack. But she was clearly irritated with the whole conversation and he felt compelled to distract her by pointing out a kestrel diving on its prey above the cove. It failed to diffuse the fog between them.

When they got to Barnhill and Avril had shed her muddy Wellingtons and Eric his boots, they pottered around at opposite ends of the house, the tension between them still palpable. Rees, nursing a cocoa by the fire, soon sensed the atmosphere and took the shotgun out with him; ostensibly to shoot rats.

After an hour of typing, Eric bent to retrieve a page of his typescript from the bedroom floor and was seized with a coughing fit. He straightened quickly to pull the handkerchief from his back pocket. As he did so, the first scarlet droplets sprayed the front of his shirt and he sat down suddenly in

                                                    ERIC IS AWAKE

his chair, facing the window. He struggled to prevent another cough, but failed and watched the drops of blood pepper the keys of his Remington, attempting to spell out his fate. He observed that his fate had no vowels and clutched the handkerchief convulsively to his thin lips. It wasn't the first time, but he had not experienced anything like it since February last year. He genuinely considered suppressing the sudden recurrence, but Avril came running in. She instantly sensed a different quality to his usual coughing fits.

He saw her take in the stained shirt, the crimson freckles across the desk and watched her shoulders slump slightly and then straighten again as she pulled herself together and led him over to the bed. He sat hunched over, knowing that lying down would only make matters worse.

'Here we go again' he managed between gasps.

Av raised a hand to pat him on the back and stopped herself, remembering that it wouldn't help.

'No more lying in bed with a bottle of whisky this time, Eric'.

He sighed huskily and passed one hand over the day's growth on his shrunken chin.

'I know, Av. I know. Better tell Rees.'

'I'll fetch him. We are going to have to get you down to Ardlussa. Have to borrow the car again.'

'What a fuss.'

'No choice. We're not taking any of the usual nonsense from you this time. Will you co-operate?'

'If it stops me finishing the book, no.'

'I thought there was no bloody point?'

'I talk a lot of rot'

'Yes.'

Rees was visibly upset by the news but quickly set about organising the car, subsuming his emotions in activity. Getting Eric into the vehicle, bundled up with a scarf and heavy coat, was a slow business and Avril worried that at least one of his lungs had collapsed completely.

The journey was utterly unbearable as far as Eric was concerned, despite Rees's attempts to move slowly and evenly across the rough track. The Fletchers were solicitous as always and insisted he stay in the spare room whilst a specialist was summoned from the mainland. Robin Fletcher opted to help him into bed, knowing that Eric would be intensely embarrassed if his wife Margy were left to do it. Eric was reluctant, but forced by the stabbing pain in his chest to concede. The room was small and clean with a view of the sea and Robin was soon sat on a chair next to the bed, shaking his head as usual.

'Told you a winter on this bloody island was too much for you. Dear God, it's too much for me sometimes.'

Eric grimaced as he levered himself painfully up on the piles of pillows. Although they conversed as equals, he was conscious of how much older and more experienced Robin really was. He had been a tutor at Eton, although years before Eric attended. He found himself deferring to him in the same way he would to a fondly regarded housemaster. Analysing the reason for this, he realised that he respected a look in Fletcher's eyes that spoke to a hundred appalling experiences that could not yet be voiced.

'I love Jura. The air is cleaner.'

'..and you're miles away from the nearest doctor. '

'The food is certainly better.'

'That is true. But you look skinnier than I did when I got back from Burma. It comes to a pretty pass when you're the same weight as I was after a prisoner of war camp.'

Eric looked down at himself and realised that, despite the food, he had lost some mass over the summer.

'I think it's the place, Robin. I genuinely feel more alive here. Even if there's less of me to feel so.'

Hearing this, Robin seemed suddenly evasive and looked away. But a moment later he deliberately met the eyes of the sallow faced man lying in the too small bed and tapped his own chest.

'We had chaps on the Burma Road who coughed like you. It's not good, Blair. You know that, I suppose.'

Eric lay back on the pillows and favoured his friend with a grim smile.

'I don't deceive myself. I was never going to make old bones. But I think I have a few more years in me yet. I may spend them in bed or a bath chair. But that doesn't concern me, provided I can still work.'

Robin turned to look out of the window as an eagle screeched somewhere in the fields. As he rubbed his eyes tiredly, Eric saw in his profile the craggy side of a Highland cliff.

'Are you sure this book of yours is worth killing yourself for?'

Eric hesitated. 'Too early to say. Perhaps not. Maybe if given enough time, it will be.'

It took a few days for a specialist to arrive from Glasgow. A large man, Bruce Dick, in his late forties with greying windswept hair and a shell-shocked expression from the long journey, told him there was to be no return to Barnhill. A fatal haemorrhage was very likely if he were physically taxed in any way. There would be a bed for him at Hairmyres hospital in East Kilbride and the journey was to be undertaken as soon as possible. The diagnosis could not yet be confirmed without further tests, but he recommended keeping the Fletcher's children away from the room.

As soon as he was gone, Eric called Rees and struggled out of bed. Robin did his best to dissuade him and Margy told him repeatedly that there was no need, but he was adamant. He did not want to risk infecting the family and after extracting a promise that his bed linen would all be burnt after he left, he insisted on returning.

The journey back and the next few days in Barnhill were agony and Eric struggled to write as much as he could before they had to leave for the arduous trip to the hospital. Avril frequently tried to stop him and even contemplated hiding the typewriter and pencils, but resisted. To deprive him of his one reason for living would be cruel.

Eric's dreams were full of dread and darkness as he realised that perhaps he would never see Barnhill again. The night before they were to leave for the ferry, he awoke from a nightmare that left him shaking and sweaty with foreboding. He was in a prison cell and a camera in the corner of the room watched as he cried and screamed and beat his head against the whitewashed walls. Then he dreamt he was standing on a high point in Africa with a lion's placid face bearing down on him. Just as he felt its breath on his cheek, a shot rang out and a fierce blow hit him in the neck, just as it had in Spain, leaving him breathless and unable to swallow the rising tide of blood in his throat.

22 Last Post

Article – As I See It column
Hackney & Haringey Advertiser 27 April 20--

The Battle of Warwick Castle was, in the end, unnecessary. Had the authorities agreed to continue negotiations, the Hoodies might have agreed to disperse without further violent action being necessary. Once faced with such overwhelming military might and a will to exact extreme force on the Data Pirates, valour would have taken second place to discretion. As it is, the blood of 78 people including five children lies entirely on the conscience of the Cabinet, the MOB, InfoSec, the police, the B & C and the army.

I was able to observe the overall layout of the action from a vantage point atop Guys Tower where I managed to escape the worst of the tear gas and the concussion grenades to command a small cohort of French Student Socialist Workers in the task of securing the main entrances to the building.

The walls of the castle had, by necessity, been breached by the Hoodies as they were left with nowhere else to go after the main body of security forces pushed them back from the centre of the camp. As there were still around 800,000 camp dwellers still on site, the building from the Great Hall to the undercroft quickly became dangerously overcrowded and many, unable to get in, held their ground all around the castle walls as the troops formed a line around the perimeter, preventing anyone from escaping.

It was not clear what they expected to do with so many Data Terrorists as the vehicles lining up behind them would not have taken a tenth of the activists imprisoned behind the line. It was this indecision that led to them falling back some distance and digging in for a temporary siege.

As morning broke and the full extent of the damage done to the camp became apparent, the mood became angry and defiant with the anarchists leading the missile throwing and catapult assaults on the forces facing them. Most of their efforts fell short and several advance parties of Chinese students making sallies out to the line of uniforms found they were quickly surrounded and dragged off to be placed in trucks and police vans.

The Hoodlab and the Lab Rats were clearly the subject of the first assault. A policy of containment and waiting it out had soon been abandoned once the MOB realised that their precious data was being corrupted, perhaps irrevocably. The tent and all its equipment lay in a blackened ruin, two Rats amongst the wreckage and three more in the police mortuary, who, we are told died on the way to hospital.

The bodies of the fallen were being slowly removed by army paramedics in small jeeps armed with stun grenade launchers manned by a couple of Welsh Fusiliers. I recognized none of those being loaded into body bags until they reached the few tents still standing to the east of the front entrance. Under an onslaught of fireworks launched by a group of Derbyshire Muslim leftist youths, one of the paramedics leapt from a vehicle and dragged two bodies out of a tent that was charred and blackened on one side, a pirate flag hanging limply from a pole where a tethered line of police tape fluttered loosely in the wind.

I borrowed an MC and used the zoom facility to focus on the first corpse as it was laid out on the grass, waiting for the body bag to be extracted from the jeep. He was wearing his red hood and when Mo was laid alongside him and their crow black hair mingled, they looked like a pair of slumbering gypsy brigands.

A groan went up from the Castle walls as word spread and the Muslim youths firework display was momentarily pointed skywards to avoid hitting the couple and perhaps to provide a valedictory celebration of their lives. It wasn't enough.

While waiting for daylight and sheltering in the undercroft with hundreds of others, I fought off grief and exhaustion by reading a brochure about the castle. I was not surprised to find that it had played a part in rebellion before. The Gunpowder plotters apparently once stole horses from the castle stables in an attempt to escape their certain execution. Scratch would have enjoyed the detail. I do not think he really understood the significance of what he was doing or the inevitable response. I knew exactly what civil warfare and direct action would produce. We felt it in Spain and in the war at home. In the AW I thought the consequences would seem insignificant and nebulous. Perhaps that makes me more dangerous than anyone else involved. To me, this is a fantasy, a dream with no real deaths and where nothing is really true. But I feel it as if it were happening, so maybe that doesn't really matter. In the BW perhaps I would have stood aside. A commentator, observing only and finding fault through the pages of 'Tribune'.

Readers will have seen the iconic symbol of those last hours on the Viewsites and on their telescreens. The trebuchet replica I ordered dragged inside the castle walls by the Whitechapel anarchists and a troop of trade union Olders was 60 foot tall, made from over 300 pieces of oak and weighing over 20 tons. I knew that the Olders, who were all local, had always wanted to get their hands on it after seeing a demonstration some years before and I appealed to their innate love of engineering and medieval weaponry. They became fired up by the idea that they could beat the record of 817 feet and loaded it up with a tar soaked collection of debris from the camp. It was supposed to take eight men half an hour to load and release. To their credit they fired load after load for nearly four hours at a rate of five projectiles every 30 minutes. One of them lost all the fingers on his left hand and another had his skull fractured by a rubber bullet, but their remarkable rate of fire was maintained.

The distraction, combined with the entire crowd (barring some women and children remaining in the undercroft) rushing in one force to the perimeter with any improvised club or projectile they could muster, saw almost two thirds of the Hoodies escaping through the line to disperse in dribs and drabs across the country back to their homes or to safe houses and temporary camps. I slipped away through the woods and climbed a tree to watch the end. As they charged the line of khaki and blue, they chanted 'Mayday. Mayday'. I did not really understand the significance of this until afterwards when the Hoodsites on the Interverse distributed the details.

And so now everyone knows that the 1st May, once known as International Worker's Day is to be the date of the next great gathering. Over four million people are expected in London and the Government seems to have conceded that the location is an open secret and that appeals to stay away are likely to be ignored. Given the state of the police and the number of forces still fighting abroad, they know they cannot prevent the demonstration happening and have therefore tried to defuse the almost universal condemnation of their actions at

Warwick by making noises about primary legislation to reduce the number of databases and ensure greater personal privacy. They even posit the idea of reducing the amount of information exchanged with the European and American intelligence agencies. No one is fooled. It was an American president James Madison who said ' I believe there are more instances of the abridgement of the freedom of the people by gradual and silent encroachments of those in power than by violent and sudden usurpations.'

I beg all those planning to attend, to do so in the spirit of remembrance for those who died at Warwick. There will be speeches of course, I am scheduled to make one myself, but let there be no more direct action for now. The Hoodies have sent a very potent message to the Government and we must wait to see what arises from that, if anything.

There were nearly two million people camping around the castle at the height of the Hoodcamp. The online petition launched in the 24 hours following the deaths, has so far gathered over 11 million names. Ironically, this particular database is far from private. It hangs in the ether like everything else in the After Wigan. Even though I know it may not be real, I will play my part to the end.

I have been asked to advise protestors that the routes leading to Trafalgar Square will be furnished with telescreens so that all may see and hear the contributions without risking the crush that will inevitably occur closer to the West End. Please take advantage of the many satellite gatherings in Hyde Park, St James and Green Park as well as Victoria and Brockwell Parks in the East and South, Chiswick House and Turnham Green in the West and Finsbury and Alexandra Palace Parks in the North.

Those coming from outside London should be advised

that the forced blockade of the M25 will begin early in
the morning so that routes into the city will be accessible only on foot. Those of you untouched by all this who
think that they will be able to make it into work or to
worship at the altars of Westfield, Bluewater, Lakeside
and Brent Cross shopping malls, are advised to leave
your cars at home. You might otherwise be forced to live
in them for some days.

This will be my last column. In the past, journalism
has often been a chore to me, but, for the most part, this
has genuinely been enjoyable. I would like to thank the
thousands of readers who have contacted me through
the Carolan Portal and the poor overcrowded Advertiser
post room on the Lower Clapton Road. After May Day,
you will not be hearing from me again. I intend to go
far away, where no one comes, because no one wants to.
I will spend my time resting and perhaps, if I am lucky,
I will sleep at last.

Editor's Note: Readers should note our usual disclaimer
that 'Mr Blair' is a writer who has adopted the persona
of a more celebrated (and dead) author. It is in this guise
that he has been commissioned to write for this paper.
Please note that his perspective and indeed his adopted
identity are literary devices that do not represent the
views of this publication. However, we are sorry to lose
him after what may best be described as a quite extraordinary year for this publication and for the UK at large.
That our most eccentric correspondent should have been
at the heart of things and able to bring you his impressions of these historic events, has been pure serendipity.
We will miss his division of the world into the Before
Wigan and the After Wigan, his odd (and largely indi-
gestible) recipes and his reflections on issues that would
have been well beyond the comprehension of Orwell,
wherever his crystal spirit now lies.

                                              ERIC IS AWAKE

ON THE MORNING of May 1st, Emily wasn't going to go. She was still at her flat, nursing Simon who had been found in a tent between three beautiful girls, his asthma making him particularly susceptible to the gas. As he never tired of telling her, he was a shade of blue that exactly matched his bathroom wallpaper and as soon as he was well enough to redecorate, he was going to invite the three girls round to help him strip it off.

He tried constantly to make her laugh because he knew she was as depressed as she had ever been and he feared another breakdown. Snooping in her MC, he found a new message from Eric and read it out to her from his sick bed as she fought him for possession.

'Emily, I'm so sorry. I know now that even in my dreams, a woman like you is out of reach. Perhaps the BW is a better world with Sonia married to me, if not actually in love. I'm now convinced there is only one way. After the next gathering, I will go to my beautiful Scottish island somehow and try to get back to my life. I don't know if a man like me is capable of real love. I loved Eileen, but I wasn't always faithful or kind, so maybe I didn't love her enough. I only know I am done with the AW and with love. I am only sorry that I may have frightened you and made you hate me. Forgive me, if you can. EAB.'

Simon realised when she threw a flask and several rounds of film-wrapped sandwiches at him, that he was being abandoned.

'You'll never find him in this and why would you want to?'

'I can't leave it like this. He mustn't think I hate him.'

'Good God, what does it matter, sis?'

'It matters to me. It really does.'

He watched her cramming her backpack, not knowing how long she would be trapped in the crowds and suggested she take his old skateboard with her. She kissed him lightly on his long nose and called him an imbecile. He waved her off from the bedroom window and as she set off jogging down Upper Street, he noticed the clock on the tower of St Mary's was broken again. Its chimes began as he watched her figure disappear around the bend of the road towards the Angel. He counted thirteen.

Eric arrived at Hairmyres on Christmas Eve and quickly succumbed to the rigors of the journey by sleeping for a straight nine hours, which was far longer than he usually managed. The hospital was a large, two-storey, gable-fronted house set off the road in East Kilbride. The weather was filthy and he had a view of the grey sleeting rain through the window facing his bed.

He also slept most of Christmas Day after sending Rees home and Bruce Dick didn't start testing until the day after Boxing Day. It was almost a week later that the pepper haired surgeon sat uncomfortably on the edge of Eric's bed, took the cigarette from his mouth and gently removed the typewriter from his lap. Eric bore the deprivation with a wry smile and lay back on the pyramid of pillows.

'I take it we are not about to discuss the Beveridge Report?'

Dick smiled and toyed a little with the notes on his clipboard. Without looking up he said 'TB, of course. Chronic, with a deep cavity in the right lung. Are you surprised?'

Eric frowned.

'Not really. I always knew it would happen one day. My lungs have been pretty useless for years, so I suppose when I got that scare last year...'

Dick's head jerked upward and he leaned forward with interest.

'A scare? What happened?'

'I supposed Avril would have told you. It was the first time I coughed blood.'

'What treatment did you receive?'

Eric smiled sheepishly, like a guilty school boy.

'Self administered. I lay in bed for a week with an ice pack on my head.'

Dick frowned and then gave a short barking laugh.

'I can see I'm going to have trouble with you.'

'Very probably. So, what's to do?'

'Collapse therapy. We Latin babblers call it artificial pneumoperitoneum. We introduce air through the abdominal cavity and up into the diaphragm to collapse the affected lung whilst crushing a nerve in your spine called the phrenic... look, it's not pleasant or dignified. But it allows the lesions in the lung to recover. '

Eric grunted as he levered himself forward to cough.

'I haven't been either pleasant or dignified for some time. Not sure I ever was. So am I to have an operation to put me on one cylinder?'

'No. I don't think you're robust enough for that. We use a rather medieval looking apparatus to introduce gas into the body. Anally, I'm afraid. I said it was undignified. But no cutting and therefore less risk of sepsis. Not the best treatment available, but the best we have in this country.'

'I presume this is painful?'

'It's an uncomfortable procedure.'

Eric laughed.

'I've never met a Doctor yet who dares to say "this is going to be very painful and you will yell like a stuck pig several times a day." When does this torture start?'

'Tomorrow, I think, would be best.'

'And have me anticipating it all night? No thank you. Let's get it done now.'

'Very well. I'll organise it for later this afternoon.'

'Will you do it, or some unfortunate nurse?'

'A nurse will assist me, yes.'

'I'd really prefer it to be a male only experience if possible. Frankly the idea of yet more young women having to stare at my arse is not as attractive an idea as it may seem. There are several nurses around the world who may never recover.'

Dick smiled and promised to try and find a male orderly.

The following day, Eric woke at dawn and made a single brief entry in the tattered, handwritten journal he kept by his bed.

'Ghastly business and much more painful than expected. They have confiscated my typewriter, which hurts even more.'

Even this brief effort exhausted him and he resolved that, in another hour, when the nurses changed shift, he would ask for some more medication for the stabbing pains in his back and chest that kept his nerves in a state of rising tension, blind panic lurking only a breath away. He closed his eyes, the image of the ward window hanging on his retina. He tried to see through the phantom aperture and glimpsed briefly the same serene face of the lion from his dream. It calmed him and he drifted off for a short while, the fretting over his typewriter forgotten.

23 Lions

THE OFFICIAL START of the demonstration was mid-day and although it was still only 10:45 when Emily made it down past UCH in Gower Street to Charing Cross Road, it was already almost impossible to make any further progress towards the square.

The crowd, many of them from out of town, milled around aimlessly, uncertain of the location of the various parks. They gawped at landmarks, listened to the musicians set up to entertain on impromptu stages and held placards and banners, occasionally dashing into shops for refreshments.

Police were situated in concentrated clumps and sweated on coaches down backstreets, riot shields obscuring the windows, but their numbers were clearly inadequate to the task.

Shops and restaurants accepted that their toilets were an opportunity and some charged a dollar a time for access. Every available space seemed to be occupied by static knots of people or slow moving ant trails at the edges on both sides of the road. The May sunshine was not warm, but the heat of the heaving humanity beneath it made the thoroughfares steamy and humid. Helicopters clattered overhead, their cameras sweeping the terrain and feeding the waves of movement beneath back to the command centres located around the city in underground bunkers and commandeered vantage points within Government and municipal buildings.

Even with every available officer, bolstered by four other constabularies from the Shires, the stewardship of such an unprecedented influx into the city meant that the orders were principally to manage the worst bottlenecks and to quickly engage with smaller snatch helicopters if officers needed to be airlifted out of any potential flash-points. Most of the police just wanted to get through the day without getting caught in an impossibly one-sided riot. They seemed fearful and cowed by the sheer numbers to be managed. Unofficial stewards in red hoods were gratefully given free rein to relieve overflow-ing statues of the more exuberant drunks and even allowed to take charge of whole sections of the city, their exhortations to the crowd for calm and good humoured protest giving them some measure of credibility with the operational commanders.

Emily despaired of ever getting close enough to the podium in Trafalgar Square to attract Eric's attention. It took her almost two hours to make it as far as the last theatre in Shaftesbury Avenue, where the show playing was yet another revival of Les Miserables. The cast had gathered in costume on the roof of the theatre and were giving well received renditions of French revolutionary songs whilst raining free tickets down on the crowd. Ticket touts were desperately trying to gather them and various scuffles with American tourists were quickly broken up by the stewards, who gathered in numbers around the touts and intimidated them into giving them up to the onlookers. Emily wondered what the tourists would tell people about their little European vacation. 'We saw the British Civil War and Harrods, but best of all, we got free tickets to Les Mis!' Almost the same account, she suspected, as 18th century English aristocrats on the Grand Tour gave of the Terror on their return.

Working her way slowly down towards the junction with St Martin's Lane, she found herself forced up against the doors of the National Portrait Gallery. Breathless with the pressure on her ribs, she managed to convince one of the staff controlling the doors to let her in, despite the numbers already streaming in to the building.

In the coolness of the air-conditioned rooms, she wandered in a kind of daze, exhausted by the struggle to get this far as figures in paintings seemed to drift through her vision like just another coach party amongst the whispering crowds. Larkin peeped over the shoulder of a German climate activist in a purple beanie, the snow white hair of Papa Hemingway mingled with the grey head of a member of the Streatley and Goring Women's Institute, munching a tuna sandwich, despite the protestations of a tearful curator.

She found Eric's spoor in one of the middle galleries. At least, she felt it might have been Eric. So many people now knew his story that they elected to speak and act on his behalf, so the random acts of pointed vandalism could have been done by proxy. A large portrait of a blonde woman kneeling naked on a velvet curtain, her face in shadow from the light of a skylight in a paint spattered studio, had been defaced with a black marker pen, the eyes scored out with a bar across the nose. Lucian Freud's signature had also been scrubbed out with angry black lines. Outside, the din of the guest musicians had died away and she could hear the harsh metallic clamour of the megaphone as the speeches began.

Glancing around her, she thought she saw the back of a tweed jacket disappearing through the far room towards the door that connected with the National Gallery itself. She ran towards the gift shop and struggled against the slow moving mob to follow.

As she reached the edge of one room, she passed a portrait of General Franco with a scrawled message across his chest in the same black marker – 'Visca P.O.U.M.'

April 1948 – Hairmyres Hospital

Eric sat propped up on pillows with the Remington on his lap and a cigarette between his lips. He could see the spring blossom on a tree almost half a mile away and in the pauses between paragraphs, speculated on the species.

His typing was punctuated by fits of coughing and spitting, but these had abated somewhat after the new treatment. The Streptomycin had been administered at the rate of one gramme a day for three weeks and Eric realised, guiltily, that all this had been achieved with the usual wire pulling.

David Astor had personally obtained the authority of Aneurin Bevan to allow Bruce Dick permission to obtain sufficient quantities of the wonder drug he had discovered in an obscure medical pamphlet passed to him by a colleague in America. Astor then came to the rescue again when a supply of dollars were required to purchase the substance. He disguised the gift by pretending to commission an article for 'The Observer' that both he and Eric knew would never be written.

Eric had railed against this and asked Dick why the Americans couldn't accept sterling. The surgeon had smiled wryly and remarked that as the Yanks were lending Britain the money being used to introduce the National Health Service and rebuild bombed housing, they were likely to regard the pound as something of a dud currency for the rest of the century.

At first, the improvement was immediate and there were no side effects beyond a slight darkening at the base of his nails. Now, he felt his body was playing a game not worth the candle as complications increased.

'This is getting ridiculous' he said to Dick during morning rounds, 'I feel like the man visiting the dentist who is told his teeth are fine but he's losing his gums.' The surgeon hadn't laughed. Neither had Eric. They knew they were gambling and a wager is a serious matter. The drug was so new that no one knew what dosage was appropriate.

He worked until just after lunch when he was usually encouraged to sleep for at least an hour before the next injection. When he woke, he took a penicillin lozenge for his sore throat and lay for a while, just staring at the sky through the window, wondering how much more of this he could take.

Listening for signs of an approaching nurse, he got out of bed, leaving yet more of his hair in clumps on the pillow and took off his pyjama jacket. This operation alone took him almost twenty minutes. When he was finally standing before the sink, he manoeuvred himself in front of the small mirror so that he could see his entire face and torso.

A kind of virulent psoriasis covered his face, chest and back with flaking scarlet skin. His lips were covered in blisters and partly stuck together with blood from where they had burst in the night. He looked down at his pajama bottoms and pulled them up slightly to reveal sore red shins, one pulsing varicose vein and discoloured ankles that looked purple and bruised in a manacle pattern. His toes were a mess, with black toenails bleeding slightly from swollen globes of pain.

He raised his hands to the mirror and observed the ropes of veins showing through the red and blue mosaic of his skin. He pulled experimentally at the worst of the blackened nails on his right index finger and suppressed a yelp of agony as it came away in his hand, the blood dripping into the sink, the skin below shriveled and pinkish. He looked hard at his face, the caved in cheeks showing new etched lines down to his swollen mouth. He felt as if he were rotting from the inside.

He ran his finger under the tap and wrapped his handkerchief around it. As he turned to put his pajama jacket back on, he noticed a new patch of grey on the back of his head. He tossed the decayed nail into the waste bin and slumped back to his typewriter. It was time for O'Brien to show Winston Smith how futile his resistance had been.

He had taken it into his head to put Smith in front of a mirror by the time the nurse entered with a small kidney dish containing another large syringe. He grimaced as he stubbed out his cigarette and rolled up his sleeve to reveal one skeletal pockmarked arm. Unlike Smith, he thought, I am forced to pay 'top dollar' for this torture.

As he reached painfully to pull the Remington off his lap, he ran his raw, aching tongue over a tooth and found it was coming loose.

Eric emerged beneath the portico of the National Gallery and levered himself up next to two young female stewards standing on the railings between the columns and saw how far away he was from the podium. He spotted several steering committee members waiting to speak amid a gaggle of celebrity activists. It seemed impossible. One of the women next to him suddenly grabbed his arm and he recognised Helen Boden, the Australian reporter from the Hackney & Haringey Advertiser, who first bearded him in his cosy little billet by the canal.

'Eric? Is it really you? What are you doing here? They are still looking for you, you know. InfoSec turned over our offices twice.'

Eric shrugged. 'It seemed the safest place. They can hardly arrest me here, can they?' She frowned and jumped down from the railings, pulling on his jacket.

'Come on. We have to get you over to the podium.'

He followed her to the foot of the steps, knowing it was hopeless, the crowd packed too tightly. She pressed her lips close to his ear as they descended.

'That bastard from B & C came round to my flat. Threatened me with all sorts. Luckily I couldn't tell him where you were. He said they had an arrest warrant out for Carolan too for refusing to hand over the security codes to his access portal. O'Brien's here, Eric. I've seen him. He's with another man, both of them wearing wireless earpieces. You'll have to be careful when you leave.'

They reached the foot of the staircase and could go no further.

'I'll never get through this.' he yelled above the powerful PA system. One of Scratch's sisters was speaking, her voice breaking with emotion.

'Of course you will' shouted Helen. 'You're one of the people they've come to see. Surf's up, Eric.' Helen grabbed a megaphone from another steward.

Eric shouted back in bewilderment. 'Surf?'

'OK folks…'

A screech of feedback had the rear ranks looking backwards and holding their ears.

'Sorry, sorry. Look, people, look who's here.'

A cheer went up as people recognised him. His identities clashed as always amongst the chorus. 'George is here. It's George. Look, Eric is over at the back. It's Eric. It's George. It's Orwell. It's Eric. Is he awake?' Laughter. 'Is it Eric? Is it George?' Helen pointed at her feet and then up towards the podium.

'He needs to get from here, over to there. Surf's up, everybody. Come on, surf's up.'

Eric found himself being upended by the legs and manhandled over the heads of the crowd in front. Almost paralysed with embarrassment, he tried to relax as people passed him hand to hand above their heads. At times they were shouting encouragements into his ear and a chant went up – 'Eric the loon, Eric the loon. We want a toon from Eric the loon.'

As he reached the stage, his clothing disarrayed and his hair windswept and awry, they passed him up over the audio monitors to a line of Hoodie stewards. As he found his feet and caught his breath, he could see a man gesticulating wildly about three rows back from the stage. It was a familiar face, although the hair and beard were now albino white and the face lined and weather beaten. But the eyes were the same, burning fiercely beneath the wrinkled brow.

'Eric! Eric, it's me. What a fucking business, huh? What a fucking business. Still got my gun you sonofabitch?' Papa laughed throatily and elbowed the jostling youths around him. 'You sonofabitch bastard, Eric. What the fuck are we doing here? What the fuck…' Then he was gone, swallowed up in the seething mob struggling to get nearer to the front. Eric searched the sea of faces but did not see him again.

As he waited for the previous speaker to finish, he looked up at the roof of St Martin-in-the-Fields where police could be seen, chattering into headsets and watching the scenes below. As his gaze moved across to the left, he saw, far up to the right of the National Gallery portico, two figures side by side, only their heads and shoulders visible above the stone parapet. They both seemed to have binoculars trained on the stage, but as one of them lowered the instrument, he thought he saw O'Brien. At a distance, it was hard to tell, but the figure next to him was unmistakable. He had on a flat cap and a scarf obscured his lower face, just as it had in the lobby of the Hotel Scribe in 1945. He knew that if he could have seen behind the binoculars, he would have observed two burning amber eyes.

Eric was suddenly conscious of someone pushing him towards the centre of the podium and finding a microphone being raised slightly higher to a point just below his truncated moustache. He saw himself on the telescreens around the square, financed and erected by Carolan's advertising agencies and, even to himself, the face staring back, the dark luxuriant hair and the lined cheeks were only too familiar from a host of T-shirts. As his head appeared on all the telescreens across the city, like Big Brother during the Two Minute Hate, a rumble of cheering rose and seemed to shake all the pigeons from their roosts.

He cleared his throat, his mouth suddenly dry and his nervous harrumph sounding even more ridiculous, magnified and echoing back to him. Looking desperately at the faces all turned to him, expectant, he was bitterly aware of how inadequate anything he might say would be to these people of the AW. He was out of his time and out of joint with the world.

When he perceived Merrett, perched up where he had previously stood on the National Gallery steps, a camera to his bruised right eye, he placed a hand over the microphone and stepped back. But as he did so, his eyes fell on Emily, perched on the edge of one of the fountains, her blonde hair loose and fluttering in the spring breeze. She was looking straight at him and as he caught her eye, she smiled and nodded slowly. Almost without thinking, he stepped back to the microphone and looked down at his boots, trying to gather his thoughts.

'It is not important that you know who I am or who I claim to be.' There were cheers again and chants of 'He's Eric. He's Eric. He's Eric the Loon'. He faltered and searched for Emily, finding her face again amongst the indeterminate fleshy blobs swimming in front of him. He decided to address only her.

'What's important is that you realise, despite how powerful you feel today, that it will not last. It never does. I do not know what will happen next, how the Government will react. But they are now very aware that the tide must turn or at least appear to turn. The British people, in all their bloody-minded, cantankerous, class-ridden fury have spoken at last and they must listen, if only for now. This Government is the last link in a chain of administration that has finally rolled over everything that gave the state meaning and power. They have, blindly and irrevocably removed their own legiti-macy. The gap between rich and poor, between the haves and the have-nots has so widened that those who are supposed to represent us have fatally increased the number of the disenfranchised. This has been their downfall. If you can no longer get free access to treat-ment when you are ill, if you can no longer get legal aid when you are accused of a crime or evicted by a landlord, if you can no longer afford a home in the first place, if you can no longer get a job or receive help to obtain one, if you can no longer protest without being arrested, if your children are sent to fight in wars you did not vote for, if your life savings are not safe in the bank, if you are not taken care of when you get old, if your taxes rise whilst your bins remain un-emptied and your schools become the graveyards of ambition, if your leaders enrich themselves and the corporations that helped them into power and not society at large, if your children kill each other on the streets because they have no aspirations worth speaking of, if the authorities no longer police with consent, but suppress and collate your every movement and communication, if you cannot vote against any of these things because no party represents your desire, well then, why are we here? Why in the name of all that we fought for in the last war and beyond, are we here?'

On the back steps between the two plinths behind the fountains, some drunken youths began to sing 'We're 'ere because we're 'ere'.

Eric smiled and waved to them whereupon they gave a great cheer that spread around the city. Slowly it died away and three and three quarter million people, standing before telescreens in parks and squares strained to hear the odd man with the archaic clothing and curious inflection.

'The British people are an irreverent people. They express affection and display disgust in the same manner. They 'take the piss'. This is their character. No matter where you come from in the world, once you are in the drunken embrace of this infuriating nation, it is the first thing you learn.

'Britons formed tribes, then villages, then parishes, then counties, then cities, then governments to draw warmth from the flames of the campfire and to support each other; to protect their children and to make decisions collectively for the greater benefit of the people, for the enrichment of that nebulous thing 'society' and, of course, to take the piss.'

Another great cheer began to arise, but he shouted over it.

'But if you are told that society cannot afford any of these hard won basic rights to life, then the people can rightly ask the question, 'what is society for?' They will increasingly reject and live outside of it. It is already happening. Some no longer see the point of contributing to a society that offers little but requires so much of them. People are disengaging. You have disengaged. That is regrettable because when the equilibrium returns, as it always does, politicians will need you and you will need them. For better or worse, perhaps some of 'them' will be you. Have no fear, England will still be England, an everlasting, timeless creature capable of changing out of all recognition through civil war or technology and yet remaining resolutely the same. I still believe, despite all the eternal verities about mixed economies and controlled markets, in the concept of an instinctive egalitarian conscience at the heart of every human being. In all that we propose as law, there must be the Briton's visceral regard for fair play and for…'

The words clotted in his mouth as he felt the dull impact in his throat. His head jerked upwards and his eyes rose to where O'Brien stood, up to the man with his amber eyes trained along the telescopic sight of his rifle.

As Eric fell backwards and to his left, he saw that the man had removed his flat cap to reveal a high forehead beneath swept back wiry hair. The scarf had fallen away so that the bushy moustache seemed to expand as the Russian Uncle lowered the rifle and smiled knowingly. Eric knew at last that Grigulevich was too small a cog to be trusted with such a mission.

The darkness slowly closed over him as he fell onto the hard triangular monitors at the edge of the stage. As the screaming began, the last thing he saw was the placid face of Landseer's lion bearing down on him. He felt sickly sweet hot breath on his cheek, heavy with the stench of rotting flesh.

February 1949 – Cranham Sanatorium, Gloucester

The chalet was fairly basic in its way with a sink and a couple of side tables, but with the added luxury of a wireless connected to headphones which Eric enjoyed wearing whilst reading the proofs for 'The Last Man in Europe' or '1984' as he supposed he must now learn to call it.

When Rees visited one mild Thursday (Irish stew day as far as Eric was concerned) they sat listening to it together whilst attempting to finish a crossword. They talked little and Eric asked half-heartedly about how things had been at Barnhill the last time Rees had seen Jura. The thought that he might not see the island again was a physical ache in his stomach.

After a while, they pulled out the notebook and played their game again, this time with a degree of rigour, now that it might have some practical use. Rees's long serious face furrowed with concentration as they sat poring over one name or another, trying to see whether their impressions were quite as justified as they had been when it had just been a gossipy intellectual exercise. Now that the Labour Government were in power and had asked, albeit indirectly through Celia Kirwan for his help, it seemed more significant and Eric was aware that he had now become slightly obsessed by the 87 names on the list.

As Rees pondered over whether they should still categorise Tom Driberg as a devious Stalinist and possible agent, Eric discreetly rubbed out one of the names he had written in pencil whilst on Jura. Whatever grubby bargain Georges Kopp made during his long period in a Spanish prison, he fought bravely in the war and almost certainly saved his life and if Eileen had gained some solace with him, well, he hadn't been the best of husbands and shared some of the blame for that. This seemingly perverse act of forgiveness and his obsession with the list made him very aware that he was entering the final stages of the disease. A characteristic, he had discovered, of final stage TB patients, was a tendency to become monomaniacal and prone to forming abnormally intense emotional attachments. His recent impulsive pursuit of women was testament to that. Although he viewed the fact with a degree of detachment, he was worried that he could no longer trust his own judgment. This was reinforced by the news from Muggeridge's spook friends that Kopp was not Belgian as he always professed, but Russian.

Arthur Koestler poked his head around the door and let in a draught along with his loud Hungarian bonhomie and gregarious halloos. For a while they played the game together and Arthur baited Eric about some old enemies appearing amongst the ranks of 'unsound' supporters of the Popular Front in Spain.

'There has to be a better reason than that' he said dismissively, lolling on the end of the bed 'You've only put Stephen Spender in because he's queer.'

'Nonsense. I met him long after I started to denigrate his position and it's a lot harder to hate a man when you meet him face to face. But I still think he harbours some overly romantic views of the Soviet model. One couldn't recommend him as a reliable contributor to Celia's literary cabal.'

'What about Chaplin? I thought you liked Chaplin? Weren't you a tramp yourself?' said Rees, amused and happy to join in with Koestler's

teasing.

'I liked the Great Dictator. Doesn't mean he wouldn't write some tiresomely sentimental tosh about the nobility of the Soviet worker. There are enough apologists out there as it is. We're trying to stop Attlee employing a bunch of identical parrots for counter-propaganda purposes. What would be the point of that?'

Arthur lay on his back and looked sideways out of the window at the lawn. 'What's the point of anything? I'm sorry Celia didn't work out for you, Eric. She's a gorgeous girl.'

Eric coughed into his handkerchief and quickly folded it away, ashamed that his friends might glimpse the scarlet streaks of sputum.

'It wasn't to be, obviously. She's too smart for that, perhaps. Foreign Office job at her age. Her life is obviously set pretty fair as it is. I'd only mess up her prospects, I suspect. I'm more hopeful of Sonia, but she hasn't written to me for a while now.'

Arthur sat up, suddenly passionate and wagged his finger in Eric's face.

'You are too damned English with them, Eric. You have to be rough with some women. Ask any Serb. They like it. They are shocked at first, but then they melt. Any conquest has to have a small element of rape behind it, the sense that you could force them to your will if you wanted to. It excites them.'

Rees looked awkward and embarrassed. Eric smiled grimly at the enviously plump Hungarian lying next to his skinny legs and shook his head.

'Not in my experience, Arthur.'

24 Barnhill

Fever Diary – 12 May 20--

Lying here, I can see the sky through the rectangle of my bedroom window. Someone has placed a typewriter on the table in front of it, although clearly it has not been used. Apparently visitors to Barnhill like to imagine that it belonged to me. I think, if it did, I would find beneath the Remington's sticky 'L' key, a spot of dried blood that I never could reach to remove, even with a piece of flannel tied to a pipe cleaner.

This morning, when they finally left me alone to rest, I managed to drag myself out of bed and over to the chair so that I could look down at the trees and overgrown tussocks of grass in front of the kitchen and on out to the bay. The Paps of Jura lie behind and to the south of the island, but I know the mountains are there, even if I cannot see them.

Taking up the carpet beneath the desk, I tore away the layer of old lino and reached with trembling figures into the thin crack between the floorboards and the wall. The brittle yellowing slip of newspaper was still there, where I remembered it falling so long ago. I recalled trying to fish it out with Avril's nail file and eventually giving up. Now it seemed eager to leap into my hands.

As I carefully laid it on the tablecloth beneath the typewriter and tried to open up the sharp folds with the fingers of my good left arm, most of it disintegrated, until all I could see was the blonde haired woman standing below the Austrian mountains. I sat for a long hour, staring out at the bay and thinking about how I had finally made it to the mountains and the sea.

The moments after I was shot came back to me like the flashes of a camera, frozen illuminated windows of memory burned on the retina. The pain was not that bad, in fact I could not feel the bullet wound at all, but the sensation of choking on my own blood was horrible. I thought I could hear it pumping through my head with each breath until the roar of it seemed to ebb and flow. As before, my arm seemed to be the most painful part of my body and even as my head made contact with the black triangular speakers at the edge of the stage, I felt nothing except a crippling cramp in my shoulder and bicep.

I lost consciousness off and on so that each time I came to, I seemed to be in a different dream. One had me lifted up on a stretcher above the heads of the people on the podium who fell back as I surged towards them. Another had me mummified in sheets and straps, swinging lightly above the square, travelling up Nelson's column until I was almost level with the back of his cocked hat.

The next moment I was lying in the doorway of an enormous military helicopter, the downdraft making the white bandage taped to my throat flutter frantically. I remember looking up as they un-strapped me from the cable to see Emily sitting next to Carolan in the bucket seats opposite the door. Hovering on the other side, his camera trained on me, was Merrett. The young doctor with syringes tattooed on his arms that I first met at Hoodcamp, was checking the line taped to my left hand as the craft lurched away.

With the help of two other paramedics, they levered the stretcher through a bulkhead into the main body of the craft. It seemed vast and I realised that it was one of the helicopter field hospitals they were using in the Chinese war. Somehow, despite the need, Carolan had purchased one and added all the comforts to which he was accustomed.

In the white vinyl operating theatre, the surgeon removed the temporary bandage and stitched busily at the hole in my throat. The bullet had passed completely through the front of my oesoph-agus, called in at the vocal chord and exited diagonally just behind the tendon, missing the artery by millimetres. Like a cart down a well worn track, it exactly followed the furrow laid by the previous sniper's bullet I had sustained at Aragon during the Civil War. I suppose I should now say the other Civil War. Back then, I had been unable to speak for some time and this appeared to be the case once more as I struggled to make myself understood, until they grew tired of my guttural croaking and sedated me.

When I emerged again into the light from the porthole above an observation berth, I found Merrett still filming me, firing queries I clearly could not answer and chatting periodically to John Carolan, who, sleek and tanned, responded in mime as the engines roar rendered them as speechless as I. I wondered at his motives until I managed to speak briefly to Emily, her lips pressed close to my ear above the blood stained bandage.

It seemed I was in bad odour when Carolan realised how the Lab Rats had corrupted the data of his millions of users, but Merrett's footage of the Hoodcamp and the battle of Warwick had proved very popular on his networks and he had quickly responded when Merrett summoned him from his City penthouse eyrie to airlift me out of the crowd where ambulances could not have penetrated the rioting mob. The bargain was struck without my being asked. Merrett would transfer his allegiance from the BBC to the Carolan Network and my every fart and movement would be documented for the media outlets desperate for any news of Eric the Loon.

As we travelled over the green patchwork of fields, Emily got them to wheel me into the white leather 'leisure area' of the helicopter where the latest state of the art telescreen occupied much of the space. As I lay still strapped into my mobile pallet, I could see the curious effect of the projected image dancing in three dimensions in front of the curved screen and learnt from the 360 degree footage exactly what had occurred. My shooting was captured on so many cameras that I grew tired of seeing myself falling, neck sprouting scarlet flowers, from a hundred different angles.

The minute I was shot, the protestors surged forward towards Whitehall and fought pitched battles all the way down to Parliament Square where they tossed aside a last ditch police barricade to storm Westminster Hall. The carnage went on for hours and as we passed over the highlands of Scotland, the army had been called upon to drive the protesters from the burning building.

Later, I woke to find the screen filled with raging three-dimensional beasts and ogres. Emily told me the network was showing the vintage trilogy of Tolkien's 'Lord of the Rings'. I laughed silently and sent a mental note to Eileen. 'Those bloody elves again.'

By the time we landed in the field behind Barnhill, the vast metal craft flattening the heather and sending deer bounding away, the real battle was still raging with every satellite gathering trying to get within sight of Big Ben.

Emily had insisted that I be taken to Jura and Carolan had arranged access with the owners of Barnhill over the phone. They told him that they had a small problem with a squatter and as they carried me from the loading bay up to the front door, I somehow knew Pedro would be waiting. He grasped my hand as he opened the door and for a blessed moment, seemed unable to speak. Then, as they levered me up the narrow stairs and into my old bedroom, he swore and fulminated about the ordeal of his journey and the misleading information I had given him about the island.

'It never stop raining, Jorge. Bloody fuckin' rain all the time and where the bloody offie, innit? I got no shop for bloody miles and the cupboards in here got bugger all. I been living on Angel Delight and bloody eggs from these buggery chickens. You full of shit, Jorge. Mountains and bloody sea. I got constipation, man.'

As it happened, he had managed to shoot a rabbit with the shotgun he found after he broke into the side barn, but he wasn't about to admit that whilst the doctor and the two pilots unloaded crates of supplies and a healthy cabinet of alcohol which he fussed over, commandeering supplies for his planned recipes.

Over these last eleven days, I have spent a great deal of time with Emily, listening and scribbling out my responses on a notepad. My voice is beginning to come back, but the doctor, Bryn Fisher, who turns out to have been Carolan's personal physician for some time, has warned me to keep it to a minimum for now.

Things haven't really changed between Emily and I, or indeed, for England. As usual, little had really been achieved. The data we corrupted was apparently expensively repaired over time and the Cabinet wasted no opportunity to condemn the mob whilst paying lip service to the promised data legislation.

At best, the Government were forced to soft pedal the patronage showed to their corporate clients and to make a great show of destroying data gathered 'in error' on millions of citizens. But it was clear that the process would go on covertly as it always had. A new election was called and candidates offered up 'freedom agendas' and 'constitutional charters' for consideration. And Emily still regarded me as her burden of guilt. The fact that I didn't seem to be getting any better, only served to make her even sadder and I started to suffocate under the weight of it.

Dr Fisher took samples and listened to my chest daily. Only Pedro noticed the blood soaked tissues beneath my pillow and disposed of them discreetly. He sat for one afternoon watching the rain with me as it fell steadily on, goose bumping the grey waters of the bay. After a particularly fierce coughing fit, he showed me his own secret cache of scarlet spattered tissues and I wished I could say something to comfort him. He didn't seem at all surprised or worried. Maybe that was the bottles of Calvados we shared from Carolan's supplies. Maybe we just didn't care. Not for us the 'natural death' in a hospital ward, slowly diminishing like a flickering candle collapsing in on itself as it melts away.

It was therefore with some detachment that I listened to Dr Fisher's prognosis once my samples came back from Hairmyres Hospital. Our time spraying car windshields in Heathrow had apparently left tiny time bombs in our lungs that were now beginning to detonate. The archaic and illegal materials used in such processes, we were told, consisted of microscopic 'nanotubes'. Tiny manufactured cylinders, impossibly small, lay in the soft tissue and sprouted infections that ate away at the lung, piece by piece. In addition, it seemed our time living next to the Olympic site demolition had ensured the inhalation of long forgotten toxic particles disinterred by the army of Poles digging the foundations of the new Staycation dome.

It took me some time to manoeuvre time alone with Merrett and no one was more surprised than he to be taken into my confidence at last. I had spent most of the time abusing him with scribbled insults that I held up for his ever present camera to his increasing frustration.

When he had finished reading my scrawled request he grinned and nodded knowingly.

'I get it. Problems may arise, of course.' I watched the cogs turning behind Merrett's cold eyes and knew he would find a way to make it work. After less than a minute, he ran a liver-spotted hand over his implants and took a deep breath. 'But I think I can make a reasonable argument. As long as I have your signed release form, I'm pretty confident. Legally, I mean. '

I struggled to speak, my rusty chords croaky and wheezing.

'I'm so very glad.'

He answered in a manner I have become accustomed to in the AW. The pistol shape made with the hand, the index finger pointed at my heart.

So, Emily, you will no doubt be one of those reading this. I intend to leave it on the desk in front of the typewriter, which, frustratingly, does not work. The letter 'O' punches holes in the paper and the lower case 'e' is missing. You can't really write a love letter with such deficiencies.

But we were never really a romance, were we? The truth is, neither are Sonia and I. But somehow we came to an accommodation that works for both of us. I'm hoping that I can get back to what's left of it. Somehow I am certain this is the only route. The end of the pier at long last.

The AW was some sort of quest, at least. I thought Corryvreckan would be the last adventure. I'm glad I was wrong. Think of me often. I'd like to be a thorn in the side of someone long after I've gone. It may as well be you. I wonder if you ever existed. I wonder if I…

FINAL JOURNAL ENTRY FOUND AT BARNHILL, ISLE OF JURA – 12 MAY 20--

ERIC IS AWAKE

Celia sat beside his bed looking slightly appalled at the wooden walls of the chalet and the mean little pieces of furniture scattered around it.

'Eric, darling, this is a hut.'

Eric smiled.

'We are separated from the main house for good reason. We're all highly infectious. Aren't you scared?'

Celia reached out and held his hand, raising an eyebrow satirically.

'No. I'd be far more scared if you were healthy and active. In my experience that's when you are at your most dangerous'

She made light of it willingly, because to acknowledge the mark of death she could clearly see on his gaunt face would be hard for him and upsetting for her. After a moment, he gently withdrew his hand and reached painfully behind his pillow for the small notebook.

'Rees and I have gone over it a few times since I saw you last. I've scrubbed out a few of our more mischievous suggestions and added some others that have come to my attention since.'

Celia tucked it into her handbag. He watched it disappearing, as if he might snatch it back.

'You have to understand this started off more as a game between Rees and I. We only started to take it seriously when it became clear how many of them there were. Stalin's apologists can be found in the usual places of course, but also amongst those who one would expect to see through the lies. Is it useful, do you think to your...what are they called?

'Information Research Department. Kind of a white propaganda unit to counter some of the nonsense put up by the Russians. Hopefully your list will prevent us from employing writers who are a little too much on the side of dear old Uncle Joe. It's very helpful.'

Eric lay back on his pillows, tired. His last coughing fit had lasted almost five minutes and his bruised ribs were taking a pounding. He looked at Celia in her neat grey suit and feathered hat and wished he could tell her how humiliating it was to appear so helpless before a woman.

'I suppose it's run by the spooks?'

Celia paused.

'I suppose indirectly, through the Foreign Office, that SIS know all *about the IRD. It is connected. But only peripherally.'*

He nodded thoughtfully.

'Probably for the best. If they did a bit of cross referencing with their files, I suspect they wouldn't be awfully trusting of anything I gave them.'

Celia wanted to go. The whole ghastly place was depressing and oppressive and the wind whistling through the gap under the door didn't help. But she desperately wanted to avoid offending him. What could she say? 'Thanks awfully for the list of suspects, now I really must get to the Cafe Royale before you propose to me again.' She couldn't see this happening in an elegant way.

He relieved her of the need for an exit line by reaching out and squeezing her hand lightly.

'It's alright, Celia. You get off. I'm not much company at present, I know. If I ever get back to my island you must come and visit.'

She stood up, still holding his hand. They both knew he wouldn't see Jura again. She leaned over and kissed his sallow cheek, holding his hand up to her face. He grunted and lightly stroked her chin.

'Thanks for coming. I wish...'

She sealed his lips with her fingers and shook her head. He nodded and raised a hand in farewell as she gathered up her handbag and walked to the door. She opened it and stood for a moment, looking back with her mouth slightly open as if she wanted to say more. Then she gave a little wave and quickly closed the door behind her.

24 Reveille

THE SMELL OF chorizo still hung in the air from Pedro's improvised rabbit stew as Merrett helped Eric down the stairs and out of the back door. Eric needed support as his right arm was almost useless, but his companion was eager to maintain control of his camera, so progress was slow as Merrett struggled to keep focus.

He had switched to infrared by the time they got outside and, using a small 'G' clamp, he fixed the camera firmly to the back of the seat of the mini jeep previously unloaded from the helicopter. He then loaded Eric into the back, where he slumped awkwardly across the seats and made sure the lens was firmly trained on him before firing up the engine.

The lights in the house were coming on as they drew away, but he knew there was no other form of transport now that the helicopter had taken Carolan back to London. He had left to negotiate a plea bargain and afterlife for Eric that would include two years in prison, a lucrative book contract and a film made with a studio he had just purchased in America.

Eric settled as comfortably as he could across the leather seats and stared up at the stars overhead. It was a clear and still night with only a breath of cloud to obscure the sky. He was on his way.

October 1949 – London

Cyril had brought Eric a mauve smoking jacket purchased for him by Anthony Powell and as he put it on over his pyjama top, the gravity of what he was doing struck him for the first time. His second and undoubtedly final marriage would be a very makeshift business and he hoped Sonia wouldn't think it too lacking in care or style. He knew he had already handled things badly or, at least, in a hasty, slapdash fashion. He felt himself rubbing an imaginary bruised shin when he overheard her, yesterday evening, regaling Cyril and Lucian about his proposal. 'Can you imagine? He told me I had better start learning how to make dumplings. Romance is dead, my dears'. Not for Lucian maybe, he mused, no, not necessarily for Lucian.

'Embers can give you away' he always told his P.O.U.M militia comrades in Aragon. 'When breaking camp it is essential to ensure that no embers are left to smoulder. Moments after you leave, they may flare up again and start a brush fire or reveal your position to the enemy. Stamp on them, pour water over them, but whatever you do, don't just bury them. They can still burn, even under the dust.'

'Piss on them' Bob Smillie had suggested in typical fashion. The compadres had laughed, not fully understanding but knowing that everything the tough little Celt said, even under bombardment, could safely be regarded as another joke. Eric imagined him joking and laughing still as the Carabineri captured him in Figueres; and perhaps giving them a defiant grin before they kicked him to death in a Valencia prison cell. For a fleeting moment, he wished the punchy young Scot were here now to extinguish whatever still burned between Lucian and Sonia; but he brushed the thought aside. Ignominious jealousy now, on a day like today, was as inappropriate as the dumplings gaffe and regretted almost as much.

Eric watched Sonia and the chaplain chatting and then felt Cyril's eyes upon him. His old friend's head was flushed with a pinkish tinge that suggested he had opted for a stiffener to cope with the uncomfortable nature of proceedings. A bottle of champagne poked from a purloined Savoy ice bucket on the hospital trolley that normally held his linen. Cyril fiddled with it pointlessly, his discomfort painful to watch as he twisted and twisted the bottle in the ice.

'I'm the one who is supposed to be nervous, Connolly.'

Cyril smiled and relaxed a little.

'I sense an impending farce. I feel like it will be me who funks it, not you. My trousers will fall down or I'll laugh at the wrong moment. It's

all your fault.'

'I know. Sorry. Thanks for the bubbly.'

'Least I could do, other than dissuading you, of course'.

'But you won't do that.'

'No. No, I won't do that – not least because you've probably heard it all before from everyone we know'.

'Not really. Visiting time is a hubbub of suppressed opinion. Quite deafening at times.'

'What are they not saying?'

'Gold digger, opportunist. Sad about Eric of course but she'll be rolling in royalties before long and she can take up with Lucian again.'

'Is that what they don't say? What about you?'

Eric convulsed into a coughing fit that, for once, he found awfully convenient. He felt Cyril watching the colour leech back into his face as he drew breath.

'A short leash from the medics gives you a pragmatic perspective. I want Ricky to be financially taken care of now that the money is finally beginning to flow. That requires a competent and, dare I say, fierce literary executor with experience.'

Cyril, conscious of Sonia's occasional glance across the room lowered his voice.

'God knows she has that. Guarded my door like ruddy Cerberus at the magazine. Every Grub Street hopeful with half a crown wanted to take her out to dinner. I was never sure whether they hoped to breach my defences or hers, such as they are.'

The Chaplain raised an eyebrow and they both arranged their faces into solemn expressions designed to inspire all those present with a sense of occasion, undermined marginally, thought Eric, by the bedridden groom. David Astor was best man and seemed as uncomfortable as the rest of them; despite the inbuilt 'born to rule' confidence normally seeping from what Eric dubbed 'his Lordship's semi-reluctant nobility.'

Cyril got through the ceremony without much more than a sense of foreboding and watched Sonia kissing Eric goodbye as they all prepared to traipse off to the Ritz for a wedding dinner without him. He caught a momentary look of rueful self-pity in his old friend's drawn face, but saw him rally as she whispered something in his ear and squeezed his arm *affectionately. 'In sickness and in health,' he thought and cracked open the champagne. The cork flew through the open window and bounced off a cab in Gower Street. The cabbie thought it a funny thing to emerge from a hospital. A bloody funny thing.*

At the Ritz, Cyril danced with Sonia a while, but quickly gave way to the more nimble Lucian, who, of course, had turned up quite by chance. Cyril got a little tight and slumped at their table, watching them both as they shimmered in the throng, the lights of the ballroom blurring his vision until it seemed as if the goat-like Lucian loomed over her like a tweedy satyr. Later, tighter still, he waited until Lucian was tempted away by some tidy little art school acolyte before asking Sonia if Eric knew about their affair.

Sonia waved her hand airily.

'Of course he does. But Mr Freud and I have been very past tense for ages, Cyril. I mean look at him. Muses coming out of his ears. We are the proverbial 'just good friends' these days.

'You have so many good friends, Sonia.'

She frowned for a moment and snapped in irritation.

'If I recall, you were the good friend who advised me to consider Eric's proposal seriously'.

Cyril nodded in a regretful fashion and rubbed his reddening eyes.

'I have had reason to regret that little nugget of wisdom, since.'

He wanted to taunt her a little more, but another of the wedding guests, Janetta, returned from the bar with her husband and Cyril could see Astor breaking away from some other gaggle of aristocrats to rejoin them. Suddenly depressed, he wanted to be gone. He kissed Sonia goodbye and she whispered in his ear.

'All I want is for him to be well enough to write again. He needs to be happy. I make him happy, don't I?'

Cyril retreated unsteadily away, one hand flapping either a farewell or a dismissal – he couldn't be sure.

The mildewed boat lay at a point below nearby Kinuachdrach, moored to a rotting wooden pier that ended abruptly where the waves had slowly eaten it away. The outboard was under a canvas cover and belonged to an amateur fisherman from the farm who had obligingly tethered it at Merrett's request close to where the coast of Scarba could be seen in the moonlight. He loaded Eric into it with some difficulty and left him to remove the cover and fire up the engine one-handed as he took up a position at the prow.

Eric leaned heavily on the tiller as they pulled away and wrenched the bandages from his neck, throwing them into their wake. Merrett pulled back from a close up of the cotton wool bobbing in the dark waters to a shot of Eric, his thin shirt billowing in the wind, piloting them out around the cove towards the whirlpools of Corryvreckan. It was a far more powerful outboard than the one wrenched from its moorings all those years ago. Merrett had been assured by the fisherman that it would cope with the pull of the currents whipping around the treacherous strait.

As they came abreast of the small outcropping of rock where Eric had once searched barefoot for firewood and something to eat, he cut the engine and allowed the current to take them out amongst the eddies. A dark shape could just be discerned on the rock islet, just at the point where Eric had rescued Ricky from the boat. The shape shifted slightly and Eric heard the bark of a dog.

A single bark, like a full stop at the end of a long sentence.

December 1949 – London

The fishing rod was important – its physical being, not the idea of fishing per se. It lay across his bed, and, with the Baedeker guide to Switzerland, represented two totems of hope that Eric had begun to imbue with almost supernatural qualities. He needed them as Dr Morland was becoming more and more obliquely pessimistic. Sometimes not so oblique, as now.

'Lawrence had very similar lesions. Although his, of course, were a lot more advanced.' Morland looked so tired and old that Eric, quite unexpectedly, felt sorry for him.

Sonia made a face and Eric, trying to cover up for her impending rudeness interjected, 'Did it affect his writing?'

Morland paused for thought.

'I don't know. I never saw him write anyway. Marc Gertler managed to sketch a little though, whilst he was under my care.'

Sonia sighed in annoyance, oblivious to Eric's expression.

'Surely there's a more cheerful subject?'

Morland looked slightly embarrassed and Eric looked away, pained by his discomfiture.

'I wasn't trying to discourage you. The point I was trying to make is that getting Eric to Switzerland is the best thing you could be doing. If I'd managed to get Lawrence to higher altitude earlier, I might have saved him.'

There was an uncomfortable pause broken by Sonia standing up briskly and kissing Eric swiftly on the cheek.

'Well, I have to go. Arrangements still have to be made. Lucian has found a lovely hotel near the sanatorium but we haven't booked rooms yet. I'll see you tomorrow, Eric.'

Morland followed her out and as they walked up the corridor was momentarily startled to find her turning on him with flashing flint-blue eyes.

'I know a Doctor's mistakes are buried in the churchyard, but you might avoid drawing attention to them at this particular moment. D.H Lawrence, for Christ's sake!'

She is a beautiful thirty, thought Morland, but in her ire, you can see already how the years will bear down on that face. That soft generous jaw will soften and sag, the lines on the forehead and around those full lips will deepen and those fierce eyes will be all that remain. They understood the transience of beauty and mortality at the University College Hospital. It was their business. But he didn't have to like it.

He took a deep breath and leaned against the wall, lowering his eyes to the floor in mock penitence.

'You are quite right, Mrs Blair. I was being very crass and insensitive. But I meant what I said. You are doing the right thing.'

'I know that.'

'There is urgency, however. Truth be told, this will only be a delaying measure. The lesions are too far-gone now. All we are doing is buying him a little more time. '

'I know that too.' She bit her lip pensively and he saw her robust beauty *return as her anger dissipated. She said, more softly, 'Will he survive the journey?'*

Morland shrugged.

'Impossible to say. But every day's delay makes the possibility of a haemorrhage more likely. If he gets to higher ground where the organs can recover sufficient strength to resist the tuberculosis, then he could go on for several years.'

She seemed to draw herself up as she buttoned her fawn coat.

'Then we'd better get on with it'.

Dawn was just breaking and Merrett asked for Eric to wait until the first rays were hitting the waters. Eric took the time to loosen some strategic bolts and pointed out a photogenic puffin sleeping on a rock back behind them, close to Jura's seaweed clogged coast.

Eric felt that his right arm was a lot less painful now that he was using it and he was relieved to be finally out of bed. It seemed for far too much of his life that the people he loved had seen him only from the waist up in some hospital bed or other. If he had thought about it before he set out on this trip, he would have added a codicil to his will asking to be buried standing up, like the gypsies. But that would be academic now of course. Not only was there no valid will for this second life, but there would be no body either. Not in the churchyard in Sutton Courtenay where his Before Wigan body lay and not here on Jura in the After Wigan. When you die in a dream, you wake up. That's what they say. The bullets from the firing squad never quite reach your bound body; the ground at the foot of the cliff never quite reaches your plunging form. You wake, sweating, a heavy weight of dread on your heart. Then, you breathe a sigh of relief, roll over, but sleep no more.

Merrett filmed until he was satisfied with the establishing shot and the cut-aways. Then he turned and nodded to Eric who stood up unsteadily in the stern and walked to the prow as Merrett took his place at the tiller. It was a delicate operation in the swell and they passed each other like two BBC executives in a narrow Broadcasting House corridor.

Settling himself with both feet braced against the sides of the boat, Merrett watched through the lens as Eric placed one foot on the gunwale.

'Now, on camera please. You are doing this of your own free will?' Eric nodded slowly.

'I couldn't dissuade you, even now?' Merrett's voice had an inappropriate note of careless finality that he felt he would probably re-dub in the edit. Eric shook his head.

January 1950 – London

Sonia felt tired and slightly washed out as she walked back from the hospital. Eric had been strangely euphoric now that Switzerland was on the cards. She worried that he underestimated the toll the trip would take on him. Fine, once you are breathing the alpine air, but getting there was a bloody nightmare. As she crossed Gower Street towards the British Museum, she heard the sound of knocking on glass and saw Lucian and his friend Ann Dunn sitting in a rather down-at-heel cafe waving at her. She smiled and crossed the road. Perhaps they could go on to that shabby genteel supper club to celebrate the trip finally being settled.

Eric was alone in the side ward and for once his coughing had subsided. He felt serene and at peace beneath the moonlight streaming through the window. Visitors had crowded him out recently and he was even glad to see Sonia finally go after what seemed hours of stilted jousting about allowing Rick to visit one more time before they departed. His adopted son seemed to have grown away from him in the last few months and whilst he didn't want to risk infection, he missed the little imp and wanted him here, on his bed, playing games with him and laughing. Poor little sod loses his new mother and now has to worry about his ailing new father. Not much of a start to life so far, Eric mused mournfully. It was he that was supposed to die, not Eileen.

He tossed aside the Baedeker, suddenly sick of the bloody Alps and picked up his notebook. He wanted to write down a more descriptive passage about his fever dream. There was a good essay there about everyone having one peculiar to him or her alone. Somehow they reflected the patient's

Eric put a hand to his head and found it quite cool. Body temperature at last. Bracing himself with his left hand, he gathered himself to jump as they neared the first of the whirlpools.

'Wait, wait. Any last thoughts, Eric?'

A flock of seagulls rose above their heads, shrieking plaintively. Merrett rejoiced inwardly. He could mix the sound in with the chanting of the crowds in Trafalgar Square. 'He's Eric. He's Eric. He's Eric the Loon'

Eric smiled, thought for a moment and then said in his throaty rasp, 'The same pattern always reasserts itself, just as a gyroscope will always return to equilibrium, however far it is pushed one way or the other. Good luck with your own equilibrium, Mr Merrett'.

As Eric levered himself up and pushed himself off the side of the boat, sending it rocking back into the centre of the strongest current, Merrett struggled to his feet, eager not to miss the shock of dark hair disappearing beneath the green billows.

He held the shot for almost a minute after Eric sank and tried to keep the camera steady in the rising swell. He wanted the waves as a poignant backdrop to the closing titles, but the waters were now too turbulent for him to maintain a decent frame as the boat started to spin in the first of the moiling whirlpools of Corryvreckan. It was time to leave and start editing. Perhaps he could mock up a background for some rolling titles between the Landseer lions in Trafalgar Square.

As Merrett turned back to the tiller, the camera still on his shoulder, he was in time to see the outboard motor sucked from the loosened bolts and dragged to the bottom.

As Eric pulled himself up on the pillows to start writing, something deep inside wrenched and tore away from its moorings. He felt an implosion in his chest that filled his throat with the familiar metallic surge. It wasn't like the other times and he knew as the blood poured from his mouth and nose that something was irrevocably broken. He wasn't afraid, only desperately sad not to have seen Ricky one more time. As he gave in to the collapsing lungs and exhaled, knowing that he would not, could not, draw another breath; he remembered being shot in the throat while standing above his dusty trench in Spain and how, as he fell, his one thought was simply a profound regret.

There was still so much he wanted to do.

About the author

Dom Shaw began his media career at 21 by winning the Grierson Award for Best Documentary in 1982 for co-directing the seminal post-punk documentary *Rough Cut & Ready Dubbed*. After a few years directing music documentaries for the fledgling Channel 4, he started scriptwriting for television. In a varied career behind the camera, he has written for peak time series on the BBC and ITV networks in the UK. *Eric is Awake* is his first novel.

www.ericisawake.com